CON VICT ION

KELLY LOY GILBERT

HYPERION

LOS ANGELES * NEW YORK

All rights reserved. Published by Hyperion, an imprint of Disney Book Group. No part of this

book may be reproduced or transmitted in any form or by any means, electronic or mechanical,

including photocopying, recording, or by any information storage and retrieval system,

without written permission from the publisher. For information address Hyperion,

125 West End Avenue, New York, New York 10011-5690.

First Edition, May 2015

1 3 5 7 9 10 8 6 4 2

G475-5664-5-15060

Printed in the United States of America

This book is set in Adobe Garamond Pro

Designed by Maria Elias

Library of Congress Cataloging-in-Publication Data

Gilbert, Kelly Loy.

Conviction / Kelly Loy Gilbert.—First edition.

pages cm

Summary: "A small-town boy questions everything he holds to be true when

his father is accused of murder"—Provided by publisher.

ISBN 978-1-4231-9738-6 (hardback)

[1. Fathers and sons—Fiction. 2. Faith—Fiction. 3. Trials (Murder)—Fiction.] I. Title.

PZ7.1.G55Co 2015

[Fic]—dc23   2014042087

Reinforced binding

Visit www.hyperionteens.com

SUSTAINABLE
FORESTRY
INITIATIVE

Certified Sourcing
www.sfiprogram.org
SFI-00993

THIS LABEL APPLIES TO TEXT STOCK

For my family, and most of all for Jesse

Hebrews 11:1
Now faith is the assurance of things hoped for,
the conviction of things not seen.

PROLOGUE

The San Francisco Giants took the St. Louis Cardinals 8–3 in a Saturday game at AT&T Park ten years ago, and that was the last time my family—my dad, my older brother Trey, and me—all went to a game together. I was in first grade then, and that was before I knew too much about all the different ways your life can fall apart, but still, I don't think it's an exaggeration to say that most of what I believe now is because of what happened that day between me and God.

The game was the first time in forever that the three of us had done anything as a family, and it was a big deal to me because the way you hear how other families are into things like Christmas or relatives or whatever, baseball's always been the thing my family's had. I'm a pitcher—I'm expected to go out as a first-round draft pick when I graduate next year—and back then baseball was my whole life already. I'd been lying awake in bed thinking about the game for weeks beforehand, and when the night before finally came, I knelt on my bedroom carpet and rested my forehead on my bed and asked

God to give me some kind of sign. I know it's not like if you come up with the magic combination of words to pray he'll spit out whatever crap you ask him to, like your own personal vending machine, but all week I'd put my best into my pitching and I'd been extra careful to obey my dad, and so this was the deal I made with God: if he would give me some unmistakable sign, one that could only come from him, then I would take it as a promise that everything would be all right between my dad and Trey.

It's about two and a half hours west to San Francisco from Ornette, where we live in the Central Valley—all long, flat roads where the tule fog rises from the ground and pools at the bottom of the valley against the foothills, a place that back then I always thought was so safe. We drove out through the country club by our house and past the vineyards and the huge ranch homes up in the hills, past one of the giant billboards with my dad's face on it, and as orchards of almond trees flicked by outside the window, I kept watch for what might be my sign.

Trey was graduating from high school that year, and the whole drive to San Francisco, my dad was teasing him about proposing to his girlfriend, Emily. Well, half teasing, because my dad always wanted them to get married. He'd said more than once that she was Trey's biggest accomplishment in life.

"You want a crazy way to propose?" he said when we were passing through La Abra and he'd locked the car doors and sped up. La Abra's our rival, and every year when we go there to play them we might as well be crossing an invisible border into some third world country: small faded homes and rundown apartments all crammed together with barred windows, dirt yards with chain-link fences and vicious-looking pit bulls, a twenty-four-hour bail-bond place. We used to stop in La Abra once in a while to eat at this place my dad liked, but then he found out the owners were illegals, and we quit going. My dad's lived here long enough to remember when La Abra was still a safe, quiet farming town full of the same kind of people you'd find in Ornette, families who've been around for generations, and he's always going on about how now La Abra's proof that we're letting the country fall apart. All I know is you couldn't pay me to walk around there after dark.

"This one's in the Bible, swear to God. Go bring Em's dad a hundred Philistine foreskins. That's what King David did when he wanted King Saul's daughter as a wife. That's what Saul made him do. Except then David got two hundred." He'd winked at me in the rearview mirror and turned his eyes from the road to grin at Trey. "Michal must've been a real looker, huh?"

In the passenger seat, Trey adjusted the headphones he was wearing. He stared out the window. When the mounting silence in the car felt too thick to breathe through, I said, brightly, "Ha, good one, Dad. Good advice."

The look my dad gave me in the rearview mirror was half warning, half plea: *Don't you turn out like your brother.* Trey was always his cautionary tale about what happened if you threw away your potential, if you were lazy and didn't have integrity in how you did things. It hadn't been a great couple of months at home, but this time all he said to Trey was, "You'll regret it if you don't lock her down before you leave for college." He pressed on the word *college* like a bruise; he wasn't happy Trey was going to a school with no baseball team and a reputation for smoking pot. "I mean it," he added. "I'm just trying to help." Trey tilted his head back against the headrest and closed his eyes like he was trying to sleep.

Back then, before New York and before his restaurant, Trey was a catcher. He was good, too, which made it all the worse that he was never willing to give the game very much of himself. It killed my dad the way Trey just never cared.

We were at the park early so we could watch batting practice before the game. We bought hot dogs for all of us and a pretzel for me and a beer for my dad, and on our way down to the field level, my dad took us the long way around the concourse to point out all the retired jersey numbers on display. Trey made it a point to look as bored as possible, and my dad, who'd been talking about the game for weeks, was disappointed. He's always liked stuff like that, and I have, too; baseball's nothing if not proof of all the ways history matters to you. That's why the stats get so specific, like a guy's batting average with two men on base, a guy's pitching record against left-handed hitters in games at home when the team's up by three runs or more—that kind of thing. You're always playing against the past.

I'd brought my glove just in case, and when we made our way down the stadium steps behind home plate, I got that anxious, rattling feeling in my heart I still get sometimes when I take the mound before an important game, and just like that, I knew what I was supposed to ask for: that I would catch a foul ball today at the park. That would be my sign from God.

Where our seats were in right field you wouldn't get foul balls, so it would have to be now during batting practice. I drifted away a few steps from Trey and my dad and angled myself just behind the dugout where the protective fence dropped off, the best place to catch a ball. We stood there a while, watching the balls fly out across the field.

I was nervous. My hand was sweaty inside my glove. To distract myself, I asked Trey, "Who's your favorite player?"

"My favorite?" Trey considered it, like he figured I deserved some kind of actual, thoughtful answer. I know there's a lot you could say against my brother, but back then he was always nice like that with me. "Probably Hummer."

"*Hummer?*" my dad repeated. "Trey. You're killing me. Stab me in the heart, why don't you. That kid looks like a fairy. And he plays like a humpback whale who swallowed a whole cow." I giggled, and my dad wrapped his arm around me. "The heck do you like about *Hummer?*"

"I've always liked him," Trey said. "Maybe I'll get a jersey."

My dad snorted. "Be a cold day in hell before I buy *that* for you." He's always said you should never wear a jersey with another guy's name on it, because it's weak and unambitious to only want to be as good as someone else who's done it already. Trey knew that, obviously; he said it just to get at my dad. I agreed it's weird to wear someone else's name across your back, but I also kind of felt like if you were going to, you might as well pick someone as terrible as Hummer, because then you still know you're better.

"I'll buy one myself, then," Trey said. Then he added, pretend-casually, "Who needs your money."

I tensed. But this time all my dad said was, "Hummer, huh. Trey, that's just embarrassing. You could kick his ass."

Trey considered that, started to say something, then changed his mind. "Yeah, well, Braden could probably kick his ass."

My dad had just bit into his hot dog, and he spit it out into his cup of beer because that made him laugh, and I felt better then. He held out his spit-in beer to Trey, the half-chewed chunk of hot dog at the bottom.

"Here," he said, grinning. "Drink this. It's yours now. You earned it."

"No, you did that. You drink it," Trey said, but he started up the stairs and came back a few minutes later with another beer for my dad, and no Hummer jersey. I guess he didn't get carded; Trey always looked older, and anyway, people usually kind of go along with what he says.

"You didn't have to," my dad said. "Here. I'll pay you back." Trey waved off the bill my dad tried to give him until my dad folded it in half and slipped it in Trey's back pocket. Then my dad looked down at me and squeezed my shoulder. "So how about you, B? Tell me I've at least raised *you* right. Who's your favorite player?"

I knew it wasn't just any question; it was a test. He'd take it as evidence that I was or wasn't going to be like Trey. So I thought a little while, and it didn't count exactly, because it had been years since he played, but I said, "You." It caught him by surprise, but it also made him happy, just like I'd known it would, and the way he squeezed my shoulder made me feel like I was maybe a step closer to getting my sign from God.

We stood waiting as the balls rained down on the field. There were a few dozen close calls, and I had my glove ready each time and my heart kept picking up as I'd flash forward to what it would feel like to know God had personally promised something to me. But then each time the ball would drift back twenty rows, or it'd fall down onto the field. Each time I felt my faith eroding. When batting practice ended, I had two autographs Trey had gotten for me, but no foul balls.

The game started, and my dad settled down in his seat to talk it through with me. Maybe it's partly all the years on the radio, but when it comes to baseball, he can turn it into something no one else can, like he's stripping tarnish off an old mirror layer by layer so you slowly start to see everything reflected back at you and you start to see yourself and your own place in it, too. I was distracted that day as he went over the different pitches and plays, quizzing me occasionally and acting proud when I knew the right answers. He wanted me to pay attention to baseball's unwritten code of honor, making sure I could tell whether everyone was doing the right thing at all times.

In the fourth inning, the Cardinals second baseman, who'd just hit a ground-rule double, cut to second base across the pitcher's mound, and—because I was too absorbed wondering what I'd done wrong with God, why he'd ignored my prayer—I noticed only when my dad stiffened and sucked in his breath.

"You see that?" he said. "What'd he do wrong there?"

I knew the answer: it's pure, calculated disrespect for anyone but the pitcher to set foot on the mound. But before I could say it, Trey said, "Relax, Braden. It's just a game," and the disgust and disappointment that crossed my dad's face was so sharp it made me think I'd been wrong—that after all that, *this* was my sign that things would never be all right.

"A *game?*" my dad said scathingly, loud enough that the people around us turned to look. "That's all this is to you? You don't give a fig what I've tried to teach you all your life about integrity, is that it? You think this is nothing more than eighteen guys batting a ball around with a stick?"

Trey was going to say something unfixable. I knew he was, and I knew he'd been close to doing it for a while, for months maybe, and I was certain then that God had failed me. I was just a kid, but I knew already how sometimes you can feel the slipping point just before it happens: that vast, awful stretch of possibility that'll hang there waiting to haunt you forever once it's past.

But then, before Trey could speak, everyone around us jumped to their feet and started yelling, and the three of us broke that ugly triangle we were caught in and looked up. And then it happened: the ball Cole Hummer had just hit flew and flew, out toward where we were sitting in right field, and Trey stopped short of whatever he was going to say. On pure instinct, I jammed my glove on my hand, and then the ball was coming right to me and I reached up and caught it and it landed hard and stinging against my palm in a way that could only be my sign from God.

There's a lot that's magic about baseball. I don't mean that as in superstition or coincidence or luck, because more than anything, baseball is mechanics and effort and hard work. Even in first grade I knew that; even then my life was shaped and measured in metrics and repetitions and stats. But there's magic in the way it comes together and in the way it makes you who you are. There's magic in the way that, when you're good enough, you can stand on a mound in front of forty thousand people who've watched and lived your past with you and prove you've earned the right to be there.

But this is the thing about it that's the most magic about it of all: that it opens up a stage for God to give you moments like that. That you can go watch a game with your dad and your brother and have a night together that winds up being as close to perfect as anything in your life has ever come. That it can give you something to hold on to when you need it most. Like when you're six and in church on Mother's Day, and all the kids are told to stand up and give their moms a hug and you try to pretend you're not there; or when you're seven, and for reasons you've still never understood, your brother drops out of college and quits talking to your dad altogether and stops coming home.

Or when you're sixteen, and without warning, before you even understand what's happening, your dad, the best man you know and the person who taught you right from wrong, is arrested at gunpoint on the street outside your house.

ONE

At the police station in La Abra, I'm frisked: arms above my head and my legs spread apart while someone runs his hands across my body, my face hot and my heart thudding so hard I'm sure he can hear it, and I'm too afraid to ask what's going on. When he's done, I'm taken to a cramped, stuffy room with no windows and a door that shuts heavy and holds the sound in the room like a trap. There are two cops sitting at a long metal table under a garish fluorescent light. The cops are wearing dark blue uniforms and they're both trim and wiry-looking, men you could imagine throwing someone against the asphalt. One's black. The white one says, "Braden Raynor?"

My voice comes out scratchy. "Yes, sir."

"Have a seat."

Outside, the night is so thick with tule fog you'd think someone dragged a tarp over everything and pounded all its edges down with stakes. As I was being driven here the streetlamps and traffic signals were shrouded in that eerie gray and nothing looked familiar, not even when we drove by places I've known all my life, and everything I need to say has turned to dust on my tongue. "I need to—can—can I see my dad?"

"He's in the facilities in Grovemont."

"The facilities?"

The look he gives me is pure contempt. "Jail."

The word hits me like I'm taking a fastball to the chest. "Sir, I think there must be some kind of mistake because—maybe you don't know who my dad is, but he—"

"*Sit.*"

His tone shuts me up, not just the tone but how fast it turned like that, and I obey. The lights in this room are hurting my eyes. When I close them, I see the fear blooming on my dad's face as the cops drew their guns on him, the three officers who wrenched his arms in place while another one locked him into handcuffs. And I see myself watching it all happen, still and silent on the driveway.

If it had been me instead of him, he wouldn't have just stood there like I did.

"Tell us what happened tonight," the first cop says now, his voice breaking the silence like gunfire. My eyes fly open again.

"Nothing happened. We were just—it was too foggy to see—"

The night catches up to me then, all of it, and I run out of air. I lower my head toward my lap and try to breathe. When I raise my head, the first cop's gripping the edge of the table like he wants to dent it.

"You," he says quietly, "are going to tell us exactly what happened tonight."

I open my mouth, but I can't get enough air to speak.

The white cop leans forward, so close that if he wanted to, he could reach out and grab me around the neck. "What were you and your father doing in the car? Were you out hunting him?"

I don't know who he's talking about. "Sir, I don't—"

He leans in even closer. The corners of his mouth are pinched white. "Your father thought he'd get away with this?"

"He wasn't trying to get away with—we were just coming home, and then—I don't even know what's—"

"He was just waiting for his chance, wasn't he?"

There's something awful in his expression, and it feels like he's reached down my throat and grabbed my lungs in his fist. "Did someone—" I try to swallow. "Did someone get hurt?"

"Hurt?" he repeats, spitting out the word like it's poison. "*Hurt?* Is that what your dad told you to say when you ran Frank down? Huh?" He's shaking, his jawline vibrating like a guitar string about to snap. He curls his hands around each other as if he can barely stop himself from slamming them into something, and then something loosens in his face and before he turns away, I swear I see his eyes are wet. "Your father just murdered one of our very best men."

⸱   ⸱   ⸰

At home, even with every single light on and the alarm system activated—I checked twice—I can still feel my pulse in every one of my fingertips and I have that feeling in the back of my neck you get when you think someone's following you. All three thousand square feet of the empty house feel like they're pressing on my chest.

It's late, and it's even later in New York, but I call Trey. *Pick up,* I plead silently. *Pick up, pick up, pick up.* He doesn't. I tell myself he's just sleeping with his phone turned off, that if he saw I was calling him for the first time in over two years, he'd answer. Finally, I text: *Dad just got arrested. Please call me. I don't know what to do.*

I watch the clock. I track when it's six a.m. in New York, when it's seven, when it's eight. I fall asleep sitting upright on the couch, and when I wake up with a start, there's still no calls. I remind myself Trey always liked to sleep in late.

The knock on the door, sharp and insistent, comes just after I wake. When I get up and look out the window to see who it is, there's a woman standing on the doorstep. She's youngish for an adult, probably a few years younger than Trey, dark-skinned, kind of hot. I've never seen her before in my life. She's wearing this skirt-suit thing that clings to her chest and carrying a clipboard, and she makes eye contact. She gives a little wave.

I should've pretended not to see her. Against my better judgment, I open the door.

"Hello," she says, her lips stretching into a professional-looking smile. "I'm Melanie Ramos, LCSW." She holds out her hand. "You're Braden, I presume?"

I stare down at her outstretched hand, long enough I guess that she figures out that her name and the string of letters after it mean nothing to me.

"A social worker, Braden," she says, enunciating like I don't speak English. "May I come in?"

⸱　⸱　∘

There's a feeling every pitcher gets in a game that's spiraling out of control, when you can't find the strike zone or you're giving yourself away to your batters, and I have that feeling now. The social worker comes into the living room and plants herself on one of the leather recliners without waiting to be invited. She rests her clipboard on her knees. "You have a lovely home here, Braden."

I'm not in the mood to talk interior design. "All right."

She looks the tiniest bit amused. "Well, let's get down to business here. I understand that your father has sole custody of you, Braden?"

"Ah—yes."

"And your mother's no longer alive, Braden?"

I think the fastest way to make someone not trust you is to overuse their name. "No."

"Braden, do you have other adult relatives nearby—grandparents, maybe, or aunts and uncles?"

I thought at first that maybe she was here to help my dad get back somehow, but I don't like wherever this is going. I say, "I've got an older brother." A half brother, technically, since he has a mom, Elaine, who's lived in Connecticut ever since she left my dad when Trey was young. A brother who still hasn't called me back.

"How old is your brother?"

"He's twenty-eight."

She glances around the room like she thinks maybe I've got him stashed off in the corner or something. "And does he live here with you?"

"No." It's been nearly ten years since Trey left home. The last time I even saw him was five years ago in sixth grade when he flew out to be the best man in Kevin's wedding, and he took me to lunch and made me bike to the gas station on the corner to meet him so he wouldn't have to see my dad. "He lives in New York."

"I see." She writes something down on her clipboard. "What does he do there?"

"He owns a restaurant."

"And, Braden, what's his family situation there?"

"He doesn't have a family there."

She sets down her pen and leans forward, her hands clasped in her lap. "You've probably figured out, Braden, that I'm asking because my job here today is to make sure you're placed in the care of a temporary legal guardian right away." She pauses. "Now, am I correct in thinking that your brother sounds like the best candidate?"

"Wait," I say. I look around the room to ground myself back in my normal life: the remotes tossed on the leather ottoman, the stack of *Sports Illustrated* magazines by my dad's favorite chair. "I don't think I understand what's happening here. I know my dad's not here right now, but I mean—how long can this possibly last?"

She runs her tongue over her teeth. I can feel her thinking of what to say, and I'm about to tell her that obviously I'm fine at home by myself for the time being, I'm not going to starve or trash the house or anything, but then before I can get the words out an awful feeling like a premonition creeps in and spreads through me. The white-hot terror of all those guns drawn and aimed at our car, the claustrophobia of being questioned at the station by the cops—those things felt like a nightmare I'd wake up from in the morning. It's this moment—sitting in my own living room with this calm, professional-looking stranger in the daylight—that I suddenly realize I might have to mark as the time when I understood this wasn't going to just easily go away overnight.

I realize the social worker said something else I didn't hear. "Sorry," I say. "Um, could you say that again?"

"What I'd like for us to do right now is to contact your brother and get the ball rolling so we can avoid having to transfer custody to the state."

I try to imagine what it would feel like to ask Trey to come back here on a moment's notice. I try to imagine what it would feel like for him to say no.

There's a pounding on the door. The social worker and I glance up at the same time and see out the window what looks like—you have got to be kidding me—a news crew setting up in front of my house.

The social worker flies off the couch and across the room and has the door open before I have time to react.

"If you don't remove everything from this property *immediately*, I'll have you arrested for trespassing and harassment of a minor," I hear her yell at someone. "Get out. Do not test me. *Get out.*" She slams the door so hard I feel it shake, and then she comes back, smooths her skirt, and sits back down.

The whole interaction took less than ten seconds. But in that quick flash of time while she was gone, something invisible happened, something that's left me reeling. I rest my palms on my knees and try to breathe.

I know I need God right now, more than I ever have in maybe my whole life, so while the social worker was gone I tried to pray: *Please let all this go away. Please tell me it'll be over soon.* The thing about prayer is it always feels like an act of faith—it forms some fragile new chamber in your heart, something empty and vulnerable that bleeds loneliness if God never answers you. Most times he doesn't. The Giants game with Trey and my dad was the only time in my life I was even sure he heard me. This time, though, when I prayed, I felt something I've never felt before, some bright, distinct certainty that arrived fully formed and lit up and flashed right at me, and even though I try to tell myself it's ridiculous, I'm scared that was God speaking to me. I'm scared of what I think I heard him say.

"Now, then, Braden." Melanie's fake smile and calm *I'm-a-therapist* voice are back, like nothing ever happened. She reaches for her clipboard. "What's the best way for me to reach your brother?"

TWO

My dad doesn't come back home that night, and he doesn't call. And he doesn't come home the next night, either, or the next. I try to be patient, to ride things out—what else is there to do?—but I feel my helplessness grating me, rubbing me blistered and raw.

Reporters call, though, so many I learn to hang up as soon as they identify themselves, and a lawyer whose messages I delete along with all the rest. The story flashes out of the national news cycle after a few days, a blip on the radar. At home, though, I can feel the news settling in, the way silt sinks down through water to coat and burrow into the lake bed, but in Ornette, at least, people are on his side.

At school, people ask a lot of questions. Or, instead, they'll do this thing where they'll come up to me in the hallway or turn to me in class and say something like *My uncle is a lawyer,* or *My parents always thought the cops there had it in for us,* or *I was watching this show the other day and there was a guy in it who got wrongfully accused,* and then they'll wait, expectantly, like they've gotten the lid off a bottle of something carbonated and now are waiting for it to come frothing out. I've always thought the people I go to school with are generally decent—or maybe I've just been lucky; in a place like Ornette, when you're really good at something, when people feel like they have some small stake in your future just because they know you now, high school's going to be pretty easy for you as long as you're not ugly or completely socially incompetent. But aside from whatever happens on the pitcher's mound, I don't hang my laundry where everyone can see it and I don't know why anyone would expect me to now.

My dad's always been pretty popular at church, I guess because people listening to you every morning on the radio makes them think you're a part of their lives, and church families come by with Pyrex dishes full of chicken pot pie casserole and enchiladas made with cream of mushroom soup, so many people I start drawing the shades and pretending I'm not home. It's exhausting putting on a polite smile and telling everyone *Thank you for the casserole* and *Thank you for praying* and *Yes, I'm fine* and *No, I haven't heard from him*; it makes me feel more alone, not less.

Three days after his arrest, someone spray-paints KILLER on a billboard advertising his show, right across his face. Chase Singer goes off about how it's going to be a bloodbath when we play La Abra this year, how I'll need a bodyguard, and my catcher, Colin Sykes, smacks him and snaps, "Real sensitive. Maybe try shutting up," and tells me I have nothing to worry about, that I know they're all behind me. Dutch Hammell tacks the schedule up in our dugout and circles the La Abra game—May 12—in red.

Five days after his arrest, when I've still heard nothing from him and I'm starting to wonder if they aren't allowing him any contact, I go to the airport with Kevin Cortland to pick up Trey. Kevin's Trey's best friend from way back, and also my Civics teacher at school and—Pastor Stan is his dad—one of the youth group leaders at church. Kevin called as he was leaving to say I should come with him to the airport. One person, he said, wasn't much of a homecoming brigade. It's nine at night and mostly empty in the baggage claim. There's some TVs mounted on the walls, and every one of them seems to have the news on, so I don't look. There's a college-age girl wearing this tight black shirt and nothing underneath who I'm ignoring because I want Trey to land safely and to not hate me for having to come here, and averting my eyes is my tacit bargain with God. And, even though I'm trying not to see, there are three cops in tan-colored uniforms pacing by the security line.

"So," Kevin says, deliberately casually, "some rough news about the proceedings this week, huh?"

He's lasted longer than I expected, actually; the whole two hours here we talked mostly about baseball and some about school, and even though I could tell it was killing him, he didn't ask me a thing about my dad. I arrange my expression into something as neutral as possible and say, mildly, "Mm."

"How have you been feeling about everything going on?"

I say, "Fine." Which isn't exactly accurate, obviously. What I've been feeling is a low-grade terror, like kindling, ready to leap into flame. Although one good thing did happen yesterday: Maddie Stern, whose family moved here from Bakersfield over the summer, came up to me when I was at my locker. Right on cue, in spite of all the ways my mind was frayed and short-circuiting, I got that tingling feeling I always do when I pass her in the halls or when I see her at church. We talk sometimes in youth group and in class, and, if I'm being honest, I've been pretty into her since the first day I saw her at school. She stood out in the classroom like she was backlit, not just because she was the new girl or the only Asian person in it or whatever, but because she's beautiful in a way that makes you want to keep staring, a way where, before you even know it, you're picturing what it would be like to kiss her. I wouldn't quite call us friends, though, and so I was surprised yesterday when she asked me for my e-mail. When I got home after school, she'd sent a message: *Dear Braden, I'm sorry about the accident you were in. This is a song that made me think of you. Sincerely, Maddie Stern.* Underneath she'd typed her phone number. When I hit play, Maddie's voice filled the room. It was a song I didn't know, but something about the way the notes rose and fell and hovered, the way they kept ratcheting up like they were leading somewhere and then just hung in the air, made me think she knows something about what it's like to miss someone, and what it's like when your world bottoms out.

Not that I told her that, because it's not the kind of thing I'd normally say to someone, and it's possible she just felt bad for me. Anyway, maybe I should feel guilty thinking about a girl right now. I should just be thinking about my dad.

"Your dad's got quite the support network," Kevin says now. "My dad just forwarded me an e-mail about listeners holding an online prayer vigil."

"Ah." I got the e-mail, too. Every week, Pastor Stan sends out prayer requests to the whole church mailing list, and this week's started with: *Please pray for strength, peace, and deliverance for the Raynor family.* "A guy's on the radio every morning, people feel like they know him, I guess."

"Sure." Kevin leans forward. "It's a lot to take in, Braden. You know, it's not even my dad, and it still hit me pretty hard to hear—"

"So how's your kid, Mr. C?" He blinks at the interruption, but I say, "How old's she now again?"

"Ah—Ellie's eighteen months. But I'd really—"

"Yeah? What's she like now?"

"Well, she's—she's talking now. A lot."

"Yeah? Good for her."

He drags his thumb against a leather key chain on his key ring. It's the kind with different clock faces—New York, San Francisco—and a compass. Then, kind of resignedly, he says, "Guess what her first word was."

I'm not in a guessing mood. But he waits, so finally I say, "Mom."

"Guess again."

"Ball."

"Not even close."

I sigh. People start trickling through the gate, but the screen's still saying twenty minutes before Trey arrives. "I don't know, Kevin. Heritage. Constitution. Homework."

He smiles. "You wish, don't you? It was *shark*."

The cops have split up, all three at different gates. If one of them snapped right now—just lost it, with no warning—and drew a gun, what would everyone do? I read some of the hate mail my dad's been getting in his e-mail; I guess some people think he should've just sat there and let himself be threatened, maybe killed. "*Shark*, huh."

"It was pretty awesome—I won't lie."

I give what maybe, barely, passes for a laugh. I can feel Kevin watching me, and after a while he says, mildly, "It'll be nice to have Trey around again."

"Yep."

"I've missed that guy."

"I'll bet you have."

His raises his eyebrows at that one, but if he thought I was being rude, he doesn't say it. (I was, actually; I should've backed off that *you*.) Instead he says, "You know, I think he's glad to be coming back."

I make a sound like, *Heh.*

"You don't think so?"

"I think he must've been banking on the social worker being hot." I remember her yelling at the news crew. "Or maybe she just scared the—"

"Oh, give him more credit than that, Braden. He can't wait to see you."

Kevin's the kind of guy who'd say that just because he's nice, but I hope that part, at least, is true. I'm nervous as hell to see Trey. I don't even know what I'll say to him. I still haven't heard a word from him, and God knows how the conversation went with the social worker. It's not lost on me that he ignored all my calls and texts the night my dad got arrested, and I'm scared he'll blame me for having to come back here. I'm scared he'll think I ruined his life.

Kevin fiddles with his key chain some more. Then he says, more quietly, "Look, Braden, it's a lot for anyone to be dealing with. And what they've been saying this week about the DA's decision is just—if you feel like you need to talk about—"

"I'm going to get something from the vending machines." Before he can finish his sentence I get up so fast that for a second it feels like there's cotton balls inside my head. "You want anything, Mr. C? I'll go get you a drink."

.   .   .

I get water for myself and Cokes for Trey and Kevin, and then I pretend to still be looking at the vending machine so Kevin can't ask me anything else. The airport's quiet, but it's still better than home, where your thoughts stretch out huge like shadows and tower across the whole room.

Nothing was supposed to go like this. I'm supposed to be focusing on pitching. After we won State last year, I felt good about it for about a month, and then however bad I wanted to win before I wanted it twice as much because now I have to prove it wasn't a fluke and prove my worth to anyone who ever doubted it. Right now I should be worrying about how we're going to beat Brantley, not worrying about my dad locked up with a bunch of criminals in a cell or about my brother getting dragged back here because of me. I've always held out hope that Trey and my dad would patch things up someday— that's what God promised me, wasn't it?—but I also always thought it would be something I did that would make Trey come back. That I'd get drafted and he'd think, *Hey, maybe I should take a break from holing myself up with groceries all the time and go watch Braden play pro ball,* or that he'd just wake up one morning and realize he missed me, the same way I've felt about him all these years. It wasn't supposed to be a social worker calling to guilt him with a bunch of documents and legal warnings.

I lean over to retrieve the bottles from the vending machine, and when I straighten, one of the officers walks by. The bottle slips from my hand and clatters to the ground, hissing like a live grenade, and my heart feels like it's about to pump itself clear out of my chest. My palms are damp.

I need to get it together. Seeing random cops walk by at the airport is nothing compared to the rest of all this.

I look around to make sure no one's watching, and then I close my eyes again and duck my head. The thing I believe about God most of all is that sooner or later he brings everyone to justice; I believe he protects and rewards the people who follow him and punishes the ones who don't. And I'm scared that part of what I felt when the social worker was over was God telling me that he brought this on us to test me—that I won't be spared his anger unless I prove my devotion to him.

Get us through this, I pray, and I wait to see if I'll feel that same warning from him again. I don't. *Protect us. I'll do everything the way you'd want me to, and I won't slip up even once. I'll be as good as I know how to be, I'll work as hard as I possibly can, I won't slack off or get distracted, even with all of this. And if I do all that, and I throw my best and beat Brantley when we play them, then let that be my sign from you that I was wrong and that all this isn't because you're testing me. And please let everything be okay.*

I down my water in two gulps and crush the plastic bottle in my hand and force myself to walk by the cop to throw the bottle away. When I get back near the gate, there's a younger version of my dad coming down the walkway, with a gray T-shirt and a mostly shaved head and a wrestler's build, and there's a feeling like a snake uncoiling in my stomach—that's Trey.

.　.　.

He's carrying two big bags, and when he makes his way over to us, he sets them both on the ground and says quietly, like he's tired, "Didn't know you were coming, Braden. Hey, Kev." I take a step forward to hug him at the same time he sticks out his hand and I take an awkward step back that feels like a whole-body stutter. I shake his hand instead, and Trey says, "You got tall."

"Yeah." I can feel my face reddening after that aborted attempt at a hug. I was never short, but I hit a growth spurt right before high school. I got our dad's pitcher's build, the five o'clock shadow because I get bored of shaving, the tan even in winter from all the baseball, wheat-colored hair from the baseball, too. Trey got our dad's eyes and jawline, and he looks . . . older, I guess, different in that way that makes you wonder if maybe this is how a person's always looked and you just aren't remembering right. I say, "I guess taller than I was in sixth grade."

"Five years will do that," Kevin says, grinning broadly and nudging Trey in the side. "And I have to say, you're not looking your best. Rough flight?"

My brother runs his hand over his stubbly head, his bicep bulging. He doesn't look like he's in much of a smiling mood. And Kevin's right; Trey's got dark half circles under his eyes and deeper hollows under his cheekbones.

"Well," he says, ignoring both our comments and hitching his bags on his shoulder in a way that means business, a way that means he's doing this because he thinks he should and not because he wanted to, "where'd you guys park?"

THREE

Kevin drives a blue Outback with a baby car seat and IT'S NOT A RELIGION, IT'S A RELATIONSHIP and ROMANS 5:8 bumper stickers. It's two hours back home from the airport, the cramped gray and the noise of the city settling back into the wide-open fields and orchards and back roads of the Central Valley. I think if I lived someplace like where Trey does, I'd never be able to really breathe. In Ripon, after the water tower, we pass one of the billboards advertising my dad's show: *Mart Raynor Jr., Truth for Today's World.* No graffiti on this one.

If Kevin's been as nervous to see Trey as I've been—except why would he be? Kevin's not the one who dragged him away from his other life—he doesn't show it. He asks if Trey got things with his restaurant all worked out, and Trey says yeah, mostly; he put Adam in charge (Kevin seems to recognize the names; maybe they talk more than I realized), hired three new line cooks, and, he says, is now bleeding from the ears in payroll. Kevin says, "I saw Mona's hiring at Jag's."

"Yeah, thanks, asshole."

Kevin grins. "Hey, now. Watch your language around your little brother."

"Not all of us lead Christian youth groups." In the rearview mirror, I see Trey raise his eyebrows at Kevin pointedly. "Anyway, I told you I'm supposed to be writing that cookbook."

I lean forward. "You're making a book?"

"That's how I could afford to up and leave my job like that."

People willing to pay to have a part of you in their homes—that's got to be a good feeling. "That's pretty cool. It'd be nice to make something that didn't just disappear when people ate it."

He says, "Mm," like maybe I said that wrong. Then he says he was supposed to have it finished months ago, but I'm pretty sure he's only telling Kevin. I stay quiet, until eventually I'm not part of the conversation at all.

It's when they start talking about actual food, something Trey's doing with dehydrated shrimp powder or something else that I guess is technically food, that I start to get queasy. Tonight is the longest I've been in a car since the accident. I lean my head back against the seat and close my eyes, and it's maybe fifteen minutes later that they lower their voices and I figure they think I'm asleep.

"This is the first day all year I haven't gone in to work, I think," Trey says. "Right? It's weird as hell. I don't know what to do with my hands. I was jittery as fuck on the plane."

"I'm sure your seatmates loved that."

"Ha. So what're Jenna and Ellie doing right now?"

"They're having dinner with Jenna's folks." Then Kevin adds, "Next week's our anniversary."

"Oh." There's a pause. "Right. That's right."

"Five years."

"I know that. What are you doing for her?"

"I'm taking her camping."

"You're what?"

"Camping. Did you forget what that was since moving to your fancy city? Tent. Campfire. S'mores. Stars. Sleeping bags."

"That's it?"

"What do you mean, that's it?"

"I mean Jenna had your *baby*, and you're making her sleep in a *tent*? Making her burned hot dogs? Take her to San Francisco or something. Buy her a nice dinner. Buy her jewelry. At least get her a hotel."

"You know what, how about I'll ask you beforehand next time I'd like ideas on what to do with my wife." Kevin clears his throat. "Have you talked to your dad yet? Since—"

"Why would you even ask me that?"

"I'm guessing that's a no."

"I told you I talked to the social worker. That was plenty."

"Has his lawyer talked to Braden?"

Trey says, "No idea."

"You still haven't asked him about it, either?"

"He doesn't need to think about that. Give him a shitload of homework this week, will you? Keep him distracted."

"Right, Trey. That sounds like exactly what he needs." Then he adds, "My parents have everyone they know praying."

"You can tell your parents that's not necessary. Tell them I said no thanks."

Kevin sighs. He never finished, because he became a teacher instead, but I know he was in seminary for a while to be a pastor like his dad. "You know I'm not going to."

"Fine. Then don't." Then Trey says, "Wait, wait," and I can't tell from his voice whether he's frowning or smiling. "You're doing it, too. I know you. You're praying, too."

"Of course I am."

"Don't you have some things of your own to discuss with God already? Maybe instead you should ask—"

"Give it a rest, Trey. How'd it go explaining things to your employees?"

"It didn't."

"What do you mean, it didn't? Did you still not tell them?" I can hear the frown in Kevin's voice. "You just left? That's it? No explanation?"

We go another mile or so. Then Trey says, "People always talk. Whatever. If they know, they know."

"Well, it's your restaurant, I guess."

Trey snorts, and when he talks, his voice is mean. "Isn't that generous of you."

Kevin's quiet. Then he says, "You've had a long week."

We go over something in the road, a pothole maybe, and I'm jostled back and forth. I clench up at that feeling. Then Trey says, less meanly, "Did, uh—did Braden say very much?"

"Oh, volumes. You know him. He adores talking. There I was, trying to focus on driving, and he wouldn't let up with the—"

"Kev, come on. That was a real question."

"Then no. No, he doesn't talk about it ever. It's very clear you two are brothers. You need to talk to him."

"He seems fine."

"It's been all over the news how the DA's office is seeking the death penalty, Trey. Why would he be *fine*?"

It has been all over the news, but so far everyone's at least had the decency to not say stuff like that around me, and this is how it feels when you hear that said aloud for the first time: like someone's pouring acid down your throat. Like the words you read in the articles have come to life and are circling you with ropes and matches and gasoline.

We pull through the gates of the country club and drive up the sloping landscaped hill and past what Trey always called the McMansions to the end of our cul-de-sac. When Trey and I get out, Kevin leans closer to Trey and says to him, quietly, "I know I said it already, but I'm proud of you for doing this," and then he drives away and, for the first time in five years, it's just us.

"Does it look the same?" I say, more for the sake of conversation than anything else, but he looks around the cul-de-sac as if he's hunting for an answer. It smells a little bit like manure, the way it does sometimes here when it's warm and the wind blows east from the Niederhost ranch a few towns over in Royalton.

Trey draws a long breath, taking in so much air his chest swells up, then lets it all out in one sharp exhale. "Smells like shit."

He unlocks the side door to the garage and we go in. I'm pretty surprised he even still has a key. "Hey," he says, stopping short and frowning at the empty garage, "what happened to the car?"

I blink at him. "I mean, they—they took it for evidence or whatever, so—"

"I know *that*. I meant the other car."

"Oh." The Mustang was Trey's, originally; my dad bought it for him when he turned sixteen but gave it to me when Trey dropped out of college and stopped ever coming home. "Ah—it kind of got messed up."

"You crash it or something?"

"Uh—sort of."

He raises his eyebrows like he's not at all impressed, but he lets it drop. That's at least a small relief. I follow him in and then upstairs, hanging around as he goes into his room.

"I washed the sheets and stuff for you," I say from the doorway. "Are you hungry or anything? You want to get something to eat? I didn't eat yet, either."

"I ate about fifty packs of peanuts on the plane."

His room looks exactly the same as it did when he was in high school, which is to say, obsessively neat. Trey used to do puzzles with my dad sometimes, and he always separated every single piece into piles according to shape, which my dad always said made him look like a serial killer. On his dresser there's an old picture of Trey's mom and, next to it, one of the three of us at AT&T Park that last time we went. My dad has his arm draped around us and he's smiling, and I'm grinning with a tooth missing, and Trey's not smiling but he's looking back at the camera amused, kind of, so you can tell he had fun in the end, too.

It helps, remembering that; it gives me something to hold on to. That the three of us, him and me and Trey, we all come from the same place.

Trey takes his laptop out of his bag and sets it on his desk. "What's the Wi-Fi password here now?"

I give him the number, and his expression changes. The password's Trey's birthday. I say, "Dad set it."

He ignores that. He leaves the laptop shut and puts the bag down next to it, then reaches down to untie his shoes.

"My games start this week," I say, watching him. "We're the defending state champions. I told you that, right?"

"That's good."

"Yeah. Except it's even more pressure now. We have a big game coming up pretty soon against Brantley. You could come watch." I pick at a scab on the back of my hand. "Actually, I think the Giants game is still on right now, too. First spring training game. Four–four in the eighth."

He makes a sound like *hungh.*

"You still follow them much? Or are you, like, a Yankees fan now or something?"

"Really, Braden? The *Yankees?*"

I smile at the disgust in his voice. "Well—you want to watch the rest of the game with me? Ramirez is pitching. Just went in." Then I add, "And Brett Kirk's catching, too. He kind of reminds me of you."

"I'll pass." He says it so fast my offer still hangs in the air, blaring like it's lit up in neon, and I wish I hadn't asked. Trey reaches into the outer pocket of his suitcase and pulls out something squishy, wrapped in paper.

"Here," he says. "Brought this back for you."

It's a soft pretzel, encrusted in grains of salt. "Best one in New York," he says, shaking out a T-shirt and then refolding it neatly. "Buddy of mine has a German gastropub."

"I see." I have zero idea what that even means; it's the kind of thing my dad would have a field day with. "Uh—thanks."

"Pretzels still your favorite?"

"What? Oh—yeah. Yeah, sure." I eat some, and Trey folds more of his clothes. With my mouth full, I say, "So did you tell any of your friends you'd be around a little while?"

"I didn't keep friends here except Kevin."

"How come?"

"Because once you get out of this town, you realize all the people here are shit."

I shouldn't have asked. "Did you tell Emily?"

"Why the hell would I tell Emily?"

"I don't know. Maybe she'd want to see you." I heard she got married a while ago, but it would still be nice for him to have a friend nearby.

"You'd want to see your exes?"

I don't have exes. "I liked Emily."

"Great. You call her, then. Anyway, she's married now."

"I know." I guess, like Trey, she's almost thirty. "Sorry."

He shrugs. "You know, in other parts of America, people don't think it's normal to get married when you're still practically a teenager. I'm the one who ended it, and that was years ago anyway, so who cares?"

"Right." I shift my weight onto my other foot. "Hey, Trey—you haven't heard anything from Dad, right? He didn't call or anything?"

"Nope."

"I'm worried they aren't letting him make calls."

He grunts.

"He still hasn't called me. And that's the first thing he'd do, right? So I'm scared that—"

He stares at me like I'm growing another set of limbs right in front of him. Or maybe that's supposed to be a warning. "Or . . . we can talk about it later."

"Listen, Braden, just so we're clear, I'm here so they don't put you in a group home or whatever the hell the social worker said they'd do. Not to talk about Dad. I have zero interest in that. None whatsoever. Understood?"

I pause a second or two. None of this is going how I hoped. But when you're the reason your older brother just uprooted his whole life, you watch the way you talk to him.

"Sure," I say, as nicely as I can. "Yeah. You probably had a long flight. You want some water or anything? Want me to make juice?"

"No." He sinks down on his bed. It makes a creaking sound, one I recognize immediately from childhood. "I've been awake for thirty hours straight, okay? I need to get some sleep."

"Oh. Yeah. Okay." I wrap up the rest of my pretzel. "Well, there's towels in the hall closet, and—"

"Yeah, thanks, Braden, I lived in this house too. I know where everything is."

That shuts me up, and I turn to go. And then, despite what I just told myself ten seconds ago, I slip. "Well, that's good. Probably nothing's changed in the nine years since you've been here. Nothing at all."

La Abra played Bear Creek today.

Back in my room, I go to the league website and refresh it until the game stats go up. I read until I see that Alex Reyes went two for three against Jorge Ayala, who's got this slider that breaks so hard you could watch the same one three times in a row and still not believe it's going to end up where it does. I've faced him once or twice, and that pitch, when he can nail it, wastes me every time. But it looks like that slider was no problem for Alex tonight.

Alex is a senior and he plays second base for La Abra, so I've played against him all my life. La Abra churns out good players, Latino kids who make you wonder if they're lying about how old they are, but Alex is just mediocre and I wouldn't think much of him if it wasn't for this: despite his .249 average, he's not an easy guy to strike out, and I've never been able to figure out why.

I've talked to him exactly once, when I was twelve and we were both at an umping clinic for Little League, and they had breakfast for us there and he ate his cereal with juice. I said it was gross, and he shrugged and said maybe I was jealous. But he didn't say it like he was defensive or like he was joking around and wanted to be friends; he said it like what I'd said just didn't affect him at all. To be nice, I said, "I'm Braden," and he said, "I know who you are." Then he said, "You're a good pitcher," only he said it matter-of-factly, not as a compliment, and I didn't know what to make of that.

I read the stats with his name four times over until the words start to lose their meanings. Then I shut the computer, fast.

It's twelve more weeks until we play La Abra. I hope that's enough time to figure out how I'm supposed to get up on a mound and face the nephew of the cop my dad's accused of killing.

FOUR

There are things you can hold at bay in the daylight, but it's when you're drifting off to sleep that the thoughts and images creep up on you, slithering across your dark room from the corners where they've been lying all day in wait. Every night when I close my eyes, I see again the cops swarming over our driveway like an invading army, the flashing lights like dull explosions through the fog; I see the cops shove my dad into the back of the squad car so roughly he almost hits his head on the door as he turns back, trying to plead with them. And I see myself standing frozen on the driveway with officers surrounding me so close I can't catch my breath long enough to say *Wait* or *Please* or *Dad* before his car is swallowed in the fog halfway down the street.

I'll say this, though: it's a lot better knowing Trey's here.

The morning dawns bright and cool, and through the window I can hear the lawn mower for the golf course driving across the greens.

Today's opening day of our season, the first game in my life I've ever played without my dad there.

I hear Trey get up and go to the bathroom, and then I hear him go downstairs to the kitchen. There's drawers opening and screeches of furniture being pushed across the floor. The doorbell rings when I'm still in bed, and I hear Trey clomping down the hall, pissed-sounding, and then back upstairs. My door swings open, and he says, "Get up. The lawyer's here to talk to you."

"Right now?"

"Yes, right now." He looks exhausted. "Look, Braden, you know this isn't my deal, but he said you haven't returned any of his calls."

"That's because I really don't want to be involved in any of the trial stuff."

"This isn't like a party you don't want to go to or something. You can't mess around like that."

"Okay, well, I can't talk to him right now. I have school."

"Then I'll call you in sick. But get your ass down there. He's waiting."

When I pass through the kitchen I see Trey's moved everything around—shoved the table all the way against the wall, corralled the chairs into one corner, moved my dad's coffee mug from its place on top of the microwave and stuck it in the sink. He's done some unpacking, at least, and the sight of his knives lined up on the counter and his gleaming coppery pans resting on the stove is reassuring.

The lawyer's in the dining room, tapping his fingers on the glass tabletop. He looks at me a few seconds too long, holds out his hand for me to shake, and smiles in a way that looks practiced. He has a viselike grip. "So you're Braden."

"Yes, sir."

"I still haven't been able to get through to you on the phone."

"Oh. Yeah." I release my hand and pull out the chair across from him. "I keep missing your calls."

The lawyer's named MacDouglas Buchwald. He has glasses, and something about him, maybe his laser stare, reminds me of the ex-athletes who turn into sportscasters and argue with everyone on TV. His website's this dump of blocky text and clip art pictures of dancing Greek columns and no actual information about him or his record or anything, and every time he leaves me a message, he sounds surprised—*Oh, hi, Braden, I see I've missed you*, like he can't believe I didn't pick up.

Trey comes in with a cup of coffee and some sugar and sets it down in front of the lawyer in an exaggeratedly polite way that, if I were the lawyer, would probably annoy me. Mr. Buchwald stirs in two spoonfuls of sugar, and I guess I (stupidly) thought there was a chance Trey might sit down with us, too, but he disappears back into the kitchen. I hear the thud of a cutting board.

"Well, Braden." The lawyer takes a long sip of his coffee—I always thought it was a dick move to start a sentence and then eat or drink something so the other person has to wait—then sets the cup down on the table. "Your father's preliminary hearing has been set for Thursday, February twenty-seventh, so we've got quite a bit to cover. As you're no doubt aware by now, the charges filed against your father are one count of resisting an officer, one count of vehicular manslaughter, one count of felony hit-and-run, and one count of aggravated first-degree murder with special circumstances, because the deceased was an officer. I predict at the preliminary hearing the prosecution will demand guilty pleas on all charges and require fifty years served. I'd be downright shocked at anything less than twenty, which I wouldn't view as a tempting deal. Point being, it's quite likely a plea deal isn't in the cards."

If I was holding on to any hope that the point of a lawyer was to get him out of jail without having to go through the rest of it, that vanishes. It feels like someone's grabbed my stomach with both hands and is twisting in opposite directions as hard as possible. "So you think there's going to be a trial."

He gazes at me as if he's trying to figure out if I'm slow. "Yes."

I remind myself that I believe God raised people from the dead. Maybe it's Mr. Buchwald's job to assume the worst, but it doesn't mean God can't work miracles even when you thought there was no hope. I say, "Have you talked to my dad? How is he?"

"He's doing as well as could be expected, I suppose. Now—"

"Does he know about . . . about what they said this week? The DA's office, I mean? About the death penalty?"

"I make sure to keep him apprised of all relevant developments in his case."

"Oh," I say, and then can't bring myself to ask how he took the news. "I haven't heard from him at all. I don't even know if they're letting him make calls."

"He's not permitted conversation with potential witnesses. However, by law, he's permitted a certain amount of phone time each week, so I wouldn't worry about that. Now." He slides a folder across the table toward me, then reaches over to flip it open. The papers inside are printed on MACDOUGLAS BUCHWALD, JD letterhead. I can't imagine any situation where I'd print out papers for someone else and make sure to have my name on every single one of them, especially if my last name kind of sounded like *fuckwad*. "This is a collection of pointers I've put together for you about how to be an effective witness."

I don't look at the papers. A witness, I think, and I try to ignore the way my skin prickles—I should just take this meeting as a reminder to hold up my end of my bargain with God. "I don't think it's a good idea for me to be involved in any of that."

He gives me the blank look people give you when someone made a joke they didn't get. "You can read these on your own time. What I'd like for us to do now is begin to discuss your testimony and how it will—"

"Actually, sir, with all due respect, I really don't want to be involved in any of that. I'm not great at getting up in front of people, and I'd be too scared I'd screw things up somehow and—"

He picks out a piece of paper between his thumb and forefinger and sets it on the table between us. "Well, as it so happens, this," he says, "is a subpoena letting you know that your presence is required in court."

Oh.

I slump back against my chair. I wish Trey hadn't let him in; I had a feeling this was why the lawyer kept calling me. I wish I'd left for school already. But I guess it's too late to do anything about that now.

I glance toward the kitchen. There's chopping sounds, Trey cutting something. "At the station the cops said something about me being an accessory, or—"

"Is that what they told you?" His lips curve. "No. The funny thing about police interviews is that officers conducting them aren't legally bound by the truth. They can lie about whatever they wish to try to squeeze out a confession. You're a minor and you weren't driving; there'd be no case. But no doubt they wanted you to make some sort of statements incriminating your father, which would also likely tarnish you as a witness for the defense. And certainly they knew you'd be a critical witness. You and Alexander Reyes were the only ones who were there."

He leans forward and shuffles through the papers. "Now, what I want to begin doing today is discussing what you'll be saying during the trial so I can start thinking about how that's going to fit into my larger, cohesive strategy."

"Which is what, exactly?"

He narrows his eyes and runs his tongue along the inside of his cheek, and I get the impression he's deciding how much he feels like telling me. "I'm sure you've noticed there's . . . how shall I say this? A sizable contingent of individuals who are positively rabid in their desire to see your father punished."

I nod. Like I said, I've read some of the hate mail, a lot of it from people who seemed to take the accident personally and can barely type. And then there was the billboard, and I saw on the news there was a protest one night, even (protesting what, exactly, I don't know), and that same night on the news there was an interview with this columnist in San Francisco who's always hated my dad. I switched it off two sentences in; I didn't need to see him gloat.

"Well, what you're seeing isn't entirely unusual in a high-profile criminal case," Mr. Buchwald says. "The police and the prosecutors talk in public, and the defense waits for the trial, so it's not revolutionary for public opinion to feel tilted toward the prosecution before then." He pauses. "But my personal theory is that Laila Shah, the deputy DA who'll be prosecuting the case, is testing the waters and trying to gauge the temperature of the public. I feel quite certain she'll try to convince the jurors that an act like this is in character for your father."

The words settle around my shoulders. "She doesn't even know him."

"Laila is quite new to the position. She's supposed to be a rising young star from Hastings Law—although so far I've not been terribly impressed—but it's been my experience that her type is often . . .

bitter, really, and stridently angry, and constantly on the hunt for a scapegoat. Originally, she wanted to try the case as a hate crime. I think that's as telling as it is appalling."

This isn't how I thought court cases were supposed to work. It's definitely not what we learned in Civics. "Okay, well—is that what juries base their decisions on? Whoever just happens to seem like a better person, or what?"

"It all depends on the jury, of course, but I think her angle is going to backfire on her. She could have picked a better poster child for her crusade. I've looked quite extensively into Reyes's history. A delinquent in uniform is just a better-dressed delinquent." He picks up the coffee cup and blows on the top of it with wet, pursed lips. "Now, to return to the matter at hand. I understand you and your father had one previous encounter with Officer Reyes. Can you tell me about that?"

I would give a lot not to, but I don't make it a habit to talk back to adults. "A little while ago, I kind of went to LA without telling my dad, and he got worried and he called the cops and Officer Reyes was one of the ones who came. And Officer Reyes was—yeah. He and my dad got into it, and he told me he wished something worse had happened to me. But I wasn't there for when the two of them were—"

"Hm." He marks something down. "Your father has maintained that he was forced to flee the scene of the accident as a safety concern. Can you explain that to me? Actually"—he holds up one finger—"I'll read the statement he gave me, and you may fill in as you wish."

He deepens his voice and sits up straighter when he's reading my dad's words. I'll bet my dad intimidates him. He has that effect on people. " 'I was speeding a little bit, I'll admit that. I deserved a ticket and I would've paid one, too, but right away, when I saw him, I knew it was going to be bad. The thing is, I met this cop once before, and it was when I was worried about my kid, so we'd, you know, exchanged words. And I'll admit I said some things I shouldn't have, but I didn't think he handled the whole situation real professionally, so afterward I called up and complained to the station about him. And he knew it. You could tell he knew it and that it did something to him. That, and the fact it was late and there was no one around, that I had no protection—he thought he was above the rules. He kept getting closer and closer to me, getting more and more threatening. And I was yelling back, I was getting hot under the collar, too, but I miscalculated. He was out for me. When he went for his gun, I panicked he was going to hurt my son. I panicked. He drew the gun, and I had to get away.'"

He puts down the paper he's holding. "Sound right?"

"I mean, do people think you should just stay somewhere and let someone shoot you?"

"So you'll testify that Reyes threatened you with a loaded firearm."

There's a buzzing in my ears that makes me want to swat at imaginary bees. But then, I've always hated guns. "I really think my dad would give a better testimony than I would. He's a lot better at that kind of thing."

"It's simply too risky to have the defendant testify in capital cases." He writes something down on his pad. "Your father says he was left distressed and very shaken after the encounter with the cop."

"Yes. That's definitely true. He was really upset. It kind of . . . I mean, it sort of made him not completely—"

Mr. Buchwald holds up a hand to stop me. "Your father backed up and then drove out into the road when he was what felt like a safe distance away."

I nod.

"He says that when he felt the car hit something, he thought he'd hit a pothole."

"There's tons of potholes there."

"You felt the car hit something, too, I presume."

"I guess I—"

"But you didn't believe it was Mr. Reyes?"

"How could anyone even think he'd do that on purpose? If you knew you hit a person, you wouldn't take off. You'd get out and make sure he was okay, and if he wasn't, you'd try to save him or at least wait there with him and call nine-one-one. That's what any halfway decent person would do." My chest and face feel like someone rubbed Icy Hot all over them. I look toward the kitchen again. It would be stupid to ask Trey to come sit in here; I'm capable of having this conversation myself. And I'm not on trial *now*. This is probably nothing compared to what it feels like saying this kind of stuff in court. "I just—I really think you should have my dad talk about all this instead. He talks for a living. And he obviously has a better memory of everything that's happened, so—"

"Son, I know this is unsavory, but these questions will come up again."

I hate when people call me *son*. "Okay, but if there's a trial and I screw it up, then what? It's going to be twelve random people who've never met him and who might have made up their minds about him already, and you said yourself it's a death-penalty case. So if I mess things up—"

"You'll have ample time to prepare, Braden, don't worry. I am very heavily invested in making your testimony as clear and as compelling as possible, and you'll be seeing quite a bit of me as we prepare. Now, do you have any questions?"

"What about bail? Can he get out on bail?"

"I'll make a motion at the preliminary hearing, but it's unlikely. Judge Scherr is up for reelection in the fall, so he'll be treading carefully."

"And if my dad doesn't get bail, then I'm just . . . not allowed to see him or talk to him the whole time this is going on?"

"Most likely no. Occasionally letters are approved. Anything else?"

It's clear he's not actually asking, but I ask anyway. "Whose idea was it for me to testify?"

He blinks at me. "I beg your pardon?"

"Like, it was your idea, and my dad didn't argue? Or he was the one who came up with it?"

"There wasn't much conversation. You're an eyewitness. It's your father."

"But did he tell you in so many words that I would testify, or what?"

"Really, Braden, there's no need to be so nervous." He claps his hand on my back and smiles with his lips closed. "Your father trusts you, and so do I."

FIVE

There've been dark gray clouds gathering over the orchards at the horizon and threatening rain all day, but there's a good-size crowd gathering for the game when we head out onto the field that afternoon to warm up. Baseball is king in Ornette, the thing you talk about with strangers in line at the store and relive when you're barbecuing at the lake in the summer. Last year when we took the championship it felt like the whole town made the trip to Southern California to see us play. Something about the crowd today makes me feel safer—the normalcy of it, partly, and also I guess it feels like a sign of good faith. Everyone in the crowd's been listening to my dad announce our games nearly all my life.

I toss a few off-speed pitches to Colin, my catcher, to warm up, and I half watch who's coming into the stands. I guess this was dumb, but I'd thought maybe Trey would be here. He's not. But it's a bad habit to watch attendance, anyway—at best, it's just a lot of people to worry about letting down.

To make the playoffs again this year, we can lose no more than once, and today won't be that day. Sierra West isn't a real threat like Brantley or La Abra, and last year we took them 11–2. Today I'm pitching against Logan Marshall, a second-string pitcher who last year had nothing more than a halfway decent slider he couldn't command half the time anyway, and whose career will probably end in Tuesday night community softball once he graduates. I've already told Colin I want to throw curveballs today to practice for Brantley, since Sierra's the kind of team you can practice on.

But still, even though Logan Marshall isn't someone I'm afraid of, even though I'm not actually worried about this game, there's a stinging, pulsing anxiety building in my muscles like lactic acid. It gets worse when I take the mound and there's a loud, breathy staticky sound from the announcer's booth. Colin gets the game ball from the umpire and tosses it to me, and whoever they got to replace my dad reads my stats from a list in a way that makes me think he's never heard of me in his life. Before I can stop it, I see again my dad's arms wrenched behind his back, the way his legs buckled from pain or maybe fear.

I curl my hand around the ball. There's a place in your mind where any voices you let in slip down your spine and into your lungs and heart, become a thing you breathe and bleed, and my dad taught me this: how to stake a barricade against those ones you can't allow. I wait until I'm back in control, until there's nothing else except the next pitch.

I position my right foot against the edge of the rubber and stand straight, sheltering the ball in my glove. Colin puts down a sign for a fastball and then sets up outside, and I position my fingers around the ball's seams, and I lift my left leg and balance on my right and watch the hitter circle his bat. It's not often that you matter more than you do in that moment, when you're another person's entire world. Then I draw back my arm and shift all my weight forward at the same time as I fling my arm as hard as it will go in one calibrated explosion and the ball goes rocketing out of my hand, a pure, clean line across the grass, and it flies over the plate and is swallowed safely into Colin's glove before the batter ever moves.

Strike one.

. ` °

I escape the first inning with nothing worse against me than a single. As I go back into the dugout, Colin's talking to Greg Harmon. Greg's our only freshman this year, a quiet, smallish kid who moved here last year. He's . . . not exactly the kind of new kid who does well here, or maybe anywhere, so I started dragging him out to eat lunch with the guys after I found out he always spent lunchtime alone in the library watching anime on the computer. He has some bullpen potential, so I've been giving him pointers every now and then, and Coach Cardy's got him batting leadoff today. Greg's gulping down water and flexing his hand around the bottle, and Colin's saying, "Greg, you aren't scared, are you?"

"Um." Greg drinks more water. He makes a *glllghh* sound when he swallows, and I don't think his voice has changed yet all the way. "No. Maybe. I guess."

"Of Sierra *West*? If that's how you feel now, you'll be shitting yourself when we play Brantley." Colin grins and elbows me. "Maybe you should just sit back and watch Braden and see how it's done. What's your batting average, Raynor? Couple goose eggs up there after your name?"

"Yeah, shut up." I sink down on the bench next to them. I'm not one of those pitchers who can also hit. "You have nothing to worry about, Greg. Logan Marshall's nothing."

"Right." He pushes his sports goggles higher up the bridge of his nose. "Well, um. It's not really that I'm worried about him."

I say, "What is it, then?"

"I mean, it's kind of that, but then also . . . do you ever get nervous when someone's here to watch you and you want to impress them?"

Colin hoots. "Is it a girl?" He shoots me a look. I know some of the guys have wondered about Greg before—the way he's always smoothing his hair, his voice, just the way he seems kind of . . . different—but I shut that down pretty quick. Greg's on our team, and you don't talk like that about someone you play and share a locker room with. Colin whacks Greg on the knee with his glove. "Say it's a girl."

"No," Greg says. "It's my dad. He came today and he never comes." Then he looks at me, alarmed. "I mean, I shouldn't complain. It's not like he's—"

Colin slices his finger across his neck at Greg, who shuts up. The ump signals for the inning to start, and Cardy yells for Greg to go bat. Greg looks relieved. Before he can get up, I snag the sleeve of his jersey and pull his head down toward me. Greg blanches.

"Listen, Greg," I say, so only he can hear. "Everyone gets nervous. You're supposed to. I'm still a wreck before each pitch. If you don't feel that way, it's because you don't care. Okay? You're in a good place."

When he walks out to the plate Colin says, "What'd you say to him?"

"Nothing."

"Right." He glances at me, and then, just as quick, turns his gaze on the chain links between us and the field. I'll bet he's the reason why, except for just now, the guys on my team have been pretty good about not saying anything about my dad. "Weird kid, huh?"

Greg takes a ball outside and then a strike at the knees. Then, on a curveball that barely breaks, he hesitates for what feels to me like a second too long and then unloads. The ball sails over left field and there's a startled silence from the crowd, and then, when the ball keeps going over the fence, everyone yells. Colin's laughing.

"Greg *Harmon*," he said. "Who knew?"

That's the thing about baseball, though, is it lays you bare: play long enough and eventually who you really are will show through.

. . .

In Greg's next at bat, Logan beans him right in the thigh with a pitch so obviously intentional our bench nearly clears and it takes the umpires' threats to call the game to make Cardy sit everyone back down. When Greg comes back in the dugout, rubbing his thigh with a grimace, I grab his wrist—you don't rub a wound like that and let the other team see how much you're hurting—and tell him to pick someone for me to hit back.

"Um . . ." He drops his hand and looks uncomfortably at the field. "I don't really want to start anything."

"Hit him in the *cacahuetes*," Dutch says, and Chase snaps, "That guy's a joke." He'd jumped up when Greg got hit, ready to charge the mound. "Braden should hit him in the fucking head."

Greg looks alarmed. I say, "You're not *starting* anything, Greg. You're righting a wrong. He did that because you took that homer off of him, you know."

"Yeah, I figured. But—"

"Where you played before you moved here, your pitcher would've just let that slide?"

"Probably. My coach would've made him."

That sounds like the worst kind of person to play for. Something like that left outstanding would eat away at me all game. Cardy's like my dad; after winning, loyalty matters most. My freshman year, he overheard me say I thought we might lose to Beyer, and he had me doing push-ups until my arms gave out. I say, "Well, it doesn't work like that here, so. An eye for an eye."

Greg lowers his voice, looking uneasy. "Um, what Chase said—"

"Chase can join the football team if he wants to knock people out cold for fun. Ignore him. He knows I don't play like that."

"I just don't want anything bad to happen."

"It won't. I have two rules for how I deal with batters, all right? No intentional walks, no throwing at anyone's head. Nothing bad will happen."

I can tell he doesn't believe me. But you can ask anyone; I've never broken either rule. The first is from my dad, because giving someone a free base that way is broadcasting to the world that you think he's better than you and it's a matter of my pride, and the second's from Trey, because back when he still played, he got his jaw shattered on a wild pitch. If you look closely, you can still see how things didn't quite heal right—the left side of Trey's jaw juts out more than on the right—because he talked the surgeon into unwiring him early because, he claimed, he was sick of being hungry all the time. That's the story he's told once or twice in interviews (I always read them online; for years it was the most of him I had) when people asked him how he knew he wanted to be a cook. I was six when he got hurt, and when he got back from the hospital, he pulled me aside and said, "Don't ever throw up high like that at someone." The words came out gritted because of the jaw. "Give me your word, Braden. Don't ever even make a guy think you might."

Since Greg's batting first today, I tell him I'll go after Sierra's number one, the shortstop, in retribution. When their shortstop comes up again in the fifth, I throw inside, way inside and as hard as I can, but my throw goes wide and the shortstop leaps back just in time. He's got quick feet. I smile at him, like I meant to do that. I won't let him see that one got to me.

The next pitch, Colin jerks his thumb to his right and then sets up inside. It's a mean trick to throw behind someone, because nine times out of ten the guy'll jump back and put himself right in the ball's path. Which is exactly what the shortstop does, and the pitch gets him just between his stomach and his side. He leans over with his hands on his knees, trying to catch his breath, and then he straightens to try to walk it off.

That one was for Greg. And for myself, too—to remind myself who I am. That no matter what else in the world is shot to hell, baseball will still hold.

We win, 7–2. I got eight strikeouts and went seven innings deep, but I missed the shortstop that first time and I also gave up two runs in five hits—five hits, to Sierra West—and, most of all, there wasn't much behind my curveballs.

It's a complete din when we push open the doors to the locker room, the celebration ricocheting off the metal lockers. Chase has gotten one of the showerheads loose and is spraying water at everyone and screaming *"Suck it, Sierra West!"*

"Hey," I say to Colin over the noise. "You think we should've laid off the curveballs?"

"Seven–two, man. Come on. You were playing Ping-Pong with them out there."

Alex Reyes has been beating out the fastballs; it's the ones that break that he's struggled with. I don't say that part aloud. "You know I'm going to have to throw curveballs when we play Brantley. Our best shot is getting them to keep grounding out."

"Yeah, well, that's Brantley. Today was Sierra West, and we took them out with the trash. Today was good. I feel good about today. You should feel good about it, too."

"Yeah, but—" I exhale and cut myself off. Colin's the only person I'll let catch me because I trust he'll lay himself out to get behind whatever it is I throw, and I won't disrespect him by questioning his calls. "You're right," I say. "We'll worry about that another day."

SIX

There are a million ways you're wrecked by the absence of someone who belongs there with you—like when Trey left, the way his name died out inside the house and my dad only ever referred to Trey as *him*, or all the times my dad went on my computer when I was at school and didn't erase his search history and my computer was littered with tabs from the homepage of Trey's restaurant and every interview he'd ever given and all his Yelp reviews, or the stack of takeout menus we keep pinned with magnets over the barren fridge because now there's no one here who cooks.

With my dad, though, aside from his name in tatters on the news, the worst part is the quiet. A whole week in, I still catch myself wanting to turn on the radio in the morning like an idiot, like he's just at work and everything's fine. On his station they're broadcasting reruns in his time slot, and I can't bring myself to listen, and in the silence of the house all the things I'm scared of swell big enough to fill every single room.

My dad's a good father, always putting me first. He used to take me camping by the lake on weekends and he'd drive around an extra hour, wasting gas, just to make me feel like we were going somewhere exciting and farther away; he's taken me to see over half the Major League ballparks all across the country. And he's a good man, even when no one's looking. Once in third grade, Dutch Hammell wet his pants after a Little League game, and my dad saw it and dumped half a cooler of water on him before anyone else noticed and even though Dutch's mom got all mad at my dad about the water, all he'd say was that it was an accident, and he never told anyone what happened except me. He gives money to charities, and he can rattle off hundreds of Bible passages he's memorized by heart, and he cares a lot about what's right and isn't afraid to speak out even when he gets attacked for not being politically correct.

My dad was fourteen when his mother died of liver failure, and two years after that, his father, who was a trucker and spent most weeks pulling overtime shifts hauling garlic and tomatoes to places like Wyoming or New Mexico or Montana, shot himself to death in the garage. It was winter and my dad was watching TV in the den when he heard the gun go off, and he was the one who went in and found the body.

It was baseball that saved my dad's life after that. He had a legendary fastball that touched ninety-nine when he was seventeen, and when he went out as a first-round draft pick after high school, he left the house and the town he'd grown up in and never went back, and he was set on making something of himself. When he was working his way up through the farm system he met Elaine, and had Trey, and he was happy then, or something like happy, and they had all these dreams for what their lives were going to be like when he finally made it big. Then, in a road game in Reno, he stumbled going after a grounder that took a strange hop and hurt his shoulder so bad that he knew as he was curled on the ground, the field blurry from the pain, he'd never pitch again.

I don't know what it's like to have one real purpose in life and watch that fall apart in front of you on one bad play, but I know it messed him up. Within a few years Elaine left him for someone else, and my dad won custody of Trey because Elaine failed a drug test. When his disability money ran out, the only job my dad could find was as a janitor at a radio station, and even though that would turn out to be part of God's plan for him, he didn't know it then; faith always makes more sense when you can look back later on, but when you're in a bad place you don't know that's not where your story ends.

My dad's always told people my mom died in childbirth. He told *me* that, even, half my life. It was on Trey's birthday the year I was in third grade—after Trey quit coming home, my dad was always kind of a wreck on his birthday—that he told me the truth. What he said seeped into me like water into the land after a drought, something irrevocable, and I've remembered every detail exactly as he told it ever since.

Aureliana Stoddard-Huff. That was her name. (Later, when I turned thirteen and got a Facebook account, the first thing I did was look her up.) She showed up when I was four months old. It was August, and it was the first Wednesday of the month. My dad remembered that part clearly because three nights before that had been the last Summer Special at the bowling alley. He'd planned to go bowling with Trey and then get pizza, which he'd been saving up for, but that same day he'd caught Trey trying to buy a bus ticket to the airport. His own son had tried to leave him. It had been maybe the lowest point in my dad's whole life.

"Hi, Mart," Aureliana Stoddard-Huff said when my dad opened

the door that afternoon. She was small, like a dancer, and less pretty now that he was sober, but definitely not bad. "It is Mart, right?" She lifted the baby a little bit as if somehow he might have missed it, then said, "Yeah, he's yours. And also, I know this is kind of late notice, but I'm leaving and I can't take care of him anymore, so I thought maybe you'd want him instead."

My dad stared at her, then at the baby, then back at her. He only half heard her explanation: she was going to Los Angeles to be a dancer, and she was going to split the rent on a studio with her friend, and anyway she'd be too busy; the baby was a lot of work. Her cousin's kid was much better behaved, but this one—

"You're serious," he interrupted. "You want to leave your kid with *me*?"

"Well," Aureliana said patiently, "he's your kid, too."

The stunning part wasn't actually the kid; it was the girl showing up here to ask him this. Was she stupid? They'd met at a disgusting dive bar, for Christ's sake, and half those guys there lied about their incomes just so they didn't have to pay child support. And sure, there was a time back before he got hurt when he seemed destined to really go somewhere—he was going to rise above his crappy past and be someone—but now he was just a ruined ex–minor leaguer who drank too much and had a custodian job at the radio station and a runaway kid who seemed to hate his own father and couldn't even stand being hugged.

"Well?" Aureliana said. "I can't take him. But you're a dad already. You told me you went to court to get custody of your other son. I could bring him to the fire station, or something, but I thought he'd be better off with you." And this, he'd told me—he was gripping his glass with one hand and my knee in the other—this is something he's always been proud of; this is who he really is: he never considered saying no.

So they went together (in her car, because it was the one with the car seat) to the courthouse to change my name on the birth certificate from Stoddard-Huff to Raynor and to change my middle name so I shared it with him and to add him as my father. To sit in the back of the car with me, my dad had to shovel pillows and clothing into the passenger seat and squeeze himself between her bags of stuff.

These are all the things he told me about her: she was from Turlock. She had brown hair and brown eyes, like mine. (His and Trey's are blue.) She drove over the speed limit carelessly, changed lanes without checking her blind spot. Once she ran a red light. And there was something otherworldly about her, like she was always about to smile at a secret no one else knew, like she wasn't completely in the moment with you because she was somewhere else, somewhere better. He didn't like that—he thought it meant she felt like she was better than everyone else—but I did.

She was twenty, which was eight years older than Trey. My dad was thirty-eight.

In the courthouse, my dad held me in his arms for the first time. He was nervous, because when Trey was a baby, Elaine had done most of the work. On the way back home I cried, and Aureliana took a hand off the wheel and reached into her purse, fishing around until something crinkled, then she tossed it to my dad.

"Here," she said. "Give him this."

It was a Ring Pop, raspberry-flavored, and my dad said, "The hell is this?"

"He likes those better than the pacifiers. You can get them cheapest at Smart and Final, if you have one near you."

"You've got to be kidding me. Even I know you don't give babies candy. What kind of mother are you? You're going to rot his teeth."

"Teeth?" She laughed. "Mart, get real. He's four *months*. He doesn't have *teeth*." Then she added, "The watermelon ones are his favorite. But in the big bags you don't get to pick the flavors."

He was horrified, then furious. And he was going to tell her off, but then he looked at her one more time in the rearview mirror and she was young enough to be his kid, really, and anyway she was obviously a terrible mother if she was leaving her baby with *him*, so he said nothing. Instead, he offered his fingertip to me and, miraculously, I stopped crying.

He smiled. He leaned down and whispered, "Hey, little guy." He cupped his hand over my tiny head and stroked it with his thumb. "How about it, buddy? Huh? You want to come and live with me?"

Back at home, Aureliana gathered her hair into a ponytail. "Well," she said, "I gave you the bag with all his clothes and diaper stuff, and here's the car seat, so . . ." She glanced at her watch. She was already in LA in her mind—he could see that. "I guess that's everything. So good luck. He's not the best baby. He cries a lot."

It was just before dark when Trey got home that day, and my dad met him at the door and grabbed his arm. He'd been waiting two hours for Trey to come home. "Did you forget you were grounded?"

Trey said, shortly, "No."

"Then you better have a damn good—" My dad stopped, changed his mind. "Well, it's your lucky day, because I'm letting you off the hook. Come upstairs with me. I want to show you something."

Trey yanked his arm away. "I've got homework."

"I have a surprise for you."

"I don't care. Leave me alone."

My dad closed his eyes. "Trey. Come upstairs with me and see the surprise, or keep this up and we'll do it the hard way. Your pick."

Trey muttered, "Fine." He followed my dad upstairs. And in my dad's room, lying in the middle of the bed, was a baby. (Obviously: me.)

Trey blinked, jerked his head back. "What is *that*?"

"That's Braden. Your new brother."

"My *what*?"

"Well, half brother. But don't you dare call him that ever, because that *half* doesn't matter." Then he added, because he hadn't exactly practiced what he was going to tell Trey: "He's a baby."

"No shit." Trey took a step forward, looking shell-shocked. "Where did it . . . come from?"

"Oh, come on, wiseass, I got the letter home about how you're doing sex ed. Don't try to tell me you don't know exactly where babies come from."

"So you're its . . . dad?" A nod. "Then where's its mom?"

"Gone. Didn't want him anymore. So now he's ours."

Trey raised his eyebrows at my dad. "Really? Someone's mom actually thought it was a good idea to leave him with *you*? Did you tell her how you—"

My dad drew his hand back, and Trey flinched. He shut up, and my dad dropped his hand, relieved. He cleared his throat and gave Trey a hesitant smile. "Surprise, huh?"

Trey watched him warily for a second, then took a few more steps forward and crouched next to the bed and very, very lightly touched the top of my head. I made a sound like a baby seagull, and Trey yanked his hand back and looked at my dad, his eyes wide. "Did that hurt him?"

"Scared him. How should he know if he trusts you?"

He watched Trey watching me. He couldn't remember the last time he'd been so nervous about what Trey might think.

"Okay," Trey said finally. "Well, that's cool, I guess. I thought your surprise would be something mean. I want to hold him."

"You want to what?"

"Well, what else do you do with a baby?"

"Okay, well—" My dad swallowed, ran a hand over his head, then slid his hands under me. "Okay. Sit back against the headboard. No, scoot to the middle. Get away from the edge." He lifted me carefully. "You drop him," my dad warned, "or hurt him in any way, I will wear you out. You hear?"

"I'm sitting *down*. Where could he even *go*?"

"This baby's made of glass, understand? Don't think I don't know what you're like. I know you. So you be more careful than you've ever been in your life."

"I get it already," Trey muttered. "You never trust me."

My dad was still reluctant. This, he'd told me, was the other thing about Trey: sometimes at night he'd lock himself in his room and my dad would hear thuds like he was punching things, or muffled yells, and he kept the door locked so my dad couldn't go in and see what was wrong. You always felt like one day a kid like that would just snap. But Trey was waiting, his arms out, and this was the first time in months Trey had acted like he even wanted to be in the same room as him, so my dad took a deep breath and deposited me, painstakingly, into Trey's lap.

"Here you go, buddy," he told me gently. "This is your big brother, all right? This is Trey. Martin Raynor the Third." He paused, then added, "My firstborn."

Trey stared solemnly into my eyes and took in my stubby eyelashes and faint pale eyebrows. He held his breath and carefully petted the top of my head with his palm, and exhaled, pleased, when my eyes found him. He looked up at my dad. "His mom really just didn't want him anymore?"

"Nope."

"Dumbass." He ran his fingers over my wispy hair and fingered my earlobes, then half whispered, like he didn't want to scare me, "Hi, Braden." He stroked my arm. I flailed the arm around and he offered me his finger, and when I grasped it, he broke into a smile. He lifted my hand and inspected the fingers one by one, then said, "Dad, look, did you see he even has little fingernails? And *knuckles*. Look."

But Trey had moved too fast, or something, and I started to cry. Trey dropped my hand and tucked his arms around me tighter. "Crap. I didn't do anything to him, I swear." He looked up anxiously at my dad. "I swear. I was just—"

"Didn't I tell you to be gentle?" My back arched, and my face turned bright red as my screams got louder. My dad snapped, "Give him back."

"Dad, I swear I didn't try to hurt him. I wasn't trying to make him cry."

My dad reached out and gathered me gently into his arms so I was cradled upright against his chest, then he shot Trey a withering look over the top of my head.

"What'd I *just* tell you? I should've known not to trust you, you worthless bully. Can't you see how little he is? Wouldn't you be scared if you were him? God*damn*, you ought to be skinned alive. I should've known."

He rubbed his hand on my back and rocked me back and forth, kissed me on the nose and on the forehead. He bobbed up and down and ducked his head next to my ear.

"Hey, little man," he crooned, turning away from the look on

Trey's face, "Shhh. Shhh. You're okay, buddy, Dad's got you, Dad loves you, it's okay."

And—when he got to this part in his story, he sat up straighter—I stopped crying and went quiet and stared up at him, tears pooling in my eyes so they looked huge, and that was the first time he ever saw me smile. And that was it, he told me: that was the moment he knew he believed in God and the moment he realized God had spoken to him and the moment he knew everything was going to be different from now on. God had given him this son out of nowhere, the way he'd chosen the Virgin Mary. This new son had been sent to him to love him and be his own. This new son was God reaching down from heaven and nudging past the years of sin and past the unbelief and right into his lonely, guilty heart.

When my dad turned around, Trey was sitting on the bed still; he'd hugged his knees against his chest and wrapped his arms around them. His eyes were hollow. He didn't move when my dad turned to him.

"Here," my dad said impulsively to Trey. "Trey, here. Sometimes babies just cry. It happens. You were like that, too. Always scared me to death. Here." He pushed Trey's knees down flat and positioned me back in his lap before Trey had time to say anything, and in that moment, he told God: *I forgive Trey for saying he wanted to live with Elaine instead of me, and I forgive him for trying to run away from me, too.* "See? He wants you to play with him."

But Trey still had that same unseeing look in his eyes. My dad tried again. "We'll have a good time together, huh? All three of us. We can—" He stopped, trying to think what you could do with three people that you couldn't with two. "We can play keep-away with him. We can have a tiebreaker if we ever vote on anything. He's lucky, you know that? Every little boy should have an older brother."

But Trey still didn't answer. There was a feeling like a knife twisting in my dad's stomach. Maybe he'd been wrong, and maybe he was hoping for too much. Maybe some things you couldn't fix.

But didn't this baby mean he was forgiven? That he got another chance? That God loved him after all, and believed in him, and that maybe he could be different too? So he settled down next to Trey on the bed.

"Trey," he said, nervous. "Look. Maybe—look. I didn't mean to yell at you, all right? I'm sorry. Okay? I'm sorry. I know you were trying to be nice to him. And I know you do things you shouldn't, but maybe I'm too hard on you sometimes. You know I love you. I blew my life savings in court so I could keep you. If I didn't have you, I'd be lonely as hell. I'd have nothing. I wanted a son my whole life."

Trey turned his face toward the wall. My dad felt his heart sink, start to slip back into that swamp of guilt. Jesus, Trey was the size of this new baby once—Trey seemed so little sometimes still—and what kind of man was so hard on someone that much smaller? He fought away the memory of beating Trey with his belt after Trey had tried to run away, and his stomach turned. Of course Trey hated him. Of course he'd tried to leave.

"Trey, I want it to be different," my dad said desperately. "I really mean it. I want things to be different. I want us to have fun together, and I want you to be happy when I'm around, and I want you to trust me. I want you to come to me when you're upset or you have a problem."

His hands were shaking. "Listen—I really—I want that more than anything. How about this: I won't hit you ever again or yell at you or any of that. Okay? I swear. Just—if you stay here and don't ever try to run off like that again. Then you can look out for your new brother and help me raise him. He'll need you. And we can be a better family now. Us three."

Trey considered that. He said, tentatively, "You mean it?"

"More than I've ever meant anything in my life."

"How do I know for sure?"

"Because I'm giving you my word."

Trey looked down at the baby. "You swear?"

"I swear. I swear, Trey. A man's word is the most important thing he's got." My dad held out his hand to offer a handshake. "I swear on my life."

Trey's expression didn't change, but he shook. He said, soberly, "Okay, well, yeah, Dad, I guess I can do that. Stay here and help you take care of him." Then he looked up at my dad and then back down quickly, like he was nervous, too. "Um—I think the baby likes you. It was nice how he stopped crying for you. I think he thinks you're a good dad."

On air, my dad talks about this only vaguely. He talks about how he was in darkness, and when he found God, he was in the light, and he talks about how God blesses people who obey him. What he means is that, after that night, God turned his life around. My dad stopped swearing, started reading his Bible, and got new bumper stickers for his car. It turned out he was a good dad to this new baby, and it turned out things with Trey were better with a baby there, too. One night at the station my dad asked if he could fill in for one of the night-shift DJs who was out on sick leave, and it turned out he was good. He got his own spot on a weekly show, and then he got his own show. He bought a house, then a nicer house. His ratings kept growing and he made himself into who he is today.

And, meanwhile, he found out I had it in me to be a good pitcher, maybe even a great one, and he started developing me. He coached a break into my fastball, taught it to paint curves around the plate, taught it to come barreling forward knee-high before sinking like a plane losing steam midair. He taught me deception—how to not waste a single motion, how to shroud your movements so they don't give a thing away. And he taught me, too, that being up there on that mound with the whole game riding on your shoulders is the loneliest place you'll ever know. That it's the time between throws, when you're forced to face your own thoughts and fears, that can break you.

I think the way you know you love someone is how badly you take it when they're suffering, and it guts me to think what he's going through alone, to think of him powerless and lonely and afraid. But at least I can do this for him: play the way he taught me. Get the win against Brantley. That'll be how I keep him close, for now—that's how I'll show him I was always listening, that I still need him, that I took it to heart all those times he told me baseball is the truest test of who you are.

SEVEN

n the two weeks before my dad's preliminary hearing, we beat Bret Harte 4–1 and Ripon 5–2, and I throw my first shutout of the season (6–0) against Waterford.

La Abra, who we're slated to play May 12, takes all of their three, and Alex Reyes goes through a slump at the plate. I read through every pitch he sees.

At home, another toothbrush shows up next to mine in the bathroom, another towel on the bar. Trey buys a cheap (crappy) car from some guy off Craigslist, and the fridge fills up with stuff I'm afraid to touch: tiny, see-through orange balls Trey says are fish eggs, dried mushrooms that look like dung. He's on the phone a lot with his restaurant, and sometimes late at night when I'm in bed already he goes out, God knows where, but at home he spends nearly all his time in the kitchen cooking, and when I get home from baseball every day, the whole house smells like spices and something rich, like browned onions. He tastes things with a spoon, but he doesn't eat much of it and he doesn't offer any to me, and when I take out the trash, I find whole meals' worth of food dumped in the garbage can. I survive mostly on beef jerky and Kraft macaroni and cheese.

I'd like to tell him how much it means that he came back for me and that I miss how things used to be between us. I don't, though; instead I straighten my side of the bathroom and don't track dirt rings from my cleats through the kitchen since I know he likes when things are neat, and read articles about food on Wikipedia, hoping maybe I can find something to say to him he'd actually like talking about, and record cooking shows for him on the DVR. He doesn't watch them, and doesn't come to watch me pitch.

The morning after we play Waterford, I see Maddie at her locker as I'm on my way to Spanish, and I spend a good sixty seconds debating whether or not to go talk to her. We've had exactly two recent interactions: I told her thanks for her e-mail and teased her about how she was going to be "Sincerely Maddie Stern" to me from now on, and then, when I asked her what song it was, she told me she'd written it herself, and then I was so impressed I couldn't think of anything to say at all except that I'd liked it a lot. And then I felt like an ass the rest of the day for not telling her what it meant to me after she'd gone to all that trouble, and also for teasing her like that—because her e-mail felt protective, kind of, like maybe she'd gotten nervous sending that song to me or reaching out to me at all, and the *Sincerely, Maddie Stern* and the way it was all businesslike was her way of not giving away too much of herself. But then, two days ago, we were coming down the hallway at the same time near the end of lunch and she paused whatever story she was telling her friends and gave me this quick smile that somehow, in a hallway full of people, felt like something private we'd shared. Although maybe I just told myself that because it was something I wanted.

I know I should watch who I talk to more than ever these days, that I've got no business anyway with a girl right now. But talking to Maddie feels like one thing still unwrecked by my dad's arrest, so I make up my mind and go over to her.

"Hey," I say when she looks up. She's wearing a button-up shirt with little dots on it and the top two buttons undone, and her skin is pale and soft-looking under the collar of the shirt.

She says, "Hi, Braden."

"I've had your song stuck in my head the whole day," I say. "I was listening to it all last night."

She closes her locker, balancing her books in her other arm. "Oh yeah?"

"I really like that part at the end, you know, where the chorus breaks off into something else? Where the tune changes?" I probably sound like an idiot—singing in church on key is about the extent of my musical ability. "Hey, and Kevin told me they got you to join the worship team at youth group." I reach for her books. "I can get those. Where you headed?"

"Lit." We start walking. Her elbow brushes against mine, and I veer myself just a little bit away from her and wait to see if it'll happen again. It doesn't. She says, "Yeah, Jenna asked me to sing. I've been sneaking into the chapel after school when no one's there to practice."

"You what?"

"After school. It's usually unlocked, so I let myself in and just . . . sing and play, I guess. Before everyone else gets there."

"Breaking and entering, Stern? I didn't know you had it in you."

"It's not like *that*." She pauses. "Well, maybe don't tell anyone."

"I'm totally telling."

She reaches out like she's going to grab my arm, then at the last second—I'm disappointed—she catches herself. "Don't you dare."

I hold my grin until she smiles back, too. "That's a pretty empty threat," she says. "When was the last time you even went to youth group?"

"Touché." So she's noticed. "Yeah, I—not in a little while. Kevin's been after me to go back." I start to say I've been too busy, and then I change my mind and tell her at least part of the truth, or at least more than I've said aloud to anyone else. "It's felt weird ever since everything with my dad and all."

She makes a sympathetic expression. "Right. Of course. It must be really hard without your dad. You must be so worried."

"Yeah." I lift one shoulder, then let it drop again. "I miss him."

She studies me a moment. I think she's going to ask more about him, like most people have been doing, and I tense up a little bit, but then—I'm grateful—she changes the subject. Maybe she could tell I didn't want to talk about it. "When my grandma was dying, I didn't feel like going to church for a long time either."

It's not like that, but I say, "When was that?"

"It was before we moved here. She had Alzheimer's and didn't remember me at the end, and whenever I'd go visit her, she kept asking who that 'Oriental' girl was. I guess I was kind of mad at God."

"I'm sorry. That's pretty awful coming from someone you love."

"It was." I have my eyes fixed on the hallway in front of us so they don't stray too low and make me look like a creep, but I can feel her studying me. "I wouldn't blame you if you were furious with God."

I'm not, exactly—there's a lot of things I feel, but that's not one of them—but it's not a conversation I want to have either way. Chase and Dutch walk by then and see me with Maddie, and a huge, syrupy grin spreads over Chase's lips. I shoot him a look that means, *Not now*. It's not like I have trouble finding dates to school dances, but I've never let anything go much further than that, and so every time the guys see me so much as talking to a girl they think it's completely hilarious to make jokes about how that's basically the equivalent of me getting to third base. Sure enough, Chase thrusts his hips back and forth and mouths something I don't catch. If it weren't in front of Maddie, I'd flip him off; I plan to nail him later with a pitch or something instead. To Maddie, I say, "Mm."

She doesn't press it. "You said your brother was coming back to stay a while, didn't you? Is he here already?"

I didn't tell her that, which means she must have asked someone— sometime, when I wasn't around, she was thinking of me. "Yeah, he got back last Friday."

"I heard he doesn't come back here very much?"

"He's pretty busy. It's been years since he's been here, actually."

"Are you guys close?"

"What? Yeah." I glance around to make sure no one else over-hears. "Hey, Maddie—you have younger siblings, right?"

"My sisters."

"If you were all set up somewhere else and something happened and you had to move back for them, would you hate them?"

"Would I *hate* them? Braden, your brother doesn't hate you. Why would you even think that?"

I shouldn't have been so direct. "Yeah, no, I know. But things just feel kind of different with him than they used to, so I don't know."

"Maybe he's nervous. He doesn't live here, right? It has to be weird coming back and your little brother's all different and more grown up than whenever you last saw him."

"My brother doesn't get nervous about stuff like that."

"Doesn't everyone?"

I half laugh; I can't tell if she's serious or not. We're almost to her classroom now; I can feel her attention shifting, and I get that empty feeling you get late at night when a movie you're watching is about to end. And then, as we go past the vending machines, she bumps one, stumbles, and brushes against me as I reach out to steady her. Touching her feels like a bulb sparking in my chest.

"Whoa there, Stern," I say as her face turns pink. "Go easy on that vending machine, would you?" I dodge when she tries to elbow me. "It's been good to me all these years."

It's not particularly great, as jokes go, but it makes her laugh anyway. And it's funny about that laugh—it makes me feel a kind of calm I haven't felt much these days, like something twisting and then settling inside me. I smile back at her.

I wish more things felt like this.

EIGHT

Trey's gone when I get home that night from practice, which is unusual enough to spark a flame of panic; when you don't know what made someone leave once, you also don't know what might make him do it again. I try to relax when I see all his stuff's still laid out in the kitchen. There's no way he'd take off without his knives and pans.

He gets home around nine that night when I'm at the kitchen table going over Brantley's schedule, looking for a game I can go scout out. He's carrying a shoe box in his hands.

"Hey," he says, like he has no idea I've been sitting here worrying about where the hell he went off to. Probably he doesn't; I know it's not like he does the same for me. "You want to see something?"

It's unlike him to seem this happy, and it makes my worry seem like an overreaction. I say, dryly, "Is it shoes?"

"Funny." He sets the box down carefully on the table. "Look, but be careful. Open the lid just a little bit."

Before I can open the lid, I hear something rustling inside and then a chirping sound, which I wasn't expecting at all. When I look inside, it's birds. They're gray and green with shining black eyes and tan beaks, and they're tiny—you could cup all four in your palms.

"They're nice," I say. "But random. Why'd you decide all of a sudden to get pet birds?"

"*Pet* birds, Braden?" The corners of his mouth push up. "Those aren't pets."

"What are they, then?"

"They're ortolans."

Looks like birds to me. "I see."

"They're songbirds. You get them in France, but they're illegal everywhere to eat."

"You *eat* them?"

"If you can find them. I couldn't even find them in Brooklyn. I couldn't believe it when I found out I could get them here. Guy in a warehouse out in Alameda gets them shipped in on the black market. Hundred bucks apiece."

I expect him to tell me he's kidding, but I don't think he is. "Why would you pay that much to illegally eat birds?"

"They're not just *birds*."

"If you say so." I peek inside the box again, and they make a tiny bird stampede toward the sliver of light. "They're so small, though. They're, like, two bites."

"You keep them in a box with millet and figs, and you force-feed them until they're"—he sets the box down on the table and holds his hands apart to indicate—"about four times as big. All fat. Then when they're big enough, you drown them in really good brandy and roast them. You eat them whole, bones and all. It should take you fifteen, twenty minutes to eat." Then he adds, "You eat them with a napkin over your head."

"You what? Why?"

He ignores my question. "One's for you. You, Kevin, Jenna. When they're ready, I'm going to have a dinner for all of you. Something nice. And purees for Ellie." He pulls open the fridge and looks inside. "You eat yet?"

"Ah, kind of. I had a sandwich."

"I'll make you an omelet. What do you like in omelets?"

I try not to look surprised. "Anything. Nothing green." Then I add, "Thanks."

He pulls a bunch of stuff and a carton of eggs from the fridge and gets to work. Without turning around, he says, "You win your game today? You had a game, right?"

"Yeah, we won. Five–two."

"What was the two?"

"RBI on a triple. Left-handed batter. I missed on a cutter."

"Thought you almost never threw cutters."

"How'd you know that?"

He shrugs. Then he says, "So everything good at school and all that?"

"At school?" It's the kind of thing he would've asked me back when he actually liked sitting around and talking to me. He must be really happy about his birds. Maybe he'll keep them as pets after all. "Yeah, same old."

"How's Kevin's class? He a good teacher?"

I say yeah, and Trey kind of smiles. "Figures," he says. "He always liked telling people what to do."

"It's weird he's someone's dad."

"Why's that?"

"I don't know." His voice was weird—was that rude of me to say?

"He just doesn't seem like one. I've never even heard him raise his voice. You think he's a good dad?"

"A good dad? Sure. Just not a very good husband."

"What? Why?"

"Just always thought he could do better by Jenna. Never thought he should marry her in the first place. She was our valedictorian, you know that? She should've moved away somewhere and done something with her life. Make sure my birds are still alive, will you? They've gotten quiet."

When I pick up the box, the birds start chirping again, and when I undo the lid the four of them are huddled together there. They skid and flap around when the box tilts. "Still alive."

"Excellent."

"Yeah." I let the lid fall shut. "So . . . how'd you know I don't throw cutters?"

"I read when you told that woman from the Stockton *Record* you don't have much use for them. I"—he pauses like he's embarrassed, then makes an expression like, *Eh, screw it*—"I get it sent to me in New York."

"You what? You don't have papers there you like, or what?"

"I don't have time to read the paper. I just read about your games."

"Oh. Really?" I look down at the box again so he won't see my grin. For as much as he seems to hate Ornette, that wasn't something I saw coming. "You know you can just read that online, if you—"

"Yes, I know that, Braden, thank you. We're no *Ornette*, but when the wind blows right, we do get an Internet connection in New York. I just like having something you can actually touch."

"Well, it's your money, I guess. If you want to spend it on stupid things like that."

"Yep."

He sets down a plate in front of me. The omelet's steaming, and there's two sprigs of some green plant on top. I tell him thanks and take a bite, and he sits down across from me with his own plate, and then without warning I'm stabbed with an ache that my dad's not here for this. I used to take for granted the ordinariness of things like all three of us just being in the same room together, or sharing a meal, and for a second I let myself imagine what it would be like for that to happen again. I didn't exactly expect Trey to come back ready to call my dad and make up on the spot, but—I don't know. I guess a part of you always hopes.

Trey's watching me not eat. "You don't like it?"

"No, it's good," I say, but it comes out too quickly and makes it sound like I'm lying. I eat another bite. "It's good."

"I didn't put the chervil *in* it, you know. You said you don't like anything green. I don't serve people things they specifically told me they don't like."

"No, it's not that. I just . . ." I tuck my arms around my sides and meet his eyes. "I'm just . . . thinking about Dad."

A darkness goes across his expression again, chasing away whatever it was that made him look happy before. Maybe I should've kept it to myself. But what does he think—that we'll just never acknowledge our dad, or the trial, or anything that's happening? Who else am I supposed to talk to?

He takes a bite of his own omelet, then spears another bite with his fork and looks at it, clinically, like it's some kind of lab specimen. "Dry," he says. "Overcooked it."

I don't want to talk about eggs. "I just—I'm really worried about a trial, and the lawyer says—"

He silences me with a single warning shake of his head, and I sit back against my chair, defeated. As bad as everything is, it would help to at least have Trey on the right side. It's been nine years, and if his plan is to just stay pissed off forever, then I think that's a shitty plan. I mutter, "You know, people always say they feel better after they forgive stuff they were upset about."

"Oh, they always say that, do they?"

His tone is sarcastic. He slants his head to one side and gives me a look that means he knows perfectly well what I meant by that. I should probably back off. Instead I say, "It seems like good advice."

Trey sets down his fork. I tense, nervous he'll snap at me, but instead he reaches up and massages his temples with his thumbs like I'm exhausting. "You know what, Braden, in the right situation, sure, whatever, maybe it's great advice, but you have to be careful what you forgive. Sometimes it doesn't mean you're a good person or you're taking some kind of moral high ground, all right? Sometimes it just means you're weak."

Or maybe tearing your family apart because you want to stay pissed off forever is weak. "That's not what it means."

He sets his jaw and lets his gaze track around the kitchen, taking stock of old grievances, maybe, or maybe telling himself to not yell at me. "It means what, then? You keep letting people get away with whatever the hell they want because they know you won't do anything about it?"

"No. It means you believe God gives us more chances."

Trey snorts. "That's what you actually believe?"

"That's what the Bible says."

"That's not what I asked you."

"I—yes." Don't I? But then I know people tell themselves all kinds of things about God because they don't know him or they're afraid of who he really is.

"I could massacre a bunch of innocent people and God would forgive me and I could just go to heaven? That's what you think?"

I hesitate. "Well—yes."

"Really? All I have to do is say I'm sorry?"

"I mean, you have to *be* sorry, and ask God to—"

"I could play against you and nail one of your batters in the head for no reason and you'd forgive that?"

"I—that's different." I cross my arms and look away. "Fine. Whatever. I guess. I don't know. I just think nine years is plenty long to hold a grudge."

"You know what, I could do without the attitude."

"You're right. I'm sorry." I stab with my fork at the omelet and will politeness into my tone. "I just think if there's a trial and it doesn't go well, I bet you'll feel guilty you didn't—"

"That's enough, Braden," he says, sternly enough this time that I drop it immediately. I eat the rest of my omelet in uneasy silence while he texts someone on his phone, and I jump up when he starts to clear our plates.

"I'll do those," I say quickly. "Thanks for the omelet. It was really good."

Scrubbing the pans, my hands red from the steaming water, I'm irritated with myself for not being more careful. I didn't get anywhere with him anyway, and I know I need to watch myself. He's not happy about being back here—that much is painfully obvious—and the absolute last thing I want to do is give him a reason to think maybe this just isn't working out or a reason to cut me out of his life the way he did to my dad.

He leaves again that night, this time around two. When I hear the garage door close after him, I go downstairs and turn on the kitchen lights, check to make sure all his things are still there. The birds make noise like maybe I woke them up. I peek into their box and they skitter around, chirping louder.

I used to always want a dog, but my dad would never let me because he figured it would be too rough when it died, and when it's late enough that no one else in the world is awake, it's kind of nice to have something else there in the house with me even if it's only just birds. I sit there in the kitchen and wait for Trey to come home, and then when I hear the garage door open again, I turn off the lights and go back upstairs to my room before he sees.

꙳   ꙳   ꙳

One night when I was six, Trey's last year in high school, Trey came into my room in the middle of the night. He did that sometimes when he and my dad got into it, and earlier I'd woken up to the whole house shaking from my dad's yelling, and so that night I was only half surprised to see him.

"Scoot over," he whispered, and I rolled closer to the wall, and Trey lay down next to me on top of the blankets and murmured, "Go back to sleep." I kept my eyes closed and hugged my stuffed horse and tried not to move or touch Trey so he wouldn't go away, but I stayed awake, and tracked his breaths. After a long time he whispered, "Hey. Braden. I need to ask you something. You awake?"

I opened my eyes at him so he could see I was.

"Am I a good brother to you?"

That one was easy; Trey never yelled at me or made me feel bad and always let me hang around him even when he was with his girl-friend. I nodded.

"You swear?"

I nodded again, and we lay there for a long time. I stroked my horse's nose and played with its hooves. Trey and Emily had won it for me at the state fair, and I was always nice to it; besides the home run ball I'd caught at that Giants game with Trey and my dad, I loved it more than anything else I owned. I listened to the trickling sound of my fish tank.

Then Trey whispered, "Hey, Braden—do you think I'm a good person?"

That one was tougher. I knew a lot of people—his teachers, his principal, my dad—didn't. He got in trouble a lot at school. But I loved him, and he was always good to me, so I said yes. When I did, he rolled over onto his side so his back was to me.

"Wake me up at six if I'm not up," he said. "I'll make your favorites for breakfast."

He was up the next morning before me, and he was the one to come back in and nudge me awake. In the daylight, I could see there was a bruise starting over his cheekbone, a dark half-moon under his eye.

"Quit staring," he said, when he saw the look on my face. "I got this wrestling. It's nothing."

While Trey cooked breakfast that morning, I shadowed him as close as I could without actually touching him. Twice he almost tripped over me, but he didn't say anything. My dad's floor creaked as he rolled over in bed, the sound coming through the ceiling over the sizzling of the onions, but Trey didn't react when I looked up. My dad was supposed to be at work. A couple minutes later, Trey set two plates down on the table, with diced potatoes and onions and bell peppers, my favorite. There was toast with peanut butter and a banana he'd peeled and cut into slices for me.

Trey put his elbows on the table and leaned his head forward against his hands. I waited for him to eat. He didn't. I took a forkful of the potatoes and let it hover over my toast. "Hey. Trey. Should I make a sandwich?"

He looked up, startled, and I got the feeling he'd forgotten I was there. Then he muttered, "That's disgusting, Braden. Quit messing around. Eat."

I lowered the fork closer to the toast. He narrowed his eyes at me. I jiggled the fork so the potatoes wobbled. He said, "Don't even think about—" But I slanted the fork so the potatoes plopped onto the toast.

"I told you to knock that off, Braden. Don't make me tell you again."

I shoved half the toast in my mouth. Then I opened my mouth to show him the half-chewed peanut butter and potato on my tongue. I said, "Soooooo good."

That got him. "You're disgusting," he said, but he reached up and grasped his chin in his hand so I wouldn't see he was smiling, and I'd thought maybe things were okay again. My dad loved him— otherwise he'd just leave him alone. But before we left for school that day, we sat in the garage with the engine on, and then Trey put his hands on my shoulders and twisted me so I was facing him. It startled me; Trey never touched me.

"Listen," he said. "I want to tell you something, okay? Don't turn out like me."

"Like you how?"

"At all," he said. "I'm not a good person."

"Yeah you—"

"Shut up and don't argue, Braden. You don't know anything." His voice was rising. "You're just saying that because you're a kid. Are you listening? Just do what Dad tells you. Don't just try to tell yourself you're a good person and it doesn't matter what he thinks about you, because that's bullshit and you're just lying to yourself because you want it to be true so bad. You got that? So don't be like me, or you're just asking for it and you deserve it when he thinks you're nothing." It was the only time in my life he'd ever kind of scared me.

I don't know what that particular fight was about, but really, half the time their fights weren't even *about* anything; we could be deciding what to eat for dinner and the next thing I knew, Trey had gone cold and my dad was slamming doors and yelling. Both of them have always been the kind of people who hold on to things and turn them into something bigger, and I know they always pushed each other's buttons. Neither of them was exactly perfect.

But in the end, Trey was the one who left us. And maybe when that's the kind of person you are, your disloyalty is always there inside you, underscoring everything else you do; maybe your eventual betrayal pools inside you and bleeds out over time, until finally it's poisoned everything you ever cared about.

I should know.

NINE

My dad's been in jail eighteen days now, and it's the day before his hearing, eight days before the Brantley game, and three minutes before youth group. By the time the music starts in the sanctuary, where the adults are, I'm still trying to decide whether or not to go into the multipurpose room where we meet.

I've been avoiding church, because while it's one thing to pray for specific things, like dipping your foot in the water before scurrying back to land, it's another thing altogether to just jump all the way in. The thought of being around a bunch of people in worship or in prayer where God's close by and I'm right in his line of fire is unsettling. But with the hearing tomorrow, I started thinking about how maybe God's not real impressed with my attendance record at church these days, and I can't afford to take chances right now, so. Here I am.

Kevin comes up to me as soon as I walk in, his wife, Jenna, beside him, and I see Maddie on the other side of the room talking with some of the homeschooled girls. She doesn't acknowledge me, but I have a feeling she saw me, too. Kevin gives me a huge smile and claps his hands warmly on my shoulders.

"Well, hey, look who's here!" he says. "Great seeing you, Braden. We've missed you around here."

"I keep saying to myself, we absolutely *must* have Braden and Trey over for dinner one of these nights," Jenna chimes in. It hasn't been that long since I last saw her, but she looks thinner than whenever that was. I always thought she was pretty, but these days she's all angles, severe-looking almost. "Though I'm sure it'll be a letdown compared to what your brother's been cooking at home for you."

"That sounds nice," I say, although it kind of doesn't. I don't tell her Trey still throws out almost everything he cooks and I live on mac and cheese and peanut butter sandwiches. I step out from Kevin's hands. "Yeah, he keeps pretty busy cooking . . . stuff. I couldn't tell you what half of it is."

"Well, we're just happy to have your brother back in town," Jenna says. "And so glad you're here tonight."

I tell her thanks, and then I make my way over to the side of the room where Maddie is. When I do, she breaks away from the girls she's talking with.

I feel more nervous than I expected I would, both being here and seeing her. She's got her hair pulled up and she's wearing this blue lacy-looking dress, and she looks perfect, basically, like if you were to stick her on a magazine cover, there wouldn't be a single thing to Photoshop. All of a sudden, I worry it's weird I came over this way to talk to her, that it looks like I'm all into her and I think we have something going on when really she's just a friendly person. I shove my hands in my pockets and say, "Hey."

"Hey," she says. "We were just talking about you."

"Oh yeah?" I glance back toward the door and pretend not to see everyone watching us. A guy and a girl talking one-on-one is a bigger deal at youth group than probably anywhere else in America. "I'm not sure if that's a good thing or not."

"Joy was asking if I knew how you were doing, and I was telling her I can't believe how well you've been taking everything. I'd be a total wreck."

"Eh, I doubt that. I mean, that's just something people say. It's not like you really get much of a choice."

"Well, you aren't—I don't know—doing drugs or cutting class or streaking through the hallways or anything."

My face prickles with warmth at the idea of her thinking about me naked, in any sense. "Uh—yeah. Not yet. Keep watching, though." Dear God, that came out wrong. "Ah . . . not like that."

She laughs. "Should we all stop watching for it, then? Too bad. It sounded a little exciting." The warmth from my face spreads down to my neck and chest. Maddie twists her ring around her finger— I think it's a purity ring; we guys get copies of *Every Young Man's Battle* and accountability groups, and a lot of girls at church wear the rings—and says, "Seriously, though, how've you been holding up?"

"You excited to sing tonight?"

"Are you changing the subject?"

"Yes."

She spends a few seconds deciding whether or not she'll let me get away with it, I think, seconds I spend wondering what exactly a purity ring means you can't do. "No," she says finally. "I'm nervous. I regret saying yes."

"Really? Why?"

"I hate singing in front of people."

I laugh, and then realize she isn't joking. "You're serious?"

"I've always been that way."

"Really? I wouldn't have guessed."

"That's probably just because you don't mind getting up in front of people."

"No, it's not that. I mean, you sent me that song, right? That's almost the same thing."

"Oh. Right." I think her cheeks flush a little, but it could just be the lighting. "Yeah, I never do things like that. I'm kind of having a panic attack right now."

"How come?"

She hesitates. "You'll think it's stupid."

"Try me."

"All right." She looks around like she wants to make sure no one else can hear. "It's just . . . sometimes I kind of get scared I'll mess up enough that it'll change the way everyone sees me. Like if I play and it's bad, my friends will see who I really am and decide I'm not worth it."

I can feel a slow grin spreading across my face. I grasp my hand over my chin to hide it. "How would that work, exactly? They'd all have, like, a meeting without you? Everyone gets five minutes to offer pros and cons?"

"Braden, shut *up*. I'm never telling you anything again."

"No, hey, I mean it. Messing up a song is pretty unforgivable. As a friend."

"I hate you," she says, but she's smiling. "Okay, fine, I hear how crazy it sounds. So now I feel terrified *and* crazy, thank you. This was good. Good talk."

Before I can tell her that I'm just messing with her and that in truth I kind of get it, or that she has nothing to worry about and she's got a great voice, Micah Clementi and Jon Nessbaum get up on the makeshift stage with their guitar and drums, and Maddie says, "Oops, that's my cue."

I hope I didn't actually make her feel worse—I think she was kidding, but it's hard to know. She heads for the stage, and the rest of us sit down in the banged-up metal folding chairs they line up for youth group Wednesday nights. Colin plops himself down next to me—his parents make him go to church, but I wouldn't exactly say he's a Christian—and whispers, "Damn, Nessbaum's really rocking the Jesus-wear. Think he'd let me borrow it?"

I look. Jon's sweatshirt has the green and yellow Subway logo, but when you look closer, the lettering reads HIS WAY. My dad wears crap like that, too—a shirt with a cross on it that says THIS SHIRT IS ILLEGAL IN 41 COUNTRIES, a sweatshirt with a picture of a Bible that says LOST? ASK FOR DIRECTIONS. He used to buy that kind of thing for me all the time, and even when I was too young to care about not looking like an idiot, I'd never wear them. I know people know I don't drink or hook up with girls, but I always thought marking yourself that obviously as a Christian felt like tempting fate, like if you did something wrong wearing clothing like that, it would be doubly bad. Besides that, I've always kept what I believe to myself.

But it's hard not to wonder now if maybe I was the stupid one. If it's like my dad used to say, that you have to take a stand for God if you expect him to take one for you, and all this is happening because I didn't prove my faith. But then I've been in my dad's studio, and I think it's easier to say whatever you want into a void, into your microphone and to all your invisible listeners, than it is to people your own age right in front of you. To Colin, I say, "Yeah, well, he could still probably get more than you."

"That was cold," he whispers back. He hasn't hooked up with

anyone since he and Amye Morgan broke up over the summer. "Hit a guy where it hurts, why don't you."

"Not like anyone else is hitting—"

Pastor Stan heaves himself up onto the stage, and we shut up then, although Colin flicks my thigh with his middle finger hard enough to sting and I do it back, harder, in return. Pastor Stan's not usually here on Wednesday nights because he's with the adults instead. He scans through the rows of us, and then his eyes land on me and he smiles.

"Braden," he says, "would you come join us up here? We'd like to pray for you and your family before we get started."

I was afraid of something like this. I think of the stories I've heard all my life about what people said it was like for God to speak to them, how those stories are always about God calling them to do the last thing they ever wanted to do and how they usually start with *I was praying* or *Someone was praying for me*. But there's no actual way to tell someone you don't want to be prayed for, especially not when it's your pastor, so I make my way up to the stage and hold still as he asks Kevin and the other youth leaders to come around and lay their hands on me.

"Father," he says, still kind of out of breath from climbing onto the stage, "we know your Word tells us that we'll be persecuted and despised for our belief in you. But we also know you promise us that you'll contend with those who contend against us. We know you promise to bring about justice for those who love you. So we ask to fight for your servant Mart Raynor. We ask you to give him strength in this time of persecution. Be with him in this time."

All those hands feel like someone set a cockroach underneath my skin and now it's scrabbling around. The lights on the stage force me under a microscope: God staring down at me with a scalpel, ready to dissect. I'm grateful for that *Amen*, and I mumble a quick thanks and escape back to my seat. I feel wide open, like a wound. But then, as I'm trying to stitch myself up again, trying to tell myself that I already know what God wants from me and it's to work my hardest and win the Brantley game and that's all I need to focus on, that what I thought I heard God say before was just my own fears, the worship team starts to play. And there with her guitar, her dress brushing against her thighs and lifting over a few inches of pale skin when she raises her arm to adjust the mic, is Maddie.

On my left, Colin nudges me, wearing a grin that means *I know exactly what you're looking at.* I glare back, and his grin pushes wider. "Why, Braden, you ought to be ashamed of yourself," he whispers, exaggeratedly concerned, in my ear. "This is *church.*"

I never noticed before how easily she carries herself until she got up onstage, and I see how, there, she doesn't: up on that stage and behind that microphone she holds herself with more control, all her angles sharper and her spine straight. As the lights dim, I hear the opening to the song she sent me fill the room. She doesn't look in my direction, but all the same, I wonder if maybe that might be for me. And then, just as quick, I wonder if maybe it's actually the opposite— that it's no longer something she gave only me.

The chords drift into something else, though, a different song. And when she starts to sing, quietly, with her head bowed and her eyes closed like the rest of us aren't even there, I force myself to look down at the floor and not at her; there are ways you can't let yourself think about a girl in church. Usually at youth group they sing more modern stuff, but Maddie sings hymns: "Let Us Love and Sing and Wonder"; "Before the Throne of God Above." Her voice is breathy and deep, deeper than the way she talks, and she doesn't allow herself any tricks in her singing; her voice is steady and perfectly controlled, even and soft, and the sound of it makes me ache.

When you grow up going to church every Sunday morning and Wednesday night, there are certain things you expect from worship, and one of them's this: on a particular part in every song, the music's supposed to intensify. You feel it coming a couple beats away; the drums get louder, the singers lean in closer to their mics, the people around you close their eyes and raise their hands. (Trey's always said worship looked like a cult.) The percussion's supposed to meld into your own heartbeat until your own self's been stamped out and all that's left is the music and a roaring, empty space for God—but Maddie's not giving us that. Her notes are too quiet, too sure, and she holds you in a kind of surrender to the form and structure of them. Her chords fill the room and swell around me. And in them, in their closeness, I think for a split second that I feel something else there that's not just the trying to be good or the angling for answers to prayer or the fear of what God might want from me—something that feels more like a presence, some hopeful kind of calm.

Except then next to me, Colin, who always sings too loud because he thinks he's got a way better voice than he does, belches accidentally, and then he starts laughing silently into his fist, and next to him Hannah King slaps him in the arm and Jenna looks over and Colin puts on an innocent face. And that's it—the feeling's gone.

。　、　。

After youth group's over that night, I hang around talking to Colin and Kevin and the other guys until I finally see Maddie break away from the group of girls she's been talking to. I catch up to her as she's walking toward the parking lot, juggling her guitar case and purse. I pretend not to see the enormous game-day grin Kevin gives me—if I know him, I'm in for an awkward talk about purity and respect and guarding a girl's heart—and say, "Hey. You were great up there."

"You think so?"

"I never say that unless I mean it."

"I was worried I—oops, hang on a second." She pulls her phone from her pocket, then makes a face.

"Everything okay?"

"Yeah, my mom just got caught up in work and can't come get me. I better go back and ask Jenna or someone for a ride."

I get this feeling like a seat belt clicking into place, that same little burst of rightness. "I can take you, if you want."

"You drove here?"

"I rode." I motion toward my bike leaning against the sanctuary wall. I never did get another car. "But I've fit people on the handlebars before. And I can carry your guitar."

"You don't have to get home?"

I wasn't exactly looking forward to going back and sitting around alone all night trying not to think about the hearing tomorrow. "Nah, I'm fine a little while."

"I think my parents would kill me if I rode alone in a car with a guy they've never met. But I feel bad asking Jenna, and—a bike's different, right?"

"I mean, I don't want to get you in trouble or anything if—"

"I think it's okay. Unless you don't want to, or—"

"I don't mind," I say, maybe too quickly. "Where do you live?"

She lives over by the Safeway, about a mile and a half from church. I shoulder her guitar with the strap across my chest and wad up my jacket for her to sit on, then straddle my bike. She arranges her dress carefully and then perches gingerly on the handlebars, wobbling. "Is this safe?"

"Just don't let go of the handlebars. You can—" I clear my throat, hoping no one's watching us. My face feels warm. "You can lean back against my arms."

It's harder riding with the extra weight, and the wind is freezing against my bare arms. Her hands are touching mine on the handlebars and she feels warm and close and solid, pressed carefully back against me like maybe she's not convinced this is that safe after all. I pedal a bit slower so the wind's not too strong for her, and as we cross the parking lot and head onto Wisteria, I say, "So what do you think of living here? You like it?"

"Yeah, it's nice," she says. "It's pretty here. It feels like we drove a U-Haul into a postcard."

I laugh. "You miss where you're from?"

"Bakersfield? I miss my friends a lot."

"You've got a lot of friends here, it seems like."

"Yeah, I guess so. But it's just—it's different sometimes. Some days it's fine, and some days I realize I still don't actually know anybody all that well. I guess I just miss being around people I've known since we were little kids."

I get that; we all have somewhere we belong. "Do you go back very much?"

"Sometimes. I try to stay in touch with people, but I guess everyone's pretty busy. It's okay, though." I feel her take a long breath. "I was on the prom planning committee there and Junior Ball was last weekend, and I was really sad I wasn't there. And then—it's stupid, but my friends were going to call and put me on speakerphone at least for the limo ride, but then we got disconnected and no one noticed in time to call back, so I missed it."

"I'm sorry."

"Yeah, well." Her tone shifts into something lighter, almost airy. "It's really not a big deal. But thanks."

Maybe I'm not one of those friends from childhood she misses, but all the same I don't think she's someone who usually gives herself away too easily. And I'm pretty sure that in telling me this, she's testing me—seeing whether I'm the kind of person who can't be trusted with knowing she's someone whose friends didn't notice when she wasn't there, or whether I'm the kind of person who'll offer her something worth having in return.

I think that's pretty brave of her. Especially because I'm not even sure myself.

It's late enough that even though we're going through a neighborhood I know—Colin lives around here; his mom used to do a *Día de los Muertos* party every year and we'd run around the neighborhood chucking sugar skulls at each other—it feels a little bit like the parts I recognize were packed up and dropped off somewhere a little ways away. It's a clear night, though, starry, and from the hill we're riding on, you can look out and see all the lights of the town twinkling back at you, and even with everything going on, even with how on edge I am about tomorrow, I get that embarrassing kind of swell in my heart I get sometimes seeing my hometown all arranged out there like that, thinking how steady it's always held. A place can become a sort of family to you, if you let it.

"Hey, Maddie," I say. "You know that one song from tonight, 'Let Us Love and Sing and Wonder'? Something about the way you sang it—I haven't really said this to anyone, but lately I'm maybe . . . Things haven't been great with God, and that was the first time in a while when I kind of felt like even just for a few minutes things were okay."

She lets herself relax against me, just the slightest bit, but I catch it. "You mean because of what happened to your dad?"

I should keep quiet, maybe; it would be easy to say too much. "Yeah, and also, I don't know, I guess—I always thought if I did what I was supposed to—or like, a couple years ago I was at this baseball party and everyone else was drinking and I didn't, and the next day I was crossing the street and I felt this, like, voice telling me to stop, and right at that second, this Ram truck came barreling around the corner, and if I hadn't stopped it would've flattened me. Stuff like that, you know? That's how I always thought it was supposed to go with God, like you knew where you stood with him and you could trust him to take care of you, but now there's all this—and I know it's like the oldest story in the book that the second things get rough, I'm all like, *Where is God now?* But I guess I'm just scared of how he's testing me."

"Testing you how?"

"I don't know, I guess like—seeing how far I'll actually follow him. Every time I think about going to church, I get all scared that he's going to speak to me there or something, and ask me to do something I could never do."

"Like what?"

"Ah—" I've said too much already. Besides that, I tell myself, so far I've done everything I promised God, and the Brantley game is coming up. God's given me signs before when I asked him to, and so, no matter what happens tomorrow, I should hold fast and be faithful and trust that God will give me what I need from him this time, too. "I don't know. Can I ask you something?"

"Of course."

"You trust God, right?"

She says yes. I knew that already, though—I could sense it from how she played tonight, that God felt real to her, that she felt safe with him. I envy that. I say, "If your real parents—you know—I mean, your biological parents—" She takes a deeper breath, and it probably means I should shut up, but I say, "If you couldn't trust your own parents with everything, how can you trust God?"

She stiffens, and I regret it instantly. "I'm sorry," I say quickly. God, what is *wrong* with me? "Crap, Maddie, I'm sorry. That was such a dick thing to say. I'm really sorry. Are you mad?"

"No," she says, "just—surprised. Everyone else always tells me I should be so grateful for the way God worked everything out and that he had a plan for me. Or they think just because I was too young to remember I have no right to ever be sad."

"What? That's dumb. Just because you don't remember doesn't mean you can't feel sad about it now."

"I know. But, I mean, I *should* be grateful. Right? When I was younger, I told my mom I wanted to go back to China someday to find my mother and it made my mom cry. Sometimes I still see her face in that moment I said that to her, and every time I hate myself a little bit."

"So you think about your . . . other mom still?"

"I think about them all the time. They're always there." She lets go of the handlebars then and lets her hand rest on mine, so briefly I might've just imagined it. "Your mom died, right? When you were born?"

Maddie's close enough that I can feel the warmth of her skin, can imagine sliding my hand around the curve of her waist and losing myself with her for a little while. I wish that someday I could tell her I've never lied to her, but my dad's been saying that on the radio all my life about my mom, so I say, "Yeah."

"Sometimes I kind of hope my parents are dead."

"You don't know?"

"No. And when I think about them out there without me, or I think about them *deciding* to get rid of me—sometimes it's just easier to think it wasn't their choice." She lifts her hand off the handlebars again, this time to point across the street. "That one's my house there."

It's a ranch-style house with a long front and lots of glass. I stop shy of the driveway so her parents won't see me through the windows just in case they'd be mad, which maybe I shouldn't feel too great about, and slow to a stop. When I help her off the bike, she says, "You probably think I'm awful for saying that about my birth parents."

"No, I don't think that. I just—well—I understand, I guess."

She smiles in a way that makes it look like she doesn't believe me. I mean it, though—even if I can't say so, I understand.

Maddie says, "Thanks for the ride."

"Anytime." I hand back her guitar. She takes it, glancing toward the front door.

"Also, Braden," she says, "if you ever need to talk about things— or maybe if you don't like talking about it but you still want company, or whatever, I'm around." And there's something in her expression, something about the way the quiet, steady dark makes the night feel spread before us like a blanket, that makes me think that maybe if I did something right now—if I took her hand or leaned closer—that it might go somewhere. Like it might shift the course not just of the night, but of whatever else comes, too.

I take a step backward. I say, "Well, I'll see you at school."

She steps back, too, her face shifting. I don't know what her expression means, but I hope it's not pity. "I'll be praying for your dad."

I wait on the sidewalk until she's safely in her house. It's not until

I start biking home that the rest of the world comes sinking back down around me again.

When your dad's in jail waiting for strangers to decide his fate, you don't go after a girl; I know that. It makes you look completely disloyal, and it probably makes God quit listening to whatever else you might've prayed for because he thinks you have your priorities completely skewed. And anyway, all the other reasons I never dated anyone are still true: I don't want to lose focus pitching. I don't want to get tempted to do anything stupid I can't take back or that'll put me in a bad place with God. I don't like leaving my dad alone, even if it's just in spirit; I know it would really hurt him if I was off going on dates or whatever while he was in there by himself. And besides, I can't think of anything much worse than carving out a part of yourself for someone else you trust and then having them toss it away and leave you.

All the same, though, it was nice for a little while there to feel like not everything in the world is completely wrecked around me, that there are still parts left that are hopeful and good, and I wish I could hold on to this feeling a long time.

TEN

The next day, at one forty-five in the afternoon while I sit through Kevin's lesson on civic responsibility, trying to look like a functional human being and sending frantic half-thought-out prayers pretty much on a constant loop, Deputy District Attorney Laila Shah presents the case she's been building against my dad.

Mr. Buchwald comes by the house again that night. Sitting across from me in the living room, he reminds me of when something burned in the microwave and it's lingering: he seems to take up the whole room. I know even before he says it that Judge Scherr must have ruled there's enough evidence for a case and that he wouldn't set bail, because otherwise they would've let my dad out and he would have called me right away. So Mr. Buchwald was right about that, but it turns out he was wrong about the plea bargain: the prosecutor refused to consider anything less than life in prison, so the case is going to a trial.

I thought I was prepared for this. I kept telling myself to prepare for the worst. But I guess you always tell yourself there's still a chance; you always think things will right themselves again and go the way they should, the way they always have. I feel like someone tossed a net over me and cinched it up. I can barely move.

There were small victories, Mr. Buchwald tells me, and I struggle to pay attention. The judge struck down four of Laila's motions: one to allow the trial to be moved to another county, one to have the jury sequestered, one to ensure a mixed-race jury, and one to exclude evidence of prior police conduct. But, he says, to avoid any concerns about persuading a witness, my dad's denied bail.

"So I can't see him at all?" I say. "He can't even call me?"

"Until you testify, no." He shuffles through some papers. "And I know you had some concerns about your portion of the testimony, but I'll make sure you're utterly prepared. Do you have a DVD player?"

"Yeah, but—"

"Excellent. I'll be providing footage so you can keep abreast. I'm sure for an athlete like yourself it helps to see exactly what you're up against." He pauses. "And, Braden—it's imperative that you keep this to yourself."

"Would I get in trouble for—"

"You have nothing to worry about, but your discretion is, of course, appreciated." He stands, snapping his briefcase shut. "Now, if you have no further questions . . ."

I go into the kitchen when the lawyer leaves. Trey's pounding at a cut of meat with a mallet, hammering it into almost nothing. There's blood specks spattered across his cutting board and the white towel he's got tucked into the waistband of his gym shorts. I say, "It's going to a trial."

He grunts. I watch the meat flattening on the cutting board until my face feels tingly and my forehead feels stuffed with cotton balls.

Trey glances up at me for a second, then says, "Maybe you should sit down."

God. I'm a *pitcher*; I can't be so weak that just seeing blood does this to me. But the edges of the room have gone soft, so I lower myself onto one of the kitchen chairs. He sets down his mallet, washes his hands, and dries them on his towel, then fills a glass with water and sets it on the table next to me.

"Here," he says roughly. "Drink."

I take a couple swallows of the water. Trey picks up his cutting board and scrapes the meat and fat and bone on it into the trash and picks up his mallet again and a piece of meat from a plate. I sit for a while longer until the fuzziness in my head is gone. When the world's solid and sharp again, I say, "Do you think there's any way I can get out of being in the trial?"

"A subpoena's a legal order," he says between thuds. "So no. I don't."

"I really don't want to do it."

"Well, I don't know what you want me to tell you."

"It's just—what if I screw everything up?"

He doesn't answer me. I picture myself alone on a witness stand facing the twelve people responsible for my dad's life, and my heart lurches against my rib cage. "Can you go be there with me for the trial? When I have to go?"

Trey turns around to look at me like I just suggested maybe he go move into the jail with my dad. Guess that's a no. Before I think better of it, I say, "Trey?"

"What."

"You don't—I mean, you believe him, right? Dad? That it was an accident and he didn't know?"

"Braden, I wasn't there."

"Who cares if you were there? You know him. You don't have to have been there to know he's not—"

He picks up the meat and holds it up to study, peering at it in the light. It's so thin you can see shadows moving behind it. "You know something, Braden? I drive forty-five minutes to go to the Safeway in Merced so I don't have to run into people who want to drag me into exactly this kind of discussion. I don't want to talk about him. I don't want to have to tell you that again. All right?" He pushes his sleeves to his elbows, and when I start to speak again, he spins around to face me and says sharply, "You know what, you should probably go find something else to do."

My face is hot. I draw a long breath, listening to his birds chirping, and when he raises his eyebrows like he's waiting for my answer, it's only because of what I know I owe him that I dip my head in acknowledgment and leave the kitchen without telling him what I think—that if he doesn't believe our dad's innocent, that makes him a pretty worthless son.

ELEVEN

After my dad's hearing, we get another shutout (2–0) against Beyer and win (6–3) against McNair. La Abra's still undefeated, and Alex appears to be over his slump. But something else happened when La Abra played Ripon: one of La Abra's pitchers, a righty senior named Kyle Allison, hit the center fielder in the helmet on a wild pitch and gave him a bad enough concussion his parents got scared and haven't let him come back. By all accounts it was unintentional—we hear Allison's been too shaken up to throw since, and I know he sat out his next start—but Dutch says what everyone's thinking, which is that it doesn't bode well for us that they're throwing wild like that.

The thing about baseball is you're rarely honest with yourself about how dangerous it can be; you push it out of your mind so you can play it. You try to forget what you know of shattered bats or torn ACLs or ruined ex-players, your own close calls or the times you nearly ended it for someone else. You try to forget how forty years ago, a few miles away in the minor leagues, a prospect named

Raciel Infante from Venezuela was struck in the temple on a pitch from reliever Manny Escobar, how by the time they got him to the hospital his brain had swelled up so much they had to saw off half his skull, and he never walked or spoke again.

You can't forget, though, not really; the past is buried in shallow graves on every field, waiting to be brought back to life. I've always known that. It's why when I was a kid I promised Trey so readily I wouldn't throw up high at anyone, even though my dad's told me more than once the job might someday demand it. I never knew Raciel Infante, and I don't know Ripon's center fielder, either, but there's a certain way both of them are real to me, a certain way that what happened to them matters and lives with me and belongs to me still, and haunts me with each pitch. Baseball is a game you play with ghosts.

After practice Tuesday—two days before we face Brantley, over three weeks since my dad's seen the light of day—I have Colin go with me to scout the Hughson-Brantley game. It's forty minutes out past La Abra to Hughson, mostly orchard and farmland, small towns dotted over long, flat stretches of road. When we pass the COLINA, POPULATION 468 sign, Colin says, "You're worried about Brantley, huh?"

"I think they're even better this year than they were last year."

"They didn't have many seniors last year. Everyone came back." He's quiet as we go by the Colina dairy, the sun glaring off the long white roofs. Then he says, "Scary stuff about that fielder from Ripon."

"I feel awful for him. Probably never saw it coming."

"I'm not saying it was some kind of message, but I bet La Abra sure doesn't mind word got back to us, either." He glances at me. "You thought about our game with them at all?"

"Nope."

"All right." He doesn't believe me. "That's not for a while, anyway. You've got time."

Brantley beats Hughson, like I figured they would. It's not close. Brantley's pitching's strong, their batters disciplined, their plays pristine. They even pull off a suicide squeeze, which at this level's something you almost never see. It doesn't make me feel any better watching them like I thought it might. We're making our way down the bleachers after the game when someone steps in front of me so close our chests nearly touch.

"Excuse me," I say, but then I look up, and I recognize him right away: Vidal Medina, the shortstop for La Abra. Immediately, the thinning bleachers blur in the background. I stop so hard Colin rams into me and nearly knocks me over.

"Look who it is," Vidal says, smiling a tight, hard smile. He's tall—he's got three or four inches on me—and lanky in the way some of the younger guys are: all quick strength. "What are you doing here?"

I think you can literally see my heart beating through my shirt. I cross my arms over my chest to hide it, and I make myself smile until I feel like a jack-o'-lantern. "What's it look like? Synchronized swimming? Ballet?"

Vidal cocks his head. "That supposed to be funny?" He looks at Colin then and says something to him in Spanish too fast for me to make out.

Colin stiffens. "There a problem here?"

Vidal's smile widens, and he says something else, his tone disgusted. Then he takes a step toward me. "How's your daddy doing, by the way? He having a good time in there?"

In my chest, there's a feeling like an animal clawing to get out. "You better watch what you're saying."

"Why? You feel guilty?" He takes another step closer so there's less than six inches between our faces. "How do you *live* with yourself, huh? How do you sleep at night?"

Next to me, Colin coils, ready, like a spring. I try to tell myself it's all right, that between the two of us we could take this guy if it comes to that, but then Vidal turns abruptly, taps Colin just below his rib cage, and says, very quietly, *"Más te vale que saques tu amigo de aquí, hermano,"* and he looks back up toward the top of the stands, and that's when I see him.

I don't even have time to think. I see Colin curl his hand into a fist, and I turn and stumble over the bleachers and head blindly for the car. When I get there, I hunch over with my hands on my knees and count two breaths, four, six, and then Colin catches up to me.

"The hell was that?" he yells at me, and the people walking to the nearby car turn to stare. Colin's nose is bleeding. He shoves me, hard. "You start something like that with some thug and I jump in for you and then you *bail*? Are you *kidding* me, Braden? I don't even know who that guy *is*."

I cup my hands together and breathe into them. I still can't feel my lungs. "He plays for La Abra," I say when I can breathe again. "But Colin, the guy he was with, a few rows up—that was Alex. Alex Reyes."

It's dark in the parking lot, Colin's face shadowed and yellowish from the dim lights, but even still I can see his expression.

"Then you're a coward," he mutters. He tilts his head back and wipes his nose. "God, Braden, you didn't even try to stand up for your dad."

　　　　▫　　　ˬ　　　◦

That night I can't sleep. At three I finally get up and sit down to write my dad a letter. I copy the jail's address onto the envelope, then turn it facedown. Then I sit there for a long time.

Dad: I hope you are doing okay in there. I always have my phone with me if you're ever allowed to call.

I got into something with a guy from La Abra tonight watching Brantley, and I bailed on Colin instead of sticking around to defend him, and I guess you. I'm sorry. I've been feeling pretty bad.

Trey is writing a cookbook. Maybe you could write him.

I stare at the letter a while, then crumple it up and rip out a new sheet of paper.

Dad: How come you can talk to Mr. Buchwald all the time, but you can't write me even once?

I cross it out. *Dad: I thought you always said God protects people who follow him.* I cross that out, too. *Dad: So whose idea was it to have me come testify in court?*

I tear the sheet in half and start over.

Dad: I miss you. I love you. I'm sorry about everything. When you come back, I swear I'll be a perfect son.

TWELVE

It's warm for March the day of the Brantley game, and the stands are packed. The cheerleaders brought painted signs with all our names on them—Lindsay Tellerman, Dutch's girlfriend, has one that says MY BOYFRIEND SCORES MORE THAN YOURS and the *O*s are all baseballs. Claire Kolpowski has one with my name and number on it. I wonder if Maddie's here.

Brantley's probably the toughest match in our league, but this is why my dad's always said they're the last team you'd ever want to lose to: when I was a freshman, one of their pitchers, Devon Riley, sued the district to be able to go with another guy to the prom. The case got dismissed, but still. One time that season in practice, Jarrod shied away from a tag because he was afraid of getting blown up at the plate, and Cardy yelled, *Hey, no Devon Rileys on this team,* and everyone gave Jarrod a hard time about that forever and eventually Riley's name turned into team shorthand for playing like a wuss. One of the seniors, Keith Brockmeier, copied a bunch of pictures of him and drew speech bubbles of him saying all these gay things and taped them all over the locker room. There's still a couple in the equipment room, where no one ever cleans.

I would never say this to anyone, but the way Pastor Stan talked about stuff like this in church always made me nervous. Because if the reason people even get addicted to homosexuality in the first place is that they pick the wrong ways of filling whatever holes they have in their hearts, giving into their lust and perversions until they go after other men instead of turning to God or whatever, then, I mean, maybe that could happen to anyone if they're not careful.

Maybe it sounds crazy, but in my heart, I'm holding out hope that something might happen with Maddie after all this, when things are back to normal; the truth is, I've hoped that since the first time I laid eyes on her. So in my mind, in those darker places no one goes, I'm faithful to her; I don't imagine other girls. And even when I feel guilty and kind of dirty afterward, I still feel relieved that whatever else is wrong with me, at least that isn't. That's why Brantley's pitcher bothers me—because if I were like that, if everyone either thought I was disgusting or pitied me, I'd try to fix it instead of trying to make it spread. It's like watching someone light matches inside a burning house.

I was up late last night mentally running through Brantley's whole batting order, looking up stats on everyone I couldn't remember and going over the roster. Even if I win today, it's feeling increasingly difficult to see how everything will just be fine. But I know God works in ways you could never imagine, and I've prepared harder for the game today than maybe any other in my life, and I want to be the kind of person whose faith doesn't waver in rough moments.

As the Brantley players come out of their bus, I have Zach Hamblin, our backup catcher, warm me up instead of Colin. Since

Tuesday Colin's been going around telling everyone about getting "jumped" by guys from La Abra and how he should sue for assault; at practice he's been framing my pitches to make me look bad, too. I finally got sick of it—he swung first, and anyway has no one ever hit him in his life, or what?—and tried to nail him with a pitch, but he read me too early, and caught it. Guess he's good at his job.

I catch myself looking over my shoulder, scanning the crowd for signs of more guys from La Abra there. Coach Cardy pulls me aside as we're coming back toward the dugout before the game. I can see Brantley's lineup behind me reflected in his sunglasses.

"Listen, Seven," he says. Cardy calls us all by our numbers, and even though he could probably tell you my exact ERA at any given point in time, sometimes I half think he doesn't actually know all our names. He's not one of those coaches who cares about your grades or your school attendance or your home life. All he cares about is how you play, which is why I like playing for him: it's straightforward in a way that nothing else in my life, except for maybe math class, has ever been. "I wanted to hear it from you that your head's in the game."

He was watching me warm up, then. I say, "It is. This game's important to me."

"You're focused? Because we need a win today."

"Yes, sir. I'm feeling good about it."

"Good. Don't let me down." He lets go of my arm. "You tell your brother to come say hello."

That's random, but Cardy's coached here forever, so I remember that Trey played for him, too. Maybe it's Cardy's way of saying *good luck*. That's my best guess, anyway, until I'm glancing around the stands on my way into the dugout and I see—I do a double take—Trey's here. He's sitting with Kevin and Jenna just behind the backstop, and he gives me a nod. I'm so surprised he's here I give him this big wave that probably looks dorky as shit, and then I'm embarrassed and hope no one else saw.

But that has to mean something, right? That he's here. That feels like a small miracle all its own.

Brantley plays small ball, which means sacrifice bunts and stolen bases and advancing runners with whatever it takes. Colin's calling everything up in the zone to avoid them hitting grounders, and even though I eventually get out of it unhurt, I've walked three batters by the end of the second. Last year when we played Brantley something went wrong in my windup, and a fastball in the fifth inning slipped and went wild. Colin laid himself out trying to block it, but it went past him and I could do nothing but watch as the runner scored from second. That play is haunting me today.

I can feel Trey there in the stands, and I have to force myself not to look over every time I miss the strike zone. Trey was a catcher; he can probably read each mistake I make better than nearly anyone else in the crowd. Cardy's tenser than I've seen him all year, screaming at base runners to hustle so loud the veins in his forehead pop out. By the second inning, there's still no score. In the top of the fifth, we're ahead, but I miss the strike zone six pitches in a row and then when I try to pick off the runner on first I almost overthrow and Jarrod has to lunge for it, and when I get the ball back, my heart is thudding. You cannot—*cannot*—miss a throw like that.

Colin calls time. He jogs to the mound. "What's going on with you? You almost put up an error throwing to Jarrod right there."

"You think I didn't notice?"

"Yeah? Then pull yourself together, how about. Get your head back in the game."

He shouldn't have called for time. It makes me look vulnerable. "Just call more fastballs, will you? I think we should go at them more. There's been, like, three guys who keep reaching across the plate. If I pitch fastballs inside, they'll get jammed."

"Braden, come on. There's been *one* guy who did that, and he took a good cut off that pitch because you didn't get it inside enough. Practically every single guy who's come up has waited for his pitch. These aren't guys you can just hand over strikes and expect them to take it lying down." He looks at me closer. "Is something wrong?"

"What? No. You should just call more fastballs."

He frowns. "Are you still spooked about the La Abra guys?"

"I'm not spooked about anything. I'm not even thinking about that. We just need to win this game, is all."

His expression makes me think I'm a worse liar than I thought. "Okay, look," Colin says, glancing back at the ump to see if he's started out to break up our time-out yet. "I'm sorry about the other night, all right? I shouldn't have said that about you and your dad."

"I don't want to talk about that."

"Yeah, well, me neither. But I've been feeling like an ass for saying it. You'll have your day with La Abra, all right? And it'll be fine with your dad. Everyone knows him. This will all blow over. For now, just forget about all that." He nods toward the batter. "Put this guy away."

After that, I get their center fielder to ground out and I strike out the right fielder after he takes eleven pitches off me, but I'm struggling; things don't feel right. People don't always realize this, but pitching's hell on your body. There's that instant in every pitch when the motion takes over and your shoulder's being wrenched to pieces and you believe you could blow apart, you feel how close you are to some end, and today's the first time in a long time I haven't known I could just fight that off. It's the next-to-last inning, I've walked nine batters, and I've just thrown their shortstop two balls when Cardy comes to the mound to take me out.

"Coach, I'm feeling good," I say right away before he can open his mouth. The game's getting that desperate feeling when it careens outside of your control, but we're still up 3–1 and I know I can fix this if he'll let me stay. I can get the win, and I can take that as reassurance from God that everything will be okay and I can stave off those fears that've tethered themselves to me ever since that day the social worker came over. "I can keep going, Coach, I swear. I've got this."

"Next game, Seven." He holds out his hand for the ball.

"I've got things figured out now. I'll get out of this inning and then I'll throw more—"

"Give me the ball. I'm putting Harmon in."

I pass Greg as I'm going out and he's going in, and I motion him closer. "Hey," I say, "Colin's calling everything up high. Throw whatever he tells you."

"My command's not the best, though. I'm better with sinkers."

"Doesn't matter. Picture your dad being here again, and how you'd play, all right? Whatever you do, do not lose this game."

In the dugout, I slam my glove as hard as I can against the ground, and the other guys in the dugout fan out away from me so I'm alone on the bench. They know me; they know I don't like to talk to people when I've messed up. But things might still be okay if we just win. That's the thing about baseball: everything's forgiven when you win.

Greg inherits the 2–0 count with the shortstop, and walks him. Then he walks the second baseman, throwing a ball that misses so high Colin has to jump up off his crouch, and as he does, both base runners go.

Their catcher grounds out. I try to breathe easier. Two out; we just need one more. But then Greg gives their first baseman, the eighth man in the lineup, a failed sinker that comes practically waltzing over the plate and then hangs there like it's dangling from a string.

It's a gift of a pitch, the kind you pray to get, and the batter undresses it. Triple. Both the shortstop and second baseman score.

When their pitcher goes up and shows a bunt, the instinct I've been developing my whole life tells me they're going to try for a suicide squeeze. *Don't let him get a bunt,* I tell Greg silently. The first pitch he throws far enough inside that the batter pulls back. The second one comes across the plate and the batter makes contact, but it bounces foul. The guys are on their feet yelling for Greg to finish him. If I were Greg, what I'd do right now is hit him. I hate when people bunt on me, and we can't afford the runner to score on a suicide squeeze.

But whatever Colin signals, Greg shakes his head, and my heart plummets down my chest. There's a time in every losing game when you know it's over, and I'm pretty sure that was it. The next pitch Greg throws, their pitcher gets a clean bunt, perfectly positioned halfway between Colin and Greg so, exactly as I was afraid of, the batter has just enough time to get in safely and the ball can't beat out the runner at home. And that's it—I can feel the game disintegrate like the cloud of dust that rises over home plate as the runner collides with Colin, safe.

In the locker room, I corner Greg on the bench where he's untying his cleats. He lifts his head when my shadow sweeps over him. He looks near tears.

"I told you to throw whatever Colin called for." My blood is coursing so hard my vision's pulsing, too. "You had a two-run lead. You had to make six outs. That's it. Six outs before two runs."

He looks around to see who's listening—everyone is—then ducks his head over his cleats. "Thanks for the math. I really needed that."

"I saw you shake Colin off. You think you know better than him? He's been on this team three years, he's been calling the whole game, and you think you can go in to throw your two innings and know better?"

He drops his glove to the floor and zips his bag so hard I expect the zipper to break. He mutters, "I'm sorry."

"Yeah, well, it's too late for that. That might have helped when we were still winning, before you pissed away all the work everyone put into that game like you don't give a damn about the rest of us."

His face is red. I should just leave. He's not the kind of kid who can take being yelled at. And anyway, no matter what I say it won't change the outcome. But then he says, quietly, "It's only a game."

I stare at him. "What did you just say?"

From the guilty expression on his face, I think he knows that crossed the line. "Forget it, Braden, I—"

"You make me sick." I should just leave. I should wrestle back the words fighting their way now from the shadows and get the hell out, but there was just a thin layer of netting holding everything back and he just yanked it apart. "You know what? It's too bad Devon Riley wasn't pitching today. I'll bet you'd just love to bend over for him, wouldn't you? No one would be surprised. Because that's exactly what you did with his team."

THIRTEEN

When you're from Ornette, your roots go deep; it's home, and I'd stay here forever if I could. Trey's one of the few people I know who ever left. So when I was eleven and my Little League team hosted Concord in a regional playoff, it was the first time I ever played against someone I used to know.

Concord's shortstop was Jacob Pinkerman, a guy I played with before he moved to Concord. He was one of my favorites on the team, probably my best friend after Colin at the time, and it had been weird how one season he was there and the next he wasn't. Before the game he came over and said hi, and I'd wanted to tell him we had an extra jersey if he wanted to switch back and play for us. I was decent that day, and going into the last inning, we were up 7–2. I got my first batter to chase outside the strike zone, and the second dribbled a sad little shot right to first, and then Jacob was up.

He tapped his bat against the ground before he stepped into the box, like he always did when he was nervous. I missed on a slider and then got a fastball in the inside corner for a called strike, then he swung and missed. He swung so hard he spun all the way around, and from the announcer's box, my dad joked, "Whoa, there. Trying to make up all five in one swing?"

After that I sent him one right across the plate, and even though I knew my dad would get mad, I threw it soft. But Jacob swung too soon and it flew foul. I tried to throw the same pitch again, but my fingers slipped some off the seams, just enough that the ball went too high, but Jacob thought he knew that pitch and swung on it anyway, and that was it, the game was over. Then from the announcer's booth came my dad's voice saying, "And Pinkerman wastes the most cake-batter pitch Concord's seen all day and knocks Concord from the playoffs. Strike three."

Afterward, in the car, my dad had a lot to say: it took me too long to locate the strike zone; I should never throw that many changeups in a row; my curveball wasn't breaking low enough. He said nothing about my eight strikeouts, because he was too busy telling me how when I played in the minors I'd have to rely on strategy as much as strength, and halfway through the lecture, I interrupted him.

"I don't know if I want to do that anymore."

He raised his eyebrows. "Excuse me?"

"I don't know if I want to do that anymore. Try to get a contract right away in the minor leagues."

"That's what you've always wanted."

I kicked my feet against the floor mat. "I know. But I was thinking maybe I want to go to college first instead."

"College ball, huh?" he said. "Not like your old man?" There was maybe something kind of weird in his voice, but when I looked over, I couldn't read his expression. But I could tell I'd said something wrong.

Maybe it was that I'd made him think of Trey. Then he added, "You know they don't pay you to play in school."

"That's okay." College ball, at least, there's no trades. When you're on a team, that's your team.

He shrugged. "Well, you don't have to decide right this second."

"Okay." I pushed off both my cleats and twisted in my seat so I was facing out the window. "Dad? It felt weird playing against Jacob."

"Why? You won."

"It felt weird."

He sighed, like I was being dumb. "That's life, B. You think you're going to play with the same boys forever?"

"If it was the minor leagues, and you were my coach, would you ever trade me to another team?"

"Not if you were good."

"Only if I was good enough?"

I wasn't looking at him, but I knew from the pause he didn't like the question. He said, "You think too much."

I shrugged. One of the parents had brought Skittles for everyone after the game, so I tore the package open and ate a few. My dad held out his hand, and I dropped a single one into his palm.

He laughed. He smacked the back of his hand against my thigh. "Who the heck raised you to be cheap with your own *father*?"

"I'm just kidding. Here." I shook out a handful for him, and he popped them into his mouth. Then he screwed up his mouth and blinked one eye at a time. "You didn't tell me these were the sour ones."

"You don't like those?" I said, like I'd forgotten. Then I said, "So if I had a bad season, that'd be it? You'd be done?"

"You're still thinking about that?" He frowned. "Braden, it's a stupid question. Do I coach minor league baseball? No. So don't ask me stupid questions like that."

"Really, because you said on your show there's no such thing as a stupid question when your kid—"

"That's work," he said sternly, because he didn't like when I quoted him. Sometimes I thought he didn't even like when I listened. "You're you."

I ate a few more of the Skittles. "I just thought since Jacob used to be on our team you would've been nicer to him."

His face changed then. I never did that—questioned him that way. "Braden, I'm not in the mood for this." Then he added, "Anyway, you saw Jacob miss that throw to second by about ten feet. The kid's got shortbread cookie where his muscle should be. You care what people say about you, then you make darn sure you give them a reason to respect you. Did Jacob do that? No. So forget him. You played like that, I wouldn't be able to show my face at your games. You know what? I was ashamed of those last two pitches as it was. How do you think it feels to have everyone know the one who did that was my son?"

He went silent for a long time. He drove fast, weaving between cars and laying his foot on the gas when someone tried to get in front of him. When I worked up the nerve to look over at him, I could see something twitching in his neck. I said, quietly, "We were up five runs. I knew we'd win."

"There's no need to talk back, Braden. I'm telling you because I love you and I don't want to see you turn out a complete failure. You know that."

He did love me, he'd been there for me more than anyone, so I knew I shouldn't say it and I knew I should just shut up, but instead I said, "Well, I thought you were mean. I was ashamed of *you*."

"Oh?" He reached over and cupped my cheek in his hand, very lightly, and a prickling feeling lit up the back of my neck and landed like fireflies down every vertebra of my spine. He said, so quietly you had to strain to hear, "Care to try that tone with me again?"

I crumpled the empty Skittles bag into a ball. I tried not to move. "It's just Jacob was my friend."

"Your *friend*?" he repeated. "Your friend? *That's* what you think matters? You think God gave you a gift and I spent your whole life working with you so you could piss it all away because you think someone's your *friend*? That's how you repay us?"

His hand felt hot against my face. I stayed as still as I could, but inside I felt like a remote-controlled car going haywire—buzzing, about to crash.

"Throwing easy pitches at him was pathetic, Braden. *Pathetic.* You think you throw someone crud pitches like that it'll make them like you? Is that what you think? You want anyone to give a whit about you, you have to earn it. You hear me? You better grow up and make damn sure you're going to be good enough to ever matter. Because how could anyone but me ever like you when you do things like *that*?"

Something squeezed in my chest like all the air in the car had been vacuumed out, and before I could stop myself, before I even thought about it, I muttered, "Then I don't know why you always lie and say my mom died when really it was just that you weren't good enough for her or Elaine to stay with you."

Even before he reacted, before his expression went stunned and then hardened into something worse, I couldn't believe I'd said that. I stared at him, panicked. He looked frozen, or like a fish, his mouth moving without any sound coming out. He stared at me for so long I finally peered around him at the other lane.

"Dad, come on," I said nervously. "Pay attention." He didn't turn his head away. "Dad," I said again, and he just looked back, his expression blank, and a red Honda went by us and cut in front of us and he wasn't watching in time to brake. I braced myself and swallowed a yell, but there was no collision; the Honda accelerated, a puff of smoke escaping from its exhaust pipe, and sped away.

But he still didn't look. His car started to drift toward the lane line then, toward a pickup coming up on our left, and my heart thundered and I reached for the wheel, and then his face unraveled and he drew his hand back and hit me, hard, across the face. It was the only time in my life he'd ever done that, and at first I thought the sound was the impact of another car, and for a second I was blinded. But that was just the sun flashing off the hood, and then the throbbing started to spread across my face, and when I put my hand to my cheek, stunned, and looked through the window again, we were back between the lines.

"Braden," he said, his voice low and his eyes fixed on the road, "your mother didn't leave me, because we were never together. It was one night, I was wasted as hell, she was barely half my age, and when she showed up on my doorstep with you thirteen months later I didn't even remember her name. You really want me to say that instead on my show? You like that one better? Your mother didn't leave *me*, Braden. She left you."

*　　ˇ　　ᵒ

At school the next day, my teacher, Mrs. Yates, pulled me aside at recess and asked me what had happened to my face. I liked her; she'd told me she listened to my dad's show every morning and she never yelled at us in class, and on Mother's Day when we all made cards for our mothers, she told me I should make one and keep it and that my mom was probably watching me from heaven and feeling proud I was hers, which meant something to me even though I knew it wasn't true. But when Mrs. Yates looked at my face like that, I almost suffocated from the shame. I knew it meant everyone else was looking, too. I stared at the ground, my face hot, and said, "Baseball."

"It's from playing baseball?"

I nodded.

"Does your father know?"

I told her he'd taken me to the doctor, and she let me go. When I came home from school that day, the house was silent, and my dad's door was closed. I tried to tell myself he was just oversleeping, but I knew better.

He came out for dinner three hours later. He moved stiffly, and I could tell he was trying not to look at me. In the kitchen, he pulled out a frozen pizza. He ripped open the plastic wrap and stuck the pizza in the microwave, standing in front of it for a long time before he hit START, and then he leaned forward so his hands were resting on the counter as if they were the only things holding him up.

"Dad?" I whispered. My voice was shaking. "Are you still mad at me?"

He didn't answer. As the seconds wore down on the microwave, he stayed that way, hunched over the counter, and that was the first time I understood the worst part of hell: the rejection from God. If I ever taught math, that's how I'd explain what it means for something to be exponential, how every second that comes next is that much worse than the one before.

Finally, finally, he straightened. "Braden," he said, and he closed his eyes and then he reached up and rested his hand against his cheek and stood there like that for the whole remaining three and a half minutes before the time on the microwave ran out. When there was just a second left, I lunged for the microwave to stop it so it wouldn't beep. He opened his eyes when I moved, and he looked at me, and when he did, I saw he was crying.

That night, when he was asleep, I snuck downstairs and got the scissors from the kitchen drawer. In my room, I picked up my favorite stuffed horse off my pillow, the one Trey and Emily had won for me at the fair. I hugged my horse tight, then I was disgusted because I was too old for this anyway, and if you make your dad hurt you, you don't deserve *toys*. I cut into my horse's neck, gripping the blades hard enough to get through the fake fur, and I kept cutting until the head fell off. I pulled out all the stuffing and then I balled it up and threw it in the trash. Even though I knew it was pathetic, I was sick with grief, and I hid my head under my pillow and cried. I missed my horse already. I felt its body there all night until I finally got up and took the trash downstairs; then, an hour later, I took it outside. The garbage truck didn't come for three more days.

FOURTEEN

After losing to Brantley I skip youth group the next week. I know that looks cheap, like I just wanted something from God and now that I didn't get it I checked out, but I don't exactly have the luxury of feeling pissed off or betrayed—there's still too much at stake for that—and it's more that I feel ashamed to face him. Like I really thought I was special to him, that he'd do something just because I asked him to and because I considered myself his, and it turns out I was just deluding myself and he didn't feel the same way about me.

I've been hiding out in my room all week, too ashamed to face Trey. He hasn't mentioned the game, probably because there's not really much to say—*Hey, it was cool the way you kept putting guys on base out there, good work.* I've been lying low at school, too, keeping my eyes on the teacher in the classes I have with Maddie.

Now, instead of going to church tonight, I do something I told myself I wouldn't: listen to one of my dad's old shows. It feels about exactly as depressing as I figured it would, like something you'd go home and do after a memorial service because it was all you had left.

The episode's from a few years ago when there were some wild-fires going on nearby, and I remember it because he got a lot of flak for what he said, which was pretty much that as a country we'd brought this on ourselves—that we shouldn't expect God to stick around where he clearly wasn't wanted. I didn't pay close attention at the time, I guess because I personally hadn't done any of those things he thought God was judging us for, but I'm listening for something specific tonight. It comes near the end, when someone calls in to ask how you know when God's shutting you out because of some kind of sin in your life.

"How do you know?" my dad repeats. "When you feel that nagging guilt you keep hoping will shut up and leave you alone. When you lie awake at night feeling uneasy and you drink or smoke or watch garbage trying to drown it out and nothing works. That's how you know. That's your conscience warning you to get yourself right with God before he brings something even worse. You can lie to yourself a while, and people do it all the time, but eventually you pay the price."

I take my headphones out and shut my eyes like I'm praying, which I'm not. I don't know why I thought this would help me shake the fear and the emptiness that've been chasing me all week. I close my computer.

Around ten that night, I'm in my room getting ready for bed when there's a knock on the door. I freeze up a second, hoping it's not Mr. Buchwald again, or another reporter swooping in like a vulture. I hear Trey go answer it, and then I hear little feet padding erratically on the hardwood and Kevin say, "I brought her here to wear her out before I lose my mind."

"Would it've killed you to call?" Trey says, but he doesn't sound mad. Their voices fade into a murmur as they go back into the kitchen.

I hesitate a moment or two, then put my jeans and a shirt back on again. I know he's not here to see me, but maybe I can talk to Kevin.

I make my way downstairs to the kitchen, taking the stairs as loudly as possible so Trey knows I'm coming and has time to change the subject if he's complaining about me or anything. It smells like a bakery. When I walk in, Kevin says, "Braden, we missed you at youth group tonight!"

"Ah, yeah—I had homework."

He smiles. "I should've assigned less, you're saying? Was that a complaint?"

"Nah, it was for my other classes."

Trey's holding Ellie. We haven't had any real good moments since the night he brought home his birds, and so I check to see if he looks irritated I'm here now, but he just glances up and gives me a small nod before turning his attention back to Ellie. She's gripping one of his wooden spoons in her fist and sucking on her thumb, her legs wrapped around Trey's hip as she gazes down at what he's doing. It's noisy, stuff sizzling, and Trey stirs with one hand and ducks his head near hers to talk to her.

"Jenna's away on a women's retreat," Kevin says, "and I couldn't for the life of me get Ellie down to sleep. So, naturally, I'm reinforcing her terrible behavior, bringing her here. She gets to see her Uncle Trey, and he makes treats for her—do me a favor, Braden, and don't tell my wife this is how I handle parenting when she's gone."

I force a smile. I wish for a second I had his life instead of mine. Kevin says, "Pull up a chair. Sit with us a while."

I sit. He says, "You missed a good service. Maddie Stern was singing again tonight."

I say, "Ah." His grin goes wider. But he spares me the guard-her-heart-and-purity talk, at least, probably because Ellie and Trey are right there. I respond to his questions about school on autopilot, trying to think how I can somehow turn the conversation where I want it, which is maybe a long shot. I guess what I want is for someone to assure me, *It's fine, you're fine, God still loves you.*

I guess what I really want is for my dad to say it. You can trust him to give you the truth.

Trey sets a bowl on the table and sits down, shifting Ellie to his lap. "Quinoa and brown rice pudding with vanilla bean," he says. "Usually I do tonka bean, but I thought it might be too much for her."

Ellie seizes the spoon Trey set down next to the bowl. "Ellie, what do you do first?" Kevin says, reaching out and catching hold of her wrist. "What do you do before you eat? Do you pray?"

I watch her duck her head, her eyes peering up at Kevin, crinkled and gleeful, like it's a game. She says something I don't quite make out.

"Give us this day our daily bread," Kevin translates, then lets go of her wrist. "Say thank you to Uncle Trey."

Trey helps her eat, guiding the spoon to her mouth. It's messy and tedious, but he looks calm doing it—as close to happy as I've seen him look since coming back here.

I resist the urge to clear my throat and turn to Kevin, trying to sound casual. "So have you always taught her to pray?"

"For about as long as she could talk."

"You think she'll ever pray for something she doesn't get?"

"Ever?" he repeats. "Of course. Even people who don't consciously believe—everyone carries around unanswered prayers in their hearts. It's part of being human. Part of living in a fallen world."

"So what'll you tell her when that happens?"

"Hm," he says, and watches me more closely. I look away. Kevin's not stupid; I'm sure he can name a few unanswered prayers I might be holding on to right now, and I'm also sure he knows I'm not actually asking about Ellie.

Trey ignores us. I'm probably pushing it. I'll bet he wishes he told me to get lost when I first came in.

"Well, sometimes maybe our prayers aren't in line with God's will," Kevin says finally. "Sometimes answers come in different ways than we're looking for. I'd tell her that, I suppose, and I'd tell her that these are questions no one knows the answers to, but that what I do know is that our whole salvation rests on Christ's unanswered prayer to the Father to be spared the night before his death."

"Ah." I don't know what I wanted to hear, exactly, but it wasn't that. I say, "You think it's because God's angry at someone?"

"No."

I expected a much longer answer, not something so unequivocal. "Really, you don't think that?"

Ellie arches backward and lets out a long shriek that dissolves into a sob, and Kevin slaps his palm on the table and pushes himself up. "All right, that's our cue." He picks her up from Trey's lap. Trey looks something like disappointed, but he helps Kevin get Ellie's stuff together, and they say goodbye. As they're leaving, Kevin pulls me aside.

"Braden," he says. "You're going through a lot right now, and I know it's tempting to look for reasons why, but resist doing that to yourself. Sometimes life is difficult, but God doesn't change in his love for you. None of this is happening because he's angry, I promise. You can trust he's still good even when the rest of the world doesn't feel that way."

I tell him thanks, and to be polite I smile like I believe him and like that helped. Even if he was trying to make me feel better I don't think Kevin would deliberately lie to me, but I know what my dad thinks of that kind of theology—that more often than not you're just fooling yourself, trying to take some kind of easy way out in a way that'll only come back to haunt you later as you veer further and further from God's path.

But listening to an old show he did for strangers isn't the same as my dad telling me something directly about myself. And you can believe whatever you want and that doesn't make it true, I know that, but I also know I don't want to believe that God's already turned his back on me.

Upstairs again I find that message Maddie sent me with her phone number, and then I sit for a while in front of my laptop with the e-mail pulled up. I figured God would be irritated if I kept hanging around her, that he'd take it as a sign of disloyalty on my part, but maybe I was looking at it wrong. I know sometimes when God speaks to you he chooses something quieter and gentler than his own voice, that sometimes it's through a person he brings into your life.

I'm not going to directly pray for anything this time. But if Maddie could feel about me the way I do about her, if I could be the kind of person who deserved her—that would have to mean something, wouldn't it? I could take that as a sign I'm not alone.

Hey, I text her. *It's Braden Raynor. Are you still up?*

We beat East Union that week 6–4. Two of those runs are on me and two are on Greg, who got another shot at pitching, I think, because Cardy, of all people, actually felt sorry for him. He does better this game, so I tell him so—it's one of the best things about baseball, that you get the next game to redeem yourself—and his face turns red and he scuffs at the dirt with his cleats and says, "All right."

"I mean it, Greg, you were good. And I, um, I wanted to say—"

He turns around without answering, and the apology I've been practicing dissolves in my throat. I leave the locker room without talking to anyone else and spend lunch the rest of the week doing homework in my Spanish classroom, and at practice I avoid Greg. He never should've shaken Colin off that way, but I shouldn't have yelled at him even so; if anyone should shoulder more blame for that loss, it's me. That game was mine to win, and I know it. To make up for it, I avoid Maddie a while, too, and I don't text her the next few nights like I've been doing.

By the end of the week after we've played Pacheco—a 4–1 win— the jury's been selected, and Mr. Buchwald comes back to ask me more questions and to tell me April 30, less than two weeks before we're slated to play La Abra, is the date I'll have to go to court. And I don't know what else I have to offer God now to get me out of this, and I can feel the days between now and then vanishing and my court date sliding toward me the way a dense fog moves across the valley, blinding and close.

FIFTEEN

Even if I didn't have the date of the trial committed to memory, I'd know it from all the messages the reporters leave and the pictures of my dad splashed across the first page of the paper on our doorstep and the news van that, for an hour or two early in the morning, parks itself on our street. Colin finds me at my locker that morning and hands me a paper bag, saying, "My mom cooked tri-tip just to send to you for lunch, you lucky bastard," and says nothing about the trial even though I know he knows it's starting. And even though I try to move through the halls fast enough not to have to talk to anyone, Claire Kolpowski takes hold of my elbow as I'm going by the English wing and tells me she's here for me.

The trial starts at nine. At eight fifty-five that morning, the Punnett squares on the overhead projector in Biology burn away from my vision and instead I see my dad in shackles paraded in front of a room of prosecutors and jurors who are cold and unmoving against his fear; I see his Adam's apple sliding up and down as he tries to hold himself together in front of all those people, tries to convince himself it'll be all right. I stare straight ahead at the board and will myself not to see any of it, to imagine myself somewhere or sometime else instead. I try to picture hanging out with Trey. I imagine myself pitching. I try to replay the last conversation I had with Maddie. I think I understand something now about how people can live double lives—how when it feels like doing ordinary things ought to be beyond you, you still pick up the shell of yourself and go.

When I get home that evening, Mr. Buchwald's dropped off DVD recordings of the proceedings. I leave them on my desk untouched most of the night, uneasy about watching. But I can see their presence here isn't a suggestion, something for me to do with as I see fit; it's a direct order, and I wasn't raised to disobey those.

I wait until Trey's in his room before I watch. When the picture fills my screen, I scan the whole room for my dad. You can't see him, though, and it feels like a door slamming in my face.

The recordings are terrible, they cut off most of the room and are really wobbly—I have to keep looking away so I don't get motion sickness. I don't know exactly what I expected a trial to look like, but my dad used to watch *Law & Order* sometimes and I guess I was expecting something fast-paced, well-lit. Instead, there's a lot of standing around and a lot of instructions. Judge Scherr, a white-haired man with a mustache and a potbelly, has a monotone voice and looks tired, maybe bored. The camera makes everything dingy and depressing, and most of the jurors are older, too, and fat. I can see about half of them in their seats and they look so . . . normal. The woman in the front row looks like someone you'd picture handing out orange slices after a Little League game or something. But then, as we learned in Civics, they are ordinary—in no way especially qualified except they're citizens and over eighteen.

The prosecutor, Laila Shah, is attractive in a cold-looking way—Mr. Buchwald said something sarcastic once about how nice it must be to get jobs based on your looks, and I think he meant her—and she holds herself very straight and doesn't smile. I can't imagine her having friends, or family, or doing normal things like cooking dinner for her kids or wrapping gifts or shopping. I looked her up online one time and found out she's only a year older than Trey.

At the judge's direction, she goes first. "Martin Raynor is a dangerous, duplicitous killer who murdered an officer of the peace in cold blood."

She pauses for a second, letting that sink in. "The evidence you'll witness will demonstrate that the defendant, a man who fancies himself above accountability, is guilty of the brutal murder of a beloved family member and public servant.

"On Sunday, February ninth, Officer Frank Reyes, who had served with the La Abra Police Department for six years, was driving down Highway Fifty-Nine. He was providing his nephew a ride and, though he was off-duty, was driving his squad car as a service to the community. He was returning down Fifty-Nine when he received radio notification that the defendant's car had been flying down the highway and veering back and forth over the lanes and had been parked precariously halfway on the road in a way that demonstrated an utter disregard for the safety of others.

"Officer Reyes's first thought was that this was a drunk driver, a threat to the driver himself and to any other innocent drivers who might happen to pass. As a committed public servant, he quickly volunteered to go to the scene to offer assistance. Minutes later, as you know, he was dead. We are here to bring to justice the man responsible for his death.

"The defense would like you to believe that the defendant is an upright man being wrongfully framed for a crime he did not commit. The counsel for the defendant is going to ply you with excuses and half-truths: that Mr. Raynor had no discernible motive to commit so grisly a murder, that he acted in self-defense, that it was simply too foggy to realize one's car had hit something the size of a human being. Those blinded to Mr. Raynor's true nature will be paraded around the room to laud what they perceive as his moral rectitude.

"But the state will show you that, despite his carefully constructed public facade, Mart Raynor is a callous man who holds whole swaths of people in contempt. The state will show that the defendant acted with no regard for Officer Reyes's life and that he willingly, barbarously struck Frank Reyes with his car and knowingly left him to die on the road.

"Officer Reyes died a tragic, senseless death, and this loss of a beloved family member and community servant will haunt us for the remainder of our own lives. You must not allow a guilty man to roam free and, perhaps, to enact that same violence and brutality on other innocent lives. We must seek justice for our fallen officer and for our community."

Someone in the audience coughs, and there's a rustling sound, and Judge Scherr has Laila sit down. It's all kind of anticlimactic. I guess that's a good thing. Then Judge Scherr calls Mr. Buchwald up to give his own statement. He nods courteously at the jury, paces up and down the floor once or twice, then clears his throat.

"Mart Raynor is a highly regarded community servant. A devoted single father. A man of faith." His voice is quiet, calm, assured. He looks official and trustworthy on screen—like a teacher, maybe, or maybe a pastor. "But because Mr. Raynor was at the wrong place at the wrong time, because he bore the brunt of a resentful, violent individual's anger, he is also a man whose good name is being sacrificed on the altar of vendettas both personal and communal.

"The night of February ninth, Mr. Raynor was enjoying an outing with his son. Like many other drivers in similarly dangerous road conditions, Mr. Raynor was struggling to maintain control of his car. It was too foggy to even make out the lane lines on the road, and out of a concern for safety, he pulled over to the side of the road.

"The night should have ended there; Mr. Raynor waited out the fog and returned to the road when he deemed it safe. But when he was encountered by Francisco Reyes, the night took a severe turn. Mr. Reyes's unhinged, vengeful, and downright threatening behavior left Mr. Raynor understandably flustered, and he realized that it was necessary for him to risk the inclement weather and the conditions on the road to safely get away. In trying to protect himself and his son from a violent individual threatening him with a loaded firearm, he was forced to leave the scene.

"Miss Shah would like you to believe that just because a man lost his life, he must be a hero and a saint. She would like you to believe that Mr. Raynor, who has no criminal history whatsoever and holds an established record of community involvement, suddenly, out of the blue"—he snaps his fingers in a way that makes me think of a magician—"became a different person. That, without provocation or logic, he became a murderer. The evidence will show you, the jury, the patent absurdity of this notion. It will prove to you that in fact Mr. Raynor was correct to feel threatened by Francisco Reyes and that—while at no point did he intend for any harm to befall Mr. Reyes—he acted reasonably in self-defense and out of a desire to protect his son.

"You have a difficult job ahead of you as jurors. You will no doubt hear, during the course of the trial, Miss Shah's agenda to depict Francisco Reyes as a victim. You will perhaps be tempted by Miss Shah's maudlin sentimentalizing to assuage your own sense of grief at what has befallen a family in a nearby community. But Miss Shah would have you do this by condemning an innocent man.

"As jurors you must remain clear-eyed and focused. What happened is truly a tragedy for the family, and Mr. Raynor shares in the pain of their loss. But as faithful Americans you must acknowledge that Mart Raynor had no possible motive to commit this act, that he was unaware of the situation, and that he had the right to flee the scene in self-defense. You must acknowledge that there is reasonable doubt and restore Mr. Raynor's freedom and his life."

SIXTEEN

Trey's twenty-eighth birthday—May 30—was on a Saturday last year, the day we played Brantley. When I came downstairs in the morning, my dad had made breakfast and the Giants game was already on. It was early, because they were playing the Nationals in DC.

"Big game," he said as I spooned eggs onto my plate. He meant Brantley; we were having a good year, but Brantley would be our first real test. We took our plates into the den so we could watch the Giants while we ate, and on a commercial break, my dad said, "You know, B, I don't think it's too early to be thinking about scouting reports. I was going to start making some calls, maybe make good use of the rest of the season."

"Really, you think I'm ready for that?"

He thumped me on the back. "You've been good. I've been proud of you."

I ducked my head so he wouldn't see me grin. "Okay."

"I figure we'll get you right into the farm system," he said. "Get things in motion to get you drafted right out of senior year, like I was, and start working your way up. I'll bet you won't need more than a year or two in the minors."

"Yeah, maybe. I don't know." I finished my eggs. "Or maybe I could go to college somewhere first to play. Like maybe New York. Or maybe LA."

He looked at me sharply. "What's in LA?"

I shrugged. "Nothing," I said, even though he probably knew better. "Just thought it might be cool."

"That's it? You just thought it would be cool?"

"Yeah," I said, "that's it."

We settled back and watched the game. In the third inning, Hunter Micca homered. My dad doesn't like most Major League pitchers much—he's too critical, even of the good ones. But Micca, the catcher—that's his favorite.

"Maybe you'll play with him one of these days. He's only six years older than you, B, you know that?" He studied my arms and torso. "Probably a lot stronger than you, though. More meat on him. You've always been on the skinny side."

I sighed. "Yeah, yeah. I'll be sure to get you an autograph."

That made him laugh, a grin that lit up his whole face. "Don't you get smart with me, kid."

"I'll get you one of those mini wooden bats. 'To Mart. Love, Hunter.' You can hang it on your ceiling." I spread out my hands a couple inches above my head. "Just like this. So you can see it first thing every morning."

He smacked me on the thigh and said, affectionately, "You watch that mouth of yours." Then he said, casually, "It's your brother's birthday today."

I nodded. "I know."

He reached over and turned up the volume on the TV and stared fixedly at the screen. My dad hadn't seen Trey for eight years. The last night he ever spent in our home it was Easter. He was on his spring break from college; even though he lived in the dorms at Santa Cruz, his stuff was all at home still, and he came back on breaks and sometimes weekends, and I still thought of him as living with us, just away most of the time. That night I woke up because there was yelling. I pulled a pillow over my head and covered my ears and kept my eyes closed until the yelling stopped. There was a sound like something breaking, and a little while after, I heard footsteps outside my door, and my dad came across my room to my bed.

He reached for me, and I let myself be picked up and he gathered me in his arms and pulled me to him. He buried his head in my neck. I held myself very still. When he kissed my forehead, I could tell he'd been drinking. He held me close against him, then he arranged my arms so they were wrapped around him and brought his own shoulders in tighter like he wanted me to hug him, which I did.

He whispered, "Braden, I love you so much."

Then he whispered, "Don't go out there, B. The rest of the night. Just stay in here."

Then he said, more urgently, "Braden. Do you love me?" And it was only when I nodded that his grip on me started to relax. He reached out and held my face in his hand, like he was trying to memorize how I looked. I didn't cry or talk or move. The next morning, Trey was gone. My dad didn't come out of his room for two days, and when he finally did, he led me into the backyard and set up a row of cans, then handed me his gun and put his hands on my back to brace me against the recoil and made me practice firing into the cans. I took six shots, and it was so loud there was a ringing in my ears the rest of the night. I could tell I wasn't supposed to ask my dad about what happened with Trey, so I never did.

Now eight years had come and gone without Trey setting foot inside the house. The Giants were trailing. We watched them walk two runners. They got out of the inning with a double play, and then my dad cleared his throat again. "You talk to him?"

"I texted him this morning."

"What'd he say?"

"'Thanks.'" I made quotes with my fingers around the word. "All I said was happy birthday."

He snorted. I wasn't sure if that was meant for me or Trey. Then he got up and took our dishes to the sink.

We won the Brantley game, a 1–0 nail-biter, and I pitched one of my best games: eight strikeouts and no earned runs, and for the first five innings, I was throwing a perfect game. I thought my dad would be disappointed when I gave up my first hit, but when he came over to talk to me between innings, all he said was, "You'll get it next time. Just keep doing what you're doing, B. They're yours tonight." In the parking lot after the game, he clapped me on the back a bunch and talked excitedly with all the other dads, telling everyone this was going to be our year.

"Let's go out for dinner tonight," he said in the car. After games my dad and I always had a ritual: we'd go home and order takeout from somewhere, and we'd go over the game, and my dad would always pick out his favorite pitch. (Unless we lost, or I pitched badly—then we'd come home and avoid each other all night.) "What do you feel like eating? We'll go wherever you want." He was in a great mood, grinning through the windshield, turning to me at stoplights like a little kid. "You want steaks? You want burgers? Your choice. Wherever you want."

"Actually, Dad, is it okay if I go out with the guys instead?"

"Is it okay if what?"

"We were going to go hang out and barbecue at Chase Singer's for a while."

"Oh," he said. "Right now?"

"Yeah, just for a little while. The whole team's going."

"Oh," he said again. He blinked. "That's what you want?"

"Yeah, I—I mean, it's just everyone's going."

"Oh. Well, then, okay, B. Go ahead and go."

"I'll come back early," I said, because he sounded hurt. "Or I could—"

"No, no, you do whatever you want. You did good today. You deserve it. Go have fun."

"You sure?"

"Yeah, yeah." He'd stared through the windshield. "You go ahead."

It was a good night with the guys. Chase's parents weren't there, so everyone drank a bunch and played beer pong. I played with glasses of water, which in the end makes you feel about as sick. It was nice to relax and be a part of something, and it made me think for a while I was missing out just staying home with my dad so much. There were some girls there, too, and I spent a long time out by the pool with Claire Kolpowski, laughing about stuff we remembered from when all of us were little kids, and when I told her she'd turned out well—I always thought she was cute, and before Maddie, I figured I'd end up with someone from here, like Claire—she gave me a drunken kiss that was (I won't lie) pretty fun. Around nine I kept checking my phone, remembering what I'd promised my dad, and finally around ten thirty I went back home.

The house was dark when I came in, and I thought maybe he'd gone to bed. There were some takeout boxes on the kitchen table with a note: *Got extra in case you didn't eat enough.* I ate an egg roll and wiped my hands on my pants and went upstairs.

I found my dad in his room sitting on his bed, and there was something in his hands he was flipping back and forth the way I do with my glove. When I got closer—because he hadn't acted like he saw me when I went by—I saw it was his gun.

"Dad?" My voice came out high-pitched. "Dad, are you all right?"

He didn't answer me. He had his Bible open on his pillow, and when I looked around, it didn't take me long to find the glass on his nightstand, the bottle nearby. I said again, "Dad? Can you put that away?" He didn't move, and I said, "Dad, please. I don't—" I swallowed. My heart was thudding. "I don't like it when you get like this."

"You want to know something about God, Braden?"

I stared down at the gun. "Yes, sir?"

"He judges the whole world."

"I know, Dad, I—"

"He sees *everything*. And you know what he sees? He sees how there are some people past forgiveness. You know that? You ever think about all the people he ever destroyed? Just wiped out because he gave up on them?"

"Sometimes, I guess. . . ." I figured he must have been talking about Trey. "But doesn't it say he forgives everyone who believes in him and asks him to—"

"That's what you think?"

"I just think—I don't know. You can tell me if I'm wrong. But first can you just put away the gun? Please?"

"You think God forgets all the bad things you ever did? You think he doesn't know it if you're evil, Braden? There are people in the world God *hates*. No matter how they try to cover it up, no matter how they try to lie to themselves, they're his enemies and he hates them."

"Yeah, but those are other people," I said. "Not people like—" I hesitated. "Not people we know."

"When you sin," he said, his voice rising, and he raised a finger to point at me, "every time, when you sin, it's like you nail Jesus on his cross all over again. If you aren't right with God, then you don't even deserve to live. You think that's something to mess around with, Braden? You think that's something to take lightly?"

"No, sir." I didn't. I don't. "But—Dad, please. Please just put it away."

He'd leaned back against his pillows. He was wearing shoes on his bed. "You're sixteen," he said.

"Uh—yeah."

"You know what happened to me when I was sixteen?"

A feeling crept into the room like someone watching, someone waiting in the shadows for you to turn your back. I shouldn't have left him alone on Trey's birthday. "Um," I said, "yeah, I—you told me once—" and then I couldn't get the words out, how my dad had found his own dad's body bleeding in the garage.

"Come here," he said.

"Okay, just—put your gun away first."

He put the gun back in his drawer and closed it with a thud, and the look he gave me seared me. "I just want a hug, Braden. Come on."

I went to him. I should've stayed home all night. I shouldn't have made him sit there alone all night, thinking about Trey, thinking about his dad, because I know this about him: he's a good person. He's not the kind of man who could really hurt people. I should've proven myself to him then.

"You won't leave me," he said, gathering me in a hug I felt too old for, a hug that hurt my heart. "Right? It's you and me. You're all I've got."

SEVENTEEN

The morning of the annual church barbecue at Lake Ornette, I text Maddie to see if she's going. I was going to skip it this year—I always went with my dad, and anyway, I'm not exactly in the mood to sing worship songs around a bonfire and balance flimsy paper plates of baked beans and potato chips on my lap—but I change my mind when she says yes. We've been texting some more at night, but when I see her at school it never feels anywhere close to the way it did when I took her home from youth group that one night and so I can't tell what this is to her—a good deed because she figures I'm having a rough time, a consolation prize for not getting to talk to her real friends, or what.

I bike there, which takes an hour. The sun beats down on me as I ride, and I try to imagine what it would be like if we were together. The orchards around town are blooming, and I think about how I could bring her to places like this, show her how the trees look like clouds hovering right over the land. There's probably a lot here she hasn't seen yet. But then when I get there she's tossing around a volleyball with some of the other girls, wearing just a T-shirt over her suit, and when I go say hi she's smiling and out of breath and her hello seems distracted; I have that feeling I get sometimes around Trey, that there's a huge gap between how much you matter to a person and how much they matter to you.

I kind of wish I hadn't come. I kill time throwing a football around with some of the guys instead. Later, when everyone's gathered around the huge bonfire to eat, I'm near but not next to Maddie when Mrs. Kolpowski comes to give me a hot dog to roast and tells me she's praying for my dad.

"You know," she says, laying her hand on my shoulder, "you are the spitting image of him."

Because it's clear she means it as a compliment, I tell her thanks. I can feel Maddie watching me.

It cools down in the evening. By the time everyone gathers again around the fire I've had enough of parents coming over to ask me how my dad's doing, and I slip away and go lie down by the water and watch the sun set over the lake. When someone comes and lowers herself next to me, I know before I even look it's Maddie. My heart picks up. I turn my head back up toward the sky and say, "Hi."

"How come you aren't roasting marshmallows with everyone else?"

I shrug, my shoulder blade dragging against the ground. "Eh, I'm not that big on sweets. I always end up burning marshmallows anyway."

"I happen to make an impressive s'more. Want me to make you one?"

"I'm all right." I glance in her direction. "Why aren't you over there with everyone else?"

"I don't know. Sometimes I get tired of being around a lot of people all at once." She hugs her knees to her chest and draws neatly into herself, like she thinks maybe she was getting too close to me, and when she's farther away like that the air feels thinner. The sun dips under the waterline, and she says, "You know, I don't really think you look like your dad."

"No?"

"My parents listened to him sometimes before we moved here, and I remember being really surprised the first time I met you because I thought you'd be more like him. I didn't expect you to be like you were."

"And what was that?"

"Quieter. More private. I can't imagine you talking on a public broadcast every day." She hesitates. "And . . . nicer. I remember when we were picking lab partners in Science and you asked Austin O'Connor when you saw he was all by himself." She unfurls herself—I can trace the line of her calves in the low-lit dusk—and lies down on the sand, too. "And I remember when my youngest sister spilled grape juice on you at church when we were doing Communion and you were really nice about it. Your dad's . . . more intimidating."

Maddie's six or seven inches away from me, and when you're pressed close to the ground that way it's easier to pretend there's no one else around. My skin pulses with a desire to touch her. A breeze picks up, ruffling her hair and sending ripples across the lake. It's not dark yet, but there's a full moon hovering low in the sky. Her shirt's slipped down, and I can make out the goose bumps on her neck and collarbone and the skin just underneath, and so I take off my sweatshirt and say, "Here," and drape it over her, careful not to touch her, and she lets me.

Over from the road a car starts. And I think to myself how this feels like the direct opposite of what it feels like to be lonely, and how if I were the kind of person who deserved her, everything else would feel more clear. And, kind of suddenly, I have this image of the two of us lying places together like this—outside under the stars or maybe on the beach or maybe in our living room, maybe a couple of our kids playing nearby. I could take care of her and make sure she was never cold or scared or sad. We could get old together. We could make sure our kids knew we'd stay there with them no matter what, and each other, too; I'd prove to her that I'd be there no matter what. "Hey, Maddie?"

"Yeah?"

I don't know what I'm going to say, exactly, but then before I can shape words into something true they wash out anyway. But then, like the way I feel right now is some kind of magnet, she comes nearer so she's lying alongside me, our hips nearly touching. When I lean in closer, she stays. When I reach out and gently stroke the skin between the hem of her shirt and bikini bottom, she shivers, but she doesn't move away. And I tell myself to stop there, that her parents are nearby somewhere and all the pastors, and it would be pretty hard to explain lying alone with her this way in the dark.

But when I kiss her, she kisses back, and while it lasts that feels like everything, like hope again, and absolution, like God's presence coming down to rest on me. I think I could lie here with her just about forever, just like this.

EIGHTEEN

The prosecutor doesn't start with Alex Reyes or with any of the cops or the investigators or the coroner; she starts with Tucker Walker, the weatherman from the local news. Walker's a short man with greasy hair who wears rings on half his fingers and shiny-looking shirts—I would not be at all surprised if he turned out to be gay— and Laila Shah lets him describe the habits of tule fog as though it's an animal, what it likes and doesn't like and how it behaves. It's nothing any of us who live here need explained to us, and I catch a few of the jurors looking bored.

I know strategy. I know the way you lull a batter into complacency with softer pitches so when you give him worse, it has more impact. And I'm right—after she's drawn out the long explanations, Laila smooths her skirt and says, "Given the conditions the night of February ninth, if one were in a car parked twenty or so feet behind another car, would one expect to be able to clearly see what was happening?"

Walker says yes.

"Would one be able to see an adult male standing within striking distance of the car?"

Walker sort of laughs, a high-pitched, nasal laugh like maybe he doesn't like talking to real people instead of a camera, or like maybe he isn't quite telling the truth. "Visibility that night was calculated around two hundred feet."

"When was the last time, in your experience, that weather conditions would have been such that a driver might not notice someone in such close proximity?"

Walker blows air through his lips. "Truth be told, I'd say a good three or four years."

That's her last question, so Walker stays up there as Laila takes a seat and Mr. Buchwald stands. I've seen him talk (obviously) to me and I've seen him on the news and I've seen him addressing the jury, but as soon as he adjusts his tie and starts speaking to Walker, I realize I still probably don't know him at all. He talks in a measured voice the way people do when they're so angry they know any second they might slip. His face is expressionless, and he punctuates what he says with a pointed finger jabbing in the air, and if he were a principal or a coach or something, I think I'd be afraid of him. Watching him talk that way makes you believe Walker did something awful.

Under Mr. Buchwald's cross-examination, Walker admits that visibility can vary from point to point, that cars can slide unexpectedly into fog banks with no warning, and that there've been multiple documented instances in the Central Valley where visibility fell as low as under a foot. Laila and Mr. Buchwald battle two days over that fog. A 911 dispatcher who Laila brings up for all of two minutes claims there were no weather-related accidents that night, and Mr. Buchwald says, aloud and to everyone, *"Other."* Judge Scherr tells him sternly to remain silent, but I think he might be hiding a smile, too. After that, Laila calls on a short, squat woman who claims to have driven by my dad's car when it was parked halfway off the road that night.

"The car was fully visible, despite the fog?" Laila says. The woman says yes. Laila shows a photograph of the car and the woman nods: yes, yes, it was that one, that same car.

"A navy Range Rover?" Laila presses, and the woman moves her head up and down. She was driving home and had to swerve to miss it; she thought she was going to be killed. She keeps looking around nervously, fingering the crucifix she's wearing on her neck, and when Mr. Buchwald asks her why she didn't call the police if the car was really as dangerously parked as she claims, and if she was driving by so fast and was really that scared, how she can be sure it's the same one, she bursts into tears. Then Laila plays a 911 recording, and that's worse: a man who scolds the dispatcher, "I nearly got run off the road by some crazy driver swerving all over the lanes on Fifty-Nine. You'd better send someone out right now before anybody gets killed."

All these people who could be up there saying anything, could be lying through their teeth—I watch how they stay fast or they crumple and fall apart on the stands; I feel how they're picked apart and mercilessly cross-examined and how everything they say is held up to scrutiny and judgment. And I think how each of them holds some share of blame in whatever the eventual verdict will be, and how I will, too.

I've been working myself ragged every day at practice lately, coming home after to work out in the garage until the exhaustion's purged any errant thought from my mind. This is the longest I've gone in my life without any coaching from my dad, and while some days I feel strong and certain, hopeful about the future still, others I feel uncentered and lost. Once at practice I come too far inside throwing during batting practice and nearly take off Dutch's head, and I'm rattled all day. Dutch jokes about it, but after that he doesn't get a hit the rest of practice. That night I hunt down my dad's old game videos and watch them until I can hold the image of his pitching perfectly in my mind, and then the rest of the night I go through my windup over and over with my eyes closed, trying to superimpose his steady, impeccable mechanics over my own. At our game against Lodi the next day, my command is better, and nothing gets away from me. We win 3–0. And Maddie comes to watch.

Since the lake, it's been different with Maddie—we haven't kissed again or even really touched, but somehow just sitting in the same room as her in class it feels different, like the walls have loosened at their seams and expanded to make room for whatever new thing we're holding between us. We've been together a lot at lunch—the guys are all over that one—but whenever she texts or calls it's still never just *hi*; it's always a question about homework first. I'm not sure how to read that. Most times, though, we wind up talking for real after that. She doesn't press me about my dad, I think because she can sense I'd rather she didn't; instead, we talk about baseball or new songs she's been working on, or about things I want to take her to do when it's summer like river rafting two towns over in Lourdon or going on the rope swing out on the south end of the lake. And it's always nice—it's like visiting some other, better life—and I think maybe the way she always starts conversations like that is just that she's still giving herself an out. It's different if someone doesn't answer your question about homework than if someone doesn't answer your *hello*.

Mr. Buchwald comes over Saturday morning to bring new recordings and to go over the questions he'll ask me on the witness stand. He seems animated and crisp; he strikes me as the kind of person who enjoys working on a Saturday. He brings bagels and orange juice. I don't have any. When I ask how my dad's doing, Mr. Buchwald says, "Oh, fine," which has to be a lie. Of course he isn't fine.

He tells me Laila's work so far has been less than stellar. The testimony was dry, he says, not something that'll strike any kind of emotional high point for the jury, and the woman testifying about my dad's car was so clearly nervous some jurors won't read her as credible.

"Just because she was nervous?" I say. "Because I'm going to be nervous, too. And I really don't think it's a good idea for me to—"

"Oh, your father assures me you're excellent under pressure."

I don't know whether I believe him; I don't know if that's what my dad would say about me. "Have you ever seen a jury get a case wrong?"

"All the time. You'd expect otherwise?" He looks amused. "A jury is not an infallible machine, Braden. Picture selecting twelve people at random from your high school and you'll get an idea why. I've long believed that there should be an IQ requirement to serve as a juror. Imagine the frustration of having hours and hours of your work dismantled by a high school dropout who tuned you out after the first witness and simply thinks the accuser seems like a nice man."

"Sounds pretty frustrating for you," I say flatly, and if he catches the contempt in my tone he doesn't let on. I'm disappointed. That was as close as I'll let myself get to *Screw you.*

I'll admit he's good at what he does—he's good with the jury and you can tell he makes the witnesses nervous, and he's said a jury's less likely to trust a witness who acts afraid because it makes you look like you have something to hide. So I'll give him that, at least. I can respect that he's good at his job; the recordings he's brought me might not be aboveboard, but I can respect people who do whatever it takes to be competitive.

But when it comes down to it I don't trust him any more than

I do the prosecutor, and hearing him say that about juries, I put my finger on exactly why—this is another notch on a résumé to him. *This* being my father's life.

.   .   .

At the end of March, Laila Shah shows the jury photos of my dad's license and registration lying on the asphalt just outside La Abra near where Officer Reyes was hit. After Ornette, there's nothing but orchards on either side of the road for miles and miles before the land gives way to cramped gray apartment buildings rising up over the freeway wall, and the road is rough there and you can see potholes on the slides Laila shows. They look huge in the photographs, like craters on the moon.

After that, she calls up the county coroner, an owlish woman whose hands fly around to make pictures of her words: a cupped hand patting the back of her head when she says *basilar skull fracture*, a curve she traces under her eye when she says *periorbital ecchymosis*. I watch her testify on Mr. Buchwald's DVD, as ordered. Trey's birds keep chirping the whole time. It hurts my ears. Trey's gone, who knows where; I only watch these when he's not home.

Under oath, the coroner tells the jury that eight ribs were shattered and the entire abdominal cavity was distended with pooling blood, and that the autopsy revealed that parts of the colon were found smashed inside the spleen. She pantomimes holding a scalpel. She gives the actual cause of death as asphyxiation due to torn and punctured lungs, and says *Without doubt* when asked if the death was caused by being struck by the defendant's car.

In his cross-examination, Mr. Buchwald harps on the physical findings—were there bones shattered by motive? Blood cells lining up to spell a note telling the coroner exactly what happened?

After the coroner is the forensics investigator, who comes with an easel and a permanent marker to map out an illustration for the jury. The stretch of the road where the accident happened is torn up and there's potholes everywhere, and stretches where the shoulder disappears. The investigator has poster-size images of the road and the accident scene blocked off.

"Based on the clothing fibers and DNA traces we found, the victim was struck and fell"—he thuds the marker against the photo to punctuate—"right here, next to the car. From there, he was dragged underneath the wheels about a foot and a half, then dragged forward again. There were four spots where we picked up samples, which makes it likely the car backed over him and then drove forward again. But here"—he draws another X on the easel—"this time, instead of going straight forward, we found the evidence about a foot and a half to the right."

Laila asks what this means. The investigator caps his pen and turns away from the map he's made, then looks apologetically to where I think the Reyes family's sitting. "He likely tried to crawl away before being struck again."

The air feels thin and slippery the way it does before you black out, my lungs like mesh, and I inhale until it hurts. The investigator testifies that he found blood and hair fibers on a four-yard area of the asphalt, that my dad's license and registration were found nearby, and that Frank Reyes's gun was found in his holster and with the safety still engaged. Then he motions to someone off to the side and a photo's broadcast onto the projector screen next to him: Frank Reyes's body faceup on the ground, one hand over his chest and one splayed against the asphalt, and even though it's the last thing you'd notice about the picture, his gun's secured in his holster, untouched.

. . .

I'm rewatching the forensics investigator's testimony Sunday night, thinking about what might happen if the judge knew I'd seen all this, when Trey appears in my doorway. I slam my laptop shut, and my voice comes out weird when I say, "Hey."

"Hey," he says back, like the greeting amused him. I can't tell if he noticed me jump or not. "The Cortlands want to have us over for dinner. I told them you're coming, too."

I clear my throat and hope my voice comes out more normal this time. "Right now?"

"Yeah. Wear something nicer, will you? Put on something with a collar at least."

I'm wearing jeans and a T-shirt, but I change. Kevin and Jenna live out near Kevin's parents, near the Martinez vineyards on the west part of town, up in the foothills. From where we live, you can either drive along the outskirts of the town—the way I like, out where there's almost no people and even though you've lived here all your life you could get lost somewhere in all the oaks and the winding roads curving into the hills—or you can cut across the main artery on Oakridge Boulevard all the way there.

Trey takes Oakridge. Traffic lights the whole way.

While he's driving, I ask since when did Kevin care so much about what I wear. "Dinner was Jenna's idea. It's at Kevin's folks' place."

"Oh. Those Cortlands." I half wish I hadn't gone with him; it feels weird going to dinner at your pastor's house when you've been skipping church. But I keep that to myself since clearly it's important to Trey, and anyway I can't say I love being at home by myself, either. "Yeah, Jenna said something about dinner."

He frowns. "When did you talk to her?"

"At youth group."

"Oh. Right." He checks the time on the dashboard and then speeds up some, like he's worried we'll be late. "You know she has this blog? All stuff about, like—diet plans, and pictures of her and Kevin on their anniversary camping trip, and crap. It's depressing as hell. You know the only reason she even applied to college is so she could go with him to Bethany for two years?"

"You date much in New York?"

"No."

"How come?"

He shrugs. "No time."

"Maybe you should get out more. Go to church sometime and meet a girl."

"Yeah? Maybe you should write an advice column."

Fine, whatever, I know he thinks that's dumb. But I also think, even though he doesn't say it, that maybe he's lonely—that maybe he wishes things had gone differently for him.

When we get there, Trey checks himself in the mirror before we go in. I'm about to tease him for it, but I change my mind; I don't know why. I guess because something about him seems different.

I wonder if maybe I'm making that up, but the transformation, once we step over the threshold into their home, is complete. Trey's smiley and polite and pleasant—animated, even. He hugs Pastor Stan and Mrs. Cortland, and thanks them for having us over in a voice I can only describe as warm, and hands them this bottle of olive oil he brought as a gift. He kisses Jenna on the cheek and says hello to Ellie, who Jenna's holding, and—this strikes me as weird—barely glances at Kevin at all.

Pastor Stan shakes my hand and says how great it is to see me, how proud of me my dad must be, and Mrs. Cortland gives me a big hug and tells me how strong I'm being. I've always liked Mrs. Cortland; she's kind and smiles a lot and doesn't take herself too seriously. But the hug makes me weirdly guilty, like I wish I could somehow peel it off and give it back. Maybe it's that the last time I was here at this house, I was with my dad—it was last fall, and my dad had such a good time he loosened up in a way he almost never does with other people. Remembering how he laughed at his own jokes, how boisterously happy it made him to feel wanted and popular and liked, a purer kind of happy than he gets when fans recognize him, makes me ache. Thinking about him happy hurts even worse, somehow, than thinking about him sad.

After we all finish saying hellos, Trey follows Jenna into the kitchen to help her. She tries to push him away, saying jokingly, "Kitchens aren't for men," and when he tells her thanks a lot, she laughs. "That's different, Trey. You know what I mean."

"Well, at the expense of my masculinity, then, I'd like to help."

"Kevin and Stan are about to open some brandy. You don't want to join them?"

"Nope. I'm at your command. Tell me what to do."

She gives in. "Well, of course you'll think it's silly, but I found the most darling flower cupcakes"—she holds up a picture to show him—"because I'm throwing a baby shower next week for Hailey Cleminger—do you remember Hailey? They're having twins, can you believe it?—and I wanted to practice so I didn't mess up Hailey's big day."

She puts him in charge of coloring the fondant pink (I guess they're girl twins) and cutting out petals. Trey works carefully. I've seen him enough to know nothing he ever does in the kitchen is slow, but cutting frosting petals for Jenna, he's painstaking about it. More than once, their elbows touch.

When they're done, there's three rows of flowered cupcakes, like a garden. Jenna sprinkles some kind of glitter stuff on the tops, then surveys them. "Do you think they look all right?"

"They look great."

"In the picture they were more artistic. It's her baby shower, and I'd hate to disappoint her if—"

"What are you talking about? There's no way she'd be disappointed. You could run a business doing this if you wanted to, you know. I mean it. You've always—"

Kevin comes into the kitchen then, and Trey goes quiet. "Well," Kevin says, raising his eyebrows at the cupcakes, "haven't you two been busy."

Jenna dusts her hands on her apron and smiles at him. "Don't worry. I made a chocolate cake, too, so you boys aren't stuck eating flower cupcakes."

Kevin pulls Jenna toward him and gives her a kiss on her lips. "What a superb wife. Isn't she, Trey?"

"Superb," Trey says. He washes his hands at the sink and dries them on a towel and doesn't say anything else.

For dinner, there's pot roast, mashed potatoes, green bean casserole, and what Mrs. Cortland refers to as pioneer biscuits. There's wine, and candles, and I think how much my dad would appreciate this. For Father's Day I always try to make him dinner because he loves when people cook. I wonder what he's eating. I wonder what it's like to go so many days without talking to a single person who cares about you.

I sit down across from Trey and try to root myself here, in this house, with these people, and try not to leave any space in my thoughts for what I was watching before we came. Pastor Stan prays over the meal—Trey ducks his head along with everyone else—and when we all raise our heads, Pastor Stan lifts his glass of wine.

"I'd like to propose a toast," he says. "To the most wonderful family in the world, to our beloved friends, and"—he pauses in a way that makes me think whatever he's about to say is the real reason for this toast—"especially to our son Kevin, who next year will answer God's call on his life and return to seminary. Kevin, you make us unspeakably proud."

There's a silence: me and Trey absorbing that one. Pastor Stan's beaming. "Wonderful news, isn't it?" he says, and leans over to squeeze Kevin's shoulders enthusiastically. I'll bet Pastor Stan's the kind of dad who tells everyone *Good game, good game* even when it wasn't. "The Lord just astonishes me daily with his grace in Kevin's life."

"Seminary, huh." Trey leans back in his chair and looks over at Kevin behind Jenna, who's sitting between them with Ellie on her lap. "You didn't tell me."

Kevin glances at Jenna. "I still have to accept the offer."

"Oh, but of course you will." Mrs. Cortland smiles at me. "You're the first to hear the news, Braden, so please keep it hush-hush for now."

"Well." Trey has that same overly polite tone of voice he used with Mr. Buchwald. "Congratulations, Kevin. Everything's really falling into place for you, isn't it?"

Jenna, I notice, barely eats; Mrs. Cortland keeps offering her serving spoons, and each time, Jenna takes some food and then just pushes it around on her plate, or puts it on Kevin's. She mostly just focuses on Ellie, and sometimes strokes Kevin's hand and props her hand on her chin and smiles at what everyone's saying.

Pastor Stan asks Trey about his restaurant and what he's been doing since they last saw him at Kevin's wedding. Mrs. Cortland asks meaningfully if there are any young ladies in his life and Trey says no, that Kevin has all the luck. "We'll have to pray for that, then," Mrs. Cortland says, and under the table, a foot nudges mine; when I look up, Kevin's got his gaze trained on me, a smile tucked away.

"Speaking of young ladies," he says, "isn't prom coming up soon?"

"Ah—it might be."

"And might you have any plans to go with a certain young lady I've been seeing you with?"

"Ah—" I'm not at all in the mood to talk about that in front of everyone. But Pastor Stan chuckles and then—sensing my discomfort, maybe—he changes the subject, asking Trey what he thinks of New York. Trey kind of shrugs and says there are things he likes and things he doesn't, and I'd like to hear more about the things he doesn't, but he doesn't elaborate.

"It's probably nowhere near as exciting as what you're used to, having grown up here," Mrs. Cortland teases. "I can't imagine how you manage to fill your time. So little to do in that town. Did you know we were in New York a few years ago? After I finished my treatment and got the all-clear from my doctors, we took a week there before driving up to see the fall colors in New England."

Trey reaches out his arms to Ellie. She lights up, clambering across Jenna's lap and onto his. To Mrs. Cortland, he says, "That sounds nice."

"Oh, it was. It was just what I needed. All through that awful treatment, I felt the Lord holding me up, telling me he was going to carry me through this, and one day he brought me a vision of Stan and me in Times Square, and I just held on tight to that. I thought, *This will all be over and we'll go on a marvelous trip*, and God was faithful to his promise." She laughs and takes a sip of her wine. "And you will never guess where we stayed. Stan kept telling me, 'Linda, just relax, I'll take care of everything, you just pack your bags and *relax*,' and then we show up and—surprise! We could've just left our bags on the plane."

Pastor Stan makes a good-natured grumbling noise. "Linda, they don't need to hear—"

"It was a *clothing optional* hotel," she says, lowering her voice to an exaggerated whisper. "*Very* optional."

Kevin's eyebrows shoot up, and he turns to Pastor Stan, a slow grin spreading across his face. "Don't remember you putting that on the postcard, Dad."

Pastor Stan sighs. "I can't imagine how it slipped my mind."

"Oh, you should have *seen* the look on his face. He could barely talk to the concierge, he was trying so hard to keep his eyes down and not see anything. Delightful people, though, it turned out. We met a lovely nudist couple in the elevator, and we all went to see *Jersey Boys* together that night. And we left our Bibles in the room for the next guests when we checked out."

She pats Pastor Stan's hand, her eyes twinkling. "It was a wonderful trip, though. Oh, such a beautiful city. We got to stand where the First Congress adopted the Bill of Rights—it was absolutely breathtaking. And we went to the most amazing restaurants, and to two Broadway shows and a comedy show—our daughter Samantha was taking an improv comedy class and said, 'Oh, Mom, you have to go see this man whose tapes I've been watching.' It turned out to be a little PG-thirteen, but we thought it was quite funny. But then Sam's class put on a show at the end of her class and we thought, 'Well, it'll be like what we saw in New York—we enjoyed that,' but, oh, it was just awful. It was just so *unfunny*. After the third dreadful routine, Stan turned to me and said, 'Honey, do you think God is thinking right this second, *Whatever possessed me to send my beloved son to that planet to save* them?'"

Trey laughs, a real laugh, and Ellie cackles an echo. Mrs. Cortland says, "Oh dear." She points at Kevin. "I am still your mother, so you listen to me when I tell you not to breathe a word of that to Sam. She will go to her grave believing we were in stitches the entire night."

"It's tempting to hold on to that as blackmail, actually," Kevin says, and Mrs. Cortland shakes her finger at him.

"Oh, you watch your mouth. Everyone needs a mother to cheer them on no matter what. You ask your wife." She gives Jenna a kind smile, and her tone softens. "Ellie is such a lucky girl. Too many children these days grow up always playing second fiddle to their mothers' careers, raised by nannies, practically motherless." Then she looks at me, stricken, and puts a hand over her mouth, like I've let something show in my expression. "Oh, Braden—I'm so sorry. Both of you boys. Oh, listen to me. How insensitive." She waves her hand in front of her face, and her cheeks turn red. "Why on earth did you all let me prattle on like that? Someone else talk now."

Pastor Stan squeezes her hand, looking maybe a little uncomfortable, and, before either Trey or I have to answer, says, "Trey, what a blessing that you get this season in your life to spend with Braden. He's sure done well for himself, hasn't he?" And then he spends the next five minutes trying to talk to me about baseball even though he obviously knows almost nothing about it, which feels like a kindness—a sort of clumsy grace.

It's actually worse that I can tell how hard they're trying. I don't think I can take a lifetime of putting on a polite smile like this, pretending nothing's wrong and secretly resenting good people for somehow not being what I need. I don't even know how I'll take another few weeks.

I'm more than ready to go home, and I'm relieved when we finish dessert. But then Mrs. Cortland starts making coffee, and Pastor Stan brings out Catch Phrase, and obviously I'm stuck. There's so much yelling and it goes so fast, it's about the last game you want to play when you'd rather just be at home.

I'm on Mrs. Cortland's team. She draws her word and purses her lips, then says, "Oh," drumming both her hands on the table, spinning one finger in a circle like she thinks it'll make me guess faster, "Oh, Braden, it's big and you drive it! It has a steering wheel! It goes on roads!"

I say *car*, obviously, and she beams and gives me an incredibly enthusiastic high five—she's breathless—and then nearly drops the buzzer handing it off to Kevin while for no good reason at all, I'm stuck paralyzed in my seat. Mrs. Cortland looks closely at me. She leans over and puts her arm around me and murmurs in my ear, "God will get you through all this, honey. He's with you."

I last two more turns. Then I mumble something about needing to go to the bathroom and push my chair back so fast I almost knock it over. I hurry down the hallway, and then I shut the door behind me and sink against the floor and bury my head in my arms. Something's constricting around my rib cage, making it hard to breathe.

This is why I hate when people tell me *I don't know how you're surviving*—because that implies you get a choice. What do they think, you're actually going to die? Because that's not how it works. You don't get an escape into nothing; you get a brother who half the time acts like he can't stand you anymore and you get a seashell-themed bathroom in your pastor's house to escape to because a nice dinner with people who believe what you wish you could about God is more than you can take.

I breathe and breathe and breathe until I feel light-headed and then I cup my hands and breathe into them so I can feel the air going in and out. My phone beeps. When I pull it out of my pocket, my hands are shaking. I hope it's Maddie, even though I also hope it isn't, because I feel fragile enough I might crack open and let slip things I can't tell her, or anyone, ever. But instead, it's a text from Trey: *You fall in or something? Get your ass back out here.* I don't answer it, and soon there's a rap on the door, and then when I don't answer he lets himself in.

"You've been gone like twenty minutes, Braden." He's frowning. "It's rude to—"

"Sorry," I manage. "I'm sorry. Just please don't yell at me."

"I wasn't even close to yelling. What are you doing? They're getting all worried. Mrs. Cortland thinks she hurt your feelings."

"It's not that. I just—I'm sort of—"

"Okay, well, then, get back out there."

"Trey, I'm—I'm really not feeling that great."

"You're in someone else's house. So show some manners, would you?"

No matter what, the last thing I want to do right now is upset him. I make myself nod and make myself smile. He watches me a second, then, unexpectedly, his face softens. "You want like a code word or something?"

"What?"

"We'll pick a word and you find a way to work it into a sentence if you really need to bail, and that'll be my signal you're done."

"Like what word?"

"How about *fuck*." He hides a smile at my expression. "I'm kidding, I'm kidding. But, Braden, look—sometimes you just have to pull yourself together and fake it, but I know things aren't the greatest right now, all right? I've been there, too, and I know it sucks, so you tell me if you need to go and we'll go. I'll cover for you."

I pull the air into my rib cage. I'm pushing my luck, but I have to ask. "Hey, Trey?"

"Yeah."

"I know you don't want to, but—can you go with me to court when I have to go? You could just sit in back and you wouldn't have to talk to anyone, just—if there's any way—"

His expression closes off again. "That's your thing, Braden, not mine."

"I know, but—"

"You can take the car. Or I'll call you a cab if you want. But that one's yours."

I thought he might change his mind; if it was going to happen, tonight would've been the night. "Then will you at least come when I have to play La Abra?"

He runs a hand over his head, then lets it drop heavily against his side. "Sure. You really want me there, I'll go."

"You swear?"

"Yeah, yeah, I'll be there. And in the meantime"—he deepens his voice the way he used to when he was trying to get a smile out of me when I was a kid—"how about you get it together and come play Catch Phrase like a man."

NINETEEN

didn't recognize the name Curt Molson, but when I watch Laila call him to the stand I recognize him right away as the other officer who was there the night I came back from LA. When he walks past where I know my dad is sitting, his face contorts in hatred, but when he steps behind the witness stand his entire expression changes like a shape-shifter from a superhero movie and his voice sounds artificially soft, especially when he says "Frankie." Laila spends the first five minutes tossing him lob questions to make him look good, and he tells the jury about having served the community for decades and says Reyes was a dedicated, upstanding officer (of course he does) who was given an Excellence in Service award three years ago for antiviolence work he did with youth.

"Frankie cared so much about his job. He cared about the job and he cared about this city. He never got to have a family of his own, you know, so it mattered to him a lot. Went away to college and got a degree, then came back to join us. Six years he's been with us. Volunteers with at-risk teenagers, too."

"Had he—"

"At least he used to before he got killed by that man over there."

Mr. Buchwald objects. Judge Scherr orders the comment stricken from the record, not that it matters since the jury already heard.

Laila pulls at a thread on her jacket sleeve, then flicks it on the floor. "Would you describe Officer Reyes as a conscientious public servant?"

"Oh, yes, ma'am."

"Officer Molson, what would the procedure have been the night Officer Reyes pulled over the suspect?"

"Standard procedure, ma'am. He would've figured out the situation and maybe done a field sobriety test if he suspected a DUI. Run the paperwork. Unless the suspect was making some kind of threat, there's no reason Frankie would've ever engaged a weapon or anything of the sort."

"Can you describe physically where Officer Reyes would have been during the traffic stop?"

He pushes his sleeves up his arms to his elbows. The shirt's baggy on him; since the last time I saw him I think he's lost a bunch of weight. "Well, he'd pull up behind the car. He'd go around to the passenger side to talk to the driver so he didn't get hit by anything. You don't stand on the driver's side unless you want to get hit by a truck or something. So if you got hit by a driver trying to make a break for it, it means the driver drove away from the road instead of back on it. You can't do that on accident. Driving *into* the shoulder? If all you really want is to make a getaway? I can't picture that happening any more than I can picture Frankie pulling a gun during a traffic stop."

"Had Officer Reyes ever received any credible complaint about his conduct on the job or conducted himself in such a way that any disciplinary action was deemed appropriate?"

"No, ma'am. Never once."

Laila smooths the front of her jacket. "Was he hotheaded?"

"No, ma'am. Not one bit. Sweetest guy you ever met. Besides that, he was with his nephew that night. He was crazy about that kid. He would never do nothing risky when he was with his nephew. Or when he had no backup."

"Under what situation would an officer conducting a traffic stop pull out a gun, as the defense has claimed Officer Reyes did that night?"

"It would have to be something pretty serious. Because you don't want a situation escalating or nothing. A suspect sees you pull a weapon, he's going to lose his cool, and all of a sudden you got a situation on your hands. Frankie wouldn't do that. Frankie never discharged his gun one time on the job. Not one time in six years. You'd only do that if maybe there was a threat. Maybe if the other guy reached for a weapon or something, but only then. But you saw the pictures. He never even got a chance."

"Officer Molson, can you explain why Officer Reyes's fingerprint was found on the taillight of the suspect's car?"

"That's standard, too."

"Why is that?"

"Ah—" He looks off toward the side. I know the courtroom's filled with cops who've driven in from as far away as Reno to be there; in the papers, one of them said in an interview that even though he'd never met Officer Reyes, he'd still lost a brother. He told the reporter they want justice against my dad. "We train our boys to do that. You pull someone over; on your way up to talk to them, you stop and you mark their taillight. The fancy departments get cameras, but we can't afford that. It's half superstition. At least you hope you never actually have to use it. But that's so then we know for sure you were there just in case something ever goes wrong."

Laila says, "Officer Molson, let's go back to the night you and Officer Reyes first encountered the suspect. What happened?"

"We were called to the house because of a missing-child situation. The man couldn't get ahold of his kid, so he called us. This was back in January. So we came to the house and started asking questions. Standard stuff. You know—where'd he last see his kid, was there anything that would make him think we had a runaway situation, had his kid been talking to anyone unusual lately—all that. I mean, I got two girls and Frank's got a nephew and nieces he's close to, so we know teenagers pretty well. Now, I've been on the force, oh . . . twenty years, about, and I've seen a lot of upset parents. We see a lot of things. But there was something off about Raynor. He was all defensive, for one thing. Usually parents want as many questions as possible because they want to find their kid. They'll answer anything. But he wasn't that way. I can't say I was too shocked when I heard it was him who killed Frank."

Mr. Buchwald objects again. Judge Scherr says sternly, "Stick to the facts, please." Officer Molson gives a nod of acknowledgment, but his expression isn't nearly so polite.

"It was weird stuff about him," Officer Molson continues. "Like he wouldn't answer our questions, and he didn't like when we tried to tell him his kid was probably fine. He didn't like when we made suggestions, either. He kept saying this couldn't be happening because his kid was supposed to be at a baseball game. Reyes and I keep looking at each other, like, 'Your kid's missing and all you care about is a ball game?' Like he couldn't believe the kid's not there to be his trophy for one afternoon." The microphone screeches, and Officer Molson jerks back like it startled him. "Or maybe like he couldn't believe anyone had the nerve to cross him. And the other thing is he didn't like Frankie right away. That was the other thing. He had a real nasty attitude with him."

"Did Officer Reyes respond?"

Officer Molson flattens out his lips. "Some. Just a little. You can't get into it with a man like Raynor. It's just not worth it. But something about him—he really knew how to drag you into it. And Frank could get kind of sarcastic. Not the worst I've ever seen. All due respect, ma'am, you woulda got snippy with him, too."

The way Laila pauses reminds me of when you're behind the plate waiting for the pitcher to wind up. "After that incident, would you characterize Officer Reyes's relationship to Mr. Raynor as hostile?"

"Ma'am, there was no relationship. We just showed up there that one time. Frank's a professional. We deal with so much on that job I bet he never thought about it again. I can't imagine him getting worked up about it the next time he saw him. In the car afterward, he was his usual self, joking around. Told me he was looking forward to the weekend."

"What state was Mr. Raynor in when you left?"

"He wasn't in a good way, to tell you the truth. Just didn't seem like he had himself all the way under control. And now I know we should've stuck around, maybe made sure the kid was all right, looked at Raynor more, but at the time . . ."

Officer Molson reaches up and wipes his forehead. He's wearing a blue shirt and there are sweat stains starting to show under his sleeves. "The thing is that at the time, Raynor had no record. And he's on the radio and you see his picture, and you figure, sure, he's an asshole, maybe, but you figure he's all right. You can't arrest someone just because you don't like him. And to be straight with you I figured the kid needed to be taught a lesson and I thought, good, his old man's pissed off at him. Jesus, I would've done it different if I knew what kind of person Raynor was. Everyone keeps asking how come I didn't do nothing at the time and then maybe Frankie would still be around. But I didn't know it was going to turn out like this. I thought he was just upset about the kid and that was why he was acting that way. How was I supposed to know?"

In his cross-examination, Mr. Buchwald rubs his hands together briskly and peers over his glasses at Officer Molson on the stand. The lawyer looks bright-eyed and alert; he practically leapt up when the judge gave him the go-ahead.

"June eighteenth," he says. "Four years ago. The twenty-two-year-old son of Officer Isaac Willingham—a thirty-year veteran of your department—was accused of sexual assault. Is this correct?"

Officer Molson frowns. "He was cleared of—"

"It's a yes or no question. Is this correct?"

"Yeah, sure. He was accused."

"And yet no charges were ever filed. Is this also true?"

"Yeah, because—"

"The son of one of your colleagues was accused of rape and was never arrested, never investigated, and never formally charged with a crime. Is this correct?"

"He never—"

"Please answer yes or no."

"Of course he was investigated."

"Who did the investigating? Was it your department?"

He pauses. "Yes. That's standard."

"On August tenth, four years ago, did Officer Reyes Taser a woman's young dog to death in front of her?"

"That dog was a threat."

"The puppy's mother tried to sue your department—"

"Pal, the puppy's *mother* was a dog."

You can hear someone in the audience snicker. Mr. Buchwald presses his lips together. "I don't believe I finished my question. The puppy's *owner* tried to sue your department because she said there was no threat whatsoever." Mr. Buchwald leans closer. "Did Francisco Reyes attempt any other courses of action before attacking the dog?"

"It was his Taser. It wasn't a gun."

"Did he attempt to subdue the puppy in any other way first?"

"He didn't have time for that. Look, this wasn't some cute puppy. This was a pit bull trying to attack the neighbor's kid, okay? But it wasn't supposed to happen like that, and no one felt worse about it than him."

"The dog was shot at a distance of approximately fifty feet from any human being. Is that correct?"

"I got no idea."

Mr. Buchwald looks irritated, but he doesn't press it. "In September, two years ago, was Francisco Reyes investigated for excessive use of force during the arrest of Jordan Dadier?"

"That was a DV suspect trying to cover his—"

"Yes or no, please, Mr. Molson."

"He was investigated, sure. Then he was cleared. People say all kinds of things about us, but that doesn't make them true."

"Did Francisco Reyes receive two weeks' paid leave from taxpayers while your department conducted an investigation into the incident?"

"That's standard procedure."

"Did your department appoint its own employees to conduct its own internal investigation?"

"Well, that's how—"

"It's a yes or no question."

"Yes."

"And he was found to have acted in accordance with department policy based on the results of that internal investigation?"

"Yes."

"Was an investigation ever conducted by an outside committee?"

"Nothing like that was needed."

"So, no?"

"No."

"The night of January eleventh, did Francisco Reyes tell Mr. Raynor's teenaged son, 'If there was any justice at all in the world, you wouldn't have come back here safe'?"

"I don't remember exactly what—"

"But he said that? That he wanted Mr. Raynor's sixteen-year-old son harmed in some way?"

"I don't think he said it like that."

"You've testified that Francisco Reyes was angry and that he got"—he lifts his fingers in quotation marks—"*snippy* with Mr. Raynor, if that's what you'd like to call it. Can you categorically deny that he said that?"

"Look, if he said it, he didn't mean it like that. He meant he wanted Raynor to get his head out of his ass and he meant that his kid was spoiled. That's it."

"Would you say you enjoy a camaraderie with your colleagues?"

"Excuse me?"

"Would you say you feel a strong sense of loyalty to Francisco Reyes?"

"I'm loyal to all of 'em. And to the community." He adds, "You too, buddy. We're here to look out for all of you."

Mr. Buchwald cleans his glasses with his shirt. "Did you regard Francisco Reyes highly as a person?"

"You couldn't meet a better kid. Real family guy. Been helping support his family for years."

"Is it accurate to say you had a close relationship?"

"Yeah. He invited my whole family over to his niece's *quinceañera*, that kind of thing. My kids loved him."

"Were you the first person on the scene the night of the accident?"

"That was no accident. But yeah, I got there first."

"Mr. Molson, just answer the question, please."

"Yes."

"The official report states that you arrived at eight-oh-six, Officers Escobar and Washington arrived within five minutes, and the nondepartmental personnel were notified at that time. Is this correct?"

"Yeah."

"And at that point Francisco Reyes's firearm was found in his holster."

"Yeah."

"How long would you say you were alone with the body?"

Officer Molson stiffens. "Excuse me?"

"It's a straightforward question, sir."

He's reddening. "Look, mister, if you're asking if I tampered with—"

"How long were you and your department alone with the body, Mr. Molson?"

"We weren't. His nephew was there."

"Correct. His nephew. How long were you and your department alone with the body with only a teenaged relative as a witness?"

"I don't know."

"The records indicate the paramedics arrived eight minutes after you did. Does that sound right?"

"Sure. Fine. Eight minutes."

"How long does it take to put a gun in a holster?"

He's livid. "Listen, pal, you don't come in here and—"

"Mr. Molson, please lower your voice. How long does it take to put a gun in a holster?"

He lifts his hand, lets it drop against the podium with a thud. "Not long, I guess. Neither does running someone down with—"

"Mr. Molson, please. Does placing a gun in a holster take eight minutes?"

"No."

"Thank you. And just so we're all clear—you said, I believe, that you feel a deep sense of loyalty to Francisco Reyes?"

Officer Molson doesn't answer. Mr. Buchwald smiles.

"I believe it's already on the record that you do. Thank you," he says, his tone brisk, as if Officer Molson is just a guy behind a register ringing up his receipt. "Then, Your Honor, I have no further questions."

»   ·   ·

All my life, my dad's taught me that a person's worth is measured by what he does. The whole time he played in the minor leagues, some of his favorite teammates were the Latin American guys—proof it doesn't matter where you're from or what you look like as much as it does who you are under your skin. He gave a bunch of money to help build an orphanage in Mexico and led a missions trip there once with our church, and once when I was a kid I got my mouth washed out with soap for repeating something racist I heard at school.

So he's not a racist, and anyone who knows him can tell you that. But it turns out Mr. Buchwald was right all along that Laila never saw it that way: after they're done with Officer Molson, she plays the jury a compilation of clips from my dad's show. She plays it straight through without commentary, blinking at the ground with her arms folded across her chest.

One nation under God? Ha. I tell you what, when your nation's got a whole class of people that broke the law to get here and brought all kinds of criminal behavior across the border, and then we're supposed to reward them with health care, with free food, with ballots in their own language—what's that teach our children? You think those people care about God? They don't care about God. And they don't give a fig about everything our parents and our grandparents before us worked so hard to build. You should take that personally.

You seen what they do when they come here? They bring the third world right to your backyard. You ever seen them take over a town and not run the whole thing to the ground? Because I sure haven't. You want to live in those towns? You want to buy real estate there? You want to let your kids play there? We'd be better off rounding them all up in their barrios and shipping them back, no questions asked. Let that be a warning to all the others.

It lasts an hour. She must have combed through the past ten years of his archives to find them. Laila's so thorough, and it feels so vindictive, that it makes me think she had some kind of personal vendetta. I can't believe they let her play all that out of context this way. What my dad believes about illegal immigration is irrelevant; it has to do with laws, not race. Colin's half-Mexican and my dad likes Colin more than he does anyone else I've ever played with. And he likes Cardy, and he's Mexican, too. Cardy's short for Cardenas. But how is the jury supposed to know any of that?

I remind myself that Mr. Buchwald told me it'll always feel the worst when the prosecution's making their case. But even that's not the part Mr. Buchwald fought the hardest to keep out of the proceedings; that part comes next. On January 12, the day after I went to LA, my dad called the administrative office of the La Abra Police Department, and the jury hears the message after Laila's done with the clips from his show.

"Yeah, listen, I'm calling to make a complaint about Frank Reyes." His words are slurred, but the voice is unmistakably my dad's. "Listen. I could buy your whole department if I wanted to, and I want to see him gone. I don't need trash like him telling me I'm a bad father. Coming to my house like he's better than me and saying to my face I'm a bad father. Saying to my face I'm the reason my kid took off. None of them get away with talking to me like that. You hear me? No one gets away with that." And then a clattering, like he missed the receiver hanging up.

TWENTY

riday, just under a month before my court date, I turn seventeen. I wake up before my alarm and listen to Trey downstairs in the kitchen. My dad always gets doughnuts for breakfast on my birthday; I hate how they make your fingers sticky, but I never had the heart to tell him I don't like them. He'd always get me a bunch of gifts, too, and give a big talk about what my last year was like, and at night we'd go get steaks and then stay up late watching a movie or something.

Seventeen. I hope this year ends better than it starts.

When Trey brings in the mail that morning, there's a letter from my dad, the envelope marked with the correctional facility's return address. Trey sets it down in front of me without a word, and I tear it open right away, expecting I don't know what—I don't know what you say to someone after all this. But when I open it, it's just a birthday note, split into the same columns as his birthday cards always are. I don't read it, because I can feel Trey watching me. Instead, I fold it back up, and that's when I see the note on the back: *In the hall closet*

there's something I bought you a couple months ago. Behind the towels.
Happy birthday, B, I love you.

Trey says, neutrally, "What'd he say?"

"Nothing," I lie. "Just happy birthday." I'm not in a gifty mood, but before I leave for school, I get up and go to the hall closet. In back, I find the 1920 *Baseball Almanac*, the year that covered the Black Sox Scandal. It's in a plastic sheet to protect it, and he wrapped the box in a pillowcase so I wouldn't see. It must have cost him thousands.

I carry his letter around in my backpack, where it feels radio-active, and finally read it at the start of lunch, standing at my locker, ignoring all the people streaming by me; sometimes, in a crowd, that's when you're the most alone. I fold the letter up again and shove it in my pocket. The words feel carved into my skin.

I have some vague idea of going out to the track to run sprints or do pushups until I feel like collapsing and nothing else, but on my way down the hallway, I nearly collide with Maddie. I'm so wired already it feels like atoms sparking, rubbing against each other like flint.

"Hey," she says, stepping back to look at me. "I've been looking for you. What are you doing for lunch?"

。 　 。 　 　 °

I never told her it was my birthday, but when we sit down in the quad on a concrete planter in a corner away from where either of us usually eats, she says, "I got you something."

She reaches into her backpack, then hesitates. "I thought about getting you something basebally, but I have relatives who don't know anything about music except that I'm into it, and they buy me stuff like—violin magnets carved out of walnut shells, or these long books about Beethoven's childhood, and you can totally tell they tried to get something they thought I'd really like, and then I feel too guilty to ever get rid of any of it. So I thought maybe you didn't want baseball oven mitts or whatever I'd get for you. So instead, I got you—um—I got you—" She rummages in her backpack. "I got you this." She pulls out a small, used-looking bottle of sunscreen and sets it down in front of me. Huh.

"Sunscreen," I say. "Ah—thanks. Always a good thing to have."

"Yeah, I thought since you're outdoors all the time, you could probably—" Then she shakes her head, trying unsuccessfully to fight off a sheepish smile. "Braden, you really thought I got you *sunscreen*? And didn't wrap it or anything? For your birthday?"

"Was I not supposed to think that?"

"That would be the worst gift ever. I just panicked at the last minute and the sunscreen was what I happened to pull out of my backpack."

It makes me laugh. And I feel guilty, a little, but sitting there with her, I forget for a while about my dad. "I'll keep it forever," I tell her. "What's the real thing?"

"The actual thing I got you is, um—okay." She turns serious again and takes a long breath. Over the neckline of her shirt where her skin is pale and smooth I can see her chest rise and fall, then she glances around to see if anyone's watching. (A few freshman girls are, actually, Dutch's little sister Shannon and her friends, but they turn away quickly when Maddie looks at them.) She reaches into her backpack again, and this time holds out two of the tickets the senior officers have been selling for prom on April 19. "I know you have a lot you're going through and you don't have to or anything, but I thought maybe—"

"Wait, wait." I grab them from her hand. "This isn't—wait. I was going to ask you."

"Were you?"

"I know you were sad about missing the one at your old school, and I thought you might want to go. I just wanted to do something nicer than—well—"

"Oh, nicer than me thrusting them in your face on your birthday like this, you mean?" she teases. "This isn't nice enough for you?"

"I didn't mean *that*," I say, then I grin. "Well, maybe I did. But, yeah, if you wanted to go . . ."

"Do you want to?"

"I do if it's with you," I say, and the way she smiles at me suspends the rest of the world all around me, makes me feel like I've borrowed another life.

"My parents will want to meet you before prom, by the way," she says when the bell rings at the end of lunch and we both get up. "Also—do you care what color your boutonniere is? I was looking at different ones online, but I thought I should see what you wanted before buying one."

"Ah, whatever you think is good is okay." The flowers aren't exactly what'll occupy my imagination between now and then, that's for sure.

"Okay. You'll come over beforehand, though, right? My mom will want you to come have dinner with us."

"Yeah, sure."

"Good." We start walking back in toward the building, and she says, "I always thought flowers were kind of dumb, to be honest. It seems like such an unromantic thing to give someone."

I could read a lot into her use of *unromantic* just there. "Why's that?"

"It feels kind of wishy-washy, don't you think? Because they don't last."

We round the corner toward the math classrooms, and Maddie brushes against me then, her hand lingering next to mine in a way I think might have been on purpose. There are people in the hallway who can see us, but I reach out and take her hand. I feel electric.

This won't last, either. But it feels the way it does on the field when you dive for a ball you aren't supposed to catch, and you make it—how you're bigger than yourself in that moment, how for that breathless second there you'd swear you were created for exactly that very moment, that unexpected heat against your palm.

For dinner that night, Trey offers to cook, but I tell him it's all right. He says maybe that's better anyway; he's been working on a menu to serve with the ortolans and everything's felt off. He lists a couple places in Stockton and one in Sacramento he says he wouldn't mind trying, but I tell him I'd rather just go to Jag's instead. He's here on what probably feels to him like an extended babysitting trip; I don't want him to think I'm more work than I already am.

Jag's is run by Mona Delgado, a widow from church, and the place is like her love letter to the town. She knows everyone. Everyone I know has a spot they always sit in when they come, and if you grew up here, there are probably pictures of you framed somewhere on the walls. She has a whole baseball section; there's pictures of my dad from his minor league days, and some framed articles about me, too. By the register, there's a picture my dad signed for her with his show slogan.

In the car, on the way over, Trey says, "Should I tell them it's your birthday?"

"Ha. Yeah. Please." He knows I don't like birthdays.

"Have them sing?" Trey says. "Bring candles?"

"Do it. You'd love that even more than I would."

"In my place, I make my waiters dance for birthdays."

"Really?"

"The hell, Braden." He smacks me on the knee. "You think I'd do that ever?"

It's crowded when we walk in, and Mona makes a fuss over us, especially Trey. We order burgers, fries, and water. When Mona's gone, I say, "You don't want a beer or anything?"

"You know I don't drink."

"Not even beer?"

"Gateway drug." He glances around the restaurant. "I hate going places where you might run into someone you know."

I haven't been here since my dad's doctor said he had to watch his cholesterol, but it has that exact same familiar greasy smell and the same stale air and clinking of silverware against plates, and there's a little kid a few tables over who keeps peeking up over the booth to stare at us and then getting shy, and it makes Trey smile, and things with Maddie were so good earlier and I should be happy. But I can feel my mind dissecting everything, someone chipping at the moment so I see all it really is: I'm sitting around a scratched rectangular slab of Formica where there are silver napkin dispensers shipped in from China or somewhere, and I'm waiting for someone to bring me ground-up dead cow in a second-rate restaurant that looks and feels like the dusty attic of a half-crazy woman who has nothing and no one else. It's that same dullness when you suddenly see through a magic trick or a movie set or a room full of people you suddenly realize you'd rather not be in. But what's most terrifying is there's not a single place I can imagine going that I think would make this feeling lift.

I shouldn't have opened my dad's letter. I should've known to just not read it. What did I think he was going to say?

Our fries come. Trey offers them to me first, eats some after I do, then grimaces. "We should've gone to Sacramento. How can you have bad fries at a *diner*?"

"I like this place."

"Really, Braden? You need to get out more."

When Mona comes to refill our waters, she leans forward and puts her hand on my shoulder. "You know," she says, "every single morning I wake up and I think, Lord, I miss your daddy's show. Oh, honey, I always listen to him *religiously*. My day isn't the same without it, and I just *miss* him. It's sure not getting any easier. I can't even imagine how it is for you."

"Probably about like it is for you."

Trey gives me a look like *Behave*, and under the table he knocks his foot into my shin. I stifle a yelp. To Mona, he says, "Great fries." When she's gone, he says, "The hell was that?"

"I don't like people talking about him like that. She doesn't even know him."

"Well, what do you want, a soapbox to stand on?"

"No, I just want—"

I don't know exactly where I'm going with that one, but before I can work it out in my mind, a girl's voice says, from behind us, "I hope you got the burgers, Martin. I hear they're the best thing on the menu here," and I stop because Emily Zilker is the only person in the world who's ever called Trey that. When I turn around, she has the same pretty smile and kind eyes, but she looks older, and she's holding a baby on her hip. (A baby with a patch over its eye.) I say, "Emily. Hey."

She looks, if anything, even better than she did back in the day. For a second I'm positive Trey's going to get up and bolt. But he recovers and says, "Em. Uh—wow. You, uh, you look great."

"And look at you, Mr. Restaurateur!" She shifts the baby in her arms, its head squishing against one of her boobs. "I heard you were back in town. I tried to call your house a couple weeks and left a message. But maybe I had the wrong number, or . . ."

"Maybe you did."

"Well, how nice you're back."

I don't know if they think I'm stupid or they can't help it or what, but they're having entire conversations with their eyes. If it wouldn't be more awkward to get up and leave, I'd do it. It's Emily who looks away first. Her baby's tugging at her hair, and she removes his fist and strokes his palm with her thumb. Then she turns to me and says, brightly, "Well, if I remember right, it's someone's birthday today, isn't it?"

I clear my throat. "You have a good memory."

"I do. Seventeen now, right? Braden, do you know how old you're making me feel right now?" To Trey, she adds, "Doesn't it blow your mind? He just seems so grown-up. Playing baseball, driving . . . Martin, when we were that age, that was the year you came with my family to Tahoe, wasn't it? And you and I got lost on that awful hike, and I was sure we'd die out there, and then my parents thought we'd done it on purpose so we could be alone?"

"Sounds about right," he says, but the look he gives her means he doesn't want to go in that direction. I think she's going to ignore him—she sounds the way people get when they've been holding something in and just want to come out with it, and anyway she

184

always did that when they were together; he'd say he didn't want to talk and she'd press it—but she goes quiet.

Trey shifts in the booth like he's going to offer her a seat, but then he doesn't. "Uh—how's Erik?"

"Oh, he's fine. Still at the bank. We moved last year, so we're remodeling. And of course we have our hands full with the kids."

"What happened to your little one there? What's the eye patch?"

"Surgery. Isn't that the saddest?" She kisses the top of her baby's forehead. "I cried for days. Emma—she's three—wanted to get a matching patch because she thought he might feel lonely being the only one."

"Makes him look like a pirate." Trey winces, then adds, quickly, "In a good way, I meant. A pirate baby. Cute kid."

"Want him? I'm the youngest, remember, so I never knew how much babies just *cry*." She nuzzles her chin against the baby. "Do you want to know an embarrassing story about your brother, Braden?"

What I want, actually, is to be somewhere else. But I put on a smile. "Yeah, let's hear it."

"Once when I went to go visit Trey when he was at Santa Cruz, he took me to breakfast. We were sitting next to a mom with a little boy in a high chair, and I'd gotten up to visit the ladies' room, and when I came back Trey was sitting at their table, playing with the baby. *Complete* strangers, mind you."

I force a laugh. That's weird as hell.

"I always thought he liked little kids because they all reminded him of you."

I don't look at him and I can feel him not looking at me, too, but I think my face is going red. Obviously neither one of us says anything.

"And how about you, Martin?" Emily asks brightly, like she's oblivious, which I doubt she is. "How's your restaurant?"

Well. She has people to go home to at night, and my brother has his restaurant. Ouch. Trey says, "Holding up."

"I've heard amazing things."

"That's kind of you."

"You know, I saw you at the movie theater in Stockton last year. I tried to come say hi, but by the time I—"

"I wasn't here last year."

"In February? That weekend we had that awful storm? I thought you two saw me."

"I haven't been here in years."

"I swear, you and—"

"No."

There's a long silence between them. Emily glances toward the door. She straightens her baby's eye patch and rocks him up and down when he fusses. Then she says, quietly, "Martin, I was so sorry to hear about your father."

"It's fine."

"It isn't. I tried to call, and I wrote to you, but you just disappeared. I asked Kevin, but—I just wanted to tell you that—"

He tilts his head toward me, barely, like I'm not supposed to see, but I do. She falls silent. Then she says, "If you'd give me your number, maybe we could talk sometime."

"I don't really know how long I'll be around."

"All right." She smiles again, a different smile. "Well." She hitches her baby up on her hip. "Then I'll let you get back to your dinner. It was so nice running into you both. I'll see you around, perhaps? Martin, you don't—do you go to church?"

"Not so much these days."

"I go to a different church now. First Episcopal of Stockton. You'd be more than welcome there."

"I'll keep that in mind. Tell Erik hi."

"Of course."

She's taken a few steps away when she turns, abruptly, and comes back. She puts her hand on Trey's shoulder and he jerks away as if it's searing hot.

"I forgot to tell you," Emily says, "that when I heard you'd come back here just for Braden, I wasn't surprised at all. I really wasn't, because it felt so like you. I wanted you to know that. And Martin—please, please believe me that I'm so sorry about everything that happened with your dad."

Our burgers come flat and overcooked, the tomatoes crunchy and pink. Trey holds his up to study. "This is worse than I remembered."

"I mean, it's not birds you force-fed and strangled or whatever it is you have planned, but—"

"Ha. Don't make me kick you again." He takes another bite. "Just feels like you should be able to come up with a decent burger when you live somewhere that stinks like cow shit half the time."

"Don't talk so loud. Mona will hear you."

He surprises me then: he laughs, that little chuckle he used to have sometimes when he found something unexpected and amusing both. "You were just a little prick to her, so don't pretend you care." He holds out his water glass. "Cheers."

"Cheers." I guess.

"Happy birthday, kid."

When we finish, he lifts a couple fingers off the table to summon Mona when she walks by. I don't say it, but it strikes me as rude. Mona says, "Now, Trey, did I see you talking to Emily Fassel just now? When you two used to come in here and get milk shakes, I would tell myself, Well, *there's* a beautiful young couple. I still have that picture I took of the two of you sitting here together. I think I put it by the kitchen. I loved that picture. Erik Fassel is a lucky man." She reaches for our plates. "But things go the way they go. And, hey, you're a lucky man, too: Emily paid your check."

He jams the keys into the ignition and doesn't look back as he reverses. I say, "Thanks for dinner."

"Yeah, thank Em, apparently."

"I meant thanks for going with me." I glance at him. "Are you insulted?"

He shifts roughly into drive, then he sighs. "No. Emily always means well. One of the nicest people I ever met. Genuinely kind."

"One of the nicest people you ever met and you dumped her after six years?"

"Make me sound like a monster, why don't you."

"Why'd you break up with her?"

"Braden, that was so long ago."

"I really liked Emily a lot."

"Fair enough. She's a good person."

"Then why'd you dump her?"

"Can you not phrase things to make me sound like a complete asshole? It just wouldn't have been the right thing."

"Did you not love her?"

"That's an incredibly personal question, Braden."

He sounds annoyed, but I think for just a second that, just because it's me, I can get away with joking around with him and it'll be all right. So I say, "Sorry you're jealous you don't have your own pirate baby."

He half smiles; I guessed right. But there's something kind of sad about the smile, too. "You're right. I could've had a pirate baby."

"Nice going calling him that to his mother."

"Yeah, thanks, asshole."

I lean my head against the window and watch as we go past the school. "Anytime."

That night the nightmares come again. My nightmares mingle now— the past and the future twisted together, the night of the arrest and the day I'll have to go to court. I struggle awake, my heart pounding, and then I get up as fast as I can and go downstairs. It's stupid, maybe, but it feels like maybe they won't follow me there.

There's a scratching sound coming from the box Trey's birds are in, and I toy with the idea of trying to hold one. Probably he'd be pissed. Every day he's been feeding them carefully, holding each one in place with one hand and pouring some kind of mashed-grain-and-water mixture down its beak with paper rolled into a funnel, writing notes about his dinner with them that he sticks to the fridge. I leave their box closed, and I'm pouring a glass of water in the near-dark when there's footsteps, and then the kitchen light flicks on and Trey says, "Braden, it's four in the morning. What are you doing up?"

I start to say I had a nightmare, but stop when I realize it'll make me sound like a kid. "Just got thirsty."

"What woke you up?"

I hesitate. Because that sounds like an invitation, maybe, so I'm about to tell him when suddenly there's a noise from upstairs like someone walking, and I freeze. "What was that?"

"Nothing. It's fine."

"No, Trey, didn't you hear that? It sounded like—" Then I see his face. "Is someone . . . here?"

"Finish your water and go back to your room."

"There's someone here with you?"

"Go back to bed, Braden."

"Who's—"

"Don't make me tell you again."

"Fine, fine, I'm going." But at the foot of the stairs, I turn around, barely hiding my grin. "Is it a girl?"

He practically herds me up the stairs. Maybe it's just because I'm half asleep still, but I'm amused, even if he obviously isn't. He waits for me to close my door, and just before it clicks shut, he says, "I better not hear you come back out here again."

TWENTY-ONE

n the entire history of Major League Baseball, exactly twenty-three people have ever thrown a perfect game. More people have been to outer space or been president, and it's happened only nine times in my lifetime. A perfect game means you allow no hits, no walks, and no hit batsmen, and unlike in a no-hitter, which itself is rare, not a single batter makes it on base. You have to pitch a full game without relief. You face exactly twenty-seven batters, three in each inning, and whatever it takes, you have to beat down every single one.

The thing about baseball is that when you've worked at it, when you trust yourself and you trust it, too, there's always a part of you that believes, deep down, that anything could happen. And days when things are going well, days you put away every batter who steps up to face you and you're so dominant the strike zone belongs to you, there's a time right around the third or fourth inning when you start thinking: *Maybe.*

Of course, it never happens—a guy gets a cheap bunt off you

in the seventh, maybe, or your left fielder loses a ball in the sun, or you put a guy on first with a walk. There are infinite ways it can go wrong, but, like with everything, there's only one way it can go right.

This past June, for the first time in Cardy's career, my team made it to the state championship. We beat Brantley to take the league, Merced to take the district, Riverside to make it the championship, and then, a Saturday in Long Beach, we played San Diego Day. I was throwing pure heat all day, beating batters down with such immaculate fastballs and changeups no one even got one out much past the very tip of center field. It was in the sixth inning that I knew I had it, that I knew this game and every single player in it belonged to me, and that day, in front of eight thousand people, including nearly a dozen scouts who kept calling my dad about me for weeks afterward, I threw a perfect game.

The night we came back home, Mona kept Jag's open late for us, and half the town came out. My dad was the happiest I'd seen him maybe ever, and when I texted Trey to tell him, he wrote back right away with just two words, all caps: *HELL YEAH.* It was the first time in my entire life I'd ever felt completely good about myself. The whole night was a rush, a flare of energy I hadn't come down from even on the long ride home, and when we finally went home that night I caught my dad as he was getting out of the car and bear-hugged him so tight I lifted him off the ground, went upstairs, logged on to Facebook, and then sent a message to my mom.

Six months later, by the time I'd already given up, she wrote back. It was Christmas. My dad and I were eating steaks in front of the TV and watching *It's a Wonderful Life* when I saw the message on my phone.

Hello, it said. *Are you free on January 11th? There's a Denny's on Jefferson off the 110 that I can get to from my work. I can be there at four.*

TWENTY-TWO

I t's when Maddie tells me nine days before prom that she got her dress that I realize, way too late, that I don't have anything to wear. When I ask Colin where he's going to get his tux he looks surprised and tells me he did it three weeks ago and I better get my ass in gear, and then I worry I've waited too long and I'll ruin it for her. This is the one good thing I've been counting down toward, and I want it to be perfect. Since she doesn't like how flowers don't last I ordered something else for her, something that won't wilt and die—a flower necklace, gold-painted petals with a blue glass stone in the middle on a thin gold chain. There's going to be a party at Chase Singer's after and then a bunch of the guys on my team (at least the ones who are good at lying to their parents) booked rooms at the Woodmont Hotel; this would be an awful time to mess up like that, so I'll skip that part, but if her parents let me I'll take her to the party for a little, and maybe after, if she wants to, out to the lake again. In the moonlight when it's quiet there, you could be the only people in the world.

I bike to the nearest tux-rental place four miles away, and the man there measures me—it's uncomfortable having him get that close, wrap his tape around my hips and chest—and tells me to come back and pick it up the day of. As I bike back home, cold and tired in the dark, the headlights from the passing cars make me feel weirdly lonely. I think how preordering a tux is something my dad would've known I was supposed to do. And I think how I hope he'd be happy for me, how I hope it wouldn't hurt him that I'm doing all this without him here.

Trey's birds are making noise when I come inside, but he's not in the kitchen. Since the night I heard him with someone over, it hasn't happened again, although he's gone more at night now. I kept trying to figure out who it might have been, but he shut it down when I tried to ask and he doesn't leave any clues. I can't imagine him calling up people he used to know, and I wonder if he's the kind of guy who picks up random girls online. I can't see it, exactly, but then so much of his life feels unknowable to me.

He's not upstairs, either, but I see him through the window, out in the backyard smoking, which I didn't think he did. He sees me when I come back downstairs and waves me outside. When I open the sliding door, I realize it's not a cigarette.

"This isn't great," he says, "but come share it with me anyway."

"Uh—" I glance around, wondering if any neighbors can smell it. Good thing the houses are far apart. "Nah, I'm good."

"When's the last time I asked you to do something for me?"

Well. There's not much I can say to that. I settle down next to him, and when he hands it to me, I inhale as shallowly as I can.

"Come on," he says, amused. "Is this your first time? That won't do much."

I inhale again. I hope God won't hold this against me; I can't afford to screw anything else up right now and give God any more reason to punish me. But it would've been worse to not do the one thing Trey's asked me to do when I know full well what I owe him. We sit there for a little while, and I track each heartbeat, waiting for something to happen. I don't like the idea of something else controlling my body. Even if I weren't a Christian, I probably still wouldn't do drugs or drink. I say, "You do this a lot?"

He shrugs. "Sometimes you get too wound up."

I'm not brave enough to ask him why he feels that way. After a while, I say, "Hey, Trey?"

"Mm."

"I, um—I don't really—I know this isn't much, but I've been meaning to say—thanks a lot for coming back here. It's really . . . It's been a lot better with you here."

He doesn't answer. But then I guess it's arrogant to assume your thanks is real reward for someone, so maybe I shouldn't have said it.

I think something might be happening—I'm starting to feel weird. When I make a walking motion with my index and middle finger, you can see the tendons arc and curve mechanically on the back of my hand and the veins underneath. I feel floaty and kind of loose, too, like maybe I'm not completely in control of what I might say.

Trey says, "You know Kris Blaine?"

He was a senior when I was a freshman. "I know who he is. Why?"

"He's the guy I bought from. Turns out his dad's a cop."

"Maybe he shouldn't be selling you drugs if his dad's a cop."

"He's probably safer that way." Trey licks his thumb and runs it along the side of the rolled paper where it's burning faster. He smokes again, offers it to me, then sets it down on a plate he's using as an ashtray when I shake my head. He says, "I heard the guy has an older brother."

"What?"

"The one—you know. The cop. Reyes."

"Oh." He means Alex's father. "Yeah. I guess."

"Blaine said they're ten years apart."

"What difference does it make?"

He puts his hands behind his head and stares up at the sky. "Ten years, I mean—probably watched the guy grow up."

"So?"

"If I had reason to think anyone ran my brother down with a car like that, I'd want to see whoever was responsible put to death. While I watched."

We sit like that for a while. The pounding gets heavier in my temples, and everything sounds a little too loud. "Well, I guess you've never liked getting over things."

"What's that supposed to mean?"

"Nothing."

He snorts. "I'll bet nothing."

"Okay, fine, I just—I just think whatever it was you and Dad fought about isn't worth hanging on to all these years. I think it's time to let it go." The expression on his face is like a door slamming, but I say, "You know how Dad is, Trey. He gets mad and says stuff he doesn't really mean, but it shouldn't be forever." My dad and I understand each other, but Trey was never like that. I don't say this part, but Trey's a different person than I've ever known how to be; there's something cold and immovable at the core of him, the same place where in me whatever's there shifts and jostles like tectonic plates. "What'd you even fight over, anyway?"

"That's none of your business."

"You won't even say what happened? Was it something you did?"

"That's enough, Braden."

"All right, well, whatever it was, you've taken it way too far. You won't even go see him. You won't even talk about him. You won't even let *me* talk about him."

"Jesus. I shouldn't have tried to get you high. I was trying to help you relax."

Relaxed is definitely not how I feel. "Don't you ever miss him? Even a little bit?"

"What part am I supposed to miss, exactly?"

"He always missed you. Whatever it was you did, he still misses you. I've caught him in your room just sitting there, you know that? Whenever he washes the sheets, he always washes yours, too, like he hopes maybe one day you'll just show up. And every year on your birthday, he gets really drunk. But you just never—"

"You know I've been sending him checks every year and he never cashes them?" Trey interrupts. "I want to settle whatever he paid for college and whatever he spent on me growing up so I don't owe him anything. But he won't cash them. I work a hundred hours a week, my apartment's the size of a closet, I own a fucking restaurant and at home I eat instant ramen so I can pay it off, and he hasn't cashed a single one."

"God, Trey." I lean back against my seat. I feel sick, kind of. Dizzy and sick. If this is what it's like to be high, then I hate it. "You send him checks for *raising* you? That's one of the cruelest things I've ever heard."

He half laughs, but not like he finds anything funny. "You think I'm cruel?"

I know him well enough to see that got to him, so I tell him no. But I think he knows me well enough to know that might be a lie, too.

I'm doing laundry the next afternoon while Trey's out and when I go downstairs to get it, I see Trey's found those checks somewhere. He must have gone looking. He must have figured my dad wouldn't have just ripped them up and thrown them out—that he'd hold on to them because they were all he had of Trey. The checks are creased and lying on top of the washer, like Trey stuffed them in his pocket. There's six of them, each one dated a year apart, and I picture my dad seeing mail from Trey and getting his hopes up only to find a check inside.

I throw my laundry onto my bed and go into the kitchen. My heart is pumping with anger at him, at his callousness. He has no idea how it feels getting cut out of someone's life that way.

His birds are sluggish and swollen, but when I open the box and let the light in, they chirp like crazy. I cover the box with a napkin and pick it up carefully, holding the napkin down so they can't fly away, and I take the box outside and then flip it over, very gently, so they get out. They're slow at first, waddling around on the ground like they can't quite believe it, then two of them go off in different directions and the other two fly away.

Trey doesn't notice until that night. I hear him grinding up the grain to feed them and then I hear him say loudly, "What the fuck?" He comes pounding up the stairs and into my room before I can leave. He's holding the empty box between his thumb and forefinger. "Did you do this?"

I say nothing. What felt right when I did it feels dangerous now that he's here in front of me. Why did I do that? Was I testing him? Was I punishing him? Did I think I was proving something? I say, "Yes."

He lets the box drop to the floor. "Where are they?"

"I let them go."

He swivels his head around as if he thinks for a split second he can find them and get them back, and then he quits doing that and lasers his gaze at me instead. "Why the fuck did you do that, Braden? What the hell were you *thinking*?" His voice is dropping lower and lower. "Braden, do you not even realize how hard this is for me to be here? Or how much I've put on hold for—*God*." He smacks his hand against the wall and the whole room shakes.

I shrink back. I don't know what I'm expecting him to do—he's never hit me; he's never even really yelled at me—but what he actually does is stoop over and swipe the box up and walk away, and a couple minutes later the door slams and then I hear the garage door open and then shut itself over its new emptiness.

That's worse, actually. At least if someone screams at you or fights with you, you're in it together; this way, you're both alone.

. . .

In the kitchen the next morning he pretends I'm not there, and when I get home from practice he turns away when I come in.

But that night, he knocks on my door around ten thirty while I'm getting ready for bed. When I open it, he's holding a plate. On it there's a sandwich: grilled cheese with something else in it, too, something dark. He says, "Here."

"That's for me?"

"Fontina. With figs."

"Oh." I can't read a thing on his face. "Uh—okay. Ah—thanks."

I take the plate. He's already a few steps down the hallway when he says flatly, "The figs were for my ortolans, so. Enjoy."

TWENTY-THREE

When the bell rings for lunchtime and everyone in Precalc zips away their binders to leave, I slip away from the stream of people pouring outdoors for lunch and duck into Kevin's classroom a few doors down the hall. He's doing something on his phone when I go in, but he puts it away when he sees me. When I ask if he has a minute, he says, "Absolutely. What's up?"

"I had a question."

"Of course." He motions for me to have a seat. "What've you got?"

"It's church stuff."

He smiles. "I won't tell."

"Okay. Uh, well . . ." I shift my gaze to the Roosevelt poster he has on the wall. "You know before the crucifixion how Peter was going to deny Jesus and Jesus knew about it before he did it and told Peter it would happen?"

Kevin nods. "Sure."

"Well, then when Jesus comes back after he's alive again and he goes to Peter and asks if he loves him and Peter keeps saying yes and Jesus keeps asking—what was that about?"

"Ah. Good question." He sets his elbows on the desktop. "That's my father's favorite Bible passage, incidentally. Do you remember how many times Peter denied Jesus?"

"Three."

"Three, right. And how many times did Jesus ask Peter if he loved him?"

"Also three."

"What might that mean?"

I know that feeling you get when you know you've let someone down, how you want tear off every inch of your skin and step into someone else's, pretend you're someone else a while. "I don't know, I guess he was calling him out for all three times?"

Kevin kind of laughs, like he thinks I'm joking. "Jesus wasn't particularly passive-aggressive, Braden. When God calls you out, it's not subtle. You know."

Making sure someone knows he messed up doesn't exactly strike me as passive-aggressive—because what are you supposed to do, just pretend it never happened?—but whatever. "Then what was the point of all that?"

"It was a restoration. Jesus came for the sinners and the broken, and he wanted to transform Peter and redeem him into his better self. He was letting Peter redo the times he denied Christ before. Erasing his sin."

"But you can't erase something that happened already."

"Well, in dying for us Jesus does, essentially, erase our sin. God looks on our sin as the morning mist." He smiles. "I don't think we're just speaking academically here. Were you wondering about possible applications for your own life?"

"Maybe. I guess I was wondering for someone like—" I look across his desk, where he's got a wedding picture of him and Jenna and a bunch of Ellie. My heart's doing weird acrobatics in my chest. "Someone I guess like . . . Trey. God will still forgive him?"

Something I can't quite name changes in his expression. I shouldn't have said it—it wasn't even what I meant. "Why do you ask?"

"Forget it. I'm sorry. Never mind."

"It's all right, Braden. These feel like honest questions. What makes you ask?"

"Ah, I guess just how he doesn't want anything to do with God anymore, and—" I know they're close, but somehow I doubt Kevin knows about the drugs. (Or that Trey thinks Kevin's a bad husband.) "I don't know."

"You know something, Braden, I've always thought there's evidence of God at work in Trey's life. He's one reason I can understand God's constancy. When my mom first got sick, Trey was my rock. He shipped my mother meals packed in dry ice. He's generous. He's faithful. He's honest with himself, even brutally so. He's kind." He sees my eyebrows go up, and he laughs. "I didn't say he was *nice*."

"Fair enough." No one has to tell me Trey's done a lot for me. "But just in general, I mean, for . . . everyone, even if you're good in most ways but then you still sin—how long does God keep forgiving you?"

"God doesn't limit his forgiveness toward us."

"What about the verses that say things like if you keep sinning, then you haven't known God or there's no more sacrifice left for your sins?"

Kevin tilts back in his chair and studies the wall, thinking. Finally he says, "Do we ever deserve God's mercy?"

"I guess only if we—"

"No. Never. There's no *only if.* By definition we will never be good enough for it, we will never deserve it, and yet he gives it freely anyway. Right? You know that?"

"But what if you . . . know all that, and you still deliberately do something you know is wrong? Like Peter? You know it's wrong and you do it anyway?"

He looks at me more closely. "Braden, is there something you'd like to share? Something tells me you're dancing around your real question here."

I half knock over my chair standing up. I should have never brought this up. "No. Never mind. I'm sorry to bother you."

"It's definitely not a bother, Braden. I'm just trying to see what—"

"No, no, it is. Sorry. And, um . . . please don't mention this to Trey. He has enough to worry about as it is."

TWENTY-FOUR

t was warm inside the Denny's when I walked in that day in January
I went to meet my mom. I was wearing a collared shirt, tucked
in—I'd changed three times that morning before leaving—and I
unbuttoned and then rolled up my sleeves, glancing around the restaurant. I'd meant to get there early, but it had taken me six and a
half hours to get there because I'd hit traffic and then there was snow
coming over the Grapevine. My gas tank was running on empty and
I was scared to park because the neighborhood was maybe the worst
one I'd ever seen and I had twenty-nine missed calls from my dad,
but I was on time.

She was sitting in a booth near the window overlooking the parking lot, and—like I'd known I would—I knew her right away. She
was thirty-six, I'd calculated, or maybe thirty-seven, depending on
whether her birthday came before or after mine. She looked older. She
was heavy and shifted around in the booth tiredly, with effort, and
there were thick, dark circles under her eyes and she wore greenish

eye shadow and a blue CVS shirt and khaki pants that bulged at the waist. She looked dull and worn out.

But still: my mom. She had the same eyes as me.

She looked up and saw me and lifted her hand off the table just high enough to wave. I came over to the table—not too fast, because you never want to look overeager—and slid into the booth across from her. I said, grinning, "Wow. Hi."

"Well," she said, and inhaled. "Look at *you*." And then she did, studying me so long I felt my face heating up, and I twisted my fingers together under the table. Still, I was happy. Because if you spend your whole life thinking you don't have something and then it turns out you have it after all, you realize all those times you let yourself hope were worth it, in the end, because, I mean—my mom was here. In person, in front of me, on a Saturday afternoon, and she had my same eyes and chin, and probably everyone walking by could see that we belonged to one another. She said, "You look older than I expected."

"People say that sometimes," I said, and even though I always get awkward around adult women, I knew enough not to say the same thing back to her. I was out of breath, kind of, like I'd been running, which I hadn't. I joked, "My dad just tells me I'm not aging well."

She gave a kind of a half laugh, then glanced at her watch. "Well, listen, I don't mean to be rude, but I'm on my lunch break and I've only got about twenty-five minutes."

"Oh—that's all right." It was the longest drive I'd ever been on by myself, but even with all the traffic I hit on the way, it'd felt much shorter than it was, something I wouldn't mind doing regularly. "It wasn't very far."

"I already know what I'm going to order. You hungry?"

I told her I wasn't; I'd eaten a bunch of beef jerky in the car. Then

I said, smiling, "Isn't it kind of late for a lunch break? They wouldn't let you off earlier?"

"You sure?" she said, squinting at the menu. "On me."

"I'm okay. But thank you."

She shrugged. "Well, suit yourself." She ordered a club sandwich and a Coke, and then, as an afterthought, a second Coke for me, and I said, "Oh, thanks," and I didn't tell her I never drank soda. Then, when the waiter was gone, she sat back and tapped her fingers on the table and said, "Well."

She was watching me the way Colin looks when he watches YouTube videos, sitting back and waiting for something shocking to happen, and it was a little while before I realized it meant I should talk first.

"So, um," I said, motioning to her CVS shirt, "do you work there?"

I winced right after I said it. Sixteen years I'd been waiting for this, and that was the best I could do? I should've practiced what I was going to say. I guess I figured, sixteen years later, there'd be so much.

"Yeah. I'm a pharm tech."

"You aren't a dancer?"

"I'm not a—oh, Lord, no." She reached down and grabbed at the skin around her waist. "Do I *look* like a dancer? Lord. You need to get out more."

"But you still stayed in LA?"

"Yep, been here, oh, about fifteen, sixteen years."

"Sixteen."

She raised her eyebrows at that, and a little smile went over her face, not necessarily a happy one. "I guess so." She took a sugar packet and tapped it against the table. "Well, so, how's your daddy doing? You still live with him? He ever get remarried or anything?"

"He's good. And yes, and no."

"Does he know you're here?"

"Ah—no." I was supposed to be at a scrimmage. I'd left at nine, when my dad was at the bank; by eleven, the time I was supposed to go with him to warm up before everyone else got there, I'd already missed six calls and ignored four voice mails, too. I'd passed Fort Tejon right when the game was supposed to start, and I knew Cardy would be livid, but it was a just a preseason scrimmage and the records for those didn't matter and when I got back I'd run bleachers for him until I'd paid it back. The guys would figure I had a good reason. And I wasn't letting myself think about my dad.

"You didn't tell your dad where you were going?"

"Not yet." Something about the way she asked me made me think she didn't know who he was, but then I guess when she knew him he was just a former pitcher and a janitor who worked the night shift; he wouldn't go into radio for a few more years. I said, hesitantly, "You, um, you might know my dad, actually. Do you ever listen to the radio much?"

"Sometimes. Why—" Then it hit her—I could see it in her face—and she said, "Mart *Raynor*. My *God*. I knew that sounded familiar. That's *Mart*?"

"Yeah, that's him."

She shook her head slowly, back and forth. "Well," she said, and she let out a long, low whistle. "I'll be."

I was surprised she could forget something like that. Wouldn't you remember the name you went all the way down to the courthouse just to add to a birth certificate? I remembered everything my dad ever said about her, even the things that weren't true. The waiter came back then with the Cokes, and my mom ripped open the sugar packet and dumped it into her glass and then stirred it with her straw. I must have looked startled because she smiled wryly. "Bad habit."

I smiled back. Then I said—and I felt shy doing it, which seemed ridiculous—"You must really like sugar, I guess? My dad said, um, when I was a baby you used to give me Ring Pops instead of a pacifier."

"*Ring* Pops." She made a startled laughing sound. "I forgot all about that. Good Lord, can you imagine? It's a wonder they let me have children after that." She crumpled her sugar packet and shook her head. "Well, you know something, it's funny where life takes you."

I let that one rest between us a moment. It was warm in the restaurant, a homey yellow glow from the lights overhead and the gentle sound of the silverware clinking, and at the table next to us there was an old couple in their eighties, probably, and he was eating an omelet and she was eating soup. I watched them for a long time, their hands trembling over their silverware, then I said, "You have other kids?"

"I've got three girls." I thought maybe she was going to say more, but then the waiter came back with the sandwich and set it down on the table. My mom removed the toothpick from one half and gestured at her plate. "You want any? It's got bacon."

"No, thanks." I cracked my knuckles under the table. I realized I should've ordered something, just so I had something to do with my hands, and also because you shouldn't make someone eat alone. "So you have—you have three girls?"

Her mouth was full. "Uh-huh."

"How old are they? What are their names?"

"Ten, six, and four."

Four's how old I was when Trey was sixteen. She didn't answer when I asked their names; maybe she hadn't heard. I said, "Do they live with you and everything?"

It was an easy question—hardly even a question; really I was just giving her an opening to tell me about them—but she didn't answer right away. She picked up the little container with all the miniature packets of jam, even though she hadn't ordered toast, and studied it. There were cushions of puffy fat around her knuckles, and she wore a gold wedding band and she had pinkish nail polish that was starting to chip. She replaced the jam carefully in the container and drummed her fingernails against the tabletop so they made a clicking sound.

"Listen," she said finally, "I always figured . . ." She exhaled, then looked away. "When I was twenty, I was real wild and I did lots of stuff nice girls don't do. But now that I'm a mom, I try to teach my girls there's consequences to your actions, even if I didn't know that when I was twenty, so I knew if you ever tried to contact me, it was the right thing to do to at least own up to the past."

She took a bite of her sandwich. Mayonnaise squirted onto the corner of her mouth. Then she set the sandwich back down on the plate and reached into her purse and laid an envelope on the table.

"I don't have much for you. I never even told my own mother about you. When I had my oldest daughter, I even told the doctor she was my first. I'm not real proud of my past, but I'm a different person now. Now I try to always do right by my girls. But here." She slid the envelope across the table to me. It was thick and yellowish. "When I got your message, I remembered I had this."

My fingers weren't moving right even if I wanted them to. The envelope lay on the table between us, next to my untouched silverware and the sign advertising the limited-edition cinnamon-bun cheesecake.

"There's just about a hundred bucks in there. It's funny, I forgot all about it until I heard from you, and I had to dig all the way into my filing cabinet before I got it. But when I first moved out here, I was waiting tables to make rent, and every week I made sure to put away a couple bucks for you." She half smiled. "There was times I was down to a single can of tuna fish and I just had to eat it with a spoon, but I never dipped into that money once."

There was something settling down around my heart like that spray when you put new paint lines down on a field, like it was slowing down the valves. "I don't want money," I said slowly. "You should've bought yourself groceries. My dad does fine. I never needed that."

She shrugged, like it didn't matter, but she looked upset. "Back then and for a girl in my situation, a hundred dollars was a lot of money, you know. Sure wasn't nothing to save it up for you."

"Well, keep it. I don't need it." I slid the envelope back over to her, but my hands were damp and so my fingertips skidded on the table-top. "You really thought I wanted to see you so I could ask for *money*?"

"I knew you were asking for something. And that's what I had."

She looked around the restaurant then, and that's when I realized I should've said we should meet somewhere else. We were at a Denny's surrounded by old people, a man in suspenders and a woman with a walker jammed next to her table because no one else ate dinner that early, and it just wasn't the kind of place where good things happened, you could tell.

"You might be too young to understand this," my mother said. "In fact, I hope you are. I hope this isn't something you learn the hard way. But sometimes you make a mistake you didn't mean to and then it sticks to you and you feel like maybe it'll never go away. And I'm one of those people who's always on myself about every little thing, you know, always feeling guilty all the time. Even just this week I got the wrong color frosting for Melinda's Barbie doll cake, and I just beat myself up over it. For a *Barbie* cake. So it was hard for me, you know. What happened. I spent a lot of years not feeling real good about myself. But it's not right to live like that, and sometimes the only way you can get past things is to just turn away and start clean. You just have to forgive yourself and move on."

In my pocket my phone vibrated, startling me so badly I jumped, and the silverware clattered against the table when I knocked into it. She didn't react, so maybe it sounded louder to me than it really was.

"I play baseball," I said, abruptly, before I could stop myself. "I pitch. I throw a ninety-four-mile-an-hour fastball."

She raised her eyebrows, took another bite. "Sounds like fun."

"It's not *fun*, it's—do you know how many guys can do that in high school? Matt Cain couldn't even throw that fast as a senior, and he was still *Baseball America*'s number thirteen prospect the year he was drafted. I'm better than Matt Cain was in high school. Matt *Cain*. This year I won my team the state championship and I pitched a perfect game. No high school pitcher in the history of California has done that ever."

"Well, good for you. I mean that. It's nice to hear you're doing well."

"I'm probably going to get drafted after next year, and I'll get a contract, and if things go well this year then I'll probably get a signing bonus, too, and then—I mean, maybe you really like your job, I don't know, but—and I know you have other kids, and you're happy with just them, but—I mean, I could help out. You could stop working at CVS and taking half-hour lunch breaks in the middle of the afternoon and eating plain tuna fish. And I could learn how to play with little kids, and my catcher has a little sister and I always— I don't know. I volunteer to umpire Little League games. And I'm pretty good with dogs."

She pinched the toothpick in the other half of her sandwich between her fingernails and drew it out like you would a needle, and staring at the mayonnaise glopped onto the lunch meat, I thought, all of a sudden, that I might throw up. She stuck the envelope back into her purse and drummed her fingers on the table. She started to say something, then changed her mind, then looked down at her plate. You could see the bite mark in her sandwich. Then she looked back at me, and when she did I could see, maybe, some glimpse of all those years she spent forgetting me.

"You know, you've got a father who loves you," she said. "That's more than I had when I was your age. And it took me a long time to stop feeling awful about what happened, but that's all in the past now, and things went the way they did, and I was twenty years old and there's not much point in opening old wounds. I wish you well, and I'll give you money for gas for coming all the way out here, and it's nice to see you're doing good and there's just not much more than that to say."

*   *   *

Ornette shares a police department with La Abra, and there aren't many officers on the Ornette beat. So when you live here you see the same cops over and over again, the same way you do the cashiers at the grocery store or the postman or the teller at the bank, and so it was Officer Reyes standing in uniform in my garage with my dad and a second officer when I got home from LA.

The first thing I saw was their car parked on our curb, and then that the garage was open and the three men were backlit because of the lights from the house. From the way they were positioned, I could tell my dad was yelling. When I pulled into the driveway and turned off the ignition, all three of them turned and stepped backward from their triangle. I'm more used to this now, but that was the first time I knew what it felt like to silence a group of people just by coming in.

No one wanted to talk first. Officer Reyes folded his arms across his chest. I could tell he didn't recognize me. My dad grasped both sides of his face with one hand and then ran the hand slowly, and roughly, down over his mouth and over the stubble on his jaw.

"Well?" he said, very quietly. "Where were you?" He breathed the words more than spoke them so they didn't come to rest, exactly; they brushed against my shoulders and my ears, raised goose bumps on my skin.

"Ah—" I took a few breaths, shifted my weight from one foot to the other, and looked at the wall. "I went to Los Angeles."

"You did *what*?" He was shocked. "You planned to take off like this?"

I nodded, my throat too tight to talk. None of them liked that. Officer Reyes muttered something sharp and ugly under his breath. My dad said, still very quietly, "Alone?"

I nodded again.

"Where was your phone?"

I pulled it halfway from my pocket, then let it drop back in.

His expression didn't change. "And why did you go to LA?"

"I don't know."

My dad nodded very slowly, bobbing his head up and down in a way that made me think of a scarecrow, like a head detached partway from the neck. He flexed his fingers back and forth against his thigh. His voice dropped lower. "Why did you go to LA, Braden? Why did you go to LA, without telling anyone, and without answering a single one of my calls, when it was your job to be at your game?"

"Because I—" I could feel my pulse through every inch of my

body. The two officers looked out of place there in our garage, Officer Reyes's hand on the holster of his gun.

"No reason," I said flatly. "Whatever. I just thought it would be fun."

"You thought it would be *fun?*" Something tightened in his face. "You had a *game.* Is this how you think I've raised you?"

I said, "Apparently so."

Officer Reyes made a short, jeering laugh, his lips stretched across his teeth. He smacked the palm of his hand against the club strapped in his belt. "I told you so."

Officer Molson said quietly, "Frank. Not the time."

"No, didn't I tell you? I told you. This is a joke." He was radiating with anger when he turned to me, his face contorted in contempt. "You know what, kid? We were here three hours wasting time. We got four patrol cars out looking for your license plate on your *Mustang.* Even though as soon as I got here I told your dad I've seen this case a hundred times before. Same spoiled, rich brat with his head up his ass. I bet you never think about other people, do you? I bet you got everything handed to you your whole life."

I didn't care. Whatever. Nothing he said was going to make me feel any worse. Officer Molson said, "Frank. Frank. Come on," and patted him on the chest. "Let's go."

Officer Reyes turned away, disgusted. "If there was any justice in the world, you wouldn't have just come waltzing back in here without a care in the world, without the decency to give a damn about all the effort we all wasted for you, and your dad would've realized what an asshole he raised and what an asshole he is, too."

My dad took a step forward and grabbed my arm, squeezing so hard it hurt. "What do you have to say for yourself, Braden?" he hissed. "You have anything to say?"

I had never, not once in my life, said anything bad about my dad in public. I never had to Colin. I never even had to Trey. "Nope," I said. "Not a thing. Except he's right about one of us. And he's right I shouldn't have just come back."

My dad let go of me, his hand extended toward the officers' car, a smile plastered across his jaw.

"Gentlemen," he said, "I believe I can handle things from here. But thank you *so* much for your help."

It was dark that night, foggy, the tule fog pooling on the ground so you could barely see a hundred yards away; you couldn't quite make out the neighbors' houses. There was a near-full moon. When the officers walked down past him and past me and to their car on the curb, the night swallowed them before they'd gotten even to the end of the street.

Their taillights had disappeared when he came toward me, backing me up against the car. He yanked me by the arm and pulled his face close to mine, his breath hot and sour on my face. He'd been drinking. That was when I remembered to be scared.

"Dad, I—"

"*Dad* what?" he hissed. "*What*, Braden? You think I've worked so hard on you for you to blow off your games and ignore my calls this way? I gave you that phone and I gave you the clothes you're wearing and the car you ran away with and every last dollar in your wallet. I gave you every last thing you have, and *this* is how you treat me? What do you have to say for yourself? Huh?"

"Dad, I went to go meet my mom."

His grip froze around my arm. His lips parted. He let go of my arm and stepped back.

"That's why I went. I found her a long time ago on Facebook, and after the championship game, I just thought—I don't know what I thought. But I got ahold of her and she said I could come see her in LA, so I went."

He stared at me for a long moment, blinking, and there was a whole universe brimming underneath the blankness of his face. For that moment, the world teetered on an edge and then lay still. And that was the instant when everything caught up to me—the fact that I'd gone there, the forty-four missed calls from him on my phone, everything my mom had said—and the pain in my chest twisted even further, and I said quietly, "I thought maybe she'd—I thought she'd want to see me," and that was when his expression snapped.

We're alike, my dad and me, in so many ways, but this doesn't happen for me the way it does with him: that you lose yourself inside your anger, that it spills to the surface and rushes so fast you can drown inside it if you don't fight to somehow pull yourself out. I don't know why I didn't get that from him. But that night his anger felt like gravity to me, the way once a ball is released, you can't stop or change it and you just have to wait to see where it'll go. He went back up to the garage and leaned down to where all our baseball stuff was, my cleats and bags and the bucket of balls and Trey's old catching gear, and he picked up my bat. I froze.

"Dad," I said, and my voice cracked. "Put that down. Please. Come on. What do you need that for?"

He came back down the driveway toward the car as if he never even heard me, and he smashed the bat against my windshield. The glass cracked and then gave, hammocking inward. He was breathing hard and fast, veins puffed and snaking around his forehead, and even when he looked right at me it felt like he looked through me instead. I was fumbling for my cell phone in my pocket, my fingers wooden— but why, because who did I think I was going to call? Because the person I called when I needed anything was him—when he came around to the driver's side where I was standing. He smashed in the driver's side window and shards of glass flew at me, and I brought up my arms in front of my face just in time and my phone arced up in the air, and he had the bat raised with one arm and then he grabbed hold of me with his other and I lost my balance so badly he stumbled, too, and my blood was roaring in my ears, and I choked out, "Dad, please, I'm sorry. I'm so sorry. Please."

The way I always imagined a demon getting cast out was exactly like this: in that moment, I could physically feel something leaving him. The color drained from his face. He dropped the bat so it thudded onto the concrete, bounced once, and lay still. I was shaking so hard the hand he was gripping me with was shaking, too.

He let go and I doubled over, my hands on my knees, trying to catch my breath. *It's okay,* I told myself, *it's okay, nothing happened, he didn't mean to do that, it's okay, it's okay.* He stared at me with his eyes wide, like he was just now seeing me, then he looked behind me at the car and said, *"Jesus."* He lifted his hands and pressed them over his eyes, then dragged them down his face so his skin was taut and disfigured and his eyelids flipped out at the bottoms. When he looked at me again, he looked panicked.

"Braden," he said, "I wasn't going to hurt you. I wasn't. I swear. I swear to you." His voice was rising, going raw. "Braden, you know me—you know I wouldn't. Don't be like that. Don't look at me like that."

He put his arm on my shoulder and pulled me upright so I was facing him. I closed my eyes. I was about to hyperventilate, I could feel that, and I pulled the neck of my shirt up over my mouth and tried to breathe through the cotton.

"Braden, I'm your *father*. You know me. You know I love you. You know I'd never hurt you."

I still couldn't see. I tried to picture the cotton as a net catching molecules of oxygen like they were fish. He pulled me toward him then, and I almost tripped over the bat lying on the ground. I worked on taking calm, even breaths. He gripped my shoulders and held me at arm's length, scanning my face.

"I didn't mean to. I just—I don't know. I'm sorry. I'm sorry." He gave my shoulders a quick, frantic shake; his tone was pleading. "Don't look like that, Braden. Nothing even happened. I'll buy you another one. We'll go pick something out together. It's just a car."

Then he wrapped his arms around me and cupped the back of my head in his hand, pressing my head against his shoulder, and I closed my eyes so I didn't have to see anything anymore, not the look on his face or the glass all over the ground or the baseball bat or the sight of my own body. I pressed my arms against my side and didn't move.

"I forgive you," he said in my ear. "All right? That was a terrible thing to do, but I forgive you. I love you, B. I love you so much. I'm sorry you got scared. I'm sorry. It's just because I love you. Because you scared me."

I didn't move. I don't know if he even realized he was doing it, but he was gripping my shirt in his fist like maybe he thought I was going to try to get away. That's the part I think about now, how he did that. Because what did he think I was going to do? Where else did he even think I had to go?

I don't know how long we stood there, him retightening his grip around me every time he started to relax. I was starting to go numb, to not feel anything anymore at all. And he told me again: he loved me more than anything, and he was sorry, and everything was fine. And it was true, wasn't it? All of that. Because eventually he led me back inside, he heated up a pizza for me and scooped ice cream into a bowl and made me have seconds, he sat me down at the computer and told me to buy myself something, anything I wanted, and then we watched ESPN highlights until we both fell asleep on the couch and the cops went back to their own houses, I guess, and for that night, everyone was fine.

TWENTY-FIVE

Monday, five days before prom, we play Ceres. After this, there's only eight games left before we play La Abra.

Maddie comes to watch and waves me over before the game starts. She's with her dad, who I've seen around church but have never actually met. He's tall and serious-looking, someone who makes you want to stand up straighter and maybe tuck in your shirt.

"I've heard quite a bit about you," Mr. Stern says, holding out his hand for me to shake. "You plan to come to dinner before you take my daughter to her dance?"

"Yes, sir." I wonder if he thinks less of me for doing something like prom when my dad's still in jail, if he thinks I'm a crappy son. "Thanks for having me."

"Have you been to many of these school dances?"

"Um—" I'm not sure there's a right answer to that one. I glance at Maddie for help.

"My dad will probably talk your ears off about baseball all through dinner," she says teasingly. "He thinks someday he'll see you on TV and be able to tell people he watched you play back in high school. He wanted—"

"Raynor!" Cardy shouts from the dugout. "Wrap it up, Romeo!"

I say goodbye, and when I jog back to the dugout, Cardy grumbles, "Better not let me catch you with your head in the clouds again when you're on my clock," but he also kind of whacks me on the back in a way that means *Good for you.*

Cardy puts Greg at first while I'm on the mound. It's a demotion—you stash your worst fielder on first—but I doubt Cardy means anything by it; Greg's slated to come in to pitch again as relief. He's starting to look cleaner on the mound, and I think he has potential. He still hasn't spoken to me since the Brantley game.

I'm myself again today; I've righted whatever was off-kilter facing Brantley. Everything's going decently, and then, in the third inning, Ceres's shortstop Adrian Yamamoto gets caught between bases trying to steal. Chase gets the ball on second and makes a clean throw, and Greg plants his foot on the bag and stretches out to get the ball, and, because, it should be an easy tag, I let myself relax too soon. Adrian drops into a slide, feet first, and then just before colliding with Greg he lifts his cleats and his spikes slash right across Greg's exposed heel.

Greg goes down right away, and even before I run over, I can see the blood seeping through the cuff of his pants. I get there first, and when I reach a hand toward him, he jerks his shoulder away. He's fighting back tears.

"Hey, hey, it's all right, I'd be crying too," I say. My stomach's knotted in a rope, and I hate myself for yelling at him like I did after the Brantley game and for basically calling him gay in front of the entire team. Spiking the first baseman is the dirtiest thing a runner can do, and before today I've never seen it happen once. "We'll take care of Adrian for you. Okay? We have your back. I promise."

He doesn't answer me. Cardy and the trainer thunder over, and I step back as they kneel next to him and the trainer tries to stop the bleeding—Greg yells in pain—and then gets him off the field.

"Blue!" Cardy yells at the umpire. Today it's Jason Terry, a guy my dad's always thought is one of the worst umps in the league. "He slid in with his spikes!" He's expecting an ejection for Adrian; we all are. But instead Terry shrugs and lifts his hands like he saw nothing—unbelievable—and issues a warning to both sides that anyone coming in spikes high from now on will get thrown out. Cardy goes apoplectic, screaming an inch from Terry's face until he gets tossed. The worst part is, the next batter hits an easy fly to left field, and because the sun was in his eyes, Dutch drops it and Adrian comes in to score.

I should have never let that happen. I'm disgusted with myself. I wish it had been anyone but Greg. I'll avenge him, though—I'll make it up to him. All of it.

I'm up that next inning, and they walk me. Their pitcher's been good all day and all four balls come so far outside it almost makes me think it's intentional. But it can't be; I'm a pitcher. I barely even *have* a batting average. When I get to first base, though, the first baseman is waiting for me.

"Hey," he says. "It's Braden, right?"

His name's Rory Garcia, their captain. I say, "Yeah, what?"

"Look, Adrian messed up. That was unacceptable. I'll air him out myself. But"—Rory clears his throat—"listen, man, I know you're going to want to settle that somehow, but is there any way this time you can just let it slide?"

You can get away with talking to the first baseman as long as you both keep facing straight ahead, but that startles me enough that I twist my whole body around to stare at him. "I must not have heard you right."

"You're going to make me say it again, huh?" He runs his tongue across a lump of dip jammed inside his cheek. "I'm asking if you can let it go. Shake it off. Pretend it never happened."

"Adrian shouldn't even be in this game. Greg texted from the ER to tell us he needs thirteen stitches and two staples in his leg. That slide just ended his season."

"I'm really sorry about that."

"You're *sorry*? You play first base. What would you do if someone did that to you and the ump didn't even flinch?"

"I mean, granted, I'd expect my pitcher to take the guy out, but—"

"And you're the captain, right?"

"Yeah."

"Well, then that just doesn't make sense."

"Meaning what?"

"You're not the pitcher and not the catcher and not the shortstop; in fact you're on *first*, and I don't think you've gotten a hit off me once in three seasons. So I would've thought they made you captain because even if you aren't any good, then at least you knew the rules."

It's far and away the most insulting thing I've ever said to another player. But all Rory says is, "I'm not telling you what I think you should do. I know exactly what you *should* do. I'm asking you a favor."

"If you know, then why are you even asking me?"

He starts to answer, then stops himself. I don't know Rory, I have no idea what he's thinking, but even I can see he'd pay a lot to not be having this conversation right now.

"His sister's pretty sick," he says at last. "He just found out this week he's not a match to give her his bone marrow. He's been telling everyone for weeks how he was all set to do it, and he's not taking it well."

We watch as their pitcher steps off the mound and kneels down and does something with the laces on his cleats. He's taking long enough that it occurs to me to wonder if he's waiting for us. There's something like a clamp inside my chest. I ignore that. I glance out at the stands. "How old is she?"

"His sister? She's—"

"Never mind, actually," I say quickly. I don't know why I asked. I don't want to know. "It doesn't matter. Greg never did a thing to him, and now he won't play again this year. And you don't spike the first baseman ever. You know that."

Their pitcher steps back onto the mound. "Look, brother—forget it," Rory says, crouching forward again to get ready for the play. "I know you're probably exactly the wrong person to ask about this. In every way. So forget I said anything. Have fun."

◦ ◦ ◦

Adrian comes up again in the sixth. His last at bat, he wasn't showing any of the tells batters sometimes will when they're nervous, circling his bat or taking too long to get into the box, but this time he does both those things and then brushes his feet against the dirt, too, like he's trying to stay light on his cleats.

Colin and I settle on a two-seamer that comes up the inside corner, high and tight on him so he can't possibly mistake the message, but—he's got quick feet, which I knew—he's got just enough time to arc himself away.

Colin throws me back the ball. Adrian circles his bat in the air loosely. I know he has to know what's coming. From the stands, someone—a girl's voice—cheers and calls his name, and for a split second I imagine I can physically feel Maddie watching me.

And I don't know why I do this. I know it's wrong. I know that. But my next pitch sails right across the plate, centered and slow and right across the middle at his knees, and Adrian swings.

I was right: he was ready. I don't turn to watch, but I know from the roar from their half of the crowd that it's gone.

◦ · ◦

It's quiet at night around here, and at the junior high, with all the lights off for the night and the whole place empty, it's like being the only person left in the world. When you run on the bleachers in that stillness, the footsteps explode against the metal and the sound assaults your eardrums, piercing the night like artillery.

I'm here, obviously, for penance. Even though we won, I still betrayed a teammate, in public, on the field. I go as hard as I can. By the end of the fifteenth or sixteenth round, it's like someone's slashed through my thighs with a knife; by twenty-five, they're dousing the wounds with acid. I get to the top—I'm slowing down already—and tap the wall and then turn back around to go back to the bottom. Every time I hit another step, it pounds through me, and I feel close to throwing up. I can feel every nerve ending in my lungs lit up like a fuse.

I didn't bring water, on purpose, but I wish I had. It's on number thirty when I look down and see, in the dark, four shadowy figures coming toward me. Nothing's happened with Vidal or anyone else

226

since the Hughson-Brantley game, but I know it doesn't mean things are over. My mouth goes dry.

Maybe I shouldn't be out here alone, in the dark, when no one knows where I am. I didn't even bring my phone. I turn so I'm facing them and lean over like I'm stretching, pretending I'm not watching. They come closer and closer. It's guys, all of them walking in a straight line, and I'm looking down over the edge of the bleachers, trying to think how bad I'd get hurt if I jumped over to run for it, when they get close enough that I realize who it is: Colin, Jarrod, Chase, and Dutch. That might actually be worse. When they get to the bleachers, Colin says, "Thought we'd find you here."

"We went by your house," Dutch adds. "Your brother didn't know where you were."

"Oh." I left the game without talking to anyone. "You here to settle something for Greg, or what?"

Jarrod makes an irritated noise. "No, dumbass. We've got a bottle of JD and we're going to go out to the lake and kick back a while. And you're coming, too."

"I'm busy."

"Come on, Raynor, lighten up," Colin says. "It'll be good for you. You've been even more uptight than usual lately. Everyone got all worried the way you left after the game. Let's go. Come on."

"I'm running."

"Braden, come on. You missed *one* pitch. Ease up. No one's perfect."

"I didn't miss."

I know they know that. I know everyone does. The four of them exchange a glance. Finally Colin says, "How many of these are you doing?"

I turn my head away. "A hundred."

He sighs and shoves his cap back. "God, Braden, you're such a drama queen sometimes. How many have you done so far?"

I mutter that I've done thirty.

"Okay," he says. "Well, seventy over five is . . . crap. Fifteen? That's not right, is it."

"Fourteen, moron," Chase says. "What, did you fail fourth grade?"

"All right, fourteen, Mister Mental Math." Colin motions with his head, and the four of them come and line up on the bottom step of the bleachers, flanking me. "We'll split them with you, Raynor. Fourteen each. Let's go."

TWENTY-SIX

All week, Laila's been parading academic-type expert witnesses across the stand: a blond woman who uses plastic models to re-create something to do with the physics of the scene, a gun expert who claims Officer Reyes's gun was never discharged, more cops from other counties who talk about procedure. Mr. Buchwald is openly impatient—he checks his watch and half-asses the cross-examination with the cops, and he even declines to cross-examine the physics woman. When Judge Scherr asks him, he just waves his hand like, *Get on with it*, and I catch one of the jurors looking surprised. I wonder how that made my dad feel.

But tonight's prom. So tonight, just for the night, I'm not going to think about any of it.

At lunch, just before the bell rings, Maddie finds me and tells me to come at six for dinner with her parents.

"Great," I say. I've done my research this time and I have a corsage for her ready to go, and the necklace wrapped up. "Should I bring anything? I could pick up a pie or something."

"No, it's okay." She looks around like she realizes for the first time where we are. "What are you doing in Señora Díaz's room?"

"I'm studying."

"For Spanish? At lunch?"

"Yeah, I've gotten behind." The truth is that I can't take watching Greg hobble across the quad on his crutches, the guys slapping him sympathetically on the back. I can't tell her that, but it bothers me how easily the lie slips out. That's one way I've always thought I'd turn out different from my dad. "Hey, Maddie, what'd your dad say when he met me?"

That amuses her. "In the four seconds he spent with you?"

"He seems . . . protective."

"They just want to vet you because they don't know you. They'll like you after they talk to you."

I wonder if it'll feel at all like it will with the jury—strangers deciding on you. "How should I act around them? I want to make a good impression."

Her eyes crinkle up when she laughs. "It'll be fine, Braden. You're definitely an easy guy to bring home. Just be yourself."

That echoes in my head all day, that *be yourself*, clanging even louder when I nearly trip over Greg's crutches in the locker room at practice. That afternoon, it takes me forever to bike back home from the rental place balancing the tux across the handlebars, and finally I give up and jog-walk. I get home late and throw the tux across the couch and head for the stairs to take a shower, mentally rehearsing what I'll say at dinner to Maddie's parents, and what I'll say to Maddie after the dance. When I go through the kitchen, Trey's standing still, staring at something in his hand. From the quick, tight-lipped way he motions me over I think he's been waiting for me.

"I have to go shower," I say.

"Get over here."

I do. When I get closer, I realize what he's holding is the birthday letter from my dad, and the moment tilts and then topples over. My skin shrinks around my chest.

"'Braden year sixteen,'" Trey reads aloud in a voice tight with something that sounds a lot like rage. "'Work ethic: 8.5. Pitching: 7–9. Responsibility: 9. School: 10. Attitude: 6. Loyalty: question mark.' The hell is this?"

"Where'd you get that?" It was on my desk in my room, where I figured it was safe because Trey never goes anywhere but his own room and the kitchen. "It's nothing." I reach for it. "It's just—it's nothing."

"This is what Dad sent you?"

"And a birthday present. Let me have it back."

"This is disgusting, Braden. It's sick."

"You shouldn't have read it in the first place. It has nothing to do with you." The letter is exactly why I don't like talking to anyone about my dad: because I know no one understands him the way I do. I try to grab it, but Trey pulls it away. "Give it—"

"He sent you this for your *birthday*?" The veins are starting to jut out in his neck. "Does he do this to you every year?"

"Give me that back."

"For your *birthday*?"

"Just give it back."

"'Loyalty: *question mark*'? Braden, are you *kidding* me?" He makes like he's going to tear the letter in half. I lunge for him and grab his arm, but he wrestles the paper away. "Braden, knock it off. This is trash."

I try to twist his arm around, but he yanks it back; he's stronger than I am, and while I'm still struggling for control he rips the letter in half and in half again and it feels like getting slashed across the face. I snarl, "That was *mine*."

He crumples the quartered pages in a ball. "Listen," he says, his voice low and urgent, "you can't let him pull shit like this with you, Braden. You need to—"

"Give me those back." I'm dangerously—humiliatingly—near tears. "I *miss* him, Trey, and that's the first he's been able to talk to me since he got arrested. And if the trial doesn't go well, and he gets—he gets—"

"If he gets killed, then what? You want this garbage playing over and over in your head, following you around everywhere you go? That's what you want?"

I choke on the words, I couldn't say what I was afraid of with the trial, but it seemed all too easy for Trey to voice it. "You've been gone nine years. What do you know?"

"I know him. I know what he's like."

"Okay, well, you keep telling yourself that, but you know what? Just because you're a shitty son doesn't mean he's not a good dad."

He drops his hand, but he takes a step closer. "That's what you think?"

"Yes."

He holds the crumpled pieces of paper with his thumb and index finger. "You think he's right about all this?"

"What's it to you?" I'm shaking with anger; my brother is the one person in the world who should understand. "You think you know me better than he does? You were gone over half my life. What do you care?"

"You really think that, Braden? I packed up my whole life and came here for you, and you think—"

"You never even called me back until the *social worker* called, Trey. You don't give a shit about me."

When I say it, something floods and unleashes in his expression.

Before I can react, he hits me in the chest, his fist like a fastball to the solar plexus. I thud into the edge of the table and then I fall, and the glass on the table falls after me and shatters on the ground. I gasp like a fish, the wind knocked out of me.

Trey's never laid a hand on me, and I know it wouldn't take much for him to really hurt me. But when I look up, he looks even more scared than I am.

"God," he says. "Braden, I—" He takes a step forward and starts to say more, and then he turns and slams the door shut behind him so hard the whole house shakes. *Please,* I think to him, *please, please come back,* but I hear the garage door opening and his car starting, and I hear the car rumbling until I lose it down the street.

I was so stupid. I should know better than this by now. I should have let him say whatever he wanted, and I shouldn't have talked back, and I shouldn't have pushed him like I did. I know what that does to people, how far the consequences can reach. And I know what it is to live here with nothing more than his ghost.

Maddie was wrong, it turns out: in some ways, some of the worst ways, I am exactly like my dad.

· ˎ ﻌ

I've read everything there is to read on the Internet about my brother—every interview in every obscure magazine, every restaurant review, every old archived story about back when he used to wrestle and play baseball in high school. I've memorized every website photo of the inside of his restaurant, and once, a few years back, I subscribed to *Restaurants Monthly* because he'd been profiled in it and I wanted a copy to put up on my wall. And besides that, he's my brother. When my dad was working, Trey was the one who raised me. So I can't try to excuse myself by saying I didn't know, that I wasn't trying to upset him—I knew I'd upset him. And for a little while there, for long enough to do real damage, I wanted to.

I stay on the floor like that a long time waiting for him to come back, the minutes notching themselves like cuts in my chest. My phone rings at six fifteen, and six thirty, at a quarter to seven, and I let it ring. I know it's Maddie. I picture her, waiting and nervous and hopeful, on the other end. I picture her all dressed up and assuring her parents I'm just late, that I'm a good person and they can trust me with someone like her. I picture myself yelling at Greg, and at my dad the night of the accident, and at Trey just now. I picture Maddie thinking well of me, trusting me and giving more and more of herself to me, not knowing I'm someone who drives the people I care most about to ruin. And I picture how it felt to lie next to her at the lake, how it felt to plan out a future together over and over in my mind.

I don't know why I ever thought I could have that.

When I finally get up, I duck my head down to the faucet and run the cold water and pat it over my eyes until my face feels numb. My chest still hurts. I get the broom from the hall closet. There was still some water in the glass and when I sweep, it mixes with the dust on the floor to rub across the tile.

Please come back, I plead silently with Trey. *I'm sorry. I'll forget about the letter, I won't ever talk back like that again, I'll do whatever you want, just please don't make me go through the rest of this alone.*

I'm reaching to get a towel when I feel something stinging on the bottom of my foot, and then a streak of blood smears across the tile. I grab my foot with my hand to see where I got cut, and I don't even hear at first when Trey comes back in. He says, "You shouldn't be in here barefoot," and I startle so badly I nearly fall.

As I reach for something to say, he surveys the pile of glass in one corner, the fallen broom, the blood on the floor, then leans back against the wall and slides down until he's on the ground. He stares straight ahead. His eyes are bloodshot. I think I smell pot. He says, flatly, "You all right?"

"Yeah." I swallow. "Trey, I'm sorry. I'm really sorry. I—"

"Don't." He reaches both his hands on top of his head and then runs them over his eyes and face so his fingers leave white marks that vanish, like ghosts. "Let me see your foot."

"It's fine. It's nothing."

"Please."

So I let him. He presses above the cut until it separates, a red gash that isn't quite as deep as the blood makes it look. There's a loosening feeling in my gut. I've always hated blood.

"It'll be fine tomorrow. Stay off it tonight." He wipes his finger against his pants and drops his head back against the wall, hard enough that it thuds. "I'll clean up here."

"I can do it. I'll do it."

"Go take care of your foot."

"No, it's my fault, I'll do it, I—"

"I said go."

"Okay, if you say so. I'll go." I keep one hand against the wall and hop forward on one foot, trying not to drip blood. When I get to the door and look back, he's slumped forward, his forehead in his hands.

He hears me pause there, maybe. He looks up. I can't read the expression on his face. "Hey, Braden?"

I wipe my eyes and look away. I doubt I want to hear this. "Yeah."

"You're probably the most loyal person I know."

TWENTY-SEVEN

I know Trey's been gone all these years and there's a lot he missed, but I still thought he knew me. He's wrong about this, though: I'm not loyal. Not when it really counted.

After that night my dad wrecked my car when I took it to LA, I thought things would go back to normal. I thought I'd paid for things, and I thought we'd just get over it and we'd pretend it never happened. All I wanted at that point was to forget the whole entire thing, and I figured he'd want that, too.

But I'd misjudged him. The day after, he woke me up in the morning and told me things were going to be different, now that I'd betrayed his trust. From then on, he said, I had to come straight home after practice; I had to text him when I left and I had to be home exactly fifteen minutes later. The one day practice went late, he called Cardy to make sure I wasn't lying, and once I got paged to the front office because he'd called me through their phone to make sure I was really in school. He took to sleeping with his door open and made me give him the password to my Facebook account and my e-mail, and when I balked at all that, he ordered me to look up Proverbs 15:10, which says, *Stern discipline awaits him who leaves the path; he who hates correction will die.* So I didn't fight him on it. But I stopped speaking to him unless he addressed me directly, so for days we didn't talk—not about LA and not about anything else, either. I could hold everything at bay if I was throwing and I pushed myself hard enough, or a few times if I was around Maddie, but back at home I could never replay those moments sharp enough or bright enough to keep. At night I'd sneak out of the house and into the grounds of the country club, running as hard as I could in the dark until everything in my body hurt.

It was four weeks after I'd gone to LA when my dad came and sat down on my bed while I was in my room. Sunday, February 9, although I didn't know then the date was going to get played across the news the way it has. I had my homework out in front of me, so when he came in, I flicked up the edge of my papers to show him. It was sarcastic—*You happy now?*—but he just nodded like he thought I meant it, stared around my room a couple times, drummed his fingertips on his thighs, and finally said, "Look, B. I think—" He cleared his throat. "I think you need to tell me exactly what you did in LA."

"Nothing."

"I know that isn't true."

"You didn't want to hear it. Remember? You threatened me to never bring her up again."

"I did nothing of the kind."

He definitely had. Still, I was mad, but not quite dumb enough to contradict him. I pressed the tip of my pencil into my thumb until it hurt and muttered, "Well, there's nothing to tell."

"Braden, please. You already went behind my back and broke my trust. After everything I've done for you, please, please don't keep lying to my face this way."

That stung. "I've never lied to you in my life. There's just nothing to say."

"You left me here thinking the worst and you couldn't even be bothered to pick up your phone to tell me you were coming back? Do you know what it was like for me worrying like that? How could you do that to me, Braden? That's why you wanted to go to LA? To hurt me?"

If he was mad it would've been one thing, I figured I'd been punished enough already, but that's not how he looked—he looked pained and old and sad, and it made me second-guess myself. Was that what I'd wanted, really? I said, stiffly, "I wasn't trying to hurt anyone. But I'm sorry for what I did."

"I forgave you already. I forgave you the second you came home." My dad crossed his arms over his chest and looked down at the floor. He puffed out his cheeks and blew air through his lips. "Well?" he said. "How was it? When you saw her?"

"I don't know."

"Braden, please."

"Fine. It was stupid. She doesn't want to see me ever again. So it doesn't matter. Whatever. Who cares."

"Well, I could've told you that, Braden. She didn't want you before, she's not going to want you now. People don't change. I can't even think what was going on in your head. She dropped you off like you'd get rid of clothes that don't fit anymore. She didn't *care*. I don't know why you'd think that disobeying your father the way you did would make anyone like that change her mind."

"I just—I thought—"

"You thought what?"

I twisted away so he wouldn't see my eyes filling up. What was I supposed to say? I thought she'd want to know me, after all these years? I thought she'd *love* me?

"Nothing," I said. "I didn't think anything. I was just being dumb."

He reached out and took my chin in his hand. I tried to look away, but he tilted my head back so I couldn't. He reached out and brushed under my eyes with his thumbs.

"B," he said, "I love you. I love you so much. I believe in you. I'm the only one who sees the best in you. You have a dad who lies awake at night thinking about you and who every day of his life thanks God for you. Isn't that enough? Doesn't that mean something to you?"

I've replayed this part again and again in my mind. Because I could've changed everything, I know that, if I just gave him the answer he wanted. I could've told him yes, and he would've relaxed, and we would have stayed home that night and he would have thought things were okay. And I couldn't have said why I didn't, if I was angry about the past four weeks, or if I blamed him for the way things were, or if I'd always been a destructive kind of person or if maybe I was just exhausted from how much he always wanted from me. But all I said was, "Fine."

"Fine?" he repeated. "*Fine?* Jesus, Braden—" He dropped his hands, then he stood up. He checked his watch and stood there for a couple seconds, blinking, then something shifted in his face. "Go meet me in the car."

When I didn't move, he said, "I'm not suggesting it, Braden. I'm telling you to go get in the car. Now."

So I did. My car had disappeared that week from the garage— I didn't ask—but there were still pieces of glass in the driveway. I had no idea where we were going, and I didn't know—I still don't know—if I was going with him because deep down I believed some-how he could fix things still and he could make everything all right again and I wanted him to prove that, or if I thought he couldn't and that was the thing I wanted to prove. Maybe neither. Maybe both.

We went through Ceres, Salida, and Manteca, and I didn't feel anything except maybe numb. We got onto 205. It was when we hit Tracy, passing through the flats and the foothills with the windmills spinning on either side of the freeway, that he said quietly, "Braden, I'm not the one you're mad at, you know. I know you. You're mad at her. And you're mad at yourself."

We drove through Livermore and came up over the pass where you see the valley spread out beneath you; we drove through Pleasanton and Dublin and then in Castro Valley we cut north. We kept going past the gray concrete cities until we hit Oakland, and that's when he exited. We made enough right and left turns that I felt like a Tetris piece, spun out of shape, and I lost the map I'd been trying to keep inside my head.

Then, in the middle of the neighborhood, we stopped. It was when we stopped that the numbness thawed some and I realized how much I didn't want to be wherever this was.

We were in front of a house surrounded by similar houses with browning lawns and shoulder-high chain-link fences going around the yard. It was unmarked, no signs or anything, just 2407 as an address and, above the garage, an Oakland Raiders flag.

"Well," he said, and he took a deep breath and looked toward the door like he was trying to psych himself up, "We're here."

"We're where? What is this?"

"You'll see."

"Can we just—"

"Let's go, Braden." He swung his door open. "Get out."

The man who opened the door was wearing a leather vest with a flag stitched on one side and a bandanna tied over half his head. He had a buzz cut and a handlebar mustache, and he was huge, like a prison guard maybe, the kind of guy you'd watch carefully if you saw him in a parking lot somewhere, and it was when I saw him that I started to get scared, and started to wonder if I didn't know my dad as well as I'd thought I did. I thought how maybe I shouldn't have come, although maybe I also didn't have a choice. Either way, it was too late now.

My dad said, "Hi, Jimmy," and the man blinked at him, then laughed like he was startled and said, *"Mart?"*

"Look, I need a small favor." My dad pulled a folded slip of paper from his pocket and unfolded it, then handed it to Jimmy. "Here. Can you do this?"

Jimmy looked at the paper, then blinked again at my dad. "This? You show up here out of the blue for *this*? When was the last time I saw you? Fifteen years ago? What's the—"

"Can you do it?"

Jimmy was going to say no, I think, but he changed his mind. He sighed. "Fine, fine. No one can say I ever turned away an old friend. For you, even though it's last-minute, six hundred."

"All right." My dad reached into his wallet, and I tried to think what you'd drive two hours to pay someone you hadn't seen in fifteen years—someone who looked like Jimmy—six hundred dollars to do. Jimmy grinned.

"You're not even going to haggle, weakling? You could've worked me down to less than half." He opened the door wider. "Come in, come in. Let me go grab my stuff. Hang tight."

"Dad?" I whispered when Jimmy had disappeared down the hallway. "I'm sorry. For everything. I'm sorry. Can we just go home?"

We were standing in the den, and between the den and the kitchen there was a counter, bar-height, so you could see the dishes stacked up in the sink. The house was messy. There weren't very many windows or doors, and it was dark, and when my dad cracked his knuckles and then reached up and put his hands behind his head, the shadows his arms made went all the way across the room.

"Dad, come on, what is this? Who's that guy? What's he going to do?"

"So now you feel like talking," he muttered. He dropped his arms against his sides with a thud, then he turned and looked at me. "I try to tell you how much I love you and you tell me *fine*, Braden? That's how it is for you? You don't believe me?"

"Dad, come on, that's—"

But Jimmy came back then, so I shut up. He had a plastic tray with a couple bottles, a stack of gauze, a stick of deodorant, a disposable razor, and a tub of Vaseline. He set the tray next to the sink in the kitchen, then he said, "Changed the needle for you and everything."

My stomach knotted like a rope. I hate needles, I'd rather break a bone than get one stuck in me, and I knew my dad knew that because he's always felt the exact same way. I turned back to him, ready to do whatever he said to get out of here, but before I could say so he went to the counter and unbuttoned his left sleeve and rolled it up to the elbow. He pushed aside a half-full bottle of Pepsi and laid his arm across the counter, palm up. Even from across the room I could see his shoulders were tense and his forehead was shiny with sweat.

Jimmy rubbed his hands together. "All right," he said. "Let's go."

He poured something onto a cotton ball and rubbed it on my dad's arm, then picked up the razor and ran it carefully over the skin. He licked his middle finger and stuck it down on the tray and when he pulled it up, there was a small cutout of paper clinging to it.

He rubbed the paper over the deodorant and then pressed the paper onto my dad's skin. I still didn't understand until Jimmy picked up something that looked like a gun chamber attached to an awl, and I realized what it was. The gun made a whirring sound, like something in a toolshed or a dentist's office, and even from across the room, the needle looked sharp and huge.

My dad winced. I felt it, too, and closed my eyes. I opened them again right when the needle slid through his skin and my dad made a gasping sound and then a high-pitched, girlish yelp.

Jimmy roared with laughter and said, "Raynor, you are getting *soft*." He made a high-pitched sound like *Uhnngh!*, imitating my dad's little scream, and after that he stopped smiling and worked quietly with the tip of his tongue positioned carefully between his teeth.

The needle kept sliding rapidly in and out of his skin. Jimmy kept dabbing away what looked like blood welling up around it. After a few minutes—or maybe it was longer; I had the weird feeling that if I looked at a calendar, whole days could've passed—Jimmy leaned closer to peer at what he'd done, dabbed at the blood and ink, and switched off the gun.

"All right, you woman, there you go. Be right back." He went into his hallway again. When he did, my dad said, "Come here."

His skin had puffed up around where the needle slipped into his forearm. It was black blocky letters, two rows: MARTIN SCOTT RAYNOR III. That was Trey. And then, under that: BRADEN SCOTT RAYNOR. That, obviously, was me.

"You like it?" He watched me stare at our names. His anger had evaporated; he looked as close to nervous as I'd ever seen him look. Then he looked down at his arm and broke into a proud, tired smile. "You want to know a secret? That needle scared me half to death. Jesus, B, that *hurt*."

Jimmy came back then, holding up a bottle. "Forgot the ointment." He dribbled some onto a pad and then pressed it against my dad's skin. My dad made another high-pitched sound and Jimmy smirked and pressed harder, rubbing it in.

"How about you?" he said to me. "You want one, too? I do it free if it's a name you won't want covered up later, some girl or something." He let go of the pad and grinned. "No, I don't. I just feel bad your old man didn't even try to haggle. You want a matching one? You want your old man's name?"

My dad tried to sound like he was joking, like he didn't want me to know how much he wanted it, how much it would mean to him. "Two for one," he said, and he nudged me in the ribs. "How about it, B?"

It was like an egg cracking and spilling its contents, messy and runny, all over your hands: just like that, I was sick of everything, I was done, and whatever things I'd been pretending weren't there for I don't know how long clawed to the surface all at once and then broke loose. I'd lost the one thing I always wanted most, the one thing I couldn't even talk about to anyone because I wanted it too much, and I was supposed to be grateful for *this*? My name needled into someone who thought I wasn't good enough for anyone else to care about, ever, except him? He gave me a shy, hopeful smile and held his breath the way people do when they're caught up in something that really matters to them, and I said, "You should've saved your money, Dad," and I had just enough time to catch the way his expression collapsed before I walked out and left him, the smile dangling off his face like a broken limb.

I stay off the Internet completely the weekend of prom and leave my phone off and I mostly avoid Trey, which even though neither of us leaves the house is easy enough because he avoids me, too. But he cooks for me, platefuls of things like spaghetti and roast chicken that he brings up to my room without saying much, which I know means he feels bad about what happened. He shouldn't—I pushed him too far and got what I had coming because of it, and anyway I'd put up with him losing his temper and I'd eat canned tuna and peanut butter the rest of my life if it meant he wouldn't pick up and leave again.

I get to school as late as I can Monday morning, my dread fossilizing into a hard, painful lump inside my chest. Just before the bell rings, someone takes my arm—I jump a mile—and when I turn around from my locker, Maddie's there. The concern on her face chokes me.

"Braden, thank God." Her eyes are huge. "I kept checking the news because I was so scared something happened to you. I've been trying to call you all weekend. What happened? Are you okay?"

All weekend I've been trying not to think about this moment. And now that I'm in it, now that she's standing so close I can make out the downy hairs on her forehead, I wish for a second I'd just never met her. I kept trying to tell myself that Maddie was proof I wasn't alone and forsaken by God, but that's because I twisted things with her into what I wanted them to be. I see that now. I never deserved her; I should've just left her alone. Just because you need something doesn't make it right.

I say, "I'm fine." I pull my arm away, and doubt flickers across Maddie's face.

"We'd said—we'd said six, right? Did I miss something? We were all waiting for you, and I told my parents . . ." She reaches up to push some of her hair behind her ear. "Did I do something wrong?"

"No." I turn back to my locker, my heart lodged in my throat. What is there to tell her? It's too late to take everything back, and there's nothing I can say that'll change a thing about who I am.

"Braden—" Her hand goes uncertainly toward mine, hovers a second, and then pulls back again. "Are you okay? Are you going to tell me what happened? Say something."

"I said I'm fine." I turn back around and meet her eyes. "I just—I don't think we should talk anymore."

"Are you—are you breaking up with me?"

The words are a stake through my heart. "There's nothing to *break up*," I say, putting the words in quotes with my fingers. "It's not like we were together, Maddie. It wasn't anything big. I was just being stupid."

The bell rings. Maddie stares past me, blinking rapidly, hugging her arms around herself. The halls fill with people, and I wish right then that I were any one of them besides myself. I say, "You should go to class."

"Can't we—"

But I'm already walking away, already erasing the look on her face from my memory. I wish she'd never trusted me. I should've just left her alone. "You'll get in trouble if you're late."

TWENTY-EIGHT

The night before Alex testifies, I hear Mr. Buchwald's red Miata pull up to our street, and he's at the door before I can disappear. He comes in with takeout dinner and loosens his tie and the buttons on his sleeve, and says, "Tonight we're going to prepare you for cross-examination."

Laila Shah is going to rest her case soon after the jury hears from Alex Reyes tomorrow, and after that, Mr. Buchwald will present his. Before me, he'll bring out the woman whose dog Frank Reyes killed and who will say he was reckless and impulsive, a different weather guy who'll say my dad's account of the fog sounds reasonable, a neighbor who'll testify that Frank Reyes threw parties that turned loud and sometimes violent. He'll bring out Frank Reyes's record to show he was caught with marijuana when he was nineteen and the year after was arrested for reckless driving, and he'll question Jordan Dadier, who accused Frank Reyes and the LAPD of using excessive force during an arrest. Dadier will show medical bills and pictures of the broken cheekbone and bloodied face he'll say he got after Frank Reyes beat him, and he'll tell the jury that the department threatened and harassed him when he tried to file a complaint. Jimmy will show up clean-cut and in a suit and testify—anything, I guess, for an old friend—that my dad was calm and relaxed when he left his house. An expert medical witness who bills a thousand dollars an hour will question the coroner's findings.

And then me. Mr. Buchwald hasn't come right out and said it, not in so many words, but I know my testimony's going to matter most.

Mr. Buchwald wolfs down his dinner, a foil-wrapped burrito dripping whole pinto beans onto our table, and hammers me with cross-examination questions, interrupting me midsentence and quoting me back at myself and raising his voice. At first I try to wilt under his questioning and fumble my answers, hoping he'll decide I'm not good at this and he'll do better without me after all, but he just gets louder and louder until his words feel like an assault and I'm rattled enough to tell him what he wants. I tell myself it's just practice and that what I say doesn't matter yet, and I try to talk softly so Trey can't hear. We go through the whole process another time, and then he flips a switch and suddenly he's smiley and nice, trying to get me to go back on what I'm saying because he's being nice about it. That one's harder. Apparently I trust too easily.

After that, he makes me bring down three different shirts and pants so he can decide what he wants me to wear to my court date. He picks gray pants I rarely wear anywhere but church and a light blue dress shirt. When he's finally satisfied, he asks if there's anything else I need to go over before April 30. I tell him I don't have a ride to the courthouse, and this time I raise my voice enough for Trey to overhear. If I were braver, I'd just ask him again to come. And maybe if I were a better brother he'd come because he wanted to.

Mr. Buchwald tells me to look in the phone book to find a cab. "And come early," he says. "We don't want you stumbling in like a tardy freshman. That's not how we need the jury to view you."

I think about all the footage I've seen that I wasn't supposed to watch, about how God saw me do that. How all this time I used Maddie to try to hide. "I still don't think it's a good idea for me to get up there."

Mr. Buchwald takes off his glasses and sets them on the table. He leans back in his chair so the two front legs hover above the ground.

"Braden, let me tell you how I see you," he says. "Let me tell you why I believe you'll be a phenomenal witness. A pep talk, if you will. Think of it as a pregame huddle. You aren't skittish and emotional like the woman who claimed your father nearly hit her, or smarmy like Tucker Walker. You're not angry and vengeful like Molson. You're wholesome, dependable, and responsible. You're confident in your own rightness. A devoted son. The jury will look at you and be reminded of their own sons. You are your father's mouthpiece. And I have every confidence that you will convincingly illuminate for the jury the fear you and your father felt."

"But I'm not—"

He lets the chair thud against the floor. "Juries are sympathetic to fear," he says. "They're human, after all. I can all but guarantee that at some point during this trial, each juror has asked himself what he would have done were he similarly threatened. No one wants to live in a world where a man can't defend himself or his family. We can debate technicalities over fog all day long, but in the end, no one else was there that night besides you and Reyes's nephew. If we can convince the jury that you and your father were afraid, then I believe the case is ours. If the jury doesn't believe you, of course—then I may as well rest my case before I call a single witness to the stand."

. ` °

I've never seen Alex in anything but a baseball uniform, and to court he wears glasses and a collared shirt that make him look like more of a nerd than I would've pegged him for—like someone who probably plays chess—and a baseball cap, which is one of the things that Mr. Buchwald's forbidden me to wear. The hat says LA ABRA on it. Judge Scherr makes him take it off, and Alex does it as contemptuously as possible. He slouches and crosses his arms over his chest. He has a deeper voice than you'd expect looking at him, and twice Laila has to ask him to move closer to the microphone so he can be heard. And every word he says, every little gesture—all of it drips with disdain.

He and his uncle were close, he tells the jury. Like brothers. The night of February 9, his uncle had driven him into San Jose to hang out with a cousin of his, which they did every week because the cousin had moved recently for school and was homesick. Sometimes he and Frank slept over. That night they didn't, and they were driving home when Frank heard the dispatch come over the radio, which he always left on. They were right by where the other driver was, so he went. He flicked on his sirens and sped up.

Laila pauses him there. "Alex, what was the visibility like that night?"

"Foggy. Like every single person has already said. But you could still see a freaking *person* walking around in front of you."

"Could you clearly see the suspect's car?"

"Clearly."

"Can you describe it?"

"Blue Range Rover. Tinted windows. Lots of bumper stickers."

"Did your uncle recognize the car?"

"Right away." His lip curls, a half sneer. "Not hard when your license plate is M-R-T-R-Y-N-R."

"Did your uncle plan to confront Mr. Raynor?"

"I mean, he planned to give him a ticket."

"Did he plan to engage in any sort of conflict?"

"No. He just wanted to get it over with."

"How do you know?"

"My uncle's not a hard guy to read. He always acts the same way when he just wants to get something over with. He goes like this"—he jostles his shoulders up and down the way guys do sometimes before they go up to the plate, like when you're psyching yourself up. "And he said, 'Hey, I could eat a barn, after this, you want to stop and get Mickey D's or something?' That's the other thing he always does when he has to do something he doesn't want to. He eats. I said yeah, sure, whatever, we'll get french fries or whatever if you want, even though I don't normally eat that crap. He sat there for another second or two and then he got out. He went around to the passenger side. I was waiting for him in the car and my buddy was texting me, so I was kind of looking up and down. I could kind of hear them talking, but not really."

"Did your uncle, at any point, draw his gun?"

"No. I would've been watching if it was something like that."

"What happened next?"

"I heard the other car start. It didn't take long, so I thought he just let them off with a warning or something. But then they hit him with their car and knocked him over. I could hear him yelling. The car went up, like on a curb. Then it stopped and then it backed up and went up over him like that again. They made a U-turn over the highway and went through the middle and got away."

"Did it look like an accident?"

"It wasn't an accident. They had to swerve to hit him. They had to drive the wrong *way* to hit him, and they hit him twice. When I got to him, he kept trying to grab my hand and saying he needed CPR, but I don't know CPR. I got down next to him and tried, but he kept trying to scream because it hurt him. I called nine-one-one, and he told me to call again, so I called again. But he was having trouble breathing and then he couldn't talk anymore. So I tried to breathe into his mouth, but he kept jerking his head around like he wanted to get away and he was crying, so I stopped. I told him it would be fine. I told him we'd go get his stupid french fries like he wanted. The paramedics showed up, like, five hours later, it felt like, and at first they were moving fast and actually trying to do something for him, and then they all just gave up. They just stood around putting him on a stretcher and looking at each other and looking at me and I heard he'd stopped crying, but no one would tell me he died, so I thought he was wondering the whole way in the ambulance why I wasn't there with him and I kept texting him to tell him I was on my way. When I got to the hospital, they told me he died. And that's it."

The camera shifts then so the jury's in it, and in the jurors' box, the woman sitting all the way on top reaches up and wipes her eyes. And I freeze up then, not just because Mr. Buchwald's told me how dangerous it is when the jury responds emotionally to the opposition, but because I know the look on that woman's face. It's the same way I felt playing Ceres when Rory told me about Adrian's sister being sick right before I gave him that home run, how for a second or two before you come back to yourself, you stop caring about justice because some tempting, false emotion stabs you somewhere where you're weak.

When the prosecutor's finished, Mr. Buchwald comes up again for his cross-examination. I've seen enough of these by now to know how it's supposed to go, what you're trying to achieve. The lawyer's the one telling the story, not the witness. There are a lot of yes-or-no questions and you want to lead the witness as much as you can. You want to violate personal space and make him uncomfortable, you want to badger him into contradicting himself, you want to go so fast and pick so mercilessly at everything he's said that he stumbles and looks bad. You want him to break.

In his cross-examination, Mr. Buchwald tries. He barely waits for Alex's answers before going onto his next questions, and a few times when Alex starts to answer, Mr. Buchwald talks over him, saying, "I must remind you, Mr. Reyes, that you're under oath." But Alex doesn't stumble even once. He watches Mr. Buchwald with a detached, disdainful coldness, and nothing catches him off guard.

When it's over, I sit in my dark bedroom, blue-tinged shadows rearing up on the wall from the glow of my screen, and I feel so sick with fear I nearly pick up my phone to text Trey. If he were here, I could tell myself that things will be all right again. But it's two in the morning and he's out God knows where; I heard his car leave before I started watching.

I try to imagine telling the judge about everything I've seen, what the fallout would be. Whatever trouble I'd get in, I don't know if it would be worse than having to testify. I back up the video again and pause on a screenshot of the woman crying. Would someone like her believe me that Frank Reyes had it in for my dad? That out there on that road in the fog, with no one watching, that whatever anger and resentment had been knotting up inside him uncoiled and lashed out into a violence my dad had no choice but to defend himself against?

I picture myself describing him for a jury as aggressive, unhinged.

I could give a whole litany of things for him to scream at my dad; the jury heard things my dad's said on the radio that would've maybe set someone like him off. I could describe my fear, how the encounter with him careened suddenly out of control and how afraid we were for our lives. I picture myself describing panic at the sight of an out-of-control officer going for his gun.

Last night after Mr. Buchwald left, when Trey was in his room for the night and I couldn't sleep, I finally read what happens when someone gets the death penalty. I've been telling myself not to even look ever since I heard the prosecutor was pushing for it, but I did, and now I can't get it out of my head.

This is what I read: it always takes place in the morning at six. There's a strict routine. For the two weeks before, people watch you; there's a psychologist who reports on your mental state, a chaplain who writes about your emotional and spiritual well-being, a doctor who performs a physical (I can't imagine why). The day before, you're allowed to listen to the radio or watch TV. You can ask for soda, if you want, or coffee. At night you're supposed to go to sleep. The next day you get two hours to see visitors. After that, they give you a new pair of pants and a new shirt; at that point you have half an hour left.

There's a room with cameras and a window and a curtain over the window, and the walls are cinder block, and in one of the cinder blocks, there's a hole, and coming from the hole there's tubes for an IV. You lie down, and someone straps you in, and someone else places heart monitors on your skin. Someone outside checks them, makes sure your heart's still going strong. The monitors are hooked to a printer outside. You lie there, strapped down, while they get you ready. Your family has to wait outside. Someone takes sterilized needles and slides them into your veins, and they're hooked to the IV with the tubes going through that hole in the cinder block. On the other side of the wall is the person who'll flush the drugs through that IV. But none of the people are nurses or doctors, just correctional officers, and maybe they're nervous or maybe they're impatient or maybe it's their first week on the job, and maybe they can't find a vein right away or they miss or they stab the needle all the way through the vein and back out the other side and they hit the muscle instead. If the needle gets clogged, then the drug bleeds into your muscles and causes excruciating pain, and then they either have to push through your yelling and wait it out and hope it works, or wait for you to calm down and then stop and try again. And then you get an extra five minutes, maybe six.

TWENTY-NINE

never told anyone this, but for the past four or five years now, I've woken up early Easter Sunday and slipped out of the house while my dad was still sleeping and watched the sun rise over the small, sloping green of the golf course you look out on from our backyard. Later we'd go to church, and we'd hear the crucifixion story and the songs about Christ rising again with the chords that would swell into your heartbeat until you felt broken and lucky and grief-stricken all at once. But before all that, every year, there was a time when it was just me and the quiet, empty space I left open hoping for some kind of glimpse of God.

When I go out this morning, it's just barely, newly light. Trey's ashtray plate is still out next to the lounge chairs. I have a piece of bread and—it was the closest thing we had—a cup of Gatorade, grape-flavored.

It's easy for someone like Kevin to talk about God's forgiveness when there can't be all that much he needs to be forgiven for. I've had too many years of my dad's voice on the radio reminding me what happens to people who reject God, reminding me how you recognize them and how you ferret out that own darkness in yourself. That's what I really believe—that love can't stretch out far enough to cover a person who cheapens it by disobeying, that if I turn away from God, that's it for me.

I think about Jesus dying his painful, brutal death, and I think about him looking a few thousand years into the future at me, and I imagine him seeing how I'm not worth it, how I never deserved what he did for me. I think how I've been skipping church all this time and how I've only ever wanted to pray on my own terms because I don't really want God to find me. All this time I've done everything I could to hide from him, and time is running out on me.

I kneel on the damp flagstone and take a bite of the bread—*my body, broken for you*—and then drink the Gatorade. *My blood, poured out for you.*

Make a way out for me, I pray. *Don't abandon me. Don't make me do this. Please don't make me choose.*

     .   .   .

Trey comes to my room a few hours later while I'm skipping church. My door's open, but he knocks gently on the frame and waits for me to look up before taking a step inside. We've been like this around each other since the night of my would-have-been prom. My dad's been gone long enough that I'd half forgotten what it's like to have to be careful like this, like balancing a heavy beaker of dangerous chemicals around your classroom lab.

"Hey," Trey says. He has a clean white towel tucked into his waistband, his cooking uniform. "Jenna and Kevin are coming at six. You'll be around?"

"What for?"

"It's Easter."

What exactly that means to him, who knows; if he remembers Easter was when everything went to hell with him and my dad, he doesn't let on. I say, "Yeah, sure, I'll be around."

"Great." He starts to go back downstairs, then he turns back. "Hey, uh—you want to come help me?"

It's warm in the kitchen and smells like garlic cooking, and there's bags and containers full of food in neat rows across the entire kitchen table. Trey motions me to stand next to him at the counter and slides a knife toward me. "Dice onions for me. You know how to dice?"

I attempt a smile. "Is that harder than scrambling eggs? Because if so, then no."

He reaches over to show me. His knife flashes and leaves behind a mound of geometric pieces, like white Scrabble tiles. "Make them look like this."

It takes me a long time to do the onions, and afterward he has me stir the pan they're cooking in so they don't burn. I can feel a rhythm unfolding in his own tasks, something that feels less ragged and frayed than the way things have felt lately with him, and with everything. I almost said no when he asked if I wanted to help, but I think I'm glad I didn't. It's better being here with him. While I'm stirring and he's dunking strips of lemon peel into a boiling pot, I say, tentatively, "So when you're in New York, do you do stuff for holidays like this?"

"Nah, I'm always working."

"But even on holidays?"

"Especially on holidays. People still have to eat." He picks the lemon peel pieces out of the pot with chopsticks and lays each one on a tray, then picks up some zucchini and a knife. "Christmas we do a dinner for people who didn't go home to family. We close early, and then around nine we open up again and everyone eats family-style. I don't advertise it. But I've been doing it every year, so people know about it. Just to give people a good place to go."

"It's your friends who all go to your Christmas dinner?"

"Strangers." He looks down at the zucchini he's shaving into paper-thin slices. "Holidays are rough on a lot of people, you know? You start remembering too many things."

There's a lot he could mean by that, but before I can stop it, my own heart pinches thinking about Maddie, as if Trey and I are having some kind of depressing, silent conversation about everything we've lost. I don't want to think about her. Her friends cross to the other side of the hallway when they see me at school or they circle around her like a hedge of protection, and from how she turns away when she sees me coming in the halls, I know she dreads running into me. Even though I know I deserve it, it still hurts. In Spanish this week we were assigned to be dialogue partners, and when she sat down in front of me, I said, quietly, "Maddie—"

"Page one twenty-nine." She looked back at me evenly, her voice cool. "I'll read the first part."

"Look, Maddie, can I just—"

She turned to Missy Winestone next to her, smiling a bright, cold smile I'd never seen from her before then. "Missy, will you please switch partners with me?" That was the last time we spoke.

To Trey, I say, "Is that why you're doing dinner today? Because it's a holiday?"

He looks kind of surprised. "I've been talking about making all of you dinner forever."

"Oh. Right. I just thought—" I cut myself off. I thought I ruined that when I let his birds go, but I'm not about to bring that up. "I just didn't know it was for Easter."

"Felt appropriate." He sweeps the zucchini into a colander and sprinkles salt on it, then stirs another pot on the stove. It smells sweet and rich, like cinnamon. "Anyway, they always have Kevin's family over and Jenna ends up doing all the work. I figured she deserved some kind of break."

I stay there with him in the kitchen the whole day. He gets quiet like he's focusing, and doesn't say much more. It's funny—before this, I would've said his cooking was about cutting and pounding and searing stuff, different ways of exerting force. But I see today how he's careful, gentle, almost reverent: when he pats a paper towel on the skin of a duck breast, when he strokes a tiny strawberry with his thumb. What he's doing feels like alchemy, and even my relatively pathetic contributions feel like some small part of it. For the first time, I can see, maybe, some of what this gives him: a kind of order he can root around for and harness, or at the very least somewhere to bury himself a while.

After my court date, I tell myself, there will still be this to come back to.

Three hours before Kevin and Jenna come, Trey unwraps a tiny headless carcass of some kind of bird about a third the size of a chicken and dabs away its blood with a paper towel. Then, out of nowhere, he turns to me.

"I've been doing this so long it shouldn't feel like this," he says, and gives me a half smile that I would maybe, almost, describe as shy. "But I always get nervous when I cook for someone."

They're supposed to come at six, and at five, Trey hands me a stack of square white plates I'm pretty sure he must have bought just for this. In the dining room, I see he's found a tablecloth somewhere—I didn't know we had one—and put some kind of white flowers on the table.

At 6:08 (Trey keeps checking the clock), Kevin comes in without knocking, holding a bottle of wine, which he hands me. He's alone.

"Ellie wouldn't go down for her nap this afternoon while we were with my folks," he tells Trey. "She's a terror when that happens, so Jenna's staying home with her."

"You came by yourself?" Trey says, and from the way he says it, I can feel the whole night tilt and shift. "There's way too much food for just you and Braden. I made some purees for Ellie, too. Give Jenna a call now and tell her to come."

"We'll do it some other time. Today it's just me."

"She decided that, or you did?"

Kevin looks annoyed. "Does it matter?" He motions toward the dining room. "Shall we?"

I know Trey wants to say more, but he doesn't push it. It's not until I see him resign himself to silence that I realize I want this dinner to go well as badly as he seems to. I want him to be calm and hopeful and at peace the way he was in the kitchen today; I want that to have signaled the beginning of some kind of redemption for me, too. I want to trust that if you really work toward something it'll fall into place the way you need.

When we go to sit down, Trey goes back into the kitchen, and I get the corkscrew for Kevin's wine. I bring just one glass, and he says, like he's tired, "It's just juice, Braden. I know Trey doesn't drink." He's kind of staring off into space. "For the record, Jenna thought it was best to stay home with Ellie, too."

I say nothing, obviously. What am I supposed to say?

When Trey comes back, he takes a deep breath and lists the dishes he's made, ticking them off on his fingers: ahi crudo with grapes. Quail and pear ravioli with candied Meyer lemon. Tea-steamed pheasant with fried arugula. Oxtail and tripe in a clear porcini broth. Surf and turf of lamb and octopus with a smoked fig glaze. Zucchini carpaccio with strawberries, hazelnuts, and duck. Vadouvan goat. Braised beef cheeks with truffled celeriac.

"Wow," Kevin says. "You cooked a petting zoo."

"Ha." Then Trey raises his eyebrows at me. "Minus the ortolans."

He disappears into the kitchen and comes back with two long rectangular plates with the ravioli, the octopus thing, some pale shiny raw fish dotted with tiny dark purple half globes that look something like blisters when they rise and fill with blood. Then he stands there and watches us eat.

"Well?" he says, when we've finished. "How was it?"

"Good," I say quickly. "Impressive."

"Kev?"

"It was . . ." Kevin pauses. And it's funny, because I would've sworn up and down Trey does whatever he wants and other people's opinions never mattered that much to him, but there's something about the way Trey looks, waiting, that makes me realize this about the way they're friends: Trey cares a lot about what Kevin thinks. "It was different."

I stiffen. Trey says, "Different bad?"

"Just different."

"Was it the texture? The flavor? What?"

"I have no idea, Trey. Are you going to come join us?"

"In a little bit. Here." He takes our plates and comes back in holding bowls of the soup.

"Watch out," he says. "They're full. I made enough for twice as many people, so."

I say, "Thanks, Trey, that looks really good," at the same time Kevin says tightly, "Can you give it a rest already?"

"Sure, whatever you say. I just think ditching your wife on Easter seems like a strange move for someone who's so big on doing everything his family expects him to. Seminary, even. Your family's lifelong dream." His voice disappears as he walks away.

Kevin's jaw twitches, and I get the feeling Trey's made his feelings about seminary clear before. Over my rising discomfort, I say, "So what made you decide to go back to seminary, anyway?"

"Ah—some reevaluation I've been prompted toward. For a long time now, I've given God less than my best, and I'd like to rectify that."

I wish I could ask what he means by that. Or maybe I don't; maybe the answer would be something like he thinks he should be reading his Bible even more, and that would just make me feel even worse by comparison. "I think you'd make a good pastor."

"That's very kind of you to say." Kevin pushes at his spoon, then lets it drop so it splashes drops of broth onto the table. "You know what I dislike about elaborate meals like this? There's a premium placed on all that solitary time locked away from the world preparing. It enables escapism."

I think of Trey preparing, how hopeful he was. "Yeah, maybe." And then I think of him waiting for Kevin to say what he thought of Trey's food, and, impulsively, I make a quick, maybe bad decision. "Hey, Kevin, could I ask you something?"

"What's that?"

"Do you think there's any way I could get Trey to come with me Thursday when I have to go in to testify at the trial?"

His eyebrows shoot up. "What do you mean, get him to come with you? He's not *going*? He's making you go by yourself?"

I was right, then: it's not something Trey told Kevin. "Do you think you could try to talk him into going? Even if he just goes and sits in back or something, I'd—"

Trey comes back in then, this time with plates of the cooked bird. He raises his eyebrows when he sees we haven't touched the soup yet. "Getting cold."

Kevin smiles in a way that doesn't seem like he means it at all. "Are you going to join us, Trey? Because if I wanted a waiter, then you know what? I would've just gone out with my wife."

Trey sets the plates down so hard the silverware clatters. "If I were Jenna, I'd sit when you said to, wouldn't I?"

"Enough."

Trey looks away first. "Pheasant with fried arugula," he says quietly. He sets down the plates and slides out the chair across from me and sits. "I hope you like it."

It's smoky-tasting, the part I'm assuming is arugula crunchy on top. Kevin takes exactly one bite. Then he puts down his fork and says, "I hear you aren't going with Braden on Thursday."

"Oh, you heard that, did you?"

"You know—" Kevin pauses, choosing his words. "I'm really disappointed."

I wanted this, didn't I? I had a feeling Trey would listen to him. But when he says it, I feel like I just knocked something breakable off a shelf. The look Trey gives me makes it clear that I betrayed him. To Kevin, he says, "You know how I feel about him."

By *him* I know he means my dad. Kevin says, "Yes. I know how you feel about him."

"And—"

"And *what*? There's no *and*. Maybe instead of concerning yourself with my marriage you should think more about where you're actually needed."

"I just don't think you've been fair to her."

"Is that so? You don't think *I've* been fair to her?" Kevin's voice is ice. "You know what, Trey, drowning yourself in guilt cancels *nothing* out."

I have no idea how we got here. In fact, I have no idea where we are. But when Kevin says that, a look I've never seen goes across Trey's face and there's a certain familiar way his shoulders square off, and it's an old feeling suddenly, this kind of triangle I feel caught in, and before I actually mean to do it I shove back my chair and stand up and they both turn like they just remembered I was there.

"Trey, I'm pretty full. I think I'll just go upstairs and—"

"Sure." His voice booms through the room. "Yep. Sure." He reaches across the table and picks up my plate and dumps everything into the still-full bowl of soup.

"Or—I can stay, if you want," I say quickly. My heart is pounding. I pull out my chair. "Everything's really good. I'll just—"

"How *loyal*, Braden." His eyes are hard. "Don't worry about it. Go."

"No, no, I'm sorry, I'll stay, and—"

"No, you know what, Braden? You got what you wanted, so don't bother. I'll go with you on Thursday, all right? It's not like you're already the whole reason I'm stuck here. It's not like my whole damn life would've been a hell of a lot easier without all of this. All right? Just go."

◦ · ◦

I hear him leave late that night, the garage door opening and closing again, and like every time he takes off at night this way there's a feeling like a fist gripping around my throat. I lie in bed with the blinds open and watch the moon outside. It's hot upstairs. It feels hard to breathe. I can't sleep, can't do anything else, either, except wait to make sure he comes back.

I'm not proud of this, especially given how I felt when he came in my room and found the letter my dad wrote me on my birthday. But sometimes, when he leaves, I go into his room and look around just because it's reassuring to see the things you keep when you live somewhere—his spare key and half-used ChapStick, the change he emptied from his pockets, the Post-it notes he sticks to his mirror to remind himself: *pay grocer, call social worker back, ask Braden about baseball more.*

This time, on a pad of paper, I find the notes he had for dinner tonight. From the different colors of ink and all the cross-outs it looks like something he had going a long time. Stapled to it there's a cutout of an old book page. The print's so small I have to hold it close to my face to read.

To consume an ortolan is an act of spiritual pilgrimage. Lift a napkin over your head to hide your cruelty from God, and eat the whole ortolan at once. The rich fat on your tongue is God, the bitterness of the organs the suffering of Christ, and as you chew the bones, your own blood mixing salt with fat and flesh is the Trinity: the separate existing as one.

This is the holiness of the divine Trinity, dwelling in mystery with us. Through this act of worship, God is made known.

                        ▫   ▪   ◦

His car finally pulls back into the garage after four. I hear him come up the stairs and sink down on his bed, and then I think he just lies down there, awake; there are no creaks in the mattress like when someone's moving around trying to sleep. When it's light out, I get up before he does. The kitchen looks like a war zone, and when I go into the dining room, the dishes from last night are still there, too.

I bring the bowls into the kitchen one at a time and pour everything down the drain. I turn the water in the sink as hot as it will go, until I have to suck in my breath even just to dip the sponge in. I scrub all the bowls and plates and pans carefully, one at a time, and as silently as I can so I don't wake him up. I sweep the floor and wipe down the counters, and then I straighten up the living room. I dust off the top of the TV, and I pick up all my crap from around the room and take it upstairs. Then I go back into the kitchen and, since I can hear Trey's gotten up, make him cinnamon toast and scrambled eggs.

Maybe I should fold my hand. I already forced him back here after he's worked so hard to get away, I drove him past his limits the night I was supposed to take Maddie to the prom—and maybe it's not just him I did that to—and maybe now I owe it to him to let him off the hook about going with me to court. Maybe that's the right thing to do.

Instead, I leave the food on the kitchen table for him, and next to the plate I put the subpoena Mr. Buchwald gave me. I circle the date and time for him so he'll know exactly when I have to go.

It's selfish, I know that, and it's weak. It can trap you to be needed. But I hope he'll forgive me, if for no other reason than when someone really needs you, that's also how you know where you most belong.

THIRTY

'm late to Kevin's class that day, but he doesn't say anything as I come in. Later, when he's walking around the room checking people's worksheets, he puts his hand on my shoulder and—whatever this means—squeezes it without saying a word.

We play Lourdon that afternoon. Their catcher's Shane Lucas, who's the best hitter in the league and whose form always reminded me of Trey's. By the time he comes up in the second, we've put two runs on the board to Lourdon's none, and I'm mowing down every-one who steps into the box. My command is as good as it ever is. I haven't yet allowed a hit.

There are different ways, when you face a batter, to go to battle. Most pitchers will try to pull the string on a changeup, send down sliders that break somewhere he's not expecting, tempt him with balls that test his patience and his greed. That's an art, and there are ways you learn to play a batter: you hide the ball inside your glove so he can't see how you're gripping it, you work with your windup so he doesn't know until your release what kind of pitch you'll offer him.

But when what you want to know is where you stand, then you show him a clean, pure pitch right down the middle. No tricks, no breaks, just a strike that hits across the plate exactly where he wants it. That's how you find out exactly who both of you really are.

Colin knows me; he puts down for a fastball inside. I throw my hardest. The pitch catches Shane looking, and he steps out of the box. I tell myself: two more.

When he comes back into the box, Colin puts down for a changeup. I shake my head. It's a smarter pitch, maybe, but I've got something to prove.

This time Shane swings, but it went by too fast for him to get even a piece of it. I'm ahead 0–2 now. The next pitch, another fastball, he swings again. He connects. This time the ball arcs over toward third, over Jarrod's head, and I'm certain—I'm certain—it's gone. I can see how Jarrod will miss it and I can see how the shot will light up on the scoreboard. But then, at the very last second, it drops foul.

Our side of the stands cheers, but my heart feels like it's lodged inside my throat. The worst mistakes are the quickest ones, where you slip just long enough to see everything you've built get blown up in a single instant. That one scared me; it felt like losing control.

I don't bother to wait for Colin's sign before I take aim at Shane's ribs. I know Shane sees it coming, but it doesn't matter, because he doesn't have time before the ball drills into his rib cage with a crack that carries all the way across the field. He goes down holding his side. The batter who was on deck flings his bat to the ground and starts forward. I think he's charging toward me—I'm expecting that, maybe I even want it—and I see Colin ready himself, too, but instead the batter drops next to Shane and puts his hand on Shane's side. His coaches and their trainer squat down next to him then, surrounding him so I can't see him anymore. Colin flips the ball back and forth between his hands. He's watching me. That was the cheapest pitch I've ever thrown in my life, and I know it. But I don't feel bad. In fact I don't feel anything, really. I thought I would feel more than this.

▫ ◦ ◦

Shane stays in the game, and when I go up to hit he lifts his mask for a second and starts to say something to me, then smiles like he's changed his mind.

"Whatever, man," he says, crouching back into position behind me, "La Abra will take care of you," and I don't even see the first pitch go by.

▫ ◦ ◦

When I come home that night from the game, the house is completely dark. When I get to the den I don't even see anyone there until I hear someone moving, and then I jump about six inches, my heart exploding into fireworks, before I see Trey lying on the couch in the dark. At first I think maybe he just fell asleep there, but when I peer into the room I see next to him, on the table, there's what's left of a bottle of Scotch and he's drinking it from one of the tall glasses you're supposed to use for juice. He looks up and sees me before I can get away. He smiles.

"*There* he is," he announces, to no one. "My brother. My golden, perfect baby brother."

"Uh—hi, Trey."

"Come here, Braden. Come sit down."

I shift my weight uneasily. I regret leaving out the subpoena for him this morning. "Actually, I think I'll just go—"

"*Sit.*"

I know when someone looks the way Trey does right now he's best left alone, but I also know that was an order. I lower myself silently on the other end of the couch as far away from him as I can. He holds up his glass to the dim light and squints at it, which if I didn't already know better would maybe be my first clue about how much he's had. Then he sets the glass down on the coffee table too hard, misjudging where the tabletop would be, and the familiarity in that particular kind of thud feels like someone's wringing my intestines like a rag.

I say, quietly, "You all right, Trey? You don't look so good."

"Oh, I'm great. *So* great."

"Do you want me to get you anything? A sandwich? Or some Advil? Or something with caffeine?"

"You are just *too kind.*"

I look down and scrape at a hangnail until it tears off. He says, "Want a drink?"

"Um—no thanks, I think I'm good."

"Oh, but of course my perfect little *brother* would never touch *alcohol*," he stage-whispers. "He does everything his father tells him. Everything! So *obedient.* So good-*hearted.* He won't even eat *birds.*"

He takes a long swallow from his glass. I start to try to get up, but he locks me into place with a look.

"So *loyal.* Your own father grades you like a book report and you tell yourself he's just being a good *dad.*"

"Maybe you should go to bed."

Trey claps. The sound's like ice cracking. "A round of applause for my brother. Such a good brother. Such a *good son.*"

"Trey, come on, don't talk like that. You're a great brother. You always—"

"You're so right, Braden. You are so right. It was *so good* of me to say my life was better without you. You are *welcome.*"

"It's not—"

"And I hit you, too—remember that one? Let's not forget *that.* I miss half your life, I don't even call, and after all that, you come to the airport to pick me up and try to fucking *hug* me, and you do my *dishes*—oh, you must just love me."

"Of course I do. You're my best friend."

He laughs like it's the funniest thing he's ever heard. "Well. Lucky *you.*" Then, abruptly, he stops laughing. "Dad was always right about me."

He pours more into his glass, then tips his head back and drains it, loudly. I don't think he hears me when I murmur that maybe he's had enough.

"I could've stayed here, you know. Right here in Ornette. Right"—he thuds the glass emphatically on the table—"*here.*"

"Sure, but you have your restaurant and everything, so—"

"I could have stayed here and married Emily Zilker and you would be happy, and Dad would be happy, and Kevin would be happy. And *Mona.* Let's not forget *Mona.* Everyone would be so *happy.*"

"You'll find someone else, Trey, come on. Don't talk like this."

"And you know what?" When I don't answer, he says, "I asked you a question, Braden. You know *what?*"

I swallow. "What, Trey."

"Then maybe that cop wouldn't be dead!" He flings out his arms triumphantly and he doesn't seem to notice when he knocks over his empty glass. "Then everyone would be happy! Or you know what else? Maybe Dad could've just finished the job and killed me the night he tried, and then everyone would be better off!"

Something cold blooms in my chest, like a bruise in fast-forward. "What are you talking about?"

"I could be exactly like Kevin. I could've done it exactly like he did. That's what he thought we both needed, you know that? I could have a *wife*, and a *baby*, and work at a *church*, and no one would know. No one would suspect a thing."

"No one would know what?"

"He told me not to tell Emily. You know that? I should've listened to him. Then her parents wouldn't have told Dad to try and save me."

All the blood's leaking slowly from my veins and into somewhere else, my lungs maybe, my abdominal cavity. "Told him what?"

"About me and Kevin."

"Told him *what* about you and Kevin?"

"I took six years of her life. Six years I led her on. I always told her we'd get married. Six *years* I said that."

"Trey, are you . . . are you having some kind of affair with Jenna?" Someone's gripping the edges of my temples, squeezing tighter and tighter like a vise. Then something occurs to me, something that's been nagging at a dark, quiet corner of my mind, and I say slowly, "Trey? Please tell me Ellie isn't yours."

"Braden." He smiles at me, a terrible smile. "You're so *innocent*. Don't be so innocent. I just said his name like thirty times."

"I don't get what you're—" And then, in one horrible moment, I do. The whole room shrinks on top of me, and for a second I can't see. "You and—oh my God. You're—you're—" But I can't even say it. Oh God. "You're completely drunk, Trey. You don't know what you're saying."

"Oh, but Braden," he says, "*Braden*, don't you want to know why Dad and I don't talk? You always ask. Don't I owe it to you to tell you? My *perfect* baby brother? My baby brother I always loved more than life itself?"

"You should go to bed. You should go to bed right now."

"It's because your father tried to kill me when he found out. You know that? He tried to choke me to death. Is that what you wanted to know?"

"Shut up, Trey. You're lying."

"Oh, no, Braden, no, no. I never lie. Just ask Emily. Just ask Kevin about the last ten years." He leans forward. His eyes are veiny and red. "And next time *you* don't have to lie about it when I ask if you think I'm cruel."

"Dad would never do that to you."

"Your father is being held without bail for *murder*, and you're going to look me in the eye and say I'm wrong?"

"You're wrong."

"Oh?" Trey says airily. "If that's really what you think, then how come you aren't answering all the reporters who want to know what happened and how come you keep asking me if I think he did it and how come you want so bad to not have to say it under oath?"

"Trey, no." I start to get up, but he yanks me back down. He says, "*No?* No? What do you mean, *no?*"

"You're just—you don't know what you're saying. You're drunk. Dad never did that. He didn't kill anybody. And you don't feel that way about . . . Kevin. You're just—fuck." I close my eyes. I can't breathe. "My God, Trey, that's not—you can't—how could you just—"

"Oh, I've tried to fix it, Braden. And Dad tried *so* hard. Thank God he didn't know it was Kevin or he would've ruined his life. He sure tried with me. I couldn't talk right for *weeks*. Did you know you burst blood vessels in your face when someone chokes you? Did you know that?"

"Stop saying that. Stop talking like this. Stop talking." I stand up so fast twin flashes flare on either side of my eyes. He reaches for me but misses this time.

"There," he says, as I stumble toward the door. "Now you know. Now you have your answers. Everything you always wanted. So there you go. I hope you're finally *happy* now."

THIRTY-ONE

This is the truth. This is what happened that night.

My dad had changed by the time he came out to the car where I was waiting at Jimmy's house. Something had gone taut in his face; he looked like he'd aged ten years, and even I could see he'd lost something. He had his sleeve rolled up, and his skin was puffy and swollen around the bandage. I couldn't look at him. It was cold, but he didn't turn on the heater. I bit the inside of my lip until I tasted blood.

There was traffic getting back onto the freeway. We inched by a Kaiser hospital and a huge building being demolished, the road ahead of us all brake lights, and then the traffic cleared and we sped up. We went by Mills College, and the zoo, and we left Oakland and still he didn't say a word.

And I don't know where I thought we'd go from there, but even though I knew I'd really hurt him I still didn't see this, at the time: I'd pushed him too far already. Because this was it. This was the night

Frank Reyes died. At that moment, as we were going through San Leandro, Reyes had less than two hours left.

We cut inland around Castro Valley, heading east away from all the concrete buildings shoved up against one another. I said to my dad, "You wanted me to be scared."

"Braden, I just tattooed your *name* on my *skin*."

"You forced me into the car and dragged me to some stranger's house and wouldn't tell me where we were."

"If you didn't trust me, then that's your own fault. I've never given you any reason not to trust me."

"That's a lie. You wanted to scare me."

"Goddammit, Braden, I wasn't trying to scare you. Okay? I thought it would make you happy. I thought it would be—" He swallowed. His eyes were wet. "I thought it would be like that time we went to Disneyland."

"And you agreed with that cop about me. You agreed with him and you let him say all that to me, and you didn't even stick up for me." I took a shuddering breath. "You were happy my mom didn't want to see me in LA, weren't you? You were *glad*."

He was starting to drive faster. There was almost no one on the road. The needle on the speedometer crept up to seventy, to seventy-five, to eighty and then eighty-five. I waited for him to deny it—I waited for him to tell me I was wrong—but we passed the signs for 84 and he said, finally, "You're right. I was."

We went up the hill in Livermore, the valley lighting up behind us in the rearview mirror. He went east on 205 and south on 99. And I didn't know this then, but Officer Reyes, who wasn't on duty that night, was driving his squad car ten minutes behind us on his way back from giving Alex a ride to San Jose. If I'd gotten that tattoo, he would've passed us; he might've already been home.

We passed Ripon, Modesto, Denair. We were almost to the city limits when I said, "As soon as I turn eighteen, I'm leaving."

There was something terrible emerging in my dad's expression, some way things were starting to unlatch, but he still didn't answer me.

"I'll do it. I'll turn eighteen and then I'll get out of here and never see you again. And there won't be anything you can do."

His face contorted like he was in pain. He closed his eyes so long I thought we'd crash, but I kept going. I said, "You and me can be just like you and Trey."

He made a choking sound. "Braden—"

"He hates you, you know. Trey *hates* you. He always will. And you know what? Maybe I do, too."

He veered across the lanes toward the shoulder so fast I was flung forward, and the seat belt cut a welt into my chest. He never checked his blind spot and a maroon Toyota barreled by so close it nearly clipped us. The driver swerved crazily, her car streaking across both lanes, then laid on her horn so the sound fell back toward us across the road. He stomped on the brake when he was still halfway in the far right lane; every car in the lane had to screech to a different lane to avoid hitting us.

"You want to be like Trey? That's what you want?" He leaned in closer so his mouth was right next to my ear, and then he screamed so loud it physically hurt, "*Is that what you really want?*"

A semi roared past us and the car rocked. I tried to twist around toward the passenger window, but my seat belt was still on and it had tightened when he braked suddenly and I couldn't move all the way around. Then he slammed my head against the door so hard that for a second I couldn't move or breathe or see.

"Every single person in my life I ever cared about has given up on me, Braden." He was out of breath, like he'd been running. "All of them have left me. Every single one. And your brother is going to *hell*."

There was a pain humming inside my eardrums, a worse feeling in my chest. I leaned forward and said, in the coldest voice I'd ever learned from him, "Like your dad when he killed himself? Because he chose that over you?"

His eyes unfocused. Two trucks went by in a row, one carrying garlic and one carrying tomatoes, and papery bits of the garlic skin rose off the first truck. A few drifted and settled on the windshield like ash. Then his eyes snapped into focus and his arms exploded toward me and I threw open the door to get away.

I stumbled doing it, my ankle getting tangled in the seat belt so I fell. We were almost to La Abra—I didn't know exactly where, on the side of the road. I couldn't get up. It was foggy—that part's true—and the cars were flying past me so fast I nearly got sucked into their wake. My head was throbbing, but in truth I barely felt it. I made myself get up, and I started to run. He was screaming after me, and I couldn't even make out the words—I didn't try. I just kept running. He pulled back onto the freeway without checking his blind spot and the tires scraped against the asphalt, the open passenger door flapping back and forth like a broken wing until the force and the speed made it close itself, and I stopped and stood still as he roared away.

I could make out the taillights for a couple hundred yards down the road. I put my hands together like a canoe and breathed into them. My palms were scraped. I was getting dizzier, my blood getting lost to gravity before making it all the way up to my head. And it was just when his car disappeared that I heard the sirens, and a few seconds later, I saw the flashing lights go after him, and I tried to scramble as far away as I could from the lanes so I didn't get hit. And I could be making this up because now I know the way things went, it could just be that now I know what came next and now I know who was in that car, but I regretted everything already and I'm pretty sure I knew, even at the time, those sirens were headed for him.

It was less than ten minutes I waited on the side of the road, and I begged God to send him back. I swore to him that if my dad came back for me I would never talk back or disobey or disappoint him ever again no matter what. I'd do anything, everything, if things could be okay. I was sick and exhausted with guilt, I was terrified that now I had no parents at all, and all I wanted to do was get home and go back to when it was just him and me and baseball and pretend none of this ever happened. I wanted to take everything back. And I guess, when I saw his car coming back toward me through the fog, I still thought I could.

I know now how I was wrong about that, of course. But the other thing I realized when I saw his car was this: that I'd known all along he'd come back for me. I had. I'd known all along that whatever I said or did he wasn't going to leave me and I'd also known he was the only person in the world who that was true about. And that part, I was right.

Before the car had stopped all the way he threw open the door and retched onto the asphalt. Then he stayed leaning over like that, shaking, for a long time. I was crying, but trying not to. When I got into the car, he pulled me toward him and clung to me and buried his head in my neck. He grabbed my arms and pulled them around him-self, wrapping them around his back. I could feel how fast his heart was beating against my chest. He was starting to hyperventilate, his breaths like gasps. In the car he kept saying *I'm sorry, I'm sorry, I never meant to, I'm sorry,* and I told him—because I didn't understand yet what he meant—I'd deserved it. I told him I was sorry, too. I pulled myself together and tried to fight off the throbbing in my head as he drove us home.

It was when we pulled onto our street that the cop cars swarmed around us. They'd been waiting there; they were waiting in driveways and around the street to close in on us. As soon as he saw them, his face went white. He covered his mouth with his hand, then shrieked, "Duck, Braden, don't let them see you. *Duck.*"

"What—"

"Oh Jesus," he said, "Oh Jesus. Oh Jesus. My license. My license." He gripped the wheel and tried to force it like he was going to turn the car around, but squad cars had pulled up behind us, cutting us off. He made a strangled noise.

"Listen," he said. His voice cracked. "Listen, Braden. Are you listening? Are you listening? I love you no matter what. I always have. You know that?"

An officer was starting to walk toward us, his gun drawn. I still didn't understand. I couldn't. Just like how for as long as possible I've still tried so hard to believe all this was some mistake, that my dad who I love isn't capable of this, how in spite of everything I hope that still. "Dad—"

"I love you. Since the very first day I laid eyes on you. I love you more than anyone ever has or anyone ever will. You know that, right, B? No matter what, you know that? You know that?"

The officer yelled for him to come out. And then there were more officers, and the car was surrounded.

"Nothing happened. Do you understand what I'm telling you? It was foggy. It was dark. You thought there was a flat tire, but we pulled over and the tire's fine. That's it." He was pressing down the lock on his door over and over, his fingers slipping off like they were sweating. "We didn't know it was him. We didn't know. Braden, please—please. If you love me. If I mean anything to you at all. If you didn't mean it that you hate me, tell them nothing happened and tell them we didn't know anything else until just now."

THIRTY-TWO

The next day, I do something I've never done in my life, which is cut class. I don't know how I'm ever going to be in the same room as Kevin again. Trey's door is shut when I get up, and I go to the workout room at the country club all day just to get out of the house. I go to school for practice and I see Maddie across the parking lot with some of her friends, and I think about trying to talk to her. But by now I'm familiar with that shadow that crosses her face when I pass her in the halls, with how sitting across the room from her in class I hear all those voices in my head rising to condemn me, whispering the truth of all my worst fears about myself. So I don't try. I don't think she'd talk to me anyway. When I get back from practice that afternoon the kitchen is silent, and the air is still. And all the things Trey brought back with him—his knives, his pans, the jars of ingredients he kept lined up on the counter—are gone.

I know right away, because there's a way that things lie still and a way that emptiness in a house sinks into you when it comes. But

I pound up the stairs anyway, trying to tell myself there's a good reason for everything missing from his room, and it's not until I go into my own room that I see the note he left there on my desk with his car keys resting on top and a stack of bills clipped neatly with a binder clip.

Braden, it reads, in his cramped uppercase letters, *Good luck with everything. Keep the money & the car.*

I'm so sorry.

—T

THIRTY-THREE

take his car that night. I fill it with gas and then I drive out past the turnoff for the lake and past Memorial Park and up half a mile into the hills, and I pull up outside the Cortlands' house. Pastor Stan's Ford is parked in the driveway and all the lights are on inside, and through the sheer curtains, I can see the two of them moving around in the living room. I park Trey's car on the street.

I called Mr. Buchwald today. My hands were shaking so hard it took me three tries to type in the right number, and when he answered I gathered all my courage, at least whatever I had left of it, and asked him what would happen if I went to Judge Scherr and told him about all the footage I'd seen. I wasn't actually asking; I was threatening. I thought he'd panic. He was driving, I think—it was loud on his end—and he was shouting into the phone like he was on speakerphone, and instead of panicked, he sounded annoyed. There would be lots of boring talk about his ego and his win-at-all-costs unscrupulousness, he told me, and he'd be subject to a disciplinary hearing. There would be a mistrial, and the jury would be dismissed and the whole thing would happen all over again and drag on, and I'd be subpoenaed again as a witness for the subsequent retrial and possibly face new charges of my own.

"You're clearly an enterprising young man, Braden," he yelled over the sound of traffic, "but unfortunately you will not get out of testifying, much as I can see you want to. A better use of your time is to run through what you'll say and then get a good night's sleep."

Deep down I'd known it wouldn't have gotten me out of this anyway, but at least I could tell myself I still had that one glimmer of hope. Now that's been stamped out, too, trampled like everything else.

Inside the Cortlands' house a light winks on in a small window I think is one of the bathrooms. I'm close enough that I could be at the front door in about fifteen steps.

If I tell Pastor Stan and Mrs. Cortland what Trey told me, it will shatter them. And I know exactly what they'll think: that my brother is a fallen person, not someone to be trusted or needed. And if that's true, then it means I shouldn't care that he left, and I shouldn't care that he won't be there at the trial tomorrow, and I shouldn't care if he keeps his word to me or not. It means I don't need him. I never needed him. I'm better off alone.

Another light flicks on in the Cortlands' living room, and I watch their shadows move like silhouettes across the curtains. I think about not going in and instead taking the car way up into the foothills, where the road drops off into the dark canyons, and driving it off the edge—clenching my hands against the wheel and waiting for everything to be over. And then I don't have to live with any of this. And then I don't have to go tomorrow.

Instead, I sit there for a long time. Not a soul knows where I am right now, and maybe that's the closest I'll come to not existing. One by one, the lights switch off in the rooms, and when the last one does something gets extinguished in my lungs. And then I drive out of town, out onto the two-lane highways held in place by power poles, the opposite direction from La Abra. I push the pedal down as far as it'll go, getting up past a hundred, so fast the poles blur into one continuous streak. I could just leave, I think; I could just drive until I wind up somewhere no one knows me. But—unlike Trey—I have nowhere else to go. And besides that, I could go anywhere in the world and I'd be the exact same person in every place. I go over a rock and the car bumps so hard it hurts my neck, and then I get scared, and slow down, and drive back home to wait.

THIRTY-FOUR

n the morning, my alarm goes off at six. I don't know why I set it. I didn't sleep.

I get up and shower and dress. I have to get there by nine. I try to eat toast with peanut butter, but I can't choke it down, so I throw it away. I put on dark socks and dress shoes, which, it turns out, are too small, so I have to go into my dad's closet and borrow his. His room is dark and quiet, a film of dust over the top of his nightstand, and I sit there in the silence and think how if I had to name the exact opposite of lying next to Maddie by the lake, it would be how it feels right now.

I'm still in his room when the doorbell rings. Then, like it's important, it rings again and there's a pounding on the door, insistent, and the sound flushes out the emptiness in the house from Trey leaving and I know without looking he's back.

I pound down the stairs. I don't care about anything that happened before, I don't care about anything Trey said or anything he did, and in the moment, I don't even care about everything he told me, either. It's enough that he's here now. But when I open the door, it isn't Trey after all.

"Oh, now, don't look so surprised," Kevin says. He lets himself in. He's got his keys in his hand. "You thought I'd let you go alone?"

In the car on the way over, Kevin turns on the stereo and says, "Do you like Jars of Clay, or is that before your time?"

I don't answer. "Did you eat?" he tries, when we pass Jag's. "Can I buy you breakfast? Would you like something to go?"

"I ate."

He glances over at me. "Did you sleep enough last night?"

"Nope."

"Do you need to go over any of your testimony to practice?"

"No."

He taps his fingers against the wheel. "Do you know what you're going to say?"

I lean my head against the window and watch in the mirror as the Jag's sign disappears. Kevin pulls onto the highway and checks his speedometer, then pulls his visor down over the windshield.

"Braden," he says, carefully, "I know you haven't spoken with your brother since—"

"You shouldn't care."

He pauses. "No?"

"You have a wife and you have a kid."

"You know, Trey's one of my oldest friends and—"

"He told me about you."

His expression doesn't change, and he doesn't answer that. But outside the row of apricot trees I'm looking at blurs and jostles, like for a second there he sped up.

"You were supposed to be his friend and you're a Christian, so you were supposed to—I don't even know. I don't understand what's wrong with you. It makes me sick to my stomach thinking about you—God." My voice is rising. "You have a *wife*. You have a kid and you have parents who actually love you, and people look up to you. You don't deserve any of that."

"Braden, you've had an extremely difficult week."

"Is that why you're here? You're bribing me not to tell anyone about you?"

"I'm here because you shouldn't have to do this alone, and because as someone who cares about you, I thought you'd need—"

"I think you're the last person I need anything from."

"Well, that's your prerogative."

"Maybe you should just pull over and let me out."

His jaw sets in a firm cleft. "Let's not make things worse than they already are."

"Was that a threat?"

"Do you really think that, Braden? Do you not know me at all?"

"I thought I did."

He starts to answer that, then doesn't. He stares out at the road, and I understand then that I hurt him. "Well," he says finally, quietly, "it's a ways away, right? Why don't you just try and get some rest."

I lean my head back against the seat with a thud. My whole chest feels hollow, but a painful hollow. All this time I've been too scared to name it into existence—I've been too scared to name it even to myself—but I can't push away anymore what I've been afraid of since that first day after my dad got arrested and the social worker was there: that God marked me for this. That he warned me that day that I was going to have to choose between him and my dad.

We're driving into the sun and there's clouds around it, everything lit up like a picture Kevin showed once in class of a napalm bombing in Vietnam. We learned how napalm's designed to be sticky, so instead of getting first-degree burns you only get the worse ones, both the kind that hurt the most and the kind that sear your nerves too fast to hurt at all. When there's an explosion, it releases carbon monoxide, so people lose consciousness and then, lying there, they burn.

I can't imagine a better description of hell.

When we get to the courthouse, I'm rattled going over the speed bump into the parking lot. Kevin parks, and when he turns off the car, it gets hot inside right away. There's a crowd outside the entrance, and I try not to look.

"Well," Kevin says, again, and then he doesn't go anywhere with it. I've unbuckled my seat belt and opened my door when he says quickly, "Braden, wait. Will you let me pray for you first?"

"Oh, anything you say, Mr. Cortland."

He ignores the sarcasm and reaches out to lay his hand on my head. I pull away; he drops his hand and closes his eyes.

"Father . . ." He pauses a long time, the silence swelling. "Father God, I ask that you be with Braden today. Give him the right words to speak. Give him courage. Give him strength. And God—let him feel your presence surrounding him. Be close to him. Bring peace to him. Please just let him know you love him, and let him know many of us love him, and let him know he's not alone. And Lord . . . be with Trey, whom we love very much, too."

THIRTY-FIVE

M r. Buchwald comes to escort me past the crowd gathered outside and through the back of the courthouse where no one will see me. He has an energy bar, which he hands me and tells me to eat.

"Just remember today not to deviate from the testimony as we discussed it, and to stay calm during the cross," he says as he ushers me down the long hardwood hallway into a dark-paneled room with no windows and nothing inside but some folding chairs. "No ad-libbing. Now. It may be a few minutes." He checks his watch. "Wait here."

My eyes feel dim and broken down and quavery, and nothing holds its shape when I look at it. I can feel my pulse in my brow. All those times I never actually said anything—with the cops that first night, with all the reporters and everyone who asked at school these past months—it doesn't matter if I never lied then. This time I can't evade the questions. And this time, it counts. And I still don't know what I'm going to say.

I've been waiting in the room for six minutes when my phone rings. This time I'm expecting Kevin, but I'm wrong again: it's Trey.

I don't pick up. I watch the seconds tick by on the clock; a minute goes by, then another. Trey doesn't leave a message. Outside I hear the click of footsteps, like someone walking by in high heels, and my heart revs up waiting for the door to open, but the footsteps pass. And then my phone goes off again: Trey left a message after all.

"Braden, it's me. Listen, I—" There's a lot of noise in the background. His voice is hoarse. "Listen, I'm at O'Hare in Chicago. I had a connection back to New York, but I didn't get on, and now I'm just—I don't know what I'm doing. Kevin told me he went with you and he didn't know if you were okay or not, and I know it's too late for me to make it back in time to be there like I said I would, and I just—look, I'm going to stick around here, so I'll just be here, and maybe you can call me if you want me to come back. I'll get on the first plane back. Or text me, whatever. I'll be here. Just—" His voice closes around itself. "Can you call me?"

There are black circles hovering for a second over my vision as I dial. My head hurts. He picks up on the first ring. "Braden—"

"Don't call me again." My brain feels suspended in the middle of my head on a rope swing, swaying and banging against the side of my skull with every motion. The stupid thing is when I first saw his name flash across my phone, some small part of me was holding on to some kind of hope maybe he was here, calling from the parking lot or something to let me know. "That's all I'm calling to say. Go back to New York, stay in Chicago, I don't care. But delete my number and don't call and from now on leave me alone."

"Braden, wait, please. Please just hear me out and—"

"I never want to see you or hear from you again."

From his phone I hear a flight being called, and then another one, and then I hear more footsteps outside my door. He says, "You mean that?"

"Yes."

"Please just let me—"

"It's too late," I say, because it is. "Don't ever contact me again."

*   *   *

I'm brought into the courtroom at nine thirty sharp. It has gleaming floors and no windows and wooden pews like in church, and it has that same feeling of the whole weight of the universe above you sinking closer and closer down toward you. There's a whole big contingent of cops in their uniforms seated in a cluster toward the back, a few people who look vaguely familiar, maybe spectators or protestors I saw on the news, and the Reyes family. My dad is seated next to Mr. Buchwald at a table in front of the room, facing Judge Scherr's bench, and when I come in, his eyes lock on me. Before my mind kicks in again, the sight of him there hits me the way I always imagined it felt for Elijah when God sent down the fire from heaven and incinerated Elijah's drenched altar: so swift and all-consuming you're left trembling and fighting for breath. He mouths, *Hi.* Then, *I love you, B.*

Laila Shah is across the aisle from my dad and the witness stand is next to Judge Scherr, a microphone in front of it, and the air in the room is stale and I might dissolve under so many corrosive stares.

I need more time. I need more time. I don't know what to do.

As I spell my name for the court reporter, my mouth so dry I can hardly choke the letters out, there's an insistent clicking of cameras going off. After that, the bailiff comes and stands in front of me and raises his right hand and waits until I do the same.

"Do you solemnly swear or affirm that you will tell the truth, the whole truth, and nothing but the truth, so help you God?"

I say yes. He leads me to the stand. I can't look at my dad. Maybe he's been wrong about a lot of things, but this is the one he got the most wrong: there are much lonelier places than a pitcher's mound, and there are much deeper tests of who you are.

The lights overhead are long, buzzing rectangles, big enough you could lay someone down in them like a coffin. Alone up here, as Mr. Buchwald asks me to introduce myself to the jury, I can feel, maybe, the choice I've always known I had to make starting to claw its way to the surface.

I struggle to push it back, to catch my breath. The microphone feels like a gun pointed at my head. I tell the jury who I am.

"And you're Mr. Raynor's son?"

"Yes, sir."

"Your father has been your sole parent and provider all your life?"

"Yes, sir." Mr. Buchwald's coached me to keep my eyes on the jury, but I don't do it; instead, I turn, without even really meaning to, so I can see my dad.

He smiles at me. And when he does, that night crashes into me again, all of it—the parts that've been replaying over and over every time I close my eyes, the parts I've sifted through to try to make them into what I needed them to be, the parts I've been trying all this time to shut away. And I feel the beginnings then of how I will be ruined for the rest of my life by what I'm about to do.

"Braden," Mr. Buchwald says, "will you please tell the jury in your own words what happened the night of Sunday, February ninth?"

THIRTY-SIX

He didn't recognize me when he came to our house that night I went to Los Angeles, I know that, but there was a time before that I met Frank Reyes.

I was eleven and it was August, one of those days in the Central Valley when the sun beats you down and grips your lungs when you try to breathe. Still, my dad and I went out to the mound to practice, just like we did every day. It was so hot I felt sluggish and light-headed, and in truth I wasn't even trying. We usually stayed about two hours, but less than an hour into it, my dad gave up. He handed me my water bottle and let me drink, then said quietly, "Well. I guess we learned something about you today, huh?"

Then I was ashamed of myself. When I started to tell him I was sorry and I'd try harder, he cut me off and said, "Calm down, Braden, no need to throw a hissy fit. Anyway, it's too late. Actions speak louder than words." He took my empty water bottle and my glove and bag. "You walk home and spend time thinking about what changes you need to start making in your character, all right?" He patted my back and said gently, "I still love you. I'll have lemonade for you at home."

There were heat waves rising off the asphalt, and my shirt was soaked through with sweat, and I was imagining myself dying and him getting the phone call that I'd literally burned to death out there—and I was really going with it; I was picturing the way he'd wail with regret, and for all the times he was too hard on Trey, too—but then at one point my heart started racing and felt fluttery in my chest, and I got dizzy and then, immediately, scared. Because I didn't actually want anything to happen, not to me and not to him. I just wanted things to be all right and him to be proud of me, not for me to actually die out here in the heat, which it felt like I might. So I tried to breathe slower and I put a hand over my chest to feel my heartbeat and I prayed, *Dear God, please send someone to help me.*

I'd made it—red-faced, my cleats dragging against the ground—to Eagle Crest Road when the cop car pulled up next to me. The window rolled down, and Frank Reyes stuck his head and arm outside the window. He had a bag of Cheetos he was eating from.

"Hey," he said, frowning and chewing, "you all right, kid?"

I looked around. Obviously he was talking to me. My heart jumped somewhere into my throat. When I got my voice back, I told him yeah, I was fine.

"It's a hundred and two degrees. What's the matter, you don't have a ride?"

I told him I was just going home, and that I lived nearby.

"How near?"

I told him twenty minutes.

"Twenty minutes *walking*? *Today*? Here, hop in. I'll give you a lift home."

I knew he was a cop, but he still looked exactly like the kind of person my dad had always warned me would just as soon knife me as pass by me on the street. I looked around to see if there was anyone who'd hear me if I yelled for help, and debated my chances running. But the streets were empty and I'd seen enough TV to know what cop chases looked like, so I figured I'd be better off going with him. I said, "Okay." Then I stood there hoping he'd change his mind until he leaned across the seat and opened the door and said, "Nothing happening today anyway."

I've thought about this since then, I've thought about it a lot, and I think maybe he stopped because he was using me to make himself look good. Because when I got in, he said into his radio, "Hey, Alicia, I saw this little kid walking home in the sun so I stopped to give him a ride, but do me a favor and tell the guys it was a bank robbery or something, huh?" And I could tell from his voice, and the way he said the last part like he was teasing, that Alicia was someone he was trying to impress.

When he asked where I lived, I told him one street over from where my house actually is, and when he asked my name, I stuttered for a second and then said it was Scott. The whole ride back, I sat stiffly in my seat and tried to keep an eye on him without him seeing. He didn't say anything reassuring like, *Don't worry, I'm not going to hurt you,* or anything like that. At the time, I thought he could tell that I was scared of him, and I thought he liked that. Even then he didn't feel like a normal adult. He wiped his crumby fingers on his seat and on the side of the car. He sang along to the songs on the radio—he was listening to rap music, which I wasn't allowed to do—and he got louder and more emphatic every time there was a swear word.

When we turned onto Liberty, he asked where I was coming from and I said baseball practice. He gave me a weird smile, like he thought I was lying.

"In this heat? They don't even let the high school football teams practice on days like this." He asked if I had water, and I told him I drank it and my dad had taken home my empty bottle along with all my other stuff so I didn't have to carry it.

He asked why I didn't take the bus, and I told him we don't have buses here, and he snorted the way people do when they think you're stupid and told me he grew up taking the bus all over. And I figured the fact that I was wrong bothered him, like maybe he didn't think it was fair that he didn't get his own car and he had to take the bus or whatever, because he started telling me stories about how already on the job he'd seen the body of a sixteen-year-old shot to death and how earlier that summer an old grandma had been knifed coming home from work on the bus.

"In his driveway, that kid. Blew off half his skull," he told me, like he wanted me to be scared. "You know who shot him? Fourteen-year-old kid. Four*teen*." I sat frozen in my seat looking at the gun in his belt. A couple miles later, he said, "Pow. Just like that. Blood everywhere. I don't know how his family ever got past that one."

When he pulled up to the intersection before my neighborhood, he ate some more Cheetos, and then without any warning, he stuck the bag right up in my face. But I read the gesture wrong, and I flinched and put up my arm to block what I thought was a blow. That's when I realized what he was doing, which was just offering me some, and because he had this weird look on his face, I tried to play it off like nothing had happened. I forced a smile and said, "Oh, okay, thank you," and took one. I felt a little bit sick.

I didn't trust him. I didn't like him. And to this day I don't know why he asked me what he did next, because to him I was just a kid walking home from baseball practice, and I'm always polite to adults and I wasn't impolite to him. I don't know if he thought it was his job to ask everyone this, or if he just didn't trust people, or if maybe everything's wrong where he comes from so that's what he was used to, or what. The best I've ever been able to come up with is that he might have been the first person I'd ever met in my life who didn't know me as Mart Raynor's son.

"So," he said, when we'd pulled onto the street before mine, "Scott." He crumpled up the rest of his Cheetos and wiped his hands on his seat, and then without looking at me, he said, "Your parents— are they good people?"

I pretended not to hear him. Normally I'd have never done that, I knew when an adult addressed you, you had to answer them, but he wasn't doing anything right either and so I pretended I didn't hear. But he slowed the car and said, "Are they taking care of you, or what? How come you aren't in the car with your water bottle and your other stuff and your dad?"

"My dad's a better person than anyone." I could hear that I sounded mad. I was; I didn't think he had any right to ask me that. "Than *anyone*."

"Whoa, kid, chill out, okay? I'm just asking."

I crossed my arms. And the thing is, if it had been anyone else or anytime else, this wouldn't have happened. But I guess I was feeling weird already from being so hot and scared and mad that way, and I still have no idea why I said this to him then because I've never done anything like it in my life, but all at once I kind of felt the way it does right before you throw up, and then before I could even think about it, I blurted out, "If your dad's going to give you away or if you upset him and he's going to kill himself, how do you know it's coming? Do you get some kind of warning first?"

"*What?*" Frank Reyes snapped. "What the *hell*, kid." And then he looked panicked in that way adults do when someone asks a question they aren't ready for.

It wasn't a big moment. In less than sixty seconds, I was going to get out of his car and go home; my dad wouldn't be there, because he'd changed his mind and gone out looking for me so I didn't have to walk. And really, nothing happened. Officer Reyes fiddled with his radio and said something about hotlines or something like that, but I was so shocked at myself that I didn't even hear what he said. I said, quickly, "This is my house right here, this one," even though it wasn't, and he slowed the car and started to say something else, but I said, "thank you for the ride," to cut him off. He didn't try to stop me when I got out; I think he was probably as relieved to see me go as I was to get out. But I'd taken a few steps when he called me back.

"Hey," he said, "Scott, wait up. C'mere."

He leaned out his window and handed me a card that had his name and LA ABRA POLICE DEPARTMENT written on it, and there was a phone number he'd scribbled, too.

"This is how you get ahold of me," he said. "If anything ever— I don't know—gets weird or whatever, you call me. Day or night. Okay? Your parents leave you out to get heatstroke again, you call me and I'll come talk to them. Anything ever happens where you think, *Fuck this, this isn't right, no one should treat me this way even if it's my mom and dad*, you call me. You got it?"

I said I did just so he'd leave, and that was it. I never called him. For some reason, though, I kept the card. I even went and found it one time a year later when my dad drank too much and got rough, but after that, when I got scared about what might have happened if I had actually made a call like that, I took a permanent marker and blacked out the number so I couldn't read it and tucked the card away in a book. And I know Officer Reyes didn't recognize me when he showed up at our house that day I came back from LA, so it doesn't matter. It was nothing. It was probably something he never thought about again.

THIRTY-SEVEN

After just two hours of deliberation, the jury reaches a verdict at one thirty p.m. on Wednesday, May 7, five days before the La Abra game. It's scheduled to be read tomorrow, and the news cycles light up with the information so fast that by the time Mr. Buchwald's number comes up on my phone, I've heard already, and the knowledge has settled into my lungs like dust.

I don't pick up his call. He leaves a message and tells me that the jury's decision was unusually fast, warns me not to speak to the press, and tells me the verdict will be read at nine a.m. I unplug the home phone. When the morning comes, I stay inside with all the dead bolts latched and the alarm system set on high and all the curtains drawn, like I've been doing since I came back from the trial. I haven't been to school, haven't returned any phone calls or messages, and for the first time in my life I've skipped two games. I've barely slept. Every time I close my eyes, the demons come; I see myself on the stand over and over, my words on the witness stand branded across my forehead to mark me the rest of my life.

I don't know how to live with what I did. I don't know if I can.

Just before nine, I go into the den and sit in front of the TV. It's raining outside, and the thud of the water against the skylights makes me feel like drowning. Both local news stations are broadcasting live from the courthouse when I finally turn on the TV. I can't let myself pray. No matter what the verdict is, it won't undo what I did. When I see my dad on-screen, my heart seizes, and I watch as he sits up straighter when the jurors come in and smiles a weak, hopeful smile in their direction. He searches their faces. His lips move without sound; I can read the words *Please God please God please God* over and over. His chest heaves.

"Good afternoon," Judge Scherr says, and to the jury, "Please be seated."

They sit. Judge Scherr says, "Mr. Foreman, has the jury reached a verdict?"

A man sitting in front says yes.

"Please provide the verdict forms to Deputy Rogers."

An officer in uniform sitting in one of the side rows gets up and makes his way to the foreman, who rises and hands him a manila envelope. The deputy takes it to Judge Scherr and holds it out.

Judge Scherr slides the paper from the envelope and reads it. He looks up over his glasses. "Mr. Raynor, please stand and face the jury."

My dad obeys. He swallows so hard you can see his Adam's apple slide up and down, and he doesn't look at any of them.

I did what I had to do, I tell myself. In the end it was the only thing, and I had to do it. But I can't breathe.

Judge Scherr pushes his glasses up his nose. "I have reviewed the verdict form and will now publish the verdict. The people of

California, plaintiff, versus Martin Scott Raynor, Jr., defendant." He doesn't look up. "We, the jury, find the defendant, Martin Scott Raynor, Jr.—"

I slam my hand against the power button just in time to cut him off. My palms are damp. The TV rocks dangerously on the stand.

I can't bear to hear him say it, for it to be final and real.

And I can't do this any longer. I can't live with what I did.

. . .

Upstairs, the rain still pounding against the skylights, I clear the history on my browser. I empty everything in my wallet—whatever cash I have, a few gift cards—and put everything, along with all my vintage baseball stuff, in a Ziploc on my desk and I write Colin's name in permanent marker on top. For Greg, the 1920 *Baseball Almanac* from my dad. For Maddie, the necklace I never gave her. For Trey and my dad, nothing. When they hear what I've done, that will be enough.

I'm moving through a haze. I'm wasting time, I should just get things over with, but there's one more thing. There's an index card taped to the underside of my desk where I copied down a verse I found a long time ago, when I was a little kid, and I peel off the tape and set it on the desk. *Can a mother forget her nursing child? Can she feel no love for the child she has borne? But even if that were possible, I would not forget you!* I write my mom's full name across it. Because you can say you forgive yourself, you can tell yourself you've moved on, but the world keeps going on and whatever you did is still part of it forever and you don't get to take that back. And she should have to know that if she'd done everything differently then Frank Reyes would still be alive today and I would still be alive tomorrow.

I take something with me: the home run ball I caught at that game all those years ago with my brother and my dad. In my dad's room, I sink down on the edge of his bed and open his nightstand drawer. It's messy, like all his stuff. There's his Bible and a couple foam earplugs and an eye mask. There's a note written on creased yellow legal paper; it looks old, and the knobby handwriting is clearly a young kid's, not mine: *Dear Dad I am sorry you yelled at me but I don't know what I did please tell me with out yelling so it isnt scaring me and then I will not do it again I love you Dad.* There's a picture of a thirteen-year-old Trey holding me up to a cake with a single candle on it; my face is screwed up like I'm crying, and I'm trying to turn away, but Trey's laughing, his eyes on me. And there's a box of lead, and—shoved to one side and loaded, like I knew it would be—there's his gun.

I can't change what I did. But I hope somehow this is penance enough.

My vision's tunneled into pinpricks and I feel flushed all over. I clutch the ball with one hand and with the other I pick up the gun and slide the safety off with my thumb. My whole head is pounding like a drum, swelling so much I can hardly even see. My hands are sweating so much my finger keeps slipping off the trigger. It'll take just a few seconds and that's it. I can't hear, and my heart is about to burst out of my chest, and I tell myself I should practice first to make sure I remember how to do it right and I aim at the wall above the bed and pull the trigger and the recoil knocks me back and the sound of the gunshot crackles hot and close in my ears and from the wall, where there's a hole, dust from the plaster balloons in the air and drifts down.

I drop the gun down on the bed next to me. I hug my knees against my chest and bury my head in my arms, gulping huge breaths that scald my lungs.

I can't go through with it. If there's one thing I'm not ready for, it's coming face-to-face with God.

▪   ˎ   ◦

I told myself I was done with Trey. I told myself God was done with him, too.

When I was younger, I used to lie awake sometimes at night, tormented over all the unsaved people I knew who were going to spend eternity in hell. I'd always try to believe that if God rejected people forever, they deserved it, that I had to respect his justice and not let feeling sorry for someone color what I knew deep down was right.

You have to try to convince yourself of that; it's the only way to live with the idea that anyone might be damned forever. Still, though, I'd curl up in my sheets, haunted by images of all those people pleading for mercy, and I'd feel panicked when I couldn't silence the questions I had about how that could be okay. Faith's always felt like a Jenga game to me, where if you try to mess with even a single piece the whole thing can crash around you all at once, and then you're lost. It feels so much safer to look for God's anger and his judgment everywhere, in everything, and to try to believe that's how you'll save yourself—by condemning whatever or whoever you can to prove you're somehow pure.

But when you're at your lowest, it's harder to lie to yourself. And now that I'm here—now I don't know. I don't know if I was ever right about any of it or why I thought it was so clear who was really God's or not. I have no idea what to do with everything Trey told me, but no matter how much all my life I might've said people like him brought judgment on themselves, I know I never could've stood by and watched what my dad did to him and thought that was somehow holy, or right, or from God. I never could've thought he deserved it.

I don't want my brother in hell. I don't want to see him punished. What I want, it turns out, after all this, is the same thing I've wanted all along—for him to be here.

I get up and find my phone. I hope I didn't blow it with him forever. I hope he didn't change his mind.

I don't know if you're still in Chicago or what, I text him, *but can you come back? Now?*

It takes him two or three minutes, but he writes back, *I'm here. Been waiting around in town. Be there asap.* After he does, I stay like that a long time, rereading the words until instead of crazed and maybe kind of dangerous, I just feel empty and numb. Then I put my dad's gun back in the drawer and wipe my palms on my pants. I wait forty minutes, and I leave the TV off. The rain lets up outside.

I look out the window when I hear a car pull into the driveway. It's Kevin's, and something twists in my stomach. He and my brother both get out, and Kevin says something to Trey and Trey nods, pats one pocket of his jeans. They talk a little longer. I don't know why I don't just look away. Mostly, actually, it's Kevin talking, his head bowed so he's speaking into Trey's ear. Trey keeps glancing toward the house. Then Kevin takes a step backward like he's saying goodbye, and then, just as I'm about to get up and go downstairs to see him, something happens. Trey kind of freezes, and then he balls his hands together and breathes into them the way people do when they're scared, and Kevin reaches out and cups his hand for a long moment, gently, on Trey's hip. It's exactly the way you'd touch a girl, something I would maybe describe as possessive and tender both, and in that moment it's just more than I can take. I have to turn away.

The thing is, it's not so different on a baseball diamond than it is everywhere else—you can lie with a lot of things, but you can't lie with what you do on instinct, and I have spent my life learning to catch the ways people give themselves away and so I don't miss the way Trey lets himself relax into that touch. And I don't know what I'm supposed to understand there, if it's just how far my brother is lost into what I've always been told was sin or if it's that I realize now I never saw him let go like that even with Emily and that if you find that with anyone I don't know how you'd ever give it up, or if maybe it's just that I don't think I've ever felt more alone in my life than I do right now and I'm not sure I will ever feel that at home with another person ever. But whatever it is, even though it's dumb, I'm kind of crying. God. I get up and wash my face.

When I go downstairs, he's in the kitchen, and already there's a mound of bloodied fish scales on a sheet of butcher paper next to him on the counter. When he sees me, he looks up, then back down, fast. "Ah—hey."

I mumble it back.

"I would've got here sooner, but I went by the store to get stuff for dinner." He looks solid and ordinary in front of me, a little closed off that way he always does, and I don't quite believe what I just saw out on the driveway in the dark. "Just fish. It's not much. I thought you might be hungry, and I figured you'd just want something fast."

"That's fine."

"I'm almost done."

"All right."

He puffs his cheeks full of air and blows it out his lips, then turns his head away again. "So, ah—I'll be finished soon."

I wait at the table with my head wrapped inside my arms while he cooks. My stomach's caving in on itself; I don't remember the last time I ate anything. Trey doesn't speak again until he raps on the table with his knuckles next to where my head is and says, roughly, "All right."

In front of me there's a platter with a whole fish. He takes two spoons and lifts the fish's head, then does the same thing with its tail, which comes away with bits of flesh clinging to it. There's peas, green beans, salad, and bread. Once I take a few bites, it turns out I'm not that hungry after all. Trey eats methodically, gripping his water glass with his other hand, which he doesn't move the whole time he eats; I'm not sure he even realizes he's doing it.

Twice he looks like he's about to say something, then he doesn't. The refrigerator is rattling and the fluorescent light overhead is buzzing and both seem louder than normal. Under the table, I press down on the joints in my knuckles until they crack.

"Still hungry?" he asks, when he's done eating. "You want anything else?"

I shake my head. Maybe I shouldn't have asked him here. I didn't mean I needed him to come bring dinner; that doesn't even touch what I need from him.

"There's more if you want it later." He pushes the leftover peas into a line. The fork scratches against the plate and the sound makes my shoulders clench together. He hasn't shaved in a couple days and he looks tired, maybe, or maybe something else. Maybe a lot of things. He sucks in a deep breath, and his cheekbones hollow out and something goes over his face, flickers for just a second, and is gone.

"Okay," he says. "Um—look, Braden . . ." He reaches into his pocket and pulls out a folded paper, which he unfolds and smooths on the table. "I'm no good at this, so Kevin made me write everything out, so, uh . . . let me just make sure I remember. . . ." He makes a fist and breathes into it, then he rubs his hands together and stares down at his piece of paper. Under the table he's jiggling his leg up and down. "Kevin said you have to . . . ask. For, um, for forgiveness. So. Uh . . ." He swallows. There's beads of sweat on his forehead. "Look, I know I don't deserve it, and I know you probably hate me for bailing on you every single time it counted, but I hope maybe someday, you'll maybe . . ." He reaches up and bites at a hangnail with his front teeth, then lets his hand hit the table with a thud. A couple seconds later he says, quietly, "Yeah, I'm not asking you that."

I tear off pieces of my paper napkin one by one, then crumple the mutilated remains into a ball. "Trey?"

He doesn't look at me. "Yeah."

"I lied about what happened. In court."

"Did you," he says, but from his expression I'm pretty sure he already knows.

"And I don't know what happened, but I know they read the verdict today, and—"

"I thought you knew." He frowns. "You didn't hear?"

"I couldn't watch."

"I see." When he speaks, his voice is measured, like he's making an effort to sound neutral. "Not guilty of aggravated first-degree murder, vehicular manslaughter, or felony hit-and-run. He got one count of resisting an officer."

Not guilty, not guilty, not guilty clangs in my ears. "You watched?"

"I went."

"You—what?"

"I thought you might be there. He got four months, with credit for time served, and a two-hundred-dollar fine."

Four months. I'd been wondering if he was just going to show up back home. "Are you surprised?"

"That he got off? No. He always does."

He must blame me for it. But I didn't mean that, exactly. I guess what I meant is I want to know if Trey knew all along what my dad did and if he knew all along what I'd do, too, but I don't say it. There's something I need to say to him, but it's something I'm scared to touch. I say, instead, "Do you want to know the truth?"

"Not really." Then he catches himself and makes a go-ahead motion with his hand. "Yeah. Tell me if you want."

"I don't know if that means legally you're on the hook for any—"

"It's fine. Whatever. Just go."

So I tell him. Everything—starting from the championship game, that first night I tried to contact my mom. He kind of nods like he's listening, but he doesn't say much. When I finish, I say, "I know it was wrong."

"Yeah," he says, matter-of-factly, "it was."

"I don't know what to do now."

He rearranges the peas on his plate again. "Doesn't sound like there's much to do."

"And we play La Abra next week, too, and I'm scared as hell of going. And I just—what am I supposed to do?"

"I don't know, Braden. Sometimes it's too late."

That's what I was scared of. Maybe I'll skip the game, maybe I'll keep hiding out, but you can only do that for so long. "The other part is—every time he was there, it was because of me. Frank Reyes, I mean. Every time he was ever there, it was when I screwed up with

Dad somehow and then I asked God for help. And I keep thinking how that night, if I didn't get out of the car—maybe it would've been me instead."

"It's possible."

"And I'm really scared that—do you think Frank Reyes took what was supposed to happen to me? Because I asked God to just erase my mistakes and I should never have asked for that?"

"No."

"But it was like he got sent every time—"

"No, Braden, come on. It doesn't work that way."

"Well, you don't even believe in God."

"I never once said I don't believe in God."

"Oh." I twist the bottom of my shirt into a knot. "Also, Trey?"

"Yeah."

This is the part I know I need to say to him. "I just—I wanted to say I don't think it's okay what Dad did to you."

His face is unreadable. "All right."

"I mean it." My chest feels tight. "And I know I let you down, and I'm sorry and I hate myself for doing it, but I couldn't—if it hadn't been the death penalty—whatever he did, even though I know it was wrong, I just couldn't—"

Without warning, I'm on the verge of breaking down in front of him. I can feel my face contorting with the effort to stay controlled. I turn my back so he won't see.

I don't just mean I'm sorry to Trey. I am sorry, but that's not all of it: it's just he's the only one I can tell it to because I can't say any of this to Frank Reyes.

In my peripheral vision I see him start up from his chair like maybe he wants to reach for me, or maybe leave, I'm not sure which. Probably leave. But he sits back down.

"It's fine," he says. "You do what you have to do. I did the same thing."

If he means he let me down, too, there's no comparison. I swipe roughly at my eyes and turn back to face him. "What do you mean, you did the same thing?"

He looks like he regrets saying anything. "All right, listen, I've never told this to a soul. Not even to Kevin. But what I told you about, what happened with Dad—the part I didn't tell you is he swore to me he'd find out who I was seeing and ruin him. You ever—" He clears his throat and starts again. "You ever feel that way about someone? Like you'd move heaven and earth to protect them? Kevin's the only one it's ever . . . been that way with, and it's always been, and it made me crazy thinking what Dad could do to him. So after Dad went to bed that night, I went into his room and got his gun, and I stood there with it about ten minutes thinking about how easy it would be to end him. I was this close."

I say, "You didn't, though," which is stupid. Obviously he didn't. I guess I just don't know what to say.

"No. I didn't. I left him to live. Just like you. So I know how you feel." He reaches for my plate, and stands. "I'll tell you what, though, it fucks you up coming that close."

He's done with the conversation, I can see it, but there's still one more thing I need to ask him first. I watch him clean up, thinking how even as I sit here time is spooling out between now and the La Abra game, how I don't know where to go from here. Maybe if I were a different kind of person I'd go to Judge Scherr now, or to the cops, and tell the truth. But if I'm being honest with myself, I don't regret what I did, not really. I hate myself for it, and I don't know how I'll live with it, but I'd also do it again. And I don't know where that leaves me now.

When he turns off the faucet and reaches for a towel I work up my nerve. "Hey, Trey—there's something I need you to do with me."

"What's that?"

I know he won't like it, but at this point I'd risk just about anything to not feel so broken this way all the time. "Will you go with me to see Dad?"

THIRTY-EIGHT

t's supposed to be a longer process to visit someone in jail. I know because I looked at the application a couple times earlier on, when he first went in and I was home by myself. But on the way there Trey tells me he worked something out with Kris Blaine, the guy who sells him the weed and whose dad is a cop; he doesn't say what, and I don't really want to know.

He's going back to New York tomorrow. He booked a red-eye last night because I told him to, after he said he'd go with me to the jail. *What about your game?* he said, and I told him I didn't think I was going to go. The game's on Monday. Colin's been texting to tell me they're trying to hire private security guards, and I know what it'll look like to not go—that I'm a coward, that I don't care about my team. But how can I get up there in front of everyone and go after Alex Reyes? I doubted Trey would blame me, considering. He said he'd stay as long as I needed him, that he figured he owed me at least that much, but I know him being here would never start feeling like real life, for either of us—it would only ever feel like penance.

A guard at some kind of security station ushers our car into a parking lot rimmed in chain-link fence and barbed wire, and Trey turns off the car and then doesn't move. I don't blame him; my legs feel padlocked to my seat.

The stupid thing is, after all this, I still think I need my dad's advice. About where to go from here, about the La Abra game. I don't know how I'll get through any of it.

"Well," Trey says, and then nothing else. He takes out a clear plastic orange canister from his pocket and shakes out three small white pills and pops them in his mouth. I say, "What is that?"

"Cocaine." He sees my face. "Braden, come on. It's prescription medication, all right?"

"For what?"

"Nosy much?"

"What is it?"

"It's Ativan, okay? For anxiety."

I say, "Oh." He didn't say this part last night, but I think I understood, after everything he told me, that it wasn't just my dad Trey's tried so hard to bury in the past: I think he was more afraid of whoever he was himself while he stood there in my dad's room that night. That's how I would feel—I think it's the same as how I can't imagine playing baseball again; baseball's home to me, the place I've always gone to find myself—and I think Trey and I are alike in a lot of ways I never saw. I know what it's like to want to get away from yourself. Only I guess I never thought I could be someone else the way Trey always has. "Well—should we go?"

He leans his head back against the seat and closes his eyes. I wonder if he ever prays. "Give me ten minutes for it to kick in."

The hallway on our way in is gray and bleak, the concrete walls rising around us like we're being sealed away from the world. When we go through the metal detector and empty our pockets and hold out our arms for an officer to pat us down, I feel like bolting. I don't, but I think I would've if Trey weren't there. A stone-faced guard inspects our IDs, turning them over in his hands and shining a flashlight on them, then walks us through double doors and another hallway and another door marked VISITATION ROOM and tells us we're allowed one brief hug or kiss at the beginning and end of the visit and that's all. Trey looks like he wants to say something sarcastic, thinks better of it, and says, instead, "All right, man, thanks."

"Wait here, and we'll bring him out."

We sit down. I wonder if Trey's pills are working. He looks—not scared, exactly, but something more like resolved. Grim. I say, "You were really going to just never see him again?"

"That was the plan."

The minutes pile like an avalanche as we wait. The visiting room has round tables and plastic chairs grouped methodically in the center, like a grade-school classroom with all the decorations torn down. There are windows looking onto the hallway and cameras on the ceilings and fluorescent lights buzzing at a high pitch, and at one end of the room there's a podium with an officer seated behind it and another officer leaning against the wall under a sign that says KEEP HANDS IN PLAIN VIEW AT ALL TIMES. We're the only ones in the room, but they don't look at us. I can feel the cutout of the chair pressing a pattern into my back, and I lean forward and sit on the edge of the seat. I don't want this place to leave any mark on me.

A phone rings. The guard behind the podium says something into a phone, then hangs it up.

The door in the back of the room opens, the sound huge in the room, and my dad comes in with a guard in uniform. My heart jack-knifes in my chest. Up close, he looks different than the last time I saw him—worn down, somehow, as if layers have melted off of him and he's a purer version of himself. Or maybe it's just that the shock on his face when he sees us—the way he jerks reflexively backward and then walks forward, slow, until he's standing in front of us—is so completely unguarded. I stand, instinctively. Trey doesn't. The guard who brought my dad in leaves, and the door slams shut behind him, echoing off the concrete walls.

"My God," our dad says, his voice hushed, and he glances back over his shoulder like he's seeing if anyone can overhear. "Here, here, have a seat," he says, even though Trey's sitting down already, and then he sits, too. Then he tells Trey, like his mind is still trying to put together the pieces, "You look so old."

Our dad must look different to Trey, too, and Trey doesn't say it but I know somehow that's worse. When you leave something behind, you want it to stay left there. Trey says, almost loud enough to be overheard, "You thought time would just stop if you weren't there to see it happen, or what?"

"I just—Jesus. It's just you show up without any warning, and you don't give me any time to—" My dad shifts in his chair, crosses his arms, and sticks them under his armpits so his elbows make sharp points underneath the baggy tan shirt he's in. He reaches up and runs his hands over his face and glances around the room, then back at Trey, and then his eyes fill. "I've missed you so much."

"Am I supposed to feel sorry for you?"

My dad pretends not to hear. "Means more than you know that you'd come here," he says softly. "B, I know it's only four months when all's said and done, but I can't tell you how much I've missed you. And I know you went through a lot with all this. I know that. Don't think it means nothing to me."

I know I need to say something; I can feel the words coiled and sharp inside me, trying to untangle. But my mind can only fumble around. I'd thought if all three of us were together again things would make sense. I'd thought I'd get more answers. I'd thought I'd at least be able to formulate the questions.

"Listen," my dad says, "there's no privacy here, but, B, I need to talk to your brother about something—I've been holding on to it all these years, so I just—if you can go sit over—"

Trey says, "You can say it to both of us."

"It's about that last night you were at home."

Trey's face goes hard, but he says, "You can say it to us both."

"In that case." My dad sucks in a long breath. "You want to know something, Trey, I still get nightmares about that night."

"*You* get nightmares?"

My dad holds up his hands, his palms out so you can't miss the scars there. "I did this to myself after." He tries to smile. "If your right hand causes you to sin—"

Trey says, "Fuck you."

"Fair enough. But, Trey, I have to tell you, I heard you come in that night. That night the Zilkers called me. I heard you come in and I heard you open the drawer and I heard you take out my Ruger. I wasn't asleep."

The color vanishes from Trey's face, and my dad says, "God-*damn*, Trey, I was waiting. You know that? I was waiting for you, and you couldn't do it. You never had that in you, did you? The one thing I tried to teach you all your life was how to fight back when it mattered, and you couldn't do it even then. And I bet you spent all this time since then telling yourself you were close to doing it, didn't you? Staying away because you couldn't stand that about yourself. I know you. But that's a lie, Trey, and you know it. Maybe you scared yourself, but you never would've gone through with it. You were always better than that."

Trey shuts his eyes. I can feel him telling himself this'll be over soon, that he's going to walk out of here and put this out of his life; I can feel him telling himself *breathe, breathe.* Finally, he says, "Listen. Braden lied for you and went to court for you and so I will swear on my life that he was telling the truth, and I don't care if it's wrong and I don't care if you never pay for any of it, but right now, to us, I want you to say you did it."

"Keep your voice down, Trey, there's—"

Trey lowers his voice. "I want you to say you did it. And I want you to tell Braden it wasn't his fault."

"Come on, Trey, you—"

"Say it."

It might be the first time that, between the two of them, I see my brother win. My dad drops his gaze, clears his throat. He closes his eyes for a moment like he's saying a prayer.

"That cop had it in for me from day one," he says quietly, his eyes still closed. "When he pulled me over, you could see it all over his face what he thought of me. He was out for me. He was just waiting for his chance."

His voice is frayed. And something about the way he says it, almost like an incantation, makes me think that all he's been doing these past weeks is turning this over and over in his mind. He opens his eyes again and reaches out his hand like he wants to hold mine, but he looks toward the guard across the room and drops his hand. "You should've seen how he talked to me. I was trying to go back and get you, B. I shouldn't have left you alone like that, and I shouldn't have—I shouldn't have done any of it. And when he pulled me over, I was scared out of my mind. I just kept thinking what if you got hit by a car, or what if you were done with me and I went back and you weren't there—I knew I already lost you for good, Trey, and, B, I just couldn't take it if anything—so I told the cop I had to get back and get you. I wasn't thinking right, I was so upset, and I told him what I did to you." It isn't warm, but sweat's beading on my dad's forehead, and when he reaches up to wipe it off, I see his hands are trembling. "And he said I wasn't fit to be a parent. He said he was going to send someone after you, B, and he was going to take me in. He wanted to take you away from me for good. I know he did. And I just—you remember how he treated you before—" He looks helplessly at me. "You have to believe me I never meant to do it and I'm sorry, I'm real sorry, and I wish I could take it back. But, B, I did it for you."

The room blurs. I say, strangled, "For *me*? You killed him because—"

Trey shoves back his chair and stands, the sound clattering across the room. "We're going. Braden, get up. We're leaving."

My dad grabs his arm. "Wait, Trey, please, please, we've still got forty minutes left—"

"*Don't touch me.*"

"We're supposed to get a whole hour. Please. Please don't leave."

The guard is coming over to us, shouting at Trey he needs to remain seated and not touch or the visit will be terminated. Trey yanks his arm away from my dad. My heart is going like a jackhammer in my chest, and when my dad turns to me, I feel frozen in place, and the look he gives me then sears me to my core. I don't think for the rest of my life there will ever be another person who loves me or needs me as much as he does.

"You've always been the only one who understood me, B," he says urgently. "And I owe you my life. I always knew that about you, you know. I always knew God brought you to me to save my life. And when I get out of here, we'll figure everything out. I know you've got a big game coming up, so you just pitch the way I always taught you, all right? I know you have it in you. I know you'll make me proud. And when I come back, we'll pick up the pieces and put everything back together again, and you'll be so busy being knee-deep in scouts all the time you'll forget any of this ever happened. But, Braden, please—promise you won't give up on me. Please. Like every other person who ever gave a damn about me. Will you promise me that?"

THIRTY-NINE

The reaching, searching sound of a guitar is coming through the sanctuary door when I walk into the church foyer that night. The sanctuary door's unlocked, and Maddie's in there practicing like I thought (like I hoped) she might be. When she sees me there, I catch the surprise on her face before her expression hardens, less like she's angry and more like she's afraid, which is worse.

"Hey," I say quickly. "Look, I know you don't want to talk to me, but can I just—sixty seconds? Then I'll leave you alone."

She lets her fingers stray along the strings, and she takes her time deciding. Just when I'm certain she'll tell me to get lost, she lets go of her guitar and it falls against her body with a soft thud, the strap tugging against her shoulder. "Okay."

"Thank you." For courage, or maybe just company, I think about Trey coming back with his notes on what he wanted to say to me. "I just wanted to tell you I'm sorry. For bailing on you, and for being an ass to you, and just for not being the person you thought I was. For a while I thought maybe I was, or at least I could be, but I was wrong about that. And I don't want to give you excuses or anything, and if you hate me, I understand, but I wanted you to at least know you didn't deserve any of that. And that I'm sorry."

Her expression is unreadable. Maybe I surprised her; maybe she was expecting something else. Or maybe it doesn't matter what I tell her. The silence rises around us like a flood.

I force myself to stand still and wait for her to say something. It feels like another lifetime that I used to sit here in these pews feeling safe, and right, and lucky. Maddie stares across the altar over my head, her face giving nothing away. She'd make a good pitcher. Her batter wouldn't know what to expect.

What I want her to say—beyond all reason—is that she forgives me. That she understands, that all along she saw all the things I never told her, all the redeemable parts of me layered underneath the things I did. That it doesn't matter as long as I care about her now. But I know most people don't understand you that way. I know you probably only get that once in your life, if you're lucky, and I guess I used mine up on my dad.

"I don't hate you," Maddie says finally. "But—" She pauses, like she's holding my paper-thin offering up to the light to see all the ways it's cracked and ruined, all the ways it's less than whole. An entire planet spins inside that *but*. "You should've let me decide for myself whether you were who I thought you were or not."

I think about all the things I can never tell anyone, never tell her. "I knew the answer already."

"You don't think it's possible to be wrong about yourself?"

"Do you?"

"Of course I do."

She picks up her guitar again and ducks her head over her music stand, which I guess means the conversation's over. It's not forgiveness, not exactly, but I guess it's as much as I can expect. I stand there a minute, hoping she might say something else, and when she doesn't, I say, quietly, "Thanks for letting me come by."

The music starts again when I turn to go, chasing out the muffled sound of my footsteps on the carpet and making the room feel smaller again. I'm at the arched doors going out when I turn back around. "Hey, Maddie?"

She stops playing and looks up.

I think of that home run ball I caught all those years ago, the one I thought was proof my family belonged to God in some fragile, special way. There's a part of me that wishes I could believe I was wrong about all of it—that God never existed to begin with, that he was just some fantasy we made up because we needed it. You can't betray someone who was never real.

But the rest of me thinks that's the easy way out. And anyway, I don't believe that. What I believe is that I've been wrong about so much, that fear and judgment don't tell you where you stand or what someone's worth the way I always thought they did, but that maybe, if I could sort through everything I always thought and throw out all the parts that were never true, I'd be left with just a few glimpses of God that still felt real.

"You can say no," I say to Maddie, "And I won't blame you if you do, but—you think I could stick around a little while and listen?"

If she says no, I'll take it as a sign. She doesn't, though, or at least not right away. Maybe she's just a kind person, or maybe she sees something of the past week written on my face. Whatever the case, she pauses, not like she's deciding, but like she's trying to think of something, and then she says, "If I remember right, you liked this one."

Her fingers move gently across the strings. The notes are soft, careful almost, and I recognize the tune from the song she sent me all those weeks ago. And something happens in me then, something so soft and so quiet I might be making it up, but it's that same feeling you get sometimes in the middle of a game when you can feel the tides start to shift—that moment you're certain you've won, or certain you've lost, even when there are innings left still. I follow the chords through the song, and I think how with my dad, and with Trey, no matter what either one of them ever does I think I'll still feel exactly the same way about them that I always have. I know it shouldn't be like that because it isn't safe, and because I think most other people get to choose who they care about and when to stop and it's not fair if you're the only one who can't, and I think that's the worst and the most dangerous thing I know.

But I hope—I hope—that's something like what God feels about me.

FORTY

This is what I kept coming back to the whole time before the La Abra game.

One morning in second grade, I woke up with a start because I was being carried downstairs. It was dark, and I flailed around; my dad was buckling me into the car.

"Shh," he whispered. "Go back to sleep." He wouldn't tell me what was happening, but even though I was struggling to keep my eyes open, by the time we'd gotten onto I-5, I was asleep. I jolted awake again when I felt him put his hand over my eyes. The car had stopped.

"Don't look," he ordered, pulling me outside. "All right. Let's go." I was going slow and trying to feel around with my feet, and he sighed. "B, come on, don't you trust me?"

It was noisy—cars, a lot of people. We walked for what felt like forever, and then we got into some kind of moving car with other people, and there were a lot of sounds from loudspeakers and some kind of music playing and people everywhere, and then the train stopped and he took his hand off my eyes and said, "We're here."

It was Disneyland. I could feel the grin spreading across my face as I looked up at him. "Really? We're going to Disneyland?"

"No, bozo, I just brought us here to look at the signs." He thumped me on the back. "You want to go in, or what?"

Inside it was thrumming with happy excitement and there were more people than I'd ever seen in my life. Actually (and I was just a kid, so I'm allowed to say this), with all the characters you could go up to and meet, the rides, the bright buildings everywhere—it felt kind of magic.

We'd been there a few hours when he went over and looked at a map, searching for something, and then he steered me in the opposite direction and we walked for a while until we came to a huge line wrapped around what looked like a mountain. We walked around it until we got to the very end of the line, and my dad looked down at me.

"This is the Matterhorn," he said. "Fastest roller coaster in the park," and that was when I understood why we were there. A month or so before, I'd gone with Colin's family to Great America for his birthday. It was supposed to be fun—we'd been talking about it for weeks—but the first roller coaster they wanted to go on, I freaked out and begged Colin's parents not to make me and I wouldn't get near one the rest of the day.

"See?" my dad said, motioning to the throngs of people in the line as they inched forward. "Look at all the kids having fun. There's *girls* going on it, for crying out loud. You think they'd go if it wasn't fun?"

"I don't think it looks fun."

"You don't think it looks fun, or you're too scared?"

"Um . . . I guess . . . both."

"You think I'd let you do something that wasn't safe, Braden? You'll like it. I'll be right there next to you the whole time. I'll hold your hand if you want, even. You'll be glad you went." He cupped my chin in his hand and lifted it to make me look at him. His eyes were clear and alert. "You didn't want to go with your friends before, that's fine, but don't you want to go with me?"

Of course I wanted him to be happy with me. I know not everyone's that way with their parents, and I never understood that, because why wouldn't you want that? Why would that not be a big deal to you? I could see how proud it would make him; it's just I was terrified.

"Um—" I swallowed. A hundred feet in front of me Cinderella had shown up; there were a bunch of girls running toward her. I looked up at the peak of the mountain again, and then I couldn't do it. "I just—I think—it doesn't really sound that fun. Maybe another time."

He dropped his hand to his side with a thud. "All right, then. I'm not going to make you. You don't want to, we won't go."

I was nervous he'd be mad all day, but he wasn't. We went to Toontown; we rode the spinning teacups; we ate Dole Whips and turkey legs; he took pictures of me next to Buzz Lightyear and Snow White. But I was uneasy, and as we were leaving a gift shop, I worked up the nerve to ask if he was disappointed in me. He stopped in the middle of the walkway to turn me to face him, holding me at arm's length to look at me. I stared down at the asphalt.

"You're like me, Braden," my dad said. "You know that? You're—" He laughed, an affectionate laugh. "Lord knows you're a heck of a lot softer, and you *think* so much all the time, and don't you get a big head about this but you have a better nature than your old man and I know it, but you want to know how we're the same?"

I asked how.

"Because you aren't your true self places like this. It's not where you really belong. For guys like us, the pitcher's mound is the only place in the entire world where you get to be the kind of man you want to be." He brought me closer and took my face gently between his hands and held me there for a second before he let me go. "Someday, Braden, you'll see."

He wasn't mad, I knew that; what he'd said was pretty close to absolution. He understood, and he forgave me for not being my best self. But I kept seeing the Matterhorn all day long out of the corner of my eye, towering above everything else. I felt guilty and sad and sick of being myself. Finally, when he told me he wanted to leave around dinnertime to make it back home, I steeled myself and turned to him.

"Dad?" I said. "I think we should go on the Matterhorn before we leave."

Everything changed—a different kind of smile came into his eyes, and he lit up. It took an hour and fifteen minutes to get through the line, and the closer we got, the worse I felt. I tried not to show it. He kept me close in line, his hands on my shoulders, and when we got to the front, he talked the attendant into letting me on even though I wasn't officially tall enough. I hated her for letting us in as soon as the bar locked over our seats and I knew we were trapped. My hands were sweating so bad they kept slipping off the bar I was trying to grip. My dad patted my leg.

"You can take anything for ninety seconds, can't you?" Then he laughed, and socked my thigh. "Guess now you don't have much choice."

There were clanging metallic sounds and jerks as we went up, up, up. My lungs seized. Then, while we were climbing, in the midst of the noise and that feeling like fish flopping around inside my stomach and like my head might float off into thin air, my dad leaned in and put his mouth right next to my ear.

"Hey," he said, so quiet that for a second everything else stopped, "B, I'm so glad you're my kid, you know that? You're more than I ever could've asked for. You're the best thing I ever had in my whole life and you can't even imagine how much I love you." And then—we were at the very top of the first huge peak—we dropped, so fast I was pressed back against the seat and he was whooping in my ear and there was air rushing past me and at me, and I felt exactly the way I always pictured astronauts feeling when they went zooming into space.

He was so happy afterward. And at the time I thought it was just that I got over something you aren't supposed to be afraid of and that I did it because he asked, because I wanted to make him happy. And that was part of it, maybe. That meant something to him. But I think even more than that, he was so happy because he felt the way you do when you've put things right in the world around you, because he'd told me something that was as true to him as anything else had ever been. Even at the time it felt like some kind of prophecy spoken over me, a truth I'd be bound by and owe something and belong to, the thing I would again and again come back home to.

And that's what I'm carrying with me right now, now that I've just arrived on the field where my team is warming up for the La Abra game and everyone's gone quiet at the sight of me and Cardy's calling me over to tell me, "Saved your spot in the lineup for you, Seven. I knew you'd be back."

*   *   *

The stands are filled solid, split by color: orange for La Abra, blue for us, and down at the bottom of the bleachers, there are cops planted like sentries in every aisle. I think nearly everyone I know is here. I asked Maddie if she'd be here, too, and I see her sitting near the top. I didn't think she'd come. But I guess if I learned one thing from Trey it's that sometimes people stay a part of you even long after you should've faded into each other's pasts.

We're the away team, so we hit first. The sun is starting to set over the backstop, the lights casting long shadows across the grass, and lined up in the dugout my team is quiet the way you are when you're standing over some kind of precipice looking down at a drop. The season won't end if we lose today—there's still four more games left if we don't make playoffs—but it might as well. It can make you feel pretty worthless playing out the string.

To the game today, I brought the home run ball I caught at that Giants game with Trey and my dad. And I'm glad I have it with me because I'm too jittery to sit still. I flip it back and forth between my palms as I watch Dutch chase two pitches outside the zone, the way he does when he's nervous, and then strike out. When Chase swings too high and gets out on a foul tip, Colin comes and lowers himself down next to me.

"Hey," he murmurs, low enough so only I can hear, "Reyes bats fourth."

I know that. I've spent the past three months combing through his stats, and there hasn't been an at bat he's made that I haven't gone over a dozen times. And all this time I thought I knew what I'd want to pitch him: fastballs, straight across the plate. No breaks, no tricks, all heat. That's the most I've got, and if there's a way to measure yourself against another person, it's that. I say, "I know."

"We can make it look like an accident if one gets away from you," Colin says. "We can afford to put one runner on base. Or maybe"— he glances around to see if anyone's listening—"whatever else you want to do. I know you won and all, but, I mean—the guy lied about your dad in court because he wanted to see him dead. So whatever you want to do, it's your call."

I'm about to answer him when Zach flies out for the third out, and everyone gets up to take the field. "Half our town's here watching," Colin says, over the noise of bats tossed against the fence and gloves swept up off the ground. "There's not that much La Abra can get away with doing back."

The dirt crunches under my cleats as I leave the dugout and cross the field to the mound. When I do, the La Abra side of the stands goes silent. I try not to hear it, try not to let it wrap around me and choke the air from my lungs. Taking the mound, I try to block everything out: the stands, the other team, even my own fielders. It's just me and the ball and Colin's glove. That's it. I don't let myself look anywhere past.

Their first batter's Nick Washington, the catcher. Nick's five for seven in his last at bats; he hit a home run last week off Jay Allen from Hilmar. On the first batter you haven't learned the umpire yet and you don't know his strike zone. So Colin signs for a fastball, just outside.

There's no one on base. There are no outs. This is their first at bat of the game. But just as I release, Nick gets into position to bunt, and because you never bunt this early I know exactly what he's doing, and when the ball gets to him he punches it forward, right down the first base line.

That's my ball. I don't have a choice; I go for it. I can feel him coming toward me, and I brace myself, but just as I get a hand on the ball and flip it up to Chase, Nick barrels into me so hard my teeth are knocked together and my eyes water and the wind's knocked out of me. Nick doesn't bother looking toward first; he gets up and walks back to the dugout, and as he does it, he cuts right across the middle of my mound.

Everyone sees it. Colin screams something at him as he comes around, but Nick just smiles. Lying on the ground, I can hear someone from our side of the stands yell, "You going to call that, Blue?" But the umpire pretends not to hear. It takes me a couple seconds to catch my breath and get up and get back on the mound. There's an ache starting in my side and my knee, where he got me with his cleats. When I look down, there's blood starting to seep through the white of my pants where I got spiked.

I need this game to mean something. It's the last thing I have left here, a last chance to get something right, and I can't quit now. But I'd be lying if I said I wasn't scared as hell.

Up next is their center fielder. He waits on a fastball that I miss outside, he swings at a changeup and gets a foul tip off it, and then, when I throw a slider that's so low in the zone he shouldn't swing, he slams it right back at me, a line drive right at my knees. I catch it, all instinct, but my hands are shaking. That wasn't a pitch he should've swung at. I know he knows that. And like Nick, he doesn't bother heading for first, either; I've barely gotten my hand on the ball before he's turning back for the dugout like he's done, like he already did exactly what he came here to do.

Vidal Medina bats third. He takes his time before he steps into the batter's box; he swings his bat around a couple times; he lets it hang to the ground and surveys the outfield. He turns around and says something to Colin, then he smiles at me. I can feel my pulse shooting like laser beams around my skull. I know for a fact Vidal gets greedy on anything up in the zone and has a tendency to roll over changeups, too. When Vidal gets into the batter's box, Colin calls for a fastball up high, but I miss. It's a ball. I'm down 1–0. Colin gives me the sign for a curveball. I position two fingers and thumb on the seams, hiding the ball in my glove so the batter can't see.

Colin flexes his glove. He's nervous. He reaches up and adjusts his mask. The umpire is crouched forward behind him to watch the pitch come in, his shirt straining against his chest protector and his mask like a cage over his face, and when I look behind him, when for just a second I let my eyes stray, Alex isn't taking practice swings, or stretching, or even holding a bat, even though he's on deck. He's standing straight up with his arms crossed, and through the chain link of the dugout I can see his whole team standing behind him, ready.

Vidal makes two small circles with his bat, and he swallows hard enough that from the mound I can see his Adam's apple shift. I know what that means in a batter: that he just realized how fast ninety-four miles an hour is, that he remembered in the batter's box you belong to the pitcher and you have to answer for what you've done, and when I see him shift his weight back onto his heels, just the smallest bit, I wind up. I watch him tense. I stare right at him and let my eyes blur so I can't see Alex. Then I release, my arm rocketing forward so hard I think it might explode out of its socket, and the ball screams forward in one long blur, a comet, but Vidal connects and like the center fielder's hit this one comes at me. But I miss it; it goes past me, I'm not fast enough, and he's safely at first.

And that's the heart of their batting order. Now Alex is up.

If I was trying to convince myself that I can hide up here, that a game is ever its own self-contained universe, I know I'm wrong because of this: when Alex walks toward the batter's box, a mediocre batter who doesn't even have a .250 average, a guy who's two for his last eight at bats, the crowd erupts. On the La Abra side, everyone starts to stomp their feet against the bleachers, slow at first, and then so fast it sounds like a bombing. My spine and shoulders feel like balsa wood about to snap. Alex takes his time outside the box, ignoring Colin, surveying the crowd. Then he steps in and lifts his head to look at me. And even though I've played this game my entire life, I understand for the first time right then that you hide nothing from your batter, that he sees everything you are.

I can't pitch him like I always planned to. When Colin signals for a fastball, high and tight, I shake him off and signal back. It's a sign we've never used once, one I always said—even just a few months ago to Greg—I never would, and I'm not even sure Colin will remember. He stares at me long enough I think he doesn't. Then he signs again for the fastball and I know he understood me, he just doesn't want to let me do it.

Three times he shakes me off, and three times I repeat it. Finally, that last time, he doesn't argue. He stands up from his crouch and holds his arm out straight, to the right, like half of a T. From the dugout I hear Cardy scream at me.

This is the thing about an intentional walk: there's no mistaking it. There's no subterfuge. The catcher never even sets up; he has to stand and point with his glove outside the strike zone to where the pitch is going to go. This is exactly why my dad thinks it means you're weak; it's broadcasting to everyone watching the game that you know you've already lost this round. And it's why I've never done this before, either, because it means you have nothing. That you measured yourself up against your batter already and you came up short.

My blood is thundering in my ears. I throw. It's supposed to be an easy toss, something that gives the catcher enough time to get behind it without much effort, and when I do, the crowd falls silent. But before Colin can catch it, Alex lunges from the box and hacks at the pitch with his bat. He misses, but the suddenness of the motion catches me completely off guard. When Colin tosses the ball back to me, I nearly drop it. You never, ever swing on an intentional walk. It's a free base.

We go through it all again, and again—again—Alex swings. The crowd's making noise again now, except I can feel how it's shifted—they aren't yelling for Alex anymore, they're yelling at me. I can hear the jeering, the way the tone's gotten ugly. The dugout feels incredibly far away.

Almost there, I tell myself. Every inch of my skin is on fire. Colin stands again, calls for the pitch, and I throw. This one doesn't make it to him; it bounces two feet in front of him, because my arms feel like rubber. But Alex swings anyway, swings so hard he spins around and the bat goes flying, and that's three strikes.

And that's it. Not in a way you could ever prove in court, but now every single person watching knows that I couldn't face him. That my best wasn't good enough, and that my worst couldn't touch him, either, because it doesn't matter to him that I'm sorry.

But I am. And now everybody knows.

⸪

Trey's waiting in the parking lot when I come out of the bathroom where I spent the last inning trying to pull myself together. He changed his flight for after the game, and when I get into the car, I know he knows the game's still going—you can hear the roar of the crowd still—and from the way he looks at me I can tell he wants to ask more, but he doesn't; after all this, I still think there's a lot we'll never ask each other. Instead he hands me his phone and says, "Get me directions to the airport, will you?"

"Yeah, okay."

He drives. It's good he does; I'm shaky still, and there's a film over my eyes. We're quiet on the way to the freeway, the suitcases rattling around in back when he hits a pothole in the road, and we stay quiet on the freeway as he passes the turnoffs for the police station, Ornette, the lake. There's a lump the size of a city in my throat. Halfway there, Trey's phone rings, and he pulls off to talk to his restaurant manager and I watch the line of cars zooming by send clouds of dust up at the sky. When he hangs up, I say, "Are they glad you're going back?"

"Yep."

"What about—you know?"

I mean Kevin; I still can't bring myself to say it, but from his silence, I'm pretty sure he knows. Trey pulls into the left lane and picks up some speed, something in the car making a whirring sound. He looks over his shoulder, and I think he's going to ignore the question. Finally, though, he says, "I think that might be over."

"What do you mean you think that might be over?"

"How many different things can *over* mean?"

It's supposed to be sarcastic, but there's no heat behind the words. When I turn to look at him, his eyes are glittering. That shuts me up. I've never, not once, seen Trey cry. I say, "You mean—I mean, because you're going to end it, or he—?"

"Does it matter?"

"Um, I guess not."

Maybe it just means I'm weak, maybe I've just shattered whatever I had left of any kind of moral compass, but I guess it turns out no matter how much I think what he's doing is wrong, I still want to him to be happy. I say, "I'm sorry."

"Not your fault."

A few miles later, it occurs to me that was kind of him to say it. I probably would've wondered if he blamed me.

The parking lot's crowded at the airport. When Trey closes the trunk, it echoes against the concrete of the parking structure in a way that feels so final, like *goodbye* is reverberating through my heart. The airport's busy, the departures flashing and then vanishing on the screens above the baggage claim, and there's a long line to go through security. Before getting in the line, Trey checks his pocket for the tickets.

"Well," he says, "I guess this is it." He hitches his suitcase up on his shoulder.

I try to force a smile. "Guess so."

"You good?"

My ribs are shrinking around my lungs. Even if maybe sometimes an ending's not all bad, I don't think it ever feels that way at the time. "I guess."

He hands me my boarding pass, checks for the dozenth time I've got ID. I kept that home run ball in my jacket pocket and I reach for it with my other hand, rubbing my thumb against it like I always used to as a kid. Up ahead there's a bin for all the contraband stuff that gets confiscated, bottles of liquid and nail clippers and pocket-knives, and I think about leaving it there. Trudging through the line, I think about my dad, how in a month when he gets out he'll find out I'm gone. I feel my eyes well up. I turn away so Trey won't see, but there are people everywhere and then the line steers us around a corner and Trey sees anyway. He stops in line for a second and ducks his head next to mine.

"Hey," he says, his voice low. "It gets easier, Braden. It does."

We get to the front of the line and the security agent reaches for our IDs. His uniform looks like a cop's, and I hold my breath—I think maybe it will always go this way when I see something that reminds me—but of course nothing happens, of course to him this is just routine, and he waves us through. Then I waver for a second by the bins. Eight hours from now, I'll get off the plane in a place I've never been and try to carve out some kind of new life there, so for a few seconds I let myself think it might mean something if I toss the ball away. That somehow I can leave all this behind.

But that was what wrecked me at the game today, that you can't. After I finished pitching to Alex, I stumbled off the field, ignoring Cardy and my teammates yelling at me and the cold, stunned silence from my side of the crowd. In the bathroom, I sank down on the ground and crouched under the buzzing fluorescent lights until my legs stopped shaking, and I thought how there won't ever be a time when I get up on a mound and all this doesn't haunt me, doesn't reach me, doesn't come rising up again with every pitch. How baseball is a game you play with ghosts.

So now, in the airport, I keep the ball. It doesn't feel right, exactly, but I don't know how long it's going to be before anything does. Later, strapped into my seat and listening to the flight attendants before we take off, I take it from my pocket again and spin it around on my lap until Trey tells me to put it away, I'm making him nervous, so I do. My palms are damp. And I'm scared, but not enough that I didn't catch the break in his voice.

The cabin doors shut. The pressure inside changes, and as the plane starts down the runway I grip the armrests on either side. When I do, Trey reaches out and pats me awkwardly on the knee, and he leaves his hand there as the engines start to roar. We start to lift off the ground and the angle makes it so the whole world is pressing against my chest.

And then we're ascending. We climb high enough that when I

look outside, the whole world I'm leaving can fit through one of the plane's windows. Before we level out again the plane dips, and there's something familiar in that feeling, that suspension. I grip the ball in my pocket and try to quiet the trembling near my heart, and it feels, just for a second, before the plane rights itself again, like the universe has whittled itself down to one long arc of possibility—like that moment right before you throw a really good pitch.

ACKNOWLEDGMENTS

Writing books has been my dream since I was six years old. Thank you, thank you for reading this one and for holding a piece of my heart in your hands.

In addition, my most heartfelt thank-yous to:

The inimitable Adriann Ranta for her unwavering confidence, keen insight, and all-around amazingness, and for believing in this story from day one.

Laura Schreiber for her wisdom, vision, and enthusiasm, and for uncovering the very best version of this book. Christine Ma and Mark Amundsen for their unflagging devotion to detail. Emily Meehan and the team at Hyperion for giving this story a home, and Maria Elias and Chris Silas Neal for giving it a face for the world.

Alvin Tsao, Brett Gilbert, Perla Ramos, Albert Hsueh, and Bryan Ni for fielding my questions about their respective areas of expertise. Brendan Kiley; the ortolan symbolism is based on his work.

My mother, Teri Gilbert; my aunt, Maureen Gilbert; my mother-in-law, Susan Rodriguez; Missy Loeser; and Karla Torres for their generosity in enabling me with time to write, and the Loeser-Lee family for opening their home to me while I studied.

My teachers at McAuliffe Elementary and Monta Vista High for fostering my lifelong belief in the power of stories, and Jen Ireland, for reading with me everywhere and teaching me that stories are always best shared. Renee Euchner, Nona Caspers, the community at San Francisco State, and *The Kenyon Review* for their encouragement. Emily Chen, Stephanie Chen, Colleen Dischiave, Annie Suarez, my aunts, and my grandmothers for their constant cheerleading. Bryant Look for the affirmation, and the creative writers at Eastside for the inspiration.

The YA world (bloggers, Binders, and Buccaneers), the 2015 debut community, and especially the Freshman Fifteen. I couldn't have asked to share this dream with a more wonderful group.

Annie Perez, Helena Geefay, Lee Kelly, and Anna-Marie McLemore, who not only read various incarnations of this story and helped me shape it, but who formed a chorus of encouragement that drowned out my moments of writer self-doubt. Kim Liggett, Chandler Baker, Charlotte Huang, Lori Goldstein, Jessica Taylor, Stacey Lee, and Sabaa Tahir for their camaraderie; Marci Lyn Curtis and Mary McCoy for sharing the road with me.

My family—the Gilbert, Loy, Rodriguez, and Bock clans—for their love and support. Everyone should have such a stalwart team.

Andi Heggem, Annie Perez, Christine Chong, Helena Geefay, Joe Rogel, Larry Tu, Minh and Jenn Nguyen, Ryan Yim, Serina Chang, and Tim Kim, and all their wonderful other halves, for everything.

My brother, Brett, for not choosing a lesser sport. I always knew the millions of baseball games I got dragged to to watch you play would come in handy someday.

My parents, Kirk and Teri Gilbert, for giving me every opportunity they could and for their incredibly steadfast belief in me.

Audrey, who didn't help much with the writing, but who brought me so much joy throughout the process and brightened my whole world.

And thanks most of all to Jesse, for dreaming along with me always. You are my favorite.